Chau Chun is a renowned artist and controversial painter. And rumours of new work by him has the media in a frenzy ~~~~~~~~~~~~~~ Lydia Chin and Bill Smith hired to follow the whispers to their source.

They soon discover that Chau has been officially dead for over twenty years, killed in the Tianamen Square uprising. Are Lydia and Bill really chasing a ghost?

Praise for *Ghost Hero* and the Bill Smith/Lydia Chin series:

"S. J. Rozan is one of my favourite crime writers.
Intricate plotting, great characters, smart, crisp writing.
This is a fantastic series – crime writing at its best."
Harlan Coben

"With the Bill Smith and Lydia Chin mysteries, S. J. Rozan
has written the most consistently compelling series of
traditional detective novels published in this decade."
George Pelecanos

"Excellent...engaging characters, crisp dialogue,
intelligent storytelling, and a minimum of violence
add up to another winner for Rozan."
Publishers Weekly

"Rozan delivers another thoroughly entertaining,
meticulously plotted and utterly riveting installment of
her Lydia Chin/Bill Smith series. It feels like welcoming
in old friends who have a knack for getting themselves
into the weirdest sort of scrapes..."
Romantic Times

S. J. ROZAN was born and raised in the Bronx and is a long-time Manhattan resident. An architect for many years, she is now a full-time writer. Her critically acclaimed, award-winning novels and stories have won most of crime fiction's greatest honours, including the Edgar, Anthony, Shamus, Macavity and the Nero Award.

Also by S. J. Rozan:

Trail of Blood
Blood Ties
Out for Blood
Blood Rites

GHOST HERO

S.J. ROZAN

EBURY
PRESS

1 3 5 7 9 10 8 6 4 2

Published in 2012 by Ebury Press, an imprint of Ebury Publishing
A Random House Group Company
First published in 2011 in the US by St Martin's Press

The Random House Group Limited Reg. No. 954009

Addresses for companies within the Random House Group can be found at:
www.randomhouse.co.uk

A CIP catalogue record for this book is available from the British Library

The Random House Group Limited supports The Forest Stewardship
Council (FSC®), the leading international forest certification
organisation. Our books carrying the FSC label are printed on
FSC® certified paper. FSC is the only forest certification scheme
endorsed by the leading environmental organisations, including
Greenpeace. Our paper procurement policy can be found at:
www.randomhouse.co.uk/environment

Printed and bound by CPI Group (UK) Ltd, Croydon, CR0 4YY

ISBN 9780091936389

To buy books by your favourite authors and register for offers visit:
www.randomhouse.co.uk

Acknowledgments

A big m'goi, xie xie, and thank you to

Steve Axelrod, my agent
Keith Kahla, my editor

Dr. Qian Zhijian
Xin Song

Reed Farrel Coleman, Nancy Ennis, Ed Lin,
Jonathan Santlofer,
Lisa Scottoline, Keith Snyder, Joseph Wallace

Steven Blier, Hillary Brown, Belmont Freeman, Max Rudin,
James Russell, Amy Schatz

Betsy Harding, Royal Huber, Tom Savage

The Museum of Chinese in America

And a wish for good fortune to

Liu Xiaobo and Ai Weiwei

This book is for David Thompson and Bill Reinka.
Miss ya, fellas!

GHOST

HERO

1

In a relentlessly chic and tranquil tea shop on the Lower East Side, I sat sipping gunpowder green and trying to figure out what my new client was up to. That the client, Jeff Dunbar, sat across the table laying out the case he was hiring me for, helped not at all.

"It's about art," he'd begun, stirring sugar into his straight-ahead American coffee after the pleased-to-meet-yous were over.

"Art?" I'd tried to sound intrigued, as opposed to baffled, by this revelation. Dunbar had called the day before, saying he needed an investigator and had seen my Web site. I'd expected, when we met on this chilly, bright spring morning, to hear a problem that was personal—cheating fiancée, two-timing wife—or professional—industrial espionage, embezzling employees. Straying spouses and shady secretaries are my daily bread and the Web site says so. It doesn't mention art, a specialty outside any of my areas of expertise. If this case was about art, I had to wonder, why call me?

Dunbar sent a dollop of milk to join the sugar. "I'm a collector. Contemporary Chinese art. Do you know much about that?"

Oh. This had to do with my contemporary Chineseness? "Not much, no."

He nodded and settled back. "It's a cutting-edge collecting area. Not really inside the PRC, even among the new rich, but in the West. Chinese painters, especially, but also sculptors, photographers, installation artists—they're all hot." His voice was pleasant, measured, as though lecturing at a symposium on the globalized cultural marketplace. He looked the part, too: thirtyish, short dark hair, polished shoes, the only business suit in sight. That his art and his prospective detective were both Chinese couldn't be coincidence, but the detective's ignorance seemed okay with him. My antennae went up. There's a class of Westerners who "like rice": They're attracted to Asians, or, really, to their own exotic fantasies. If Jeff Dunbar had chosen Chinese art, and me, for that reason, he was about to get a fast good-bye. And stuck with the check.

But he didn't look it, and he wasn't acting it. Those guys invariably wear something Asian, at least a tie with a double-happiness pattern. They order tea. And, during Zen-like pauses, they gaze soulfully into my slanty eyes. Jeff Dunbar came across as a guy in a boring suit conducting a business meeting.

I decided to see where this was going. "Tell me about this art. I don't think I've seen much of it." I ransacked my brain, came up with little besides misty mountains and pine trees from five or six dynasties back. "Is it like classical art? Ink on paper, that kind of thing?"

"Interesting you should ask that. Mostly, no. A lot of artists now work in Western media—oils, acrylics. But the paintings I'm concerned with happen to be inks." He set his cup down. "There's a painter named Chau Chun. Referred to as Chau 'Gwai Ying Shung'—Ghost Hero Chau. Have you heard of him?"

"I'm sorry, no." I added, "Your pronunciation is very good. Do you speak Chinese?"

"Thanks. Yes, I minored in it in college. It occurred to me that people who spoke the language would be increasingly in demand."

"And you majored in? . . ."

"Art, of course."

Of course, except for the half-second pause before he said it. "I didn't mean to interrupt. You were telling me about Ghost Hero Chau."

"Yes. Well, Chau was a young professor at the Beijing Art Institute in the 1980s. His work from that period is very valuable."

"How valuable is 'very'?"

"A piece will sell for around half a million. A little more, a little less, depending."

Yes, I thought, that would be "very."

"A lot of artists his age were doing experimental work in those days," Dunbar went on, "but Chau always worked in traditional media with traditional techniques. He made brush-and-ink scrolls: mountains, plum blossoms, lotus ponds. Classical-looking, and also traditional in another sense: They were political, but in arcane ways. Hidden symbols and metaphors, that sort of thing."

"That's traditional? I didn't know that."

"Nature painting with coded commentary goes back to the Yuan Dynasty. About eight hundred years," he added, in case I didn't know my dynasties. "The commentary's aimed at educated people of the painter's political persuasion, but the coding gives the painter deniability. But don't worry, Ms. Chin. I didn't expect you to have any expertise in this field. That's not why I called."

"I have to admit that's a relief. So tell me, what can I do for you?"

"Recently, some new paintings of Ghost Hero Chau's seem to

have surfaced. Again, inks, and again, political, criticizing the government, the Party, the economic free-for-all going on in China and the social disasters it's causing."

"I'm surprised that's allowed. Criticizing the government can get you in trouble over there."

"Very much so, if you're an activist lawyer, say. Or a writer. Artists, less often."

"What makes them special?"

"Oh, it could be liberalization. Those hundred flowers finally blooming. Or," he smiled, "maybe it's that the artists are cash cows. The West loves political work. Collectors pay a fortune and the government takes a cut."

"It does?"

"Well, so does ours, from our artists. We call it taxes. They call it something else but the result's the same. Also, there's national pride. Sky-high prices make China a player in the art world."

"But if the paintings are critical?"

"Ah, but with visual works, you can always say seeing something as antigovernment misses the point. That it was meant as ironic, tongue-in-cheek."

"Deniability, like in the Yuan Dynasty."

"Exactly."

"And that's what the artists say? To keep the government off their backs?"

"It's what the government says, to explain why someone's allowed to say in paint what a writer gets years of hard labor for saying in words. Of course, writers' manifestos aren't going for half a million U.S. dollars. The artists who get in trouble are the ones who don't keep their mouths shut. The ones who let their work do the talking are pretty safe."

"I see. So people like this Ghost Hero Chau are insulated by money. I guess I'm not surprised."

But Dunbar shook his head. "Chau's a special case. For one thing, if what I hear is true, the new paintings are here, in New York."

"If what you hear is true? You mean you haven't seen them?" I was getting a glimmer of what this was about.

"That's right. I haven't, and no one seems to know where they are. I'm hoping you can find them."

"Because I'm Chinese?"

"That sounds like racial profiling, doesn't it?" He smiled again. "I suppose it is. It occurred to me, if I wasn't having any luck tracking the paintings through art channels, there might be another way. I did an online search for a Chinese investigator."

I might have taken offense, but after all, that's why my Chinese clients come to me, too. "Tell me something, Mr. Dunbar. If no one's seen these paintings, what makes you think they exist?"

"Rumors. The collecting community's always full of rumors. Backhanded, of course, because everyone's trying to beat everyone to the prize."

"Can you give me an example?"

"Oh, someone sidles up to you at an opening and asks if you've heard this nonsense about the new Chaus, the Ghost Hero's ghost paintings that don't exist. They're hoping you'll say, *Yes, they do, I saw them*. If you do, they'll ask where, as if you must be crazy, and when you tell them, they'll laugh and say you've lost your touch, someone's passing off fakes and you fell for it. Ghost Hero Chau, for God's sake. Then it's, *Oh, look at the time, I've got to go*, and before they're out the door they're speed-dialing whoever you said had the Chaus."

"And that's been going on?"

"Variations of it. For about a week now. But I've spoken to the galleries and private dealers—I'm sure everyone else has, too—and I've gotten nowhere. Only one gallery assistant even admitted to knowing what I was talking about, and then he backpedaled. I think he realized he was in over his head. The Chinese contemporary world's pretty small and his boss must be as eager as anyone to find these paintings. If I end up with them because this kid put me on the inside track, and his boss finds out, he's up a creek. Plus, I just started collecting. He might be willing to go out on a limb for one of the big collectors, but he doesn't know me from a hole in the ground."

A creek, a limb, and a hole in the ground. Maybe these were nature metaphors with hidden political meaning.

"So what do you think, Ms. Chin? Can you find them?"

"Mr. Dunbar, you're not even sure these paintings exist. Why not wait until they either surface, or it all turns out to be smoke? I guess what I'm asking is, Why is paying for an investigation worth it?" It's not that I wanted to talk myself out of work, but something wasn't adding up here.

Jeff Dunbar regarded me. "Do you collect anything, Ms. Chin? Stamps, coins, Barbie dolls?" He added, "Guns?" Racial profiling, but carefully politically correct about gender.

"No."

He leaned forward. "For a collector, the hunt's as much of a thrill as the find. I want these Chaus, if they're real. But I also want to be the one who finds them, and finds out if they're real. Especially since I'm the new kid on the block. Does that make sense?"

"I guess so," I said, though the collector's passion, to me, is like gravity: I admit it has a pull but I don't understand it.

"Also," he said, "there's a time issue."

Ah. Time is money. And money does talk.

"Asian Art Week starts Sunday. All over town: The auction houses, the museums and galleries, two big Armory shows, and a show the Chinese government's sending over called Beijing/NYC. Mostly classical art and antiquities, but a lot of contemporary, too. The big collectors, the critics, the curators all come. From everywhere—Asia and Europe, as well as here. If these Chaus exist, whoever has them might be planning to unveil them then."

"To make a splash."

"That's right."

"And you want them so you can make the splash."

"I told you the collecting world's small? It's also closed and clannish. Some things I'm interested in I never get a shot at, because when they show up, I'm not the one who gets the call. I want that to change. If I had the new Chaus, trust me, that would change."

"All right. But there's something else. I don't know much about this, but wouldn't an artist, or a dealer or somebody, whoever has these paintings, either just put them on the market, or not? I mean, one or the other. Rumors, mystery, paintings no one's seen that may or not be real—is this how the art world works?"

"Normally, no. But as I said, Ghost Hero Chau is a special case. The possibility of new paintings by him would be bound to stir up all kinds of mystery and rumors."

"And why is that?"

Dunbar sat back. "Are you familiar with the uprising at Tiananmen Square in 1989?"

I thought for a moment. "A democracy movement that never got off the ground, crushed by the Party. That's about all I know."

"Correct. They sent the army in against the protestors. Hundreds of people were killed. Including Ghost Hero Chau. Ms. Chin, he's been dead for twenty years."

2

Back in my office an hour later, I watched Bill Smith take an evaluative sip of coffee. He used to bring his own, but last week I'd bought a coffee press and a grinder and a pound of beans to store in the tiny freezer in my tiny fridge. Bill and I have had our ups and downs over the years; buying all this coffee-producing stuff was, for me, a big commitment.

"Excellent," he pronounced.

"What a relief. So . . ." I leaned back in my creaky chair, cradling my jasmine tea, which was also excellent. ". . . what are we going to do about the late great Ghost Hero Chau and his new paintings?"

"Well, my first thought, you won't be surprised to hear, is that they're fakes." He sipped his coffee and gave a happy sigh.

"I suggested that to the client. He agreed they could be."

"If Chau's dead, and the paintings are new, they sort of have to be," Bill pointed out. "If they're real and they're new, Chau's unlikely to be dead. Unless he painted them twenty years ago and they're just turning up now, so they're not really new. Or he's dead and he just painted them, so he really is a ghost."

"Dunbar says no."

"No real ghost?"

"You sound disappointed."

"It would be something different."

"Sorry. No old paintings. Dunbar says the content refers to the problems of modern China. Internal migration, freedom of expression, corruption."

"The content," Bill said thoughtfully. "But it's coded, isn't it? He's sure he's reading it right?"

"Well, he's not reading it at all, because he hasn't seen them. Those are the rumors."

"Rumors. Which the whole collecting world's heard, but the dealers haven't."

"Dunbar thinks the dealers almost certainly have but won't admit it until one of them's got the paintings in his hot little hands."

"Okay, so tell me this: Why is Dunbar coming to an investigator instead of an art expert?"

"And an investigator with no clue about art. There, I just had to say it before you did. But it's not about whether the paintings are real or fake. It's about finding them. Which he thinks I can do because I'm Chinese. He thinks I can boldly go where no muscle-bound barbarian has gone before."

"Undercover in the teahouses and rice paddies of your people. Eavesdropping behind crimson columns. Parting the stalks in a bamboo grove."

"I actually think that's what he means."

"Well, good for him. How much does he say these paintings are worth?"

"Chaus from the eighties sell for three to six hundred thousand. And if these are real and new, meaning Chau's still alive, they could set off a feeding frenzy."

"Ah. Now chasing something that may not exist starts to make sense. Though I think your client's being a little cute about his motivation."

"By which you mean? . . ."

"The thrill of the hunt, being the new kid in town, wanting the big boys to take him seriously. All that."

"You think it's baloney?"

"I think it's worse than that, but if I use those words I might not get more coffee." He held out his mug. "You said there was something off about him."

"Well, there was. I remember the art majors from college. The studio majors were on their own planet, of course, but even the dorkiest history-and-crit major was hipper than this guy."

"People change. Maybe he swerved to the right after he graduated."

"Then why is he collecting cutting-edge art?"

"Now he has a little money and he's loosening up again?"

"What are you saying? You think I'm wrong about something being off?"

"You're never wrong about that. I'm just giving you a hard time."

"Oh, good, in case I might forget who you are. So what do we think he's up to?"

Bill considered briefly. "Well, one possibility: it's exactly what he said. He's looking to make an end run around everyone else and snap these paintings up. But—"

"But you think it's about money, not the pure love of art."

"That didn't cross your mind?"

"Actually, it more than crossed it. It lodged there." I drank some more of my excellent tea. "In our entire conversation, he didn't once say anything about wanting to *see* the paintings. Wondering what they were like. How they might be different from the older ones, better or worse. What a thrill it would be if Ghost Hero Chau really were alive, and still painting."

"So. He may be a collector, but he's not a lover. He's gambling they're real and he wants to corner the market. You're shaking your head. Why?"

"I don't think he's a collector, either. I ran a background. No Jeff Dunbars his age in any of the databases. He gave me a business card with no business on it, only his name and phone number. Not even an e-mail. Now, that could mean he's rich enough not to work, rich enough he doesn't want anyone to know who he really is. Collecting art would go along with that, and I guess so would paying my retainer in cash—"

"How much, by the way? Unless it's none of my business."

"Since I'm paying you out of it, it can be your business. A grand against two days plus expenses. More after that, or we settle up if I find them sooner."

"A trustful sort of fellow, handing over cash like that."

I shrugged. It was a lot, but clients paying in cash are not all that rare. Many people like to avoid a paper trail leading to a PI.

"But the phone," I said, "is a prepaid cell."

"Ah. Now that's damn dubious, I'd say."

"And the suit didn't scream 'too rich to work' either."

"Shiny and threadbare?"

"No, no. Perfectly fine, but strictly off the rack. A good rack, but not super high-end. Remember, I'm a seamstress's daughter."

"You do your mother proud."

"Leave my mother out of it. And frankly, if he were a Getty or something—not to display my lack of self-esteem but why is he coming to me? All the big guys have Asians on staff."

"Because you're better?"

"But how would he know that? Seriously, I'm thinking he's just a working stiff, and his work has to do with China. He said he learned Chinese because he thought it would be useful. I bet he's in import-export, or he's American legal counsel for a Chinese firm, something like that. That's probably where he heard about the paintings—at work. He's using a phony name because he doesn't want his bosses to know he's on the hunt, and he came to me, not one of the big boys, out of the same instinct. He's not the new collector on the block. He's not on the block at all. He just wants to cash in on the Chaus." I finished my tea and looked at Bill. It was a sensible theory and he nodded.

"Or," I said.

"Or." Bill didn't stop nodding, but he waited for me to say it.

"Or he's not looking for the paintings at all. He's looking for the painter."

Bill lit a cigarette and dropped the match in the ashtray I keep around for him. "So. Why?" He streamed out smoke. "Chau owes him money? Stole his girl?"

"Twenty years ago, when Chau was thirty-five and Dunbar was ten?"

"Maybe it wasn't Dunbar. It was his daddy. A multigenerational family feud. Your people go in for that, don't they? God knows mine do. Maybe this is the Hatfields and the McChaus."

"Okay. But still. Chau's well-known to be dead."

"An obstacle, but not insurmountable. Maybe he's been reincarnated. Another thing your people go in for."

"You're mocking my people."

"In case you might forget who I am."

"Fat chance." We sat in silence for a few moments. Then I said, "Here's what I propose: we take the case. But, whatever we find, we don't tell the client until we know what's really going on."

"Or, you could tell the client to go climb a tree and branch off."

"Are you kidding? May I remind you I haven't worked in nearly a month? There was that fistful of cash, you remember."

Bill didn't respond to that. He and I have both sent clients packing, retainer or not, when they were up to something we wanted no part of.

I sighed and looked into my empty cup. "I realized something. While Dunbar was talking."

"Which is?"

"The collecting thing . . . I don't get it. I never have."

"Okay."

"But the hunting thing? Being the one to chase something down? Find it first, discover a secret? That I do get. I think," I admitted slowly, "that's why I'm in this business."

Bill cocked his head and grinned. "That's your big insight?"

"What do you mean?"

"If that's news to you, you're the last to hear it."

I felt myself redden.

"No, come on," Bill said. "You keep telling me I do this so I can be Sir Galahad, riding in and saving the town. Why can't you have a less-than-pure motive, too?"

"I never said Sir Galahad. I said the Lone Ranger."

"The effect is the same, and Sir Galahad doesn't have to wear a mask."

"No, just a tin suit. Anyway, my motives are pure and we're taking the case."

"So I can be Sir Galahad and you can be Indiana Jones?"

"The Lone Ranger! And Indiana Jones, in case you missed it, is a guy. Why can't I be Lara Croft?"

"Okay, but she doesn't have a whip."

"I'm *so* not going there. And for your information, we're taking the case because at the end, when I've found the secret and you've saved the town, I can keep Jeff Dunbar's retainer and maybe even send him another big bill. Coffee-making machinery doesn't come cheap, you know. And a constant supply of beans? Please."

"Well, if that's what's at stake." Bill finished his coffee. "So okay, boss. What's our first move?"

I sat back and gazed at the ceiling. "I wish I knew more about Chau. Or Chinese art. I Googled, but Chau's story is pretty much what Dunbar said it was, and I didn't find anything else helpful. The only lead I have is this gallery assistant who backpedaled."

"Well, let's go lean on him."

"Sure, but what if he doesn't give? I don't have a clue where to go next."

"Art, according to Dunbar, is not why he hired you. Chinese-ness is."

"Yes, but he's wrong. Seriously, whatever's going on, who says anyone involved is Chinese except me and Ghost Hero Chau? It's art I need."

Bill looked at me for a few moments with something in his eyes I couldn't read. Then he shifted his gaze to his coffee cup, and the press, and the grinder. "Well, okay," he said, and took out his cell phone. The coversation was friendly and brief: he ascertained the callee was in and would remain so, and that was that. He put the phone away and stood. "Come on."

We subwayed up to a neighborhood I don't usually have much business in, the part of the Upper East Side that's waist-deep in old money. Bill, though, negotiated the sidewalks like he was right at home. That's because he was. He lives as far downtown as I do—and was born in Kentucky, for Pete's sake—but a lot of New York's museums and galleries are up here. Bill is one of those rare New Yorkers who actually spends time in museums and galleries, looking at art.

We weren't going to a gallery or a museum, though. At a brownstone on Madison near Seventy-fifth Bill pressed a buzzer. A man's voice popped from the speaker: "Hey! Come on up!" and, buzzed in, we climbed a curving staircase from the days when this was someone's grand home. On the second floor, in the open doorway of an elegantly spare office—gleaming wood floor, sunlight pouring through wide street-side windows—stood a tall and grinning Asian man.

"Bill Smith!" he said. "Way cool! Come on in." He shook Bill's hand, then turned to me. "Hi. I'm Jack Lee." His words held no trace of any Asian accent, but not a New York one, either.

"Lydia Chin."

"Bill's partner, I know." Jack Lee's hand was big, his grip solid. "Come on, sit down, you guys."

Jack Lee was around my age, nearly as tall as Bill, and in weight somewhere between us, which made him a string bean. Loose-limbed and lanky, he wore a beautiful multicolored silk tie and ironed black jeans, but no jacket. His white shirtsleeves were neatly rolled back, revealing muscled forearms. Closing the door, he pointed us to wood chairs set around a low table piled with art books. Most of what was in the waist-high bookcase behind the desk were art books, too, though some had the staid leather bindings and stamped lettering of law manuals.

Bill and I sat, and Jack Lee started to do the same, but stopped halfway. "Uh-oh. F for hospitality! I don't have coffee or anything for you guys. Drank it up, haven't replenished. You want something? There's a good place a block up." He rattled off words like a drum solo.

"Not me, I'm fine," I said. The minimalist chair was surprisingly comfortable.

"Me, too," said Bill. "I just had a really good cup of coffee."

"Cool. I'm second-generation ABC from Madison, Wisconsin," Jack Lee said to me as he sprawled onto a chair. ABC, that's American-born Chinese. I'm first generation, myself. "I may look Chinese, but think of me as an All-American midwestern college-town boy. That way you won't be too disappointed."

I had to smile. "I'm already not disappointed."

"But she wasn't expecting anything," Bill put in.

"Baseline zero, try not to make it worse, Jack, I get it. So, what can I do for you?"

"I'm not sure," I said. "What do you do?"

Jack Lee raised his eyebrows at Bill. "You didn't tell her?"

"I never tell her anything. Keeps the relationship fresh."

"'Fresh' isn't the word I'd have used," I said.

"Got you. Well, the big secret he wants me to spill is, I'm a private eye."

"Oh." I blinked. "No kidding?"

"Yeah, how about that? And Bill's been promising to bring you up here for months now. You know, so we can share mysterious Chinese trade secrets. I was starting to think you didn't exist.

That he'd invented a kick-ass Chinese partner to string me along, keep the top-shelf bourbon flowing."

"Kick-ass?"

"He was lying?"

"Not about that, no," I said.

"I was just waiting for the moment of maximum impact," Bill said. "I thought it would be most efficient for you to share those mysterious secrets while you worked on a case."

"Hey," said Jack, "you mean this isn't just a social call? You come bearing work?"

"We might." Bill turned to me. "Jack, as he says, may look Chinese, but that's actually beside the point. He's an art expert."

"'Expert' is too strong a word," Jack corrected, with Chinese modesty but an American grin. "But it's my field. Art history, Asian art concentration." I'd already taken note of the framed University of Chicago Ph.D. on the bookcase—which included the words "summa cum laude"—so that wasn't news. "Life plan was to be a big-deal dealer. Came to New York to go the gallery route. But I couldn't take it."

"It involves sitting still," Bill said, in explanation.

"Sad but true. So now instead of selling art, I corral it. Chase down the lost, stolen, or strayed. Bodyguard a vase on its way someplace. Check a bronze's provenance. Make sure the dish that comes back from the restorer is the same one that was sent to be restored. Much more fun, and it keeps me out of trouble. And out of galleries. Still, galleries have their uses. That's where I met your partner. At a Soho opening, last fall."

I said to Bill, "You hate openings."

"The gallery owner was a friend of mine. He's helped me out over the years. I had to go."

"And he's a client of mine," Jack said. "So, so did I."

I looked from one to the other. "And you guys bonded over white wine, Chex Mix, and art?"

"For that show," Jack said, "'art' is too strong a word. Installations made from rusty tools and broken dolls. Pretentious, ugly, and lethal."

"See," said Bill, "there's that Chinese problem you have, where you won't speak your mind. Same as Lydia."

I knew he was expecting me to roll my eyes, so I just sat politely, listening to Jack.

"Pretty much everyone seemed to be impressed, though," Jack said. "A lot of nodding and murmuring. 'The juxtaposition is thrillingly unnerving.' 'He brings out the feminine side of steel.' I was checking my watch to see if I could leave yet when I spotted a guy having as hard a time as I was keeping a straight face."

"Not my fault," Bill protested. "There was a critic waving his hands, going on about a piece made from doll heads and buzz-saw blades. Then he cut his thumb on it."

"It was the start of a beautiful friendship. Cemented in the bar next door."

"Though I warn you," Bill said, "Jack drinks martinis."

"Does that disqualify me from something?"

"Not by itself," I said.

"So." Jack crossed one long leg over the other. "Now that you have my CV, do you know why Bill brought you here? Besides the Chinese trade secret thing? Because if we get into that, of course we'll have to throw him out."

"Of course. Let's save that for later, in case we need it. Tell me, is contemporary Chinese art on your CV?"

Jack glanced at Bill, then back to me. "Up to a point."

"Ghost Hero Chau. Is he before or after that point?"

"Ghost Hero Chau." Jack steepled his fingers in front of his chin. "He's your case?"

"His paintings. Or, some new paintings that are supposed to be his."

"Re-eally?" Jack drew the word out, giving me an odd look.

"I know, he's dead. But that's what my client says. New paintings."

"Who's your client? Okay, never mind," he said in answer to my you-know-better smile. "But is he Chinese?"

"No. WASP, even more midwestern suburban than you are."

"Ouch," said Bill.

"But that's why he came to me. He searched online for a Chinese investigator. He thinks it'll help."

"Hmm. Hmm, hmm hmm, hmm hmm," Jack said. "What's his angle? He's been offered them and he wants you to prove the pedigree before he buys?"

"No. He hasn't even seen them. He wants me to find them."

"Re-eally." Again, he drew the word out like taffy. "Why?"

"The thrill of the hunt. And, he's the new kid in town and wants to make his collecting bones by getting his hands on them." To the look on Jack's face, I said, "No, we don't buy it either. We think he just wants to corner the market and flip them during Asian Art Week. Obviously, he's gambling they're real, or the market's not worth cornering."

"And you came to me for what? Background?"

"Yes," said Bill. "And Chinese trade secrets."

"Which *you'll* never hear, Kemosabe," Jack retorted. I snickered as Jack looked from Bill to me. "Ghost Hero Chau. Do you guys know much about him? Why they call him that?"

"He was involved in the Tiananmen Square protests in 1989," I said. "He was a big deal professor, but he stood with the students. He died when the army came in. After he died, according to my client, he was a ghost, but a hero."

"That's how he put it?"

"It's wrong?"

"It's incomplete. For months after Tiananmen, there were rumors Chau was still alive."

I gave Bill a quick look. "Oh. So if the rumors are true, the paintings could actually be his."

"It's unlikely, though." Jack rearranged himself again, throwing one leg over a chair arm. "The PRC government admits to two hundred and forty-one people dying by the time Tiananmen was over. Rioters and hooligans, every one of them, threats to the public order and enemies of the revolution. But about a thousand more were never heard from again. The government says they were more rioters and hooligans and they ran away. Their families say they were killed, but no one's been able to prove it. Those people are the 'ghosts.' But Chau was one of the two hundred and forty-one. He's on the official list, his body was identified, he's buried in his hometown."

"Then where did the rumors come from?"

"People claiming they'd seen him. In different parts of the country, over the next few months. Rumors were flying everywhere that summer. They had a news blackout; no one knew what was going on. For anyone looking for a symbol to rally around, Chau would've been perfect. The rumors were probably started by underground student leaders trying to keep the movement going. Eventually, though, they died out."

"Were there paintings?" Bill asked.

Jack's thin face had been wearing a brooding look, but now he broke into a grin. "Smith, two points! No. That's one of the things that finally convinced people it wasn't true. If Chau had been alive, he could've signaled that and rallied people by making new paintings. Even under another name, his work's that distinctive. But there weren't any."

"Okay," said Bill. "Now I have another question. How come you're a walking encyclopedia about Tiananmen Square? Which happened when you were eight?"

"Nine." Jack considered him. "If I told you we studied Tiananmen at art school because the Beijing art school was in a leadership role in the movement, would you believe me?"

Bill shook his head solemnly. Jack turned to me.

"I would have," I said. "Except I never believe anybody who asks if I'd believe him if."

Jack regarded me another moment, then ejected himself from his chair. He strode the length of the room, turned, covered the distance again. He stopped with his back to us and stared at the full moon glowing from the only thing hanging on the wall, a Japanese woodblock print. "Okay." He spun around. "Weighing the demands of client confidentiality against the possibility of actually solving the client's case, and against the *im*possibility of maintaining confidentiality when I bump into you guys every ten minutes in the course of this investigation, here's the answer: I know all that because my client told me."

"Client? What client?"

He grinned and folded his arms. "I'll show you mine if you show me yours. I have the same case."

3

For the rest of our discussion we repaired to the café on the next block because Bill and Jack both thought the situation called for caffeine. Bill also wanted a smoke. I, of course, was completely self-sufficient and needed nothing, but I went along for the ride. Jack ordered and waited at the counter while Bill and I colonized a table.

"The truth," I said, as I unwound my scarf. "Did you have any idea?"

"That Jack had a similar case?"

"The same case, he says."

"No. And I'm not sure I like it."

"Why? You have a problem with him you're not telling me about?"

"Absolutely not. Jack's a wild man, but he's stand-up. He's also really good at what he does."

"Then why have you been holding out on me?"

"Holding out what?"

"Him."

"It's my job to make sure you know every Chinese person in New York?"

"Oh, forget it. What is it you're not sure you like?"

"Two people with enough sudden interest in the same set of facts—no, rumors—to hire investigators."

"Maybe his client's interest isn't sudden."

"Or maybe it's not two clients. Maybe it's the same client, hedging his bets."

I'd thought of that, too. "That would be a weird vote of no confidence. In both investigators."

Jack came back to us, spread mugs around, and plopped onto a chair. "Okay," he said. "Cards on the table?"

"What do you mean? Share information? You're suggesting we work the cases together?"

He shook his head. "I don't think we can go that far. This is the race to the pole! Scott and Amundsen. Mush! You guys can be Scott."

"Who won?"

"Amundsen."

"Not only that," Bill said, "Scott died on the way back."

I said, "I thought you liked this guy."

"I thought I did."

"No, listen." Jack tested his two-shot macchiato. "There's an obvious conflict if we work together. Whose client gets the gold from the mummy's tomb when we find it?"

"Let me point out that, personally," I said, "I haven't been hired to deliver the mummy's gold. Just to locate it."

"Ooh, Talmudic," Jack said with admiration. "But I still see a conflict. I mean, don't you?"

"Yes," I admitted.

"But what I said before is true—we'd be running into each other anyway. It would get embarrassing after a while. And if I blow you off, tell you I never heard of Ghost Hero Chau, who you gonna call?"

"Ghost Hero Busters?"

"My client. The minute you scratch the Chinese contemporary art surface, you'll find him. He's the go-to guy. Bernard Yang, at NYU."

"Oh. I think his name came up when I Googled."

"Told you. You'd show up in his office looking for background on Ghost Hero Chau. Next thing, he has a cow and calls me. Then I have to say I have no idea who you are but I'll check it out, which is a lie and makes me look a step behind besides. Or I have to tell him I know all about you but no worries, which makes my judgment in not warning him suspect. Or, I do warn him, and tell him to pretend he's out of town when you call. Then I have to pretend to you I didn't do that, and—man, you guys are putting me in a bad position. Some friends you are."

"We'll make it up to you," Bill said. "When this is all over I'll buy you a drink."

"Not good enough."

"*I'll* buy you a drink," I said.

Jack brightened. "Now you're talking."

"Well," I said to Bill. "At least they're different clients."

Jack said, "That's why I asked before if yours was Chinese."

"Is Yang Chinese-Chinese, or ABC?"

"Chinese-Chinese. From the mainland, here about twenty years."

"From the mainland, Bernard?"

"No, Ji-tong, but he's an American now. Hey, is your name Lydia?"

"No," I admitted. "Chin Ling Wan-ju."

"Ling Wan-ju? 'Sparkling doll?'"

"More like the buzz-saw blades," Bill put in.

Jack stuck out his hand to me. "Lee Yat-sen."

We shook hands a second time. Maybe it was from his coffee mug, but now his grip seemed not just strong, but warm. "Named after Sun Yat-sen?"

"My mother's a great admirer. What about you?" Jack asked Bill.

"Charlie Chan Smith. Your Professor Yang, what's his interest?"

"Moral outrage." Jack leaned forward, bony elbows sticking out. "Yang also taught at the Beijing Art Institute, back in the day. He wasn't involved in the democracy movement—cautious kind of guy—but of course he knew Chau. They were friends, and he admired Chau's work. He thinks these new paintings are fakes and all the mystery's just a way to build them up."

"For what purpose?"

"For some forger and some dealer to make a lot of money."

"And that makes him so indignant he's willing to pay an investigator to expose them? Before they're even on the market?"

"They may never come on the market. Lots of art is traded privately. Yang says Chau died for his beliefs and he shouldn't be resurrected to fill someone's pockets."

"So Yang's doing what, salving his conscience for not marching shoulder to shoulder with Chau back then?" Bill asked. "He doesn't have a horse in the race?"

"That's the implication."

"Okay." I looked up from my spice tea. "The reason my client gave for hiring me sounded fishy and I told you what we think his real one is. Yours sounds fishy, too."

Jack nodded. "It does."

"And?"

"My completely theoretical, backed-up-by-nothing hypothesis?"

"You have another one?"

"No."

"Then that one."

"I think he's got a closetful of Chaus from the Art Institute days. They'd lose value if there's been a miracle, the guy's alive, these new ones turn out to be real and more keep coming."

I thought about that. "Is he a collector?"

"No. He has some nice pieces in his office, probably a few more at home. But he's an academic. He advises collectors, but he can't afford to collect in a major way. What that means, though, is that if he does have a stash of Chaus, they're probably his whole retirement fund."

"So if these new ones are frauds, he'll want to expose them. If they're real, he'll want to know fast, so he can unload what he has."

Bill said, "Then why not say that? Protecting his investment by exposing frauds wouldn't be illegal, or even immoral. He might even be doing someone else a favor. Like Lydia's client."

"Who is who, by the way?" Jack asked. "I did show you mine."

I raised an eyebrow but played it straight. "Jeff Dunbar. Free-lance rich guy. Sez him."

"You don't think so?"

"He's invisible in the databases. His cell phone's a prepaid. And he doesn't look all that rich."

"Hmm. So what's up?"

"I think being found sniffing out these paintings would get him in trouble with someone, and he doesn't trust his PI's discretion."

"I hate that in a client. And I have another question. Don't take this wrong, because I know you're kick-ass and all. But why didn't he come to me?"

"Nice guy, your friend," I said to Bill. "Too bad he's so insecure."

"You say he chose you because you're Chinese. I'm Chinese *and*

I specialize in art—Chinese art, even. Any collector in this area looking for a PI, my name would pop up like the answer in a Magic 8-Ball."

"But," Bill said, "anyone not in the art world searching online for a Chinese PI would have nothing to go on but a Chinese name."

"Which Chin looks like, and Lee, not necessarily."

"Plus," I said, "it comes earlier in the alphabet."

"She's very competitive," Jack said to Bill. "Is she insecure?"

With great dignity I ignored that. "So Jeff Dunbar's likely not a player in the art world. We'd figured that out, thank you very much. Still, he could know the value of these paintings and be hoping to make a quick buck."

"Why not just tell you that? Why the song and dance?"

"Good question."

"But you didn't ask?"

"Not yet."

"Because? . . ."

"The whole situation intrigues me. If he knew I hadn't bought his lies he'd drop me and find someone else. That would be no fun."

Jack's gaze rested on me, level and appraising. He broke into a big grin. "You're right," he said to Bill. "Kick-ass."

"Hey, listen," I said. "Your client's not so straightforward, either. If all he's doing is protecting his investment, why did he give you a story?"

Jack looked surprised. "Face," he said, as though it were obvious. "Come on, he knew the guy. Chau died standing up to the tanks, Yang's making a cushy living in the capitalist heartland. Sounds better to tell me he's offended at the crass attempt to cash in on Chau's rep than to admit he doesn't want his nest egg to take a hit."

"A very Chinese motive," I admitted. "So. Interesting situation."

"Generally, or specifically?"

"Both. Specifically: I wonder what your client will do if we find the paintings, and it turns out they're real?"

"Be unhappy. Just like yours will be, if it turns out they're fakes."

We shook hands in the cool spring sun outside the café, wished one another luck, and headed off in opposite directions.

"Nice guy," I said to Bill. "We'll clobber him."

"One of your best qualities," Bill said. "Your cooperative spirit."

"I cooperate. I share."

"You didn't share our other theory. That Dunbar's not looking for the paintings at all, just the painter. And you didn't tell Jack we have a lead on that gallery assistant."

"You're his friend, and you didn't either."

"I'm your partner. Your case, your choice."

That was how we worked: The one who brought the case in took the lead. It had been that way since back when we weren't partners, just PI's who called each other in from time to time. But not really, I suddenly realized. From the start we'd discussed, argued, poked holes in each other's theories and plans. We operated from a two-person consensus, not a hierarchy.

"If it were your case," I asked, "would you have told him that stuff?"

Bill grinned. "Probably not."

On the next corner I took out my phone and called Baxter/ Haig, the gallery where our lead worked. I spoke to an ennui-filled young woman, then clicked off and told Bill, "On the late shift to-day. In at noon."

Bill checked his watch. "Okay, then, I have an idea." He told me about it, I liked it, and we both headed off to fulfill our parts. I went to the Met's Asian art galleries to inspect classical ink paintings, for an idea of what these new Chaus, real or fake, might look like.

Bill went home to shave.

4

The half hour I spent drifting through the museum's quiet rooms mostly just reminded me how ignorant I was. I read exhibit labels and bought a book that talked about brushstroke angle and ink saturation. It also discussed the concept of veiled commentary, just enough to confuse me. I looked at the paintings with it in mind, but I had trouble following how plum blossoms that were borderless gray wash instead of opaque white with black outlines expressed the sympathy of Buddhist monks for exiled officials.

What did intrigue me, though, were the poems. Because this was familiar stuff.

Chinese classical paintings often have poems on them, either the poem that inspired the painting, or one inspired by it. Sometimes the poem's by the painter, sometimes by someone else. I knew that, but I'd never spent much time with the poems. Now I tried reading them as political commentary, too. The ones in the exhibit were mostly short couplets—"Crickets and ants are on the Great Road," that sort of thing. After a few, it hit me: All the old men of my childhood talked like this. Even today, if I drop in at Grandfather Gao's herb shop, we'll sit over tea and he'll come out with something like, "A swirling feather cannot come to rest until the wind dies down," or "Beating the grass for game may stir the sleeping snake." Half the time I have no idea what he's talking about, but the other half, it turns out he's saying something I really need to listen to.

I leaned in to study the poems. The crickets and ants, those must be the riffraff you encounter everywhere, even on the Great Road. The wild goose whose call, unanswered, echoes outside the poet's hut is his yearning for his hometown, far away. The poems made me feel considerably less dim than the paintings did. I was reading one about centipedes and spiders that ended, "Pity the ones caught in the world's web/Those with poison are not lenient with each other," when a voice in my ear whispered, "Don't turn around. There's a ghost behind you."

"No, it's only you," I said to Bill, whose reflection I'd seen in the glass as he was sneaking up on me. "It's just that, spiffed up like that, you look so unreal."

"You're adorably ephemeral, too. Shall we go?"

A bus, a subway, and a little walking—together faster than a midday cab—put us in the heart of the Chelsea gallery district. This part of lower midtown, way over west, is where the art dealers fled after SoHo went all upmarket.

Baxter/Haig occupied prime real estate, the ground floor of a renovated warehouse on West Twenty-fifth. We pulled open glass doors and strolled into a high-ceilinged space hung with huge, vivid canvases. The paintings all offered clichéd—or, I suppose, iconic, depending on your point of view—images of China. Tiered pagodas, terraced rice fields, moon-gated gardens, the slithering Great Wall. Busy folks swarmed everywhere, numerous as insects. Another icon/cliché: the vast industrious Chinese masses. Only when I looked closely I saw these weren't people. They were American cartoon characters. Mickey Mouse, in his white gloves, harvested rice. Donald Duck, along with Daisy, Huey, Dewey, Louie, and an army of shirted and pantless waterbirds, strolled the Wall. Yosemite Sam inspected the terra-cotta warriors. Outside the Temple of Heaven the Simpsons posed for a family photograph.

Bill, jeans exchanged for pressed wool slacks, lifted his eyebrows in bored recognition as we walked around. Giant letters on the wall announced this show as COLONY: NEW WORKS BY PANG PING-PONG.

"Please tell me that's not his real name," I whispered.

Bill glanced over a price list and artist's statement he'd lifted from the reception desk. "You're in luck. Pang's his family name. He uses the name 'Ping-Pong' as an integral part of the ironic self-referential essence of the meta-situation on which his paintings comment."

"Oh," I said. "That's much better."

Besides us, the giant room held only five people. Four were in the back, among the canvases: an elegant older woman in high-heeled boots, frowning at the Fantastic Four in Buddhist robes; the rotund man beside her, gesturing and murmuring in what seemed to me a smarmily intimate fashion; and a pair of young men whose clothes and haircuts were so painfully hip they had to be art students. The place had the hushed, intense feel of a library. No: the anxiety-tinged air of a classroom during a final exam.

The gallery's fifth occupant was a fashionably emaciated, lank-haired young man at the front desk. When we came in he gave us the narrowed eyes of a proctor; when that didn't chase us out, he iced us, going back to whatever important work he'd been doing before we'd had the effrontery to walk through the door. This charmer, as

I knew from my Googling, was Nick Greenbank, the fellow we wanted to see.

We took an unhurried, but in Bill's case pointedly apathetic, turn around the gallery. I tried to interest him in this painting or that, showing him details like Captain America and Superman in coolie hats. He shook his head and waved me off each time, until finally he sauntered back over to the desk, me in frustrated tow.

It's hard to ignore Bill when he looms, though Nick Greenbank did a better job than most. Finally looking up from his computer screen in badly hidden exasperation, he asked, "Can I help you?"

Bill leaned on the counter, smiled, waved a hand around, and in a conversational tone and a thick Russian accent, said, "Thees ees crep."

"Vladimir, please!" I hissed. "I'm sorry," I said distractedly to the affronted young man. What had affronted him was Bill's rude dismissal of the work; what was distracting me were the blindingly ostentatious gold rings on Bill's fingers, which matched the chains around his open-shirted neck, but which I was sure he hadn't been wearing a few moments ago. "Mr. Oblomov hasn't had much exposure to recent Chinese works. I brought him here hoping—"

"She vass hoping I buy, den she make fet commission. But I don't buy crep. Leessen, boychik." Bill leaned in closer and dropped his voice. "I like beautiful. Vy you tink I let her take me around? She ees beautiful, dah? Now, deess Chinese, dey used to paint beautiful. Pine trees, bamboo, all dat. Not Meekey Fucking Mouse. Now I hear"—he let the smile fade and drilled the young man with his eyes—"I hear det von of dem still does."

Bill can do a good eye-drill, especially in Russian gangster mode. Nick Greenbank blanched, making his already-pale skin a nice contrast to his black silk shirt.

"You're talking about classical Chinese art." He swallowed and tried to recover, drawing on reservoirs of disdain to soothe his rasping voice. "From the dynasty periods. We don't handle that. I suggest—"

"I suggest you pay attention, boychik. Dere's a fellow I'm very, very interested in."

From a position a discreet step behind Bill, I frantically but subtly signaled to little Nick. *Don't cross the dangerous Russian mobster,* I tried to say with my eyes. There may be people whose eyes could say that; I'm not one of them, but I did manage to get across some sense of panic. Nick paused, looking both confused and apprehensive.

"He vass dead," Bill mused. "Now he's not dead. Chau Chun, but you know dat, dah? Dey call him da Ghost Hero."

"I don't know—"

"Dah, you do!" Bill smacked his hand on the counter. The impact wasn't hard enough to make the art students or the booted lady turn around—the round gent had vanished—but Nick yanked his head back as though he'd been bitch-slapped.

"Now, come on, boychik. Someone hass a bunch of paintings, supposed to be by diss Ghost Hero Chau. You"—Bill's jabbing finger stopped just short of Nick's nose—"know who dat iss. You tell me, I buy, you get fet commission, just like her. You play stupid games, I get annoyed. My friends, dey get annoyed, too." He pulled a cigarette from his pocket and stuck it in his mouth. Then he lit a match. He didn't bring the flame to the cigarette, though, but instead lifted his arm and swept a slow semi-circle. "Ven dey get annoyed, dey can be very annoying, my friends." Unhurriedly, he drifted the match in until it was very near Nick's nose. Nick seemed paralyzed; nothing moved but his eyes, which crossed, watching the flame. After a moment, Bill grinned and shook the match out. "I forget, diss iss America, can't smoke any damn place." He opened his fingers and dropped the match on Nick's desk. "So," he said, unhurriedly restoring the cigarette to the pack. "Be a good boychik. Who hass dese paintings?"

"I—" Nick shook his head, glancing frantically to the back of the gallery. The art students and the booted woman showed no signs of having noticed. Nick whispered, "I could get fired!"

"Hah!" Bill bellowed, poking me in the shoulder. I staggered. "Fired! Good sense of humor, dah?" Bill's arm repeated the semicircle. "Fired! He gets fired, gallery gets fired! Ha! Dat's pretty funny!"

"No! All right, listen, I don't know who's got them—"

Bill sighed and shook his head.

"No, really. But I know who knows."

"Oh?" Bill smiled. "Now vee get someplace." He leaned on the counter again and placidly waited.

"This girl," said Nick. "She's at some gallery uptown, I don't remember. Wait, Gruber, I think that's it. Anyway I have her number." He was thumbing a BlackBerry as he spoke. "I met her at an afterparty, some opening. She was trying to impress me." He said that as though that was the usual reaction to meeting Nick Greenbank at an afterparty. "She tried to show me work from some studio visit. Bunch of Chinese-American artists, a group open studio. Like I'd care."

"You vouldn't? Vy not?"

"Hybridized," Nick scoffed. "Mongrel work, no real grounding in place. We don't handle Chinese-American shit, just real Chinese."

Bill had better wrap this up fast, I found myself thinking, or I might have to shove my Chinese-American fist down Nick Greenbank's throat.

"Here, Shayna Dylan, that's her." Nick turned the phone so Bill could see the screen. Bill entered Shayna Dylan's number into his own phone. Nick, meanwhile, had managed to reinflate his punctured superiority. "She's an airhead. Yadda-yadda about this shit, and then she drops that my boss saw her photos, too, and got all excited, wanted to know where the open studio was. So then I said, okay, whatever, and looked at what she was trying to show me. Of course I knew right away what he was hot for. Not the crap she was photographing. There were three Chaus, hanging on the wall behind."

"You could tell dey were dat? From a tiny picture on a leetle phone?"

"Chinese contemporary is what I do. It's the hottest area around." When Bill still looked skeptical, Nick added defensively, "Chau Gwai Ying Shung had a very distinctive style. Unmistakable, *if* you know what you're looking at."

"And boychik knows?"

Nick made a comically insincere attempt at a modest shrug.

Bill winked. "Did you tell da pretty girl? Vat she hed pictures of?"

"Of course not. She's too dumb to know, why should I tell?"

"But your boss, he's seen dem? Meester Bexter, or Meester Haig?"

"There's no Baxter," Nick said smugly. "Doug Haig bought him out years ago."

Bill nodded. "And Haig has seen dese paintings?"

"On that girl's phone, absolutely. But you mean, did he go out there, wherever the open studio was? How would I know? I certainly wouldn't have gone. There's no question these pictures are fakes." With a curled lip, as though the artist had made a career blunder, he said, "Chau's dead."

"Dey could be real, chust old," Bill suggested. "From da old days."

"Oh, yeah, right." Condescending to connect the dots for the muscle-brained mobster, Nick explained, "If you happen to have a pile of vintage Chaus, and you're some bridge-and-tunnel freak who wants to make it in the art world, you *sell* them. Get a studio in Manhattan. Where someone who matters might actually see your work. Trust me."

"Vell, maybe you don't sell dem iff you love dem?"

Nick looked at Bill as though he'd said the Easter Bunny was hopping through the door. "Yeah. Sure. Whatever."

Bill's eyes flared. Nick shrank back. Then Bill relaxed. "Yess, of course," he said soothingly. "You must be right. Terrible rotten fakes. But I vant to see dem anyvay, dah?" He looked at me, as though for confirmation, and then back to Nick before I could answer because what did he care what I thought, anyvay? "I appreciate your help, boychik. Now I tink ve go talk to Meester Haig. Dat vass him, in da beck, dat fetso?"

So Bill had noticed the round guy, also, his proprietary air and how he'd disappeared. Nick panicked. "Yes, that's him, but you can't tell him! You can't tell him I told you! If he does care—if the paintings are real—"

"Den vat? He vouldn't vant to sell dem to me, make fet commission?"

"He doesn't have them."

Bill stopped. "Oh? How do you know det?"

"He may be negotiating with the owner but if he had them I'd know, I'd have accessioned them."

"Maybe dese paintinks are so important, da big boss accessioned dem himself?"

"No! He doesn't know how to use the computer. He won't learn. He thinks it's beneath him." Nick allowed himself a superior smirk. Then he remembered why we were talking about this. "But please, you can't—"

"Oh, hush, hush. Vy so upset? Ve don't say nothing. Ve say ve're looking, not ve found. Don't vorry, boychik."

With that Bill turned and headed back. I threw Nick a commiserating look and hurried after.

"I think we're supposed to wait until the guy in the front calls the guy in the back," I whispered as we crossed the gallery.

"Oh, I promise you, he did," Bill said.

He was right. Before we reached the rear office another emaciated assistant, this one a harried-looking young woman, came trotting around a wing wall. She established position in front of the opening and, though she looked like a mild breeze could blow her over, she didn't move. Bill walked right up to her and grinned.

Nervously, she said, "Mr. Oblomov?"

"Dah, dat's me." Bill winked at her. "Leetle Neeky gafe you a ring?"

Her uneasy smile faltered but didn't fail. "Mr. Greenbank said you wanted to talk to Mr. Haig. I'm sorry, Mr. Haig's in a meeting. I can give you an appointment—no, stop! Wait, you can't go in there!"

Bill had wrapped his hands around her arms and slid her aside. "Sure ve can, sveetie. Meester Haig, he can't vait to see us."

Bill, with me trotting behind, strode through the outer office—presumably, hers—and gave a perfunctory two knocks before throwing open the inner door. The portly man we'd seen in the gallery could be found now leaning over a table, or rather, leaning over a young Asian woman who was seated at the table. His thick hand rested on her shoulder, thumb gently rubbing the back of her neck. He wore black slacks and a dark blue band-collared shirt buttoned up to his double chins. His clothes fit him so well, despite his bulk, that they'd clearly been made for him. The young woman, in a demure long-sleeved dress, seemed to be trying mightily to click through photos on a laptop, not reacting to his touch or the closeness of his mountain of flesh. I caught a sheen of perspiration on her brow. Both their heads turned sharply when the door flew open, hers in hope, his in anger.

"Dammit, Caitlin!" he roared. "I said no interruptions!"

"I'm sorry, Mr. Haig." The assistant trembled. "He wouldn't—I couldn't—they didn't—"

"No, I vouldn't and she couldn't and ve didn't," Bill agreed, striding forward, hand thrust out. "Vladimir Oblomov," he beamed. "Heppy to meet you."

Haig obviously didn't share Bill's delight. Staring at Bill, Haig said, "Caitlin, go. We'll talk later."

"I really am sorry, Mr. Haig. I—"

"Go!" He waved Caitlin off like a bad smell. She faded meekly out the door. After another few moments of eyeball-chicken with Bill, Haig took his hand off the young woman's shoulder and growled, "You, too. Get out. This work is shit."

She looked up at him, not comprehending. "But, Mister Haig." Her English was heavily Mandarin-accented. "You say you interested."

"In you, honey. Not in this crap you do. Last night was fun but the magic's gone. Get lost."

"But my paintings—"

"Won't be shown at this gallery. Eco-humano-we-are-the-worldo? Are you serious? Unfortunately I think you are. Beat it." The young woman sat openmouthed. "Your English doesn't include 'beat it'?" He turned to me. "Tell her what it means." Taken by surprise, I said nothing, barely managing to keep my own jaw from dropping. "What the hell's the matter with you people? What is this, Chinese Don't Talk Day? You, honey. Leave."

Uncertainly, the young woman stood, her face ashen. "I come all way from China because you say—"

"I said I'd give you a shot. I did. It's over. Leave and I'll do something for you: I'll forget your unpronounceable name. Hang around and argue, I'll remember it and you'll never show anywhere in New York, not even in the grade Z galleries that specialize in this shit. Never, honey. Ever." A two-second pause. "Why are you still here?"

Her cheeks flushed scarlet. Blinking fast, she gathered up her laptop and her handbag and made a stumbing exit. As she passed I could see tears glazing her eyes.

Haig surveyed us. He took obviously displeased note of Bill's open shirt, his rings and chains. I used the time he spent staring at Bill to breathe, lower my blood pressure, and unclench the fist that wanted to punch his lights out. After he'd made his point, he turned his small, devouring eyes from Bill to me. I forced myself to stick my hand out. "Lydia Chin. I work with Mr. Oblomov when he's in town."

Haig's smirk said he knew exactly what my work involved. While his damp, fleshy hand groped mine, Bill, uninvited, pulled a chair up to Haig's worktable. After forever, Haig's fingers opened and I found myself wondering how soon I could wash. Bill, blissfully uncaring, craned his neck to see the prints spread along the table. He picked one up to have a look. Though he held the purple-and-green extravaganza only at the outermost edges, Haig still snapped, "I'm sorry, I have to ask you not to touch that. If you want to see something I'll be glad to show it to you."

Bill's eyes met Haig's. Slowly he put the print down. "Forgiff me." He gave a thin smile. "Sometimes I forget American rules."

"Yes, well, no harm done." Haig's smile was as bogus as Bill's.

"So." He seated himself at the table, too. "Now that you've invaded my office and ruined my meeting, who the hell are you and why shouldn't I throw you out?"

"Leetle Neeky don't tell you?" Bill spread his hands in surprise. "Vladimir Oblomov. I'm new collector."

"How nice. So what?"

"Sorry about meetink, by da vay. Looked interestink."

"Forget it. She's pathetic, and so's her work. You saved me a wasted afternoon. Which doesn't mean I owe you anything."

"No," Bill said, grinning. "But I'm looking for someting, maybe you hev it."

"*If* I don't throw you out, and if it's a question of what's in our inventory, Nick has the complete catalog and can sit you down with a PowerPoint presentation."

Bill shook his head cheerfully. "Leetle Neek tells me he got no idea vat I'm talking about. Dah?" Bill looked at me and I nodded. "But I'm theenking, Meester Haig, he knows everytink about dese Chinese. Maybe he can tell me."

Haig waited, and finally asked, "Tell you what?"

Bill's smile split his face in two. "Tell me vether you got new paintinks by Chau Gvai Yink Shunk."

It took Haig a few moments to figure out exactly what Bill had said, he'd mangled the Chinese so badly. "Gwai Ying Shung? The Ghost Hero? New? What are you talking about? Chau's been dead for twenty years."

"So efferybody says. But I hear somebody has new paintinks."

"You mean, just found?"

"No, Meester Haig, I mean chust painted. New."

"That's absurd."

"So you don't know nothink?"

"Of course not. Mr.—Oblomov?—if someone's told you that, they're joking. Or they're trying to separate you from your money."

"Taking edvantage?" Bill seemed unable to comprehend the idea. "Of Vladimir Oblomov?"

"Almost certainly." Haig gave Bill a patronizing smile. Then it faded, replaced by a contemplative look. He sat back, folding his hands and crossing his ankles. "If there *were* new Chaus," he said, as if rolling this idea around in his mind for the first time, "of course that would have to mean that Chau was alive. I suppose that's possible. In the sense that anything's possible, I mean." He frowned to himself, then asked, "Who did you say told you about these paintings?"

"I don't remember." Bill's smiling apology was patently false. "Chust, I hear dis, and I tink, Vladimir, iff dere really are such tinks, you vant dem very much, don't you?"

Haig nodded slowly. "Mr. Oblomov, wanting is one thing. Being in a position to have? That's another."

"Vat are you saying? You're esking iff I hev money?" Bill pointed to himself with a be-ringed finger. "You Americans, alvays beating da bush. Meester Haig, my friend, I got *lots* uff money. Lots uff money, and lots uff friends vit lots uff money. Iff Chau got new paintinks, I vant dem. And I'm, vat you said, in a position to have dem. In fect," he leaned forward, lowering his voice, "I'm not in no position not to have dem. If you see what I mean."

I saw he meant nothing at all, but Doug Haig wasn't so sure. Also, he'd heard the word "money" a number of times.

"Well," Haig's pudgy hand rubbed both his chins, "why don't we do this? I'm intrigued. I'll check around. Leave me your contact information, and if I come up with anything, I'll give you a call."

"Dah." Bill nodded. "Dat sounds fine. You got pen?" Bill always carries pen and paper with him, but he waited patiently while Haig, after an irritated look, swiveled his chair to his desk and picked up a pen and one of his own business cards. Bill gave him my cell phone number, then stood to leave. "You find da Chaus," he instructed Haig amiably, "den you call Brown Eyes here. Vould be a pleasure to do business vit you."

In the crashing silence of Doug Haig not urging us to stay we strode through the office, trailed by Caitlin's nervous gaze. As we were recrossing the gallery to Nick Greenbank's desk, I heard Haig bellow, "Caitlin! Get in here!" At least the gentry weren't allowed to behead serfs anymore.

Leetle Neek had his eyes glued on us from the moment we emerged from the inner sanctum, but when we got back to his desk I can't say he greeted us like long-lost friends.

"I was right, wasn't I?" he asked, smug even before the answer. "He thinks they're fake?"

"He says he never heard uff dem. But he says he's goink to look."

"But you didn't say anything about me?"

I just shrugged, but Bill said benevolently, "No, boychik. Vat you tell me, eet's our leetle secret. Dah?"

"Dah. I mean yes!"

"Good boychik. Now, vile your boss—charmink man—ees looking, ve're going to see your leetle Shayna. Meanvile, if you suddenly theenk of something maybe I should know, you giff Brown Eyes a call, how about dat?" Bill reached over the counter, lifted a pen from a steel tube, peeled a Baxter/Haig business card from a steel box, and scribbled my number again. He tucked the card in Nick's shirt pocket and patted him on the cheek. "Okay. Now chust tell me diss. Your little Shayna, ven ve get dere, iss she going to say she hass no idea vat dat cute guy from Baxter/Haig iss talking about?

Or maybe, Shayna don't even remember no cute guy from Baxter/ Haig?"

"She'll remember me," Nick said savagely, already angry with Shayna for stabbing him in the back.

"I'm gled for you. But you're not gonna remind her? You're not thinking right now, maybe you'll give dat cute Shayna a call? Because I'll be very disappointed iff I get dere and Shayna suddenly vent home sick."

Nick shook his head. "No, no."

"And diss won't be, vat do dey say in English, a vild bird chase? Vee get up dere, Shayna don't got no photographs on her phone, and vee come back here and little boychik iss da vun vent home sick? Because . . ." Bill swept the room with his arm one more time.

"No," said Nick. "It's what I said. You ask her where that open studio was that Doug Haig got excited about. That's who has the Chaus. But I'm telling you—"

"Fakes, yess, yess, thenk you, boychik. Now, you get back to verk, so Meester Haig, he don't fire you, dah? Hah, fire you! Det's pretty funny." Bill socked me in the arm again, turned, and left. I hurried after him. Too bad Bill had told Nick to stay put. He looked bad enough to go home sick.

5

Bill and I stayed silent until we'd rounded the corner onto Ninth Avenue and put another block between us and Baxter/Haig. Then I exploded. "That sleazy, twisted, pervy horn-dog! Ugh ugh ugh. Creeparama! Can I burn his gallery down myself?"

"After we're through."

"That poor woman! Unbelievable! All the way from China and she had to put up with that! And your rings are hideous. Where did you get them?"

"Chinatown, where else?"

"And the accent? Did you get that in Chinatown, too?"

"Come on, girlchik. Dat's vun of my besst."

"Vun uff your most ridiculous, enyvayz. I can't believe either of them bought it."

"Haig was hearing the clink of coin. That drowns out a lot. And little Nicky saved his boss's business. He's a hero."

"Thanks a bunch, by the way, for giving both those jerks *my* phone number."

"That was payback for 'Oblomov.' Russian Lit. 101?"

"First time it's ever come in handy."

We'd almost made it to the subway when Bill's phone rang. "Well, it can't be either of those, um, jerks." He checked the screen and told me, "Jack." He answered, listened, stopped walking, and said, "Jesus Christ! Are you okay?"

I stopped, too. "What happened?"

He waved me silent, listened another few moments, then said, "Okay, we're on the way," and clicked off.

"On the way where?" I demanded. "What happened?"

"Someone took a shot at Jack."

Twenty minutes later we were back on Madison. For a few moments we hung back, getting the lay of the land: warning cones, crime scene tape, glass-covered sidewalk. A crowd milled, snapping cell phone pictures of the glittering shards of Jack's front window. As we watched, the door to the stairs opened and a pair of unmistakable NYPD detectives emerged, sticking notebooks away. Without discussing it, but by mutual consent, Bill and I waited until their car pulled out. That seemed to cue the crowd, too. The sidewalk began to clear and we made our way to the door. A few seconds after we buzzed, Jack appeared above us, sticking his head out the ragged opening where his window used to be. "Oh, look! It's Job and Calamity Jane! Go away."

"No," Bill said.

"Oh. Well, all right." Jack disappeared and a moment later we were buzzed in.

"Wow," I said, walking into his office. As opposed to the mess on the sidewalk, this was the same serene and tidy place I'd seen two hours ago, except for the sharp glass daggers sparkling in the otherwise empty window frame, and the long thin groove in the plaster ceiling. "Is repelling debris one of your superpowers?"

"I swept up because you were coming. Wanted to make a good impression."

"You did that already today."

"Good, because I don't think it would work out now. Look, you guys, does this kind of thing happen to you much?"

"Never," Bill answered.

I shook my head, too.

"Liars." Jack waved an arm. "The chairs are safe, if you want to sit down."

Bill settled onto a chair. "Chilly in here." Jack, his leather jacket on and halfway zipped, glared at him.

I hesitated, but it was the more Chinese move to risk my tender behind to an overlooked glass splinter than to imply I didn't trust Jack's housekeeping. "So what happened?" I asked as I sat.

Jack didn't sit. He spoke while striding the room. "I was at the desk going through auction catalogs online—tracing Chau's sales history, thanks for asking—when POW! the window exploded. I ducked and covered"—he threw his long arms over his head, to demonstrate—"and waited until it stopped raining glass. When nothing else happened I peeked up to check on the Hasui." He tapped the Japanese print on the wall as he passed it. "You're lucky it's okay. If anything had happened to it I'd have been really pissed."

"At us?" I protested. "We had nothing to do with it."

"No? I run a genteel uptown art investigation business for three years with nothing worse than papercuts, then Bill Smith introduces me to his kick-ass Chinese partner and people start shooting at me. Coincidence? I don't *think* so." He stopped and stared at Bill. "What are you dressed as?"

"Beeg-time Russian gengster."

"Are you serious? You look like you got run over by the bling truck."

"What do the police think?"

"About your outfit?"

"About someone shooting at you. Try to stay on point here."

"Hah! They think it was random. Someone showing off, maybe trying out his new gun, just happened to hit my window."

"A gangbanger? On Madison Avenue?" I was incredulous.

"Not a gangbanger. A private-school wannabe. Some punk brings Daddy's gun to St. Snooty's, shows his goods to a hot cheerleader, has an accident."

"You're on the verge of talking dirty," Bill warned.

"The cops took the slug," Jack thumbed over his shoulder at the furrow in the ceiling, "which was a twenty-five, by the way. But unless a matching one turns up in a stiff someplace, I don't expect to hear from them again." He stopped, rubbing the back of his neck with a scratched hand. "Look, you guys, I don't even know how to shoot a gun."

"Point, cock, pull," Bill said.

"Oh, thanks."

"Did anyone see anything?" I asked. "Gunshots aren't an everyday thing up here."

"If they did the cops didn't find them. No one heard the shot. *Lots* of people heard the glass break." He pointed accusingly at the empty window frame.

"A twenty-five's pretty quiet," Bill said. "Relatively speaking."

"I think it's a dumb theory," I said. "About the private-school kid."

"I happen to agree with you, but the police don't. Or at least, they're refusing to budge until I come clean."

"Come clean about what?"

"The real reason, of course! Which must be related to my shady profession. They jumped all over me. Like getting shot at was my idea."

"They wanted to know about your enemies, that sort of thing?"

"Me? Enemies?"

"Oh, right, of course. So what did you tell them?"

"What you're trying subtly to ask is, did I tell them about the case, about Ghost Hero Chau?"

I nodded, admitting it.

"I would've, if I'd had an idea how to say it and not sound like a wackjob. 'This ghost is painting pictures and two clients want to find them, one who wants them to be real and one who doesn't. I think one of them, or someone else, or the ghost himself, is responsible for this outrage, Inspector Lestrade.'"

"Works for me," Bill said.

"Yeah, well, I didn't think it would work for the Nineteenth Precinct."

"That's why you didn't tell?" I asked.

Jack stopped crisscrossing the room. He stood for a few moments, looking at me. "No." He threw himself into a chair, legs splayed out, arms dangling. "I didn't tell because it's not just my case. Not that I owe you guys anything, but I thought I ought to wait until we talked."

"We appreciate that," I said.

"Besides, I'm a private eye. Don't we have some kind of code? One for all, all for one, none for the cops? Something like that?"

"Something like that," Bill said.

"Okay. I waited, we're talking. So what the hell's going on?"

"I can't imagine," I said. "This case is barely started. Are you sure there's nothing else you're working on that could've—"

I stopped because he was shaking his head. "I don't have any other open cases. I'd just started this one and all I've done is a little research."

"It doesn't have to be an open case. It could be an old case, someone you made unhappy who's been stewing about it and finally decided to get you."

"This isn't how art people get you. They'd either have stabbed me with a jeweled dagger in the heat of the moment, or they'd cool down and get all baroque about it. Start rumors about what a stoner I am, what STD's I have, how I plagarized my Ph.D. thesis. That kind of thing. So they could see it happening. Art people like to watch."

"What about an old girlfriend?" Bill asked.

"I don't date girls who carry guns."

"That seems a little narrow-minded," I said.

Jack turned to me in surprise. For the first time since we'd arrived, he smiled. "Really?"

Now I shrugged, to cover the fact that I was a little surprised that I'd said that, myself.

"Personally, I consider it sound policy," Bill elbowed back in. "So look: If this is the case that got you shot at, then what about this case?"

Jack said, "My money's on you guys."

"If it's us," Bill asked, "why didn't they shoot at us?"

"That's a damn good question. Second only to: How do I get them to next time?"

"Look," I said. "When this kind of thing happens it's usually because someone's cage has been rattled."

"I thought you said this kind of thing never happens."

"Um, hypothetically. The point is, Bill and I hadn't rattled anything yet."

"If you're asking what *I've* rattled since last night, the answer is also nothing."

"Last night?"

"When I was hired."

Reluctantly, I said, "Oh. Well, that makes my theory that it's you a little shakier, if they could have shot at you any time since last night, but they waited until now."

"You mean, until after I met you. Hah!"

A short silence; then Bill said, "Okay, here's the big question. Do you want out?"

Jack frowned. "What? You mean me? Are you nuts? Ditch a client? Never." He sat up and pounded the arm of his chair. "And besides, no one shoots at Jack Lee and gets away with it!" He slumped back again. "There, isn't that what I'm supposed to say?"

I nodded approvingly. "And well delivered, too."

Jack squinted at me. "It's really true, what Bill said? You're not afraid of anything?"

I glanced at Bill in surprise. "A complete fabrication," I told Jack. "I just hide it well."

He kept his narrowed gaze on me. Finally he said, "Anyway, quitting, besides ruining my self-image, would only mean I'd be out of the loop. I wouldn't feel any safer, just lonelier. No, I want to be right in the middle of finding out what the hell is going on here. Right in the middle, with one of you guys on each side. With a gun."

"You mean, we should work together?"

"Why not?"

"For the same reasons as this morning."

"This"—arm waving from broken window to drilled ceiling—"makes it not the same as this morning. Look, you don't trust your client and I don't trust mine. It's perfect. Though at least I didn't just meet mine today."

"No?"

"I've known Dr. Yang for years. No way he'd shoot me. He doesn't shoot people anyway, just vaporizes them with his eyes. But there's definitely something he's not telling me. Listen, you guys, if people are firing away in the middle of Madison Avenue, this whole thing is even farther from what we thought it was than we thought it was. Don't!" He pointed at Bill, who'd been about to speak. "You know what I mean. What I'm saying is," his voice and eyes grew serious, "I don't trust my client, but I trust you guys."

"You just met me this morning," I said.

"Technically correct, but I'm willing to take a chance. How about it? If we combine our info and resources maybe we can figure out what's going on before we all get killed."

"What do we do when we find the paintings?" I asked.

"We worry about it then."

We sat in silence. A chilly breeze charged through the empty window frame and spiraled some papers off Jack's desk. He gave them a glare but didn't go after them.

I looked at Bill. His eyes were telling me *your case, your choice*. I knew that; what I was searching for was *but I wouldn't recommend it*. I didn't see that.

"Okay," I said.

"Yes!" Jack fist-pumped. "Porthos, Athos, Aramis." He pointed at each of us. "The Three Musketeers."

"Weren't there really four of them, though?"

"We're better."

"Okay," Bill said, standing. "Good to be working with you, Aramis. Come on, you need a drink. I'll buy you a martini."

Jack cocked his head. "A pickletini?"

"For me to pay for that," Bill said, "there'd have to be blood."

Jack spent a few minutes locking his computer and his Hasui in a closet, in anticipation of the emergency window repair and the inevitable sawdust. Then we headed downstairs. Jack spoke to the manager of the ground-floor chocolate shop. "Sorry about the mess," he said, giving her his key for the window crew.

She shrugged in a very French way. "Some excitement. Good for the neighborhood."

While that was going on, Bill crossed the street. He prowled the sidewalk, looking at Jack's building from various spots. Jack and I followed on the next light.

"Something up, Sherlock?" Jack asked.

"That shot came from over here."

Jack scanned the ground. "Footprints?" He sniffed. "Gunshot residue still in the air?"

"The length of the track in your ceiling. A shot fired from your side of the street would've gone straight up. Probably right through the floor above."

"And plugged poor Mischa, who rebuilds violins up there. I'll be sure to tell him how lucky he is. Listen, not to diss your detecting genius or anything, but the police already worked that out."

"Which must be why they think their 'random' theory's reasonable. If you were at your desk, there's no way anyone over here would've seen you."

Jack gave Bill another brief look, then glanced across at his own window. "Well. Damn. Do you think maybe they're right, then?"

"Not for a minute. I think it wasn't real."

"A mass hallucination? Group hypnosis? No, wait, you mean it was me! A grab for attention? A cry for help?"

"If it were you it would've been more theatrical."

"Well, thanks for that, anyway. Though how much more theatrical could it get?"

"You weren't supposed to get hurt. Just scared."

"A complete success, then! Can I ask who? Why?"

"You can ask, but I can't answer. Someone who wants you off the case."

Jack sighed. "Though it hurts my ego to say it, there are other people in New York who do what I do. Scare me off and my client would just hire one of them. Why not shoot at my client and scare him off? Then he'd fire me and run away, and we'd all be happy."

"I don't know."

"Maybe," I said, "we should ask him."

"Dr. Yang?" said Jack. "You want to go charging down to NYU and ask Dr. Bernard Yang why someone's shooting at me?"

"Yes."

"Well, I think that's a damn good idea." He took out his iPhone and poked a number. When he spoke it was obvious he was leaving a message. He clicked off and said, "Voice mail. He's probably in class. I said to call me."

We headed up the street. Both Bill and Jack seemed to know exactly where we were making for. I could only assume it was one of their male-bonding taverns.

"So," Jack asked, "what did you guys do today? Tell me you haven't been goofing off while someone tried to take me out."

"Hey," said Bill. "We've been busting our accents working this case."

"Actually," I said, "if you can hold off on that drink, when you called we were on our way to see someone."

Jack stopped. "You have a lead?"

"We got it from our other lead."

"You have *leads*? That you didn't tell me about?"

"We weren't working together then."

He waited, then said, "Are you going to tell me now, or do I only get to know things that happen from now on?"

"Sure," I said. "We leaned on a kid at Baxter/Haig and he broke like a twig."

"Baxter/Haig? That repulsive little Nick something?"

"You know him?"

"He's been there a long time. Haig's a walking oil slick and he generally hires people from the same toxic gene pool. Baxter was better, but in the end he couldn't stand Haig—"

"No, really?"

"—and he demanded to be bought out. Haig must have found someone else to finance him and now the place is all his."

"He had to be financed?" Bill asked. "You don't think he bought Baxter out himself?"

"Doug Haig only spends other people's money. Count on it." He looked Bill over again. "So Nick whatever, he was what the Russian gangster gag was for?"

"Greenbank. Gangster and his art consultant." Bill thumbed at me. "Worked, too. He gave up Shayna Dylan. A gallerina at Gruber. You know her?"

"Nope. Must be new."

"She's reputed to have photos of these Chaus on her cell phone. Nick doesn't know where she took them."

"Gallerina?" I asked. "Is that really what they're called?"

Jack nodded, verifying.

"Does that make Nick Greenbank a gallerino?"

"No," said Jack. "It makes him a yellow-bellied sapsucker, if he gave up his girlfriend."

"She's not his girlfriend. According to him he hardly knows her."

"My judgment doesn't change."

"Stubborn consistency in the face of facts," said Bill. "I like it."

"We also talked to the monumentally revolting Doug Haig himself," I said. "You should have heard Bill say 'Gvai Yink Shunk.'"

"Sounds like a Yiddish curse. You're not telling me Haig bought it?"

"What Haig bought was the idea that *I* could buy anything I wanted," Bill said. "And that what I want are the Chaus."

"Well, he's a greedy enough bastard that I can see that. Blinded, by the radiance of rubles, to the ridiculousness of your Russian ruse."

"Not bad," Bill said.

"But I'm guessing he wasn't any help, or we wouldn't need to see this gallerina."

"Not only wasn't he any help," I said, "he completely destroyed a woman we interrupted his so-called meeting with." I replayed the scene for Jack.

"Wow," he said when I sputtered to a halt. "I guess he made you mad."

"I'm going to stick a pin in the pompous pig and watch him deflate like a balloon."

"Okay then. As soon as we're done with the case."

"That's what Bill said."

"That doesn't make it wrong."

"Then let's get done fast."

"All right." Jack executed a sharp U-turn. "We'll go to Gruber. And after that, you'll still owe me a martini. How's that?"

Bill said, "Wouldn't have it any other way."

Jack's instinct was to step into the street and hail a cab, but I stopped him. We were only twelve blocks from Gruber Arts. It was faster to walk.

Three people making tracks on a midtown sidewalk is like running a team obstacle course. Especially when the other two have long legs and one of them is on an adrenaline high from being shot at for the first time. There was no way I was being left behind, though. Jack reached our destination first, me second, and Bill, who'd stopped to light a cigarette, last.

Gruber Arts was one of about a dozen galleries stacked vertically in a limestone-faced building on Fifty-seventh Street, the heart of New York's uptown gallery district. For an artist, to have any gallery is a great thing, even in the East Village or Williamsburg. If yours is in SoHo or Chelsea, you've arrived. If it's uptown, you're annointed.

"Okay." Jack spoke as the elevator rose. "I'll provide covering fire and you two go in and take out the enemy."

"You know," I said, "this getting shot at thing may have had more impact on you than we thought."

"Either that," Bill said, "or Jack knows the gallery owner and is offering to distract him while we talk to Shayna."

"Her," said Jack. "Jen Beril. Lots of white wine under that bridge."

"Maybe Shayna Dylan's just a step on the way to her," I suggested. "Maybe Jen Beril's the one who's got the paintings and is going to be unveiling them next week."

"Contemporary's not a period she generally deals in. Her focus is strictly pre-Republic, mostly Tang through Yuan, but she'll extend as far as the Han in one direction and the Ming in the other."

I blinked. "Show-off."

"I'm overcompensating for not knowing how to shoot. Anyway, believe it or not, I did think of that. I'll probe discreetly. Are you guys going to use funny accents?"

"Lydia always uses one," said Bill. "She's a New Yorker."

"Oh, I have to put up with that from a guy who sounds like Barney Fife?" That wasn't really accurate; Bill's speech still carries a trace of Louisville, but only a trace. But civic pride was at stake here.

"Vell, don't vorry. I tink I better make like Vladimir Vladimirivich Oblomov. In case da pretty girl compares notes vit Leetle Neek."

Jack snorted. "Oblomov? Russian Lit. 101?" The elevator opened and both men stood aside for me to step out first. At a door labeled GRUBER ARTS I waited with great dignity for these white knights to fight over who got to open it. Luckily for them it was a double door.

The atmosphere inside the gallery was infused with the same serenity as Jack's office, and for a similar reason: There wasn't much there. Plexiglas cases on white pedestals held here a porcelain vase painted in delicate peonies, there a pottery camel piled with Silk Road trade goods. Three scroll paintings hung on the walls, all of misty mountains and rushing streams. Acres of polished wood floor attested to the value of the art on offer: In Manhattan, nothing says wealth like empty space.

The young woman at the reception desk wasn't as immediately imperious as Nick Greenbank had been, but we didn't inspire in her a strong need to be of service, either. She glanced at us through

golden hair curtaining the sides of her face. "Yes?" Her copy of
ARTnews stayed open in front of her; clearly she intended to get
back to it soon.

"I'm Jack Lee. Is Jen here?"

She arched an eyebrow. "Can I ask what this is about?" Her
glance slid over me as though I'd been oiled, lingered a few moments on Bill, then returned to Jack.

"Jen knows me," Jack said in affable nonanswer.

The young woman raked her fingers through her glistening hair.
She gave Jack, and Jack alone, another microsecond look, then
pressed a button on the phone. She murmured into it, and a few
seconds later a white wall at the far end of the gallery swung open,
revealing a room of bookshelves and files. Another golden-haired
woman, also dressed in black, walked across the floor with the ease
and dignity I'd been trying to muster at the elevator. On her it was
natural, and she was twice my age, and in heels. She wore her hair
pulled smoothly back. Her skin was silkily smooth, too, though I
suspected both the gold and the silk had help. Smiling as she reached
us, she took Jack's hand in both of hers. "Jack! To what do I owe
this pleasure?" She and Jack shared a double-cheek kiss.

"Hello, Jen. These are friends of mine. Lydia and Vladimir." Bill
and I shook her hand in turn. "I told them about the Han tomb
figures." Jack nodded toward a glass case in the corner, occupied by
clay figures about six inches high. "And I wanted another look at
those Luo Pings anyway. So here we are."

"It must be kismet, how lovely. I was going to call you. I have a
Jin Nong I've just gotten, a lotus pond, from the same year as the
one at the Met. Shayna, will you take charge of Lydia and Vladimir?
If you need me"—she included me and Bill in her smile—"we'll be in
my office. Come." She took Jack's arm and drifted off to the back.

A cloud crossed Shayna Dylan's face as Jen Beril made off with first prize. But she dutifully stood, though I thought leaving the magazine open was a little pointed. Hair cascading over her shoulders, she led us across the floor to the glass case.

"It's a complete set," she said, sounding a little weary, as though she wished she didn't have to tell people things this obvious. "From a duke's tomb. Five musicians and three dancers. All women. In the Eastern Han, as you probably know, the musicians were often women." She was examining Bill with a newly appraising gaze. "And the dancers, always. The Han understood that beauty and grace could go hand-in-hand with talent and power."

I made a note to ask Jack if that was true. About the Han, I mean.

"The musicians would have had their instruments when they were placed in the tomb. But the instruments were wood and wood rarely survives burial." She was speaking exclusively to Bill, so I decided I might as well actually look at the figures. Traces of colored paint still clung to them; they must have been riotous when they were new. Even now, their odd, flat faces, squared-off edges, and empty hands didn't detract from their exuberance. Shayna took a step closer to Bill. "But I'm sure you know that. Are you a collector?"

"Not of antiquities," I said, partly to hear my own voice to make sure I was still here.

Shayna turned slowly to me. "Oh?" She couldn't have been less interested and still conscious.

"I wish we were. I love these old pieces. So much history, such subtlety."

"Yes." Shayna gave me a cold, customer-is-always-right smile.

I sighed. "But Vlad is the real collector." Bill grinned like the Cheshire cat, to underline my meaning: He was the one with the money. "He gets bored easily. He's only interested in what's flashy and new." I looked Shayna up and down, then gave Bill a smile sweet enough to cause a toothache. "Our focus is contemporary Chinese art. Because that's what Vlad loves."

"Oh?" Shayna said in a totally different tone, swiveling back to Bill.

"Dat's right." Bill winked. "Lydia doesn't like it, but I can't get enuff."

"Is that so?" Shayna eyed me with pity. "Well, many people are skittish. Unhappy with anything outside their comfort zone."

"Absolutely," Bill agreed. "But dey don't know vat dey're missing. Me, personally, I don't care about comfort."

"No?"

"Not exciting, comfort."

"I can hear the passion in your voice." Shayna swept her glossy hair. "I feel the same way."

"Dah. I tink I could tell dat as soon as ve came in."

"The edgy, the transgressive. The very newest. That's what I love."

"Iss dat so?"

Their eyes met with a spark that made me want to remind them they were talking about art.

"Vell," Bill smiled, "iss possible you could help me out vit something."

"I'd certainly like to try." Shayna shifted her weight from one Jimmy Choo to the other, thrusting forward, ever so slightly, the hip that came between me and Bill.

"Sveetie," Bill said to me, "dis von't interest you. Ve came here so you could look at dis stuff." He waved a vague hand. "Take long time, look at vatever you vant." His hand came to rest on Shayna's elbow. He steered her across the prairie of gleaming floor, toward her desk, where he, with no hesitation, slipped behind the counter to sit beside her as though he were working, too.

Which he certainly was.

I spent twenty minutes wandering lonely as a cloud, absorbing ten centuries of my heritage. What Bill was absorbing, I didn't know. Or Jack either, until the rear wall swung open and he emerged with Jen Beril. They were both smiling, though her smile tightened as she glanced around the gallery and took in the situation. Jack's smile, on the other hand, widened.

"Shayna?" Jen Beril's voice rang across the oak-floored miles with the silver sound of tinkling icicles. "Have you shown our guests what they wanted to see?"

Shayna's head, and Bill's, popped up, both with guiltier looks on their faces than the situation seemed to warrant.

"Absolutely," Bill answered.

"Yes," I agreed from beside a shelf of snuff bottles. "We've seen more than enough."

I wouldn't have been surprised if my words had just echoed and faded away; by now I'd concluded I might be invisible. But Jen Beril said, "I'm glad," and Bill stood, though he didn't look happy about it. I waited, kind of icily myself, until he walked over to where I was. Just as he reached me I turned and stalked away, to the door. I yanked it open and strode with great majesty down the hall, where I punched the elevator button. Before Bill and Jack had left the gallery I'd stepped through the closing doors and started my descent.

6

Bill and Jack came out onto the sidewalk laughing. I was behind them, sitting on a planter near the door. They stopped and looked around; I let them be confused for a minute, then I spoke up.

"All I want to know is, did you see the photos on her phone? The rest can stay in Vegas."

They spun around like a two-man dance routine. "Awesome," Jack grinned. "I wish I'd seen the whole thing. Do you guys run that gag often?"

"It changes," Bill said. "Sometimes she's the boss, and I'm all crude and Neanderthal."

"It's easier that way," I said. "Closer to reality."

"I was expecting the art-consultant routine that you pulled on Nick Greenbank."

"One look at Shayna, I could tell this would get Bill next to her faster. Cutting me out made her day."

"Did you know it was coming?" Jack asked Bill.

"I just go with the flow."

"Hey, I wasn't the one who hauled out the Uncle Vanya accent and the Jersey Shore jewelry when we started this," I said. "So? The photos?"

"Not yet. We were interrupted at a delicate moment." Bill looked at Jack, who shrugged an apology. "But I'm buying her a drink later."

"You're kidding me."

"Hey, she's not the kind of girl who shows her phone to a guy on the first date."

"Why not? She shows everything else."

"Oh, snap," said Jack. "Do I smell the sickly sweet scent of jealousy?"

"Impatience. What good is later going to do us? Why didn't you just swipe the phone?"

"I thought about it. But seeing the photos wouldn't have told us where they were taken. Or would it? Is there some way—could Linus—"

"You ask that as though, if there *were* some way and Linus could, you'd actually go back up and steal it."

"I would."

"Who's Linus?" Jack asked.

"Well, there's not, so don't bother."

"Who's Linus?"

"My cousin."

"Ah." Jack nodded sagely, as though that had clarified something. "Who's Linus?"

"Linus Wong," Bill said. "Runs a computer security business. His motto is, 'Protecting people like you from people like us.'"

"He's a hacker?"

"At heart."

"Really. Is he good?"

"The best," I said stoutly.

"In that case," Jack said, "I think we could use him anyway."

"Why?"

Jack leaned beside me on the planter. "Shayna's the daughter of one of Jen's big collectors. Jen's assistant is out on maternity leave, so she gave Shayna the fill-in job to keep Shayna's daddy happy. Shayna knows enough about the art to avoid making a fool of herself, and she's decorative enough that a lot of collectors don't care what she knows. But she's also wildly ambitious. According to Jen, who's counting the days, she's everything you think she is."

"You mean, a man-eating coldhearted calculating—"

"Yes."

"—backstabbing brownnosing—"

"Exactly."

"—kind of woman who, if she had a date with a new guy, would totally Google him."

"Totally."

"Ah. And might share valuable information with the new guy, if she thought there was something in it for her?"

Bill said, "Getting to spend an hour with me at Bemelmans Bar isn't enough in it for her?"

"If you're planning to expense this you'd better choose someplace cheaper than Bemelmans Bar." I took out my phone. "I'm not sure we have time, though. She's probably Googling already."

"No," said Bill. "I thought of that. I never quite gave her my last name."

I stared. "You thought of that? I had no idea you even knew what Google was."

"I don't know how to play the accordion, either, but I've seen it done often enough to know it's possible."

I looked at Jack. "Two Chinese people standing here, and the white guy talks in convoluted metaphors." I called Linus.

"Hey, Cuz! What's going on? Hey, Trell, it's Lydia!"

I heard Linus's friend Trella call a greeting across the room—his parents' garage, actually, where Wong Security operates from—and I said "hi" back, which Linus passed on. "I'm calling on business, Linus. I have a job for you guys. You busy?"

"We're always busy. Big growth industry I'm in here. But never too busy for you. Especially if it's gonna be fun."

"Well, you tell me. Bill needs a new identity."

"Awesome! He steal a billion from the Colombian cartel? Or he's on the run from the FBI?"

"He wants to date a pretty lady."

"Oh. You know, lots of people do that without being in Witness Protection. Besides, I thought . . . I mean . . ."

"It's business, Linus. We have a case. *I* have a case. Anyway," I said, suddenly annoyed at myself and not sure why, "we think she'll Google him, and we want to be careful about what she finds."

"Business. Gotcha. Way cool." Linus sounded a little unconvinced, but he asked, "What do you need? I can't do, like, Social Security numbers. I can do a driver's license, but it'll take time."

"I don't think we need that. This isn't a background check. I just want whatever she finds to make him look like what he says he is. Vladimir Oblomov, Russian with cash. Probably in import-export, something where there'd be money sloshing around. If you implied he was connected to the Russian mob that would be okay. He collects contemporary Chinese art, that's the important detail. He can keep a low profile, she'll believe that, but we want him to pop up enough that when she searches, she takes him for real, a collector, and rich."

"Rich?"

"Loaded."

"Excellent. How long do I have?"

"A couple of hours."

"Piece of cake. Call you when I'm done."

I thanked him and pocketed the phone and, his "piece of cake" echoing in my ears, I said to the guys, "I'm hungry."

"Well," said Jack, "we could go have lunch. Or, we could grab a pretzel and go downtown and talk to Dr. Yang."

"I thought he was in class."

"He was. He called while I was in with Jen. He's back in his office and available for the next couple of hours."

I hopped off the planter. "Why didn't you say so?"

Again, Jack started to hail a cab; again, I stopped him. "You have some elitist problem with mass transit? You enjoy breathing car exhaust? The six train will get us to NYU in ten minutes."

"Sorry. Occupational hazard. In my business the clients look at you oddly if you come up out of the subway. Like you might be a Martian."

"Those come down from spaceships. Listen, did Jen Beril have anything to say about the paintings? You asked her, right?"

We stopped, not for pretzels, but for gyros from the Rafiqi's truck. Garlicky lamb, with white sauce and hot sauce, wrapped in pita—fantastic, if you can keep it from dripping on your shirt.

"I asked her," Jack confirmed, as we made our many-napkined way down the block. "She said because it was me she'd admit she'd heard the rumors."

"Nice to be so important," Bill said.

"Wouldn't it be? What's really going on is, she's major in antiquities and classical but she's not a name in contemporary. If the

Chaus do exist, she has zero chance of getting her hands on them—she wouldn't know where to look and no one's going to bring them to her. So she's watching this action from the sidelines. Some day she might need a favor from me, so why not help me out?"

I asked, "Is it really that calculated? You guys looked like you actually liked each other."

"What's love got to do with it? Seriously, sure we like each other. She really would have called me to see that Jin Nong just because she knew I'd be interested, even though I can't buy it. But if she had any chance at getting her paws on the Chaus, you'd better believe she'd have iced me faster than you can say 'Frost Jack.'"

"You didn't just make that up."

"Not bad, right?"

"He's used it before," Bill said.

"So"—I led the descent into the subway—"having decided she could afford to be helpful, how helpful was she?"

"Hard to say. She heard the buzz at an opening last week, but she can't remember who from. Contemporary Chinese sculpture, at Red Sky Gallery in Chelsea. We can go over there later if you want, though I've seen the show and it's awful."

"She didn't hear it from Shayna? Right at her own front desk?"

"Interestingly, no. Possibly interestingly also," Jack said, swiping his MetroCard, "Red Sky is a couple of ambitious, currently penniless young guys on the top floor of the same building with Baxter/Haig."

The six train, obviously not wanting to make a liar out of me, swept in, scooped us up, and hauled us down to Astor Place. We picked our way along the student-clogged sidewalks over to Washington Square Park, where we manuevered past a steel band, a fire-eater, a mournful guitarist, and about a million dogs and their walkers to reach the nineteenth-century department store turned temple-of-learning where Dr. Yang was holed up.

Jack took us up to the fourth floor and along a hallway lined with posters of Japanese anime characters and Hong Kong movie stills. Bulletin boards held tacked-up announcements for summer study programs in Taipei, Seoul, and Ulaanbaatar. I stopped at a theater bill featuring an angry Asian woman waving a big dripping knife, for a show called *Alice in Slasherland*.

"I can't help noticing there are no misty mountains."

"This isn't the art department." Jack knocked on a door. "It's A/P/A Studies. Asian/Pacific/American," he expanded, ostensibly for Bill's benefit, though I'd have had to stop and think about it, myself. "Culture in context."

The door opened, revealing a large park-facing office with bookshelves and big windows. Behind the desk sat a tallish Asian man with brush-cut gray hair. In front of us, her hand on the doorknob, was a young, also tall, Asian woman. Her high-cheekboned face lit. "Jack! Daddy didn't tell me you were coming."

"Hi, Anna. He didn't tell me you'd be here, either." Jack and Anna exchanged a quick kiss.

"Hello, Jack," said the man behind the desk, in a deep and Mandarin-inflected voice. He didn't smile, just gave me and Bill a narrow-eyed glance; apparently we were another thing nobody had been told about.

I looked around. Artwork hung on the walls, divided by bookcases like battling siblings better off separated. I found a canvas of subtle gray stripes soothing, and a calligraphic scroll seemed downright antiquated until I realized the flowing ink strokes formed, not Chinese characters, but character-shaped English words. That struck me as funny, but maybe I was missing some profound point.

The neon-colored oil of a garish peony in a parched desert, on the other hand, would definitely take some getting used to.

"Are you hot on the trail of something?" Anna asked Jack.

I shifted my focus from art to people in time to see Dr. Yang flash a warning look behind Anna's back. "Not really," Jack said. "These are friends of mine. They're interested in new Chinese art so I thought they'd better meet Dr. Yang."

Anna's smile widened to include me and Bill. "Hi, I'm Anna Yang. The great man's daughter." We shook hands all around. "He is a great man, too," she said. "He can be opinionated, though. But I guess that's what people want, his opinions. Just don't let him bully you."

Professor Yang frowned. "I don't bully."

"Yes, Daddy." As Anna Yang walked back to her father's desk, I considered her. Her smile seemed genuine enough, but I got the feeling it wasn't telling the whole story. Her eyes weren't joining in. Anna kissed her father's cheek and said to us, "Sorry I can't stay to offer dissenting views in case you need them. Jack, I'll see you sometime soon?"

"You have anything new? I'll come out and take a look."

"You mean, if I don't, you won't?"

"Go all the way to Flushing to see work that's ten minutes ago? Oh, okay. Soon."

Anna smiled and left, closing the door behind her.

At a nodded invitation from Dr. Yang, Jack and I settled into the office's two visitor chairs, leaving Bill to lean against the windowsill overlooking the park.

"How's she doing?" Jack asked Dr. Yang.

"It's a difficult situation," Dr. Yang replied. I didn't know what the question referred to, but I could tell that wasn't an answer.

Jack tried another: "Any word from Mike?"

"Would we expect that?" With those words and a sharp shake his head Dr. Yang closed out the subject of his daughter. "Jack, go down the hall to the faculty lounge and bring your friend a chair."

"It's all right, sir," Bill said. "I like the view."

Dr. Yang swiveled to Bill for a moment. "Very well." He turned back to Jack. "Tell me how I can help you."

Jack paused before he answered. I hadn't known him long, but I'd gotten the impression that, with the possible exception of flying bullets, nothing fazed him. This hesitation was something I hadn't seen before.

He plunged. "You probably guessed it's about Chau Chun."

Dr. Yang's face darkened. "Jack. I asked for discretion. Did—"

"I know," Jack said. "I'm sorry. But Lydia and Bill are also investigators. I didn't go to them. They came to me."

"I don't understand."

"I brought them here so you could meet them, and they could meet you. In a minute they'll leave and you and I can talk privately. This morning a man I don't know, a collector, hired Lydia and Bill to find the new Chaus."

I'd have given Bill a raised-eyebrow glance, asking if he'd known he and I were going to leave in a minute, but I was busy watching Dr. Yang for his reaction to this news.

He wasn't delighted, that's for sure. His brow furrowed and his dark gaze fixed first on Jack, then on me, Bill, me again. He could give Bill's eye-drill a run for its money. In case he was unsure which of us to address, I helped him out.

"We went to Jack for background. We had no idea he'd been hired to do the same thing."

"And now you do." Dr. Yang shot Jack an angry look, then asked me, "What does your client want with the paintings?"

...he wants to beat out the other collectors."

...now about them?"

...e says."

...sn't seen them?"

...How do you know about them, Dr. Yang?"

"The same way. Rumors." Dismissing the question, as well as, it seemed, my right to ask it, the professor stared at the gray-striped canvas on the wall. Maybe he needed to be soothed. "Who is he?"

"My client? I'm sorry, I can't tell you anything more than that he's a collector. New in the field, he says."

Dr. Yang gave an impatient head shake. "Why does he want the paintings?"

"Because they're worth a lot."

"They're worth nothing. They're forgeries. He can stop wasting his money."

Hmm. Paying me was wasting my client's money? "If you haven't seen them—"

"Chau Chun is dead!"

"I know that's what everyone says, but—"

"He is dead!"

"Isn't it possible—"

"No. It's not." The force of his glare almost knocked me off my seat. He pinned me with it another moment, then let out a long breath. "I was there."

Jack's eyebrows rose. "You didn't tell me that."

"Did you need to know it?" The professor swung the Jupiter-gravity stare to Jack. "That I held my friend's hand as he died?"

The room crackled. "I'm sorry," Jack said. "But I think I did need to know. I thought you weren't involved in the democracy movement."

"In the movement! No. I was a painter. I cared only for my art. My students. And my friends." Dr. Yang turned to the sardonic canvas of the barren desert with the bright, impossible bloom. After a long moment, he spoke. "The students—Chau's, and mine, everyone's, from the universities of Beijing and from the countryside—had been occupying Tiananmen Square for days. With such hopes, such sense of power and possibility! Chau was with them from the first, teaching his classes on the paving stones, believing with them that things could change." Yang's face darkened. "I thought he was a fool."

None of us spoke, waiting.

"Then the rumors: tanks, troops, the army on the way. People laughed. Send the army against a peaceful protest? That was the old way. This is the New China. But people coming in from the countryside reported it breathlessly. Tanks, massing nearby, undeniable. The crowd became uneasy. Then the loudspeakers, the warnings: Clear the Square! Public order will be maintained! The mood changed again. Anger and defiance. The students were doing what the law allowed. They would stay!" He shook his head. "People went to the Square, people of influence, to beg them to leave. I went, also, to Chau, to our students. What you've done is noble and courageous, I said, but you've lost. Go home, wait for another chance. They wouldn't go. *This* is the chance! I stayed, trying to persuade. Finally, the tanks came." Another long pause. "The soldiers were weeping. When the order came, some fired into the air, over the students' heads."

In the silence, Dr. Yang stared at the painting, but we could all tell he wasn't seeing it. Finally he spoke again, in changed, cold tones. "There, Jack. Is that what you needed? Tell me, does that help you?"

In a quiet voice, but a firmer one than I could have found, Jack said, "I'm sorry. I appreciate how hard that must have been. But it does help and I wish you'd told me sooner. For one thing, if you were with Chau when he died, it makes it a lot less likely that he's alive and painting these paintings."

"*Less likely?* It was never possible!" Dr. Yang pressed his palms on his desk as though he had to keep it from lifting off. "Is that the hypothesis you've been working on since I hired you? That Chau's not dead and the paintings are real? That's a problem, Jack."

"Maybe. There's another problem, too. Someone shot at me."

"Someone—what?"

"Shot a bullet through my office window. About two hours ago."

It took Dr. Yang a moment to catch up. "I—was anyone hurt?"

"No."

"Who was it?"

"I have no idea. Or what the point was, either."

"Did you call the police?"

"Of course. Bullets in my ceiling?" Jack added, "I didn't mention you."

Dr. Yang's lips compressed into a thin line. He nodded curtly and said to me and Bill, "Will you excuse us?"

If I'd conjured up a semireasonable excuse to stay I might have tried it, but it wasn't hard to see that nothing would work. Bill pushed away from the windowsill and I stood from my chair. "Of course," I said. To Jack: "We'll be outside."

Jack gave a distracted nod. He and Dr. Yang sat staring at each other as we left.

———

I shut the door behind us, then said to Bill, "Can I listen at the keyhole?" He didn't dignify that with an answer. We sat on a bench and watched students walk by. "What did you think?" I asked.

"Tough customer."

"I had professors like him in college. I did well in their courses because I was scared not to. But from your *I-Spy* perch by the window, I mean."

Bill came up with this trick and we do it routinely at interviews now, especially the first time we meet someone: We try to sit far enough apart that the person can't see both of us at once. Then one talks, the other watches. We can't always pull it off, but it's particularly convenient when the interviewee doesn't have enough chairs.

"He's way more angry than I'd have expected," Bill said.

"Jack said he's an angry kind of guy."

"Still. Now we know he's Jack's client. So what? It may be irritating but it's not a disaster. He's overreacting."

"Maybe." In my mind I heard Dr. Yang's dark voice as he told his story. "What he told us; it makes his reason for hiring Jack more convincing, doesn't it?"

"You mean, protecting Chau's rep?"

"Protecting Chau, I get the feeling. The way he couldn't, back then. Maybe he's so furious out of helplessness. This situation is getting out of control. The way that one did, and look what happened."

Bill nodded. "Possible."

"And speaking of protecting people, here's another question: What about his daughter? Anna? You saw how he stopped Jack from telling her what was up. Why wouldn't he want her to know?"

"She seems to have her own problems. Whatever Jack meant

when he asked how she was doing and if anyone had heard from Mike. Sounds like her boyfriend ditched her. Maybe Yang doesn't want to complicate her life right now."

I thought about Dr. Yang as an overprotective dad. High walls and lattice-screened windows came to mind, but Anna's affectionate teasing didn't strike me as coming from either the cowed and timid or resentful and rebellious young woman that that approach would have been likely to produce. She'd probably been wrapping him around her finger her whole life. "Well, maybe," I suggested, "he really *is* only protecting his investment while he pretends to care about his dead friend, and he feels guilty enough about it that he'd just as soon his daughter doesn't know."

"Maybe so."

"What did you think of the art in his office?" I asked, but my phone rang, so Bill didn't get a chance to answer. I flipped it open. "Hi, Linus."

"Hey, Cuz. So, Bill's all hooked up. Vladimir Oblomov, shady Russian, Chinese art honcho. You want to hear?"

"Of course." I did; but also, he clearly couldn't wait to tell me.

"First I went to the Wikipedia pages for two hot Chinese artists. Wow, you know how weird that stuff is? Anyway, I made Oblomov a buyer on one and a seller on the other. Bill might want to check out their stuff, you know, so in case his squeeze wants to talk about them." He gave me the artists' names. "Then I made a Web site for Vassily Imports. They sell food from Russia and, like, Eastern Europe and the Stans. Caviar, black bread, pickles, cheese—whatever, I looked up what one of the real sites sells and made it like that. Oblomov is on the board of directors, and he's also VP for International Corporate Communications. No one ever knows what that means so I figured it was cool. And the Web site, I made it so it sort of takes you in circles if you try to go too deep. So if you were really trying to find who the boss man is, you couldn't. That's the shady part, you dig? Then I grabbed a shot of Bill from when we went to the park that time and Photoshopped it into some gallery opening in Hong Kong I found online, then put the whole thing on Flickr and tagged him along with the other VIPs. I got him listed on Yahoo .com and WhitePages, but no address, no phone. You think she'll pay to do the search? I might be able to get something in there, but only maybe."

"No, I don't think she will. By the time she Googles him it'll be after he's called her. She won't be trying to find how to contact him, just to make sure he's not some kind of phony."

"Good luck with that." I could hear Linus's grin. "So, anyhow, the next thing, Trella opened a blog on JournalScape, backdated like six months: She's an art student, yadda yadda yadda and OMG she met this Oblomov dude, older but God is he loaded. They kicked it for a while but it cooled."

"Good, Linus."

"And I started a Facebook fan page for the Russian mob and made him one of the fans."

"What?"

"Kidding! Joke! Winking emoticon!"

"Oh." I breathed out. "Thanks, Linus. This all sounds terrific. Send me a bill."

"Nah. Family's free. Just tell me if it works?"

I promised to do that, and clicked off.

"You're in business," I told Bill. "When Shayna Googles Vladimir Oblomov, she'll get more than if she Googled the real you."

"As it should be." He checked his watch. "This is probably a good time to call her. She gets off in half an hour."

"Well, then, absolutely. She has to have time to check out Linus's hard work."

Bill did call Shayna, who, from where I was sitting, seemed delighted to hear from him. The first thing he said was, "Eet's Vladimir Oblomov," as if he had no idea she didn't know his last name. Things went all murmuring from there, which was a little revolting, so I got up and checked out the posters and flyers on the walls. This might not have been the Art Department, but apparently a lot of events coming up around Asian Art Week considered themselves of interest to A/P/A Studies students. Auctions, lectures, panels, gallery shows, led off by a glittering benefit gala I couldn't imagine college students attending except as cater waiters. Capping the week was "Beijing/NYC," which my client had mentioned: an offering of the government of the People's Republic to the art lovers of New York. Paintings, sculpture, photography and installations, all so new their paint, or ink, or gluey emulsion, wouldn't be dry. I was considering the civilized nature of cultural exchange when Dr. Yang's door opened and closed, leaving Jack standing in the corridor.

"Aramis," I said. "How'd it go?"

"Wow."

"You look a little dazed."

Jack shook his head slowly. "All I could think while he was reaming me out was, thank God he wasn't on my thesis committee."

Bill, spotting Jack, whispered some ridiculous sweet nothing into his phone and thumbed it off. I asked Jack, "Why is he so upset? It's not your fault we went to you. Did you explain your reasoning, why you told us about him?"

"Reasoning's not high on his list right now. But I gather he'd have preferred door number two: I tell you guys 'Ghost Hero Chau? Never heard of him,' and then call Dr. Yang and tell him to hide under his desk if you come by."

"We wouldn't have bought it," Bill said. "Seriously, Jack, an artist who died at Tiananmen, whose paintings are worth hundreds of thousands—"

"Worth nothing, says Dr. Yang."

"No, I mean the ones from twenty years ago. The real ones. What I'm saying is, this is your field. By the time we got to you we already knew enough about Ghost Hero Chau that we wouldn't have believed you if you'd said you never heard of him. So we'd have wondered why you were lying."

"Cool. Would you have tapped my phone or something?"

"We'd have gotten Linus to," I said.

"Well, don't bother. I have some pretty fancy blocking equipment up there."

"On your cell phone, too?"

"He can tap a cell phone?"

"He can do anything as long as it plugs into something."

"Well, now, that sounds useful." Jack stuck his hands in his pockets and started down the hall. Bill and I flanked him. "Anyway, in all humility I mentioned that to Dr. Yang. That you guys came to me for the same reason he did. He wasn't impressed. He doesn't care what you think of me and he thinks I should've stonewalled you until I found the Chaus." Jack shrugged. "Maybe he's right."

"It's not about what we think of you," I said. "It's about what we'd have thought of *him,* meeting him under even less auspicious circumstances than we did, after you led us right to him when we tailed you to find out what you were hiding."

"Tailed me? The hell you say, little lady. Maybe your hacker cousin's all that, but a penny-ante surveillance? I'd have slipped you like a greased pig."

"Who're you calling a greased pig?"

"He's the greased pig," Bill said, peacemaking. "You're the farmer trying to hold on to the pig."

"That's a charming image. Is it a midwest suburban thing?"

"Anyway," Bill told Jack, "I've tried shaking her. She's hard to lose. And look at it this way: If you'd done that, we wouldn't owe you a martini."

"On the other hand," I said, "if he'd done that, he might still have a client."

Jack looked at me, surprised. "I still have a client."

"You do? Up one side and down the other, but he didn't fire you?"

"Through the steam coming out of his ears he reluctantly conceded I'm still the man for the job. Partly because if he cans me and hires someone else, that's yet another person who knows he's looking for these paintings."

"Why is that such a problem?" Bill asked.

"Beyond the idea that his possible real, as opposed to stated, motivation doesn't put him in the best light? I don't know."

"I'm having second thoughts about my second thoughts about his motivation," I said. "After that story."

"I know." Jack nodded.

"Tell me this," Bill said. "How much of his anger was with you, and how much was with us for even knowing about the paintings?"

"He's pretty pissed at you," Jack admitted. "Especially for not telling him who your client is."

"Did you tell him?" I asked.

"I thought about it, because we don't even think Jeff Dunbar is your client's real name, do we?"

"No, but—"

"Oh, chill. I didn't. I would've, but he threw me out before he got to the bamboo under the fingernails. Anyway, we had a bigger fight to have. He wanted me to ditch you guys from now on."

"He did? Even though the cat's out of the bag?"

"Yup."

"What did you say?"

"I said, I don't carry a gun and I'm not used to getting shot at."

"And he said?"

"He went through the whole thing we did, how the gunshot probably had nothing to do with this case. I stopped him halfway and said that wasn't the real point."

"It's not? What is?"

"Come on. If we're all looking for the same thing, and we know it, how ridiculous is it to be sneaking around trying to outsmart each other?"

"Sneaking around is kind of what we do," I pointed out. "How did he respond?"

"He was still against it. So I had to use my other big, as it were, gun. I said, maybe it was a mistake not to play dumb when you came to me, and if it was I'm sorry, but that ship's sailed. Now aren't I better off if I know what you guys are up to? Your client most likely wants to make off with these paintings, find someone to authenticate them, and sell them fast. If he can, they'll be on the market with a provenance. Very soon they'll be almost impossible to debunk. If Dr. Yang's out to protect the memory of his friend, that would *not* be the outcome he was looking for."

"Well, but here's a question. How could someone authenticate them? If Dr. Yang saw Chau die. How can this still be an issue?"

"They'll say he's mistaken. He's exaggerating. That it was chaos in Tiananmen when the tanks rolled in, he doesn't know what he saw. They'll say he was with Chau until the shooting started, then he ran away, now he's out-and-out lying. How can he prove none of that is true?"

I thought about the clenched muscles in Dr. Yang's jaw. "When he talked about holding his friend's hand? I don't think he was lying."

"Maybe not. But it's not proof."

"But Chau's buried in his hometown, didn't you say? What about DNA from the body?"

"You're going to ask the PRC government to exhume an enemy of the people so you can prove he's still alive?"

"Besides," Bill said, "DNA's only useful if there's something to compare it against. Unless someone's got Chau's toothbrush, that wouldn't help."

I thought about it. "Well, so what did Dr. Yang say?"

"He wasn't happy. He didn't like being backed into a corner and he was furious at the idea he might not be believed. But he couldn't argue. He told me to go ahead."

"With us?"

"With you." Jack looked from me to Bill. "Though if your client disappears with these paintings before Dr. Yang gets a shot at them, you guys, trust me: I am *so* dead."

"So the reason you gave him for going ahead with us, it's actually true?" I asked. "Not the synergy of shared effort? The serendipitous sparks when bits of data collide? You're just keeping an eye on us?"

"Damn correct. Also, Athos here still owes me a martini."

7

We headed north where Bill, to no one's surprise, knew a quiet bar.

"Let me ask you something," I said to Jack. "After the Tiananmen story I'm inclined to think Dr. Yang's motives are legit. But I'm hung up on his reaction when Anna asked what you were doing. If he's being noble, why doesn't he want her knowing about it?"

"I'm not sure. But things between them aren't the greatest right now and she has her own problems."

"That's what it sounded like. Can you tell?"

"It's not a secret. She went to Beijing last year to study. Dr. Yang was against it but she can be bullheaded when it comes to her work. There were old-school masters she wanted to get to before they're gone."

"Given his experience, I'm not surprised he felt that way. But things have changed over there."

"Maybe not so much. She met a poet. Liu Mai-ke. Part of a loose network of activist artists. He—"

"Wait." I stopped walking. "That's the Mike? Mike Liu?"

"You know about him?"

"Who's Chinese and doesn't?"

"I'm not Chinese," Bill said. "Fill me in."

"A dissident," I said. "He wrote an open letter to the government about artists' rights. Last fall. They closed down his Web site, but too late, and the letter went viral. Mike Liu Mai-ke. But he's in prison."

Jack said, "And it's sort of her fault."

"Hers?" I began to see why Anna might have her own problems. "I thought it was the letter. Wasn't that what the trial was about?"

"The letter went up a few weeks before he met Anna. They shut down his Web site, followed him, tapped his phone, things like that, but they didn't arrest him until after they were married."

"*Married?* Wait, Jack—Anna Yang's married to Mike Liu? Why didn't I know that?"

"They realized their mistake and now they keep it quiet."

"What mistake?"

We stepped apart for a pair of hand-holding students. "They were married at a wild wedding banquet in a hip café in Beijing," Jack told us. "*Tout le* art world, also *tout le* dissident world, was there. Even Doug Haig."

"He's a friend of theirs?" The needle on my Anna Yang respect-o-meter, which had jumped, started to slip.

"Haig? Somebody's friend? He goes to China four or five times a year just to scoop up the hot new artists. He was in Beijing then, and it would've been mass career suicide for every artist there if he wasn't invited. The whole thing was less marriage ceremony than art world happening anyway. Everyone drinking, shouting slogans, singing revolutionary songs. Belting out 'La Marseillaise' and 'The Star-Spangled Banner' in Chinese. Tweets flying, photos on Facebook, MySpace, mad blogging."

"Sounds like fun."

"Probably was. After the wedding Anna and Mike planned to ship out here to meet the in-laws."

"The Yangs? They weren't there?"

Bill said, "I bet they couldn't get visas. That whole crowd that left after Tiananmen, China doesn't want them back."

"Right," said Jack.

"Even for their daughter's wedding?" I said. "Hey, you guys, don't look at me like that. It's sad."

"Gets worse," Jack said. "One reason Anna and Mike got married, besides true love, is they figured marrying a foreigner was the only way a troublemaker like Mike could get a passport. Big mistake."

"He couldn't?"

"Not only couldn't he, when he applied he got arrested. It dawned on them too late that the marrying-a-foreigner thing, the public-wedding-banquet thing, the who's-who of the dissident world all-together-now on YouTube, that was the problem."

"Oh. That's what you meant, realized their mistake?"

Jack nodded. "Mike had been small potatoes. Now suddenly his political writing, his poems, the open letter, they were high-profile. The PRC couldn't let him travel and they couldn't ignore him. They decided to deal with him publicly, as a warning. He was convicted of subversion of the state. He got seven years, and Anna got kicked out of the country."

I looked around at the students strolling under the early spring trees. "Poor Anna. And poor Mike. And why do I get the feeling there was a lot of I-told-you-so when she got back?"

"Great heaping piles of it. Dr. Yang had been against the whole thing from the start. Not that he knew Mike from Adam, or cared. It was the idea of Anna involved with a dissident, on the other side of the world, where he couldn't protect her—I'm just sayin', that was no semester to defend your thesis."

"What about Anna's mother?" Bill asked. "Did she object, too?"

"She and Anna are pretty close. She was in on it longer than Dr. Yang, watching the romance bloom. She wasn't happy, either, because she was afraid Anna would get hurt. But she tried to soften Dr. Yang up. When Anna got back, she bombarded the Chinese consulate, her senator, everyone she could think of with phone calls, letters, e-mails. Eventually Dr. Yang gave in. He was furious, but she's his little girl. He called some people he knows, and he knows some serious people. But no one could do anything. The PRC's not backing down."

"Even though Mike Liu's small potatoes?"

"*Because* he is. He has no huge international following, no one claiming he belongs to the world, not to China. They're calling this a purely internal matter and no one's cashing in the political chips to challenge that."

The swirling student traffic thinned as we walked north. We stopped for a light a few blocks away, across the street from Union Square.

"Now I get it," I said. "Why Dr. Yang might not want to tell Anna about the Chaus. Stir up the whole subject of dissident artists."

"Anna's sort of back to a normal life. Basically, she's making art and waiting for Mike. Between you and me I get the feeling Dr. Yang hopes she'll forget him and fall for somebody else. Also between you and me, though, Anna's still in touch with dissident groups here and in China, not a word about which she breathes to Dr. Yang."

"Poor Anna," I said again. "And poor Mike."

Jack's eyebrows went up. "You don't even know Mike. He might be a self-righteous confrontational jerk with a martyr complex."

"He's a political prisoner. That makes him one of the the good guys. And I hardly know Anna, either. Is he really that bad?"

"No idea. I never met him. From what I hear he's a serious, sweet guy. Talented writer, too."

"Then why did you say that?"

"You felt bad for him. I was jealous."

"Go get arrested, I'll feel bad for you, too."

"Getting shot at's not enough?"

"That's getting old."

I got no answer because Jack's and Bill's phones both rang at once. I wouldn't have put it past Jack to orchestrate that but it was for sure beyond Bill.

Jack finished his call first. "That was Jacqueline. At Chocolat. They finished the temporary window and she told them to hang around so I could approve it. About that martini—"

"We'd have to put it off anyway," Bill said, folding his phone. "I have a date."

It took Jack a beat, but he caught up. "With Shayna Dylan? Seriously?"

Bill gave a modest shrug. "I'm too sexy for Vladimir's shirt."

"Hah," I scoffed. "You think Shayna dating you is about anything as high-minded as sex?"

"Um, well, good luck," Jack said to Bill. He glanced at me and added, "With everything. Talk later, when you're done? I'll be in my office, doing whatever I was doing when all hell broke loose." Then, habit overcoming reason, he stepped into the street and hailed a cab.

"I still think it's weird," I said as Bill and I crossed to the subway, Bill to go uptown, me to go down.

"That Jack prefers cabs?"

"No, he had a deprived childhood where they don't have subways. But based on what he said, I can see why Dr. Yang didn't tell Anna what he's doing, but it doesn't seem like it would be a big deal if she found out. And why does he care if we know?" A thought occurred to me. "Uh-oh."

"Uh-oh what?"

"'Based on what Jack said.' Maybe he's holding out on us. Maybe something completely else went on in there besides what he told us."

Bill looked at me. "I guess it's possible. I don't think so, though. That wouldn't be like him."

"You haven't known him that long, have you? Just a couple of months?"

"No, that's true. But, for example, I knew *you* were on the level from the minute I met you."

"Proving my point: You're a rotten judge of character."

"You may be right," he said. "Because I'm actually looking forward to my date with Shayna."

8

Bill and I split up at the subway entrance, promising to call each other later. I caught the N and stood the few rattling stops to Chinatown, meditating on my client. I didn't think Jeff Dunbar had given me his real name, or any reason to trust him, but I'd taken his money. Maybe he had a right to know someone else was on the trail of the paintings and I was working with that someone else's PI. Or maybe that was just an excuse to call him, because there were some things I wanted to know, too.

I got off at Canal, called, got voice mail, left a message. I wondered if Dunbar was in his office, doing whatever he didn't want me to know he did, and whether he'd have to slip away to call so the people he did it for wouldn't find out about me, either. A lot of people in this case, I reflected, not supposed to know about each other. I was putting the phone away when it chimed. That meant that while I was underground someone left a message the phone had just found.

"Ms. Chin? This is Samuel Wing. I'd very much like to speak with you. Would you give me a call at your earliest convenience?" I had no idea who Samuel Wing was, but he had a nice voice, a Mandarin accent, a desire to talk to me, and a phone number. So I called it.

"Ah, Ms. Chin, good to hear from you. I'd appreciate a few moments of your time."

"Can I know what this is about, Mr. Wing?"

"Certain paintings. I don't want to say anything more over the phone, but I'm fairly sure you'll be interested."

Unless the guy was going to try to sell me a hot Picasso, I was fairly sure he was right.

"I'll be happy to come to your office," he said. "Canal Street near Broadway, is that correct?"

He'd done his homework, the well-spoken Mr. Wing. "Yes. six-nine-three Canal, buzzer number two."

"Fifteen minutes? Is that convenient?"

For me, very. For him, that either meant his base was downtown—office or home—or he was already in Chinatown, hanging at the noodle shop or the tea house, waiting for me to stroll by. I checked the faces of the noodle-eaters and tea-drinkers on my way up the block, so if one of them appeared in my office attached to Samuel Wing I'd know I'd been, if not quite ambushed, at least waited for a little hard.

I pushed through the street door at 693, checked my mailbox, and waved to the ladies at Golden Adventure Travel. This is really their space, this whole ground floor, and their name is on the door. I'm their subtenant and buzzer number two has no name on it at all. That way, if anyone should chance to see a client of mine come in here, he can always claim he was looking into a package tour to the casinos of Macao.

In the office I put on the kettle and closed the barred airshaft window. Mr. Wing might not enjoy the Hong Kong back alley atmosphere: Beijing opera CD's; crying babies; spring onions and pork stir-frying in sesame oil. I switched the computer on and checked the phone. Interesting: no calls. My landline message gives my cell phone number, which is where I'd assumed Samuel Wing had gotten it. Evidently I'd been wrong. Putting that away for further thought, I speed-dialed Golden Adventure.

Andi Gee answered. "Hi, Lydia! What's up?"

"I have a guy coming in I don't know. Can I check the panic button?"

"Sure. Hey, girls, Lydia's checking the panic button. Don't panic!" I pressed my foot down on the button Bill wired under the desk the last time I had a little trouble in here. I've never used it, but I like to check it occasionally to make sure it works. A loud buzz sounded down the hall and also in my ear, where Andi said, "Works great! You get problem, you press, we come save you!"

"No, you don't! You call the police."

"Yeah, yeah. Who this guy? He dangerous?"

"I doubt it. Just a precaution." Because, I didn't tell her, someone already got shot at today.

I turned to the computer and searched the local databases for a Samuel Wing. I came up with four, none of them jumping out at me as possibly connected to this case. I archived them anyway, to recheck after I'd met him.

Of course, he might not be local.

Or his name might not be Samuel Wing.

I did a little more computer work, since I had the time. Precisely fifteen minutes after we'd hung up, here came the buzzer, and when I asked who was there, I heard, "Samuel Wing." Between the panic button and the .22 in the small of my back, I felt I was ready. I buzzed him in and stuck my head out the door so he'd know where to head for.

"Ms. Chin?"

"Pleased to meet you, Mr. Wing." We'd spoken so far in English, so I kept it up. His accent told me it wasn't his first language, but my bilingual phone message would have told him I speak Cantonese. I guessed we weren't speaking that because he didn't, and he wasn't trying Mandarin because if I wasn't fluent that might embarrass me.

Samuel Wing sat, pulling at his trouser knees in that way men have. He was thin, medium-height, fiftyish, gray hair, nice suit. Not a face I'd just seen on the block. Looking around, he said, "What an interesting office." Actually, I have fairly standard, if battered, desk and filing cabinets, plus laptop, lamps, and Lucky Tiger Tofu Factory tear-off calendar. If you were an anthropologist from outer space this room might be interesting, but I wasn't sure what Samuel Wing was getting at until, nodding with satisfaction, he said, "Very discreet."

So it wasn't the office, it was location, location, location. "I find my clients appreciate that. Can I offer you some tea?"

He seemed pleased to find this courtesy extended. Before I was old enough to walk I'd understood that no Chinese people could decently sit down together, for business, gossip, or companionable silence, without tea. Even Jack Lee, from the midwest suburbs, had felt inadequate when he'd realized he had no refreshments for guests. I'd been a little surprised not to have been offered anything by Dr. Yang, but maybe the rules were different for angry academics.

I scooped some oolong into a pot, poured water from the kettle, and while the tea steeped I brought out the Chinese-client cups: bamboo-painted porcelain with lids and no handles. They add a touch of elegance to my office. That I buy them by the dozen in the basement of Kam Man supermarket because I break them regularly was not Samuel Wing's concern.

"How can I help you, Mr. Wing?"

"It is I, Ms. Chin, who can help you."

I was perfectly willing to believe that and only slightly annoyed at his smug air, as though by turning the tables like that he'd made a clever pun.

"It's come to my attention, Ms. Chin, that you have an interest in certain paintings."

"I'm an art lover," I said, swirling the tea in the pot. I poured for both of us.

He smiled. "Of course." He lifted, sniffed, and tasted his tea, cradling the cup in one hand and shifting the lid aside with the other in a move my mother had made me practice my whole childhood. He sat in silence to permit the tea to occupy his thoughts and senses. "Quite good," he said, as though he hadn't expected that. Just because of the back-room-on-the-alley thing? Another sip, and then he replaced the lid and set the cup gently on the desk. "I'm speaking specifically, of course, about the paintings of Chau Chun. Chau Gwai Ying Shung, the Ghost Hero."

"Yes, I thought you might be. May I ask how my interest in Chau came to your attention?"

"No, I'm sorry, that must remain confidential. Nothing so dramatic as an electronic surveillance or anything of that nature, I assure you," he said with a dry smile. "In any case, this is an interest that the people I represent would prefer did not go further."

"Really?" I sipped and said, "I thought, Mr. Wing, you'd come here to help me."

"I have. The people I represent are prepared to show their gratitude if you abandon your search for these paintings."

"Are they? Who are these people?"

"I apologize, but that also must remain confidential. But they're serious, I assure you." He took a wallet from his jacket pocket, fat with crisp new bills. He fanned a few out: They were hundreds. "Whatever compensation you've received for your efforts thus far, my principals are prepared to exceed it. They believe ten thousand dollars is a fair recompense for the trouble you've taken."

Well. Now there was an intriguing offer. I could hand Jeff Dunbar back his thou and kiss not just him good-bye, but also the slimy Doug Haig, the angry Dr. Yang, and whoever was making like Annie Oakley uptown. Ten large, that would buy a lot of coffee beans. Jack could go ahead and find the new Chaus by himself. And Bill wouldn't have to date Shayna anymore.

"I'd be interested to know, Mr. Wing, why these people care so much."

"Yes, I'm sure. Although you don't expect that I'm prepared to tell you?"

"No. But you can appreciate that I'd have to know who, and why, before I could consider your generous offer."

"Actually, no, I don't see why that should be true. In this country, don't they say 'money talks'? Is this"—he lifted the cash—"not loud enough? I think, though I'm merely an agent acting on their behalf, I can confidently say my principals would be prepared to . . . raise the volume. An additional fifty percent, would that be acceptable?"

Part of me wanted to see how far I could push this. For one thing, how high Mr. Wing's "principals" were willing to go would be the true gauge of their interest. For another, I didn't know what the going price of integrity was these days.

But I've never been one to string a man along. "I'm sorry, Mr. Wing. I value your principals' directness and their generosity. Please express my great regret at being forced to decline."

Samuel Wing didn't put his wallet away. "Ms. Chin, I'd urge you to reconsider."

"I'm sorry."

"No. But you might be."

"Excuse me?"

"Another expression they use in this country, I believe, is 'the carrot and the stick.' This"—raising the wallet—"is the carrot."

"You're telling me," I said slowly, "that you also have a stick? Mr. Wing, are you threatening me? In my own office, while you're drinking my tea?"

"No, of course not." He smiled at the absurdity. "But I'd very much like to report to my principals a successful conclusion to this affair."

"You can *report*," I said, "that you delivered the message you were sent with. You can *report* that I considered the offer most generous and I was sorry I had to decline. And you can *report* that you got the hell out of here."

I stood. He didn't, immediately, but spoke looking up at me. "Ms. Chin, your loyalty to the client who's already paid for it does you credit. As does your natural curiosity. However, I very much hope you'll reflect on this conversation. When you do, you'll come to understand where your true interests lie. You have my number. I expect to hear from you soon." He tucked his wallet away, and stood. "Thank you for the tea. It was delicious. Good day."

He pulled open my office door, strode into the hall and out onto Canal Street. Before the street door closed behind him, I saw him turn right. I counted to ten, not to calm myself down, but to give him a chance to get far enough that he wouldn't notice me. Then I hit the street, too.

I ambled a block behind him for a while. At Hudson, he turned north. He didn't look around and, intriguingly, he didn't take out his cell phone. I hoped he'd take advantage of the spring weather to stroll back to wherever he was going, but three blocks later, he flagged a cab. I watched it roll up Hudson, then headed back to my office. I called Bill, got voice mail. Well, I certainly wouldn't want to interrupt his tête-à-tête with Shayna. I left a message telling him to be careful and to call me when he came up for air. Then I called Jack.

"Lee."

"Chin."

"Hey."

"Hey. Should I stick to one syllable, or can I use sentences?"

"Whatever flies your flag."

"How's your window?"

"Smaller than it used to be. Plywood and plastic. But at least it won't rain in here before I get a real one. I put the Hasui back on the wall so I could contemplate the peaceable life I had before I met you. Is that why you called?"

"No. Is it bulletproof?"

"The Hasui?"

"The window."

Pause. "I don't think so. Does it need to be? I thought that act was over."

"It never hurts to be prepared. I just had a visit from a gentleman calling himself Samuel Wing. Does that name mean anything to you?"

"No, but I get the feeling it's about to."

"I don't know. He offered me a boatload of money to abandon this search."

"Re-eally?" In a way I was beginning to recognize, Jack drew the word out. "How big a boat? The *QE2*? Or a kayak?"

"I'd say the Staten Island Ferry. He started at ten thousand, went to fifteen at the drop of a 'no.' He'd have kept going if I let him."

"Well, that's not chump change. What's his angle?"

"According to him, he doesn't have one, he's working for 'some people.' His 'principals,' he said, would pay handsomely if I dropped the case. Then he suggested rather pointedly I'd be sorry if I didn't."

"Damn. Did he suggest specifically that he'd shoot your uptown partner?"

That tripped me up. It had taken years for me and Bill to start using the word "partner."

"Um, no," I said.

"That's a relief."

"It wasn't clear exactly what would happen. Earthquakes, tornadoes. But Mr. Wing made himself suspicious to me in oh so many ways."

"Tell me one."

"He came here with a fat wallet stuffed with hundreds. I booted him out with it untouched but he didn't call in to report to his principals."

"How do you know?"

"I followed him, dummy."

"Oh, of course you did. And you saw him not call?"

"For at least ten minutes. If they were so anxious to have me sign on that they sent him with cash, not just the promise of cash, wouldn't they have been anxious to know my answer? Also, his language is Mandarin, he drinks tea like a mainlander—I gave him the lidded-cup test—but he knows enough about New York that he walked north of the tunnel before he tried to get a cab."

"Which says he's been here awhile."

"Bill told me you were smart."

"On the other hand, I've been here all my life and I don't think I could pass the lidded-cup test."

"Your mom didn't make you practice?"

"Who were we going to impress in Madison?"

"I'll teach you. So I'm thinking Mr. Wing's from China, but he's spent serious time in New York. Also, he didn't threaten my mother."

"Well, now, that *is* suspicious. What?"

"Think about it. A pro working for people who want to intimidate a Chinese woman, the first thing he'd do would be threaten my family. I don't have kids, but a couple of my brothers do, and I have an aged mother. He didn't mention any of them."

Jack was silent for a few moments. "So he's an amateur. Not actually an enforcer."

"Exactly. I don't think he's used to threatening people and I don't think he's working for anyone. Except, possibly, for someone who's also not used to threatening people." I paused as a thought struck me. "At least, not with violence. Maybe with failing grades."

"Wait. You think he's working for Dr. Yang?"

"Is it crazy?"

"I think it is," Jack said slowly.

"Not all that many people know I'm looking for the Chaus. And only one, as far as I know, is seriously upset about it. Samuel Wing had my cell phone number."

"Which I didn't give Dr. Yang. If that's what you're calling to ask."

"I wasn't. Honestly, I wasn't. That only just occurred to me. I was calling to tell you to watch your back."

"Really?"

"Yes."

"Really really? Because I'm starting to get the feeling you don't trust me."

"Bill says you're stand-up."

"He said I was smart, too. Do you always believe him?"

"Ninety-nine percent of the time."

"What happens the other one percent?"

"I'm wrong."

"Well, you're wrong now. I'm the good guys. We have a deal. I didn't have my fingers crossed or anything."

My cheeks burned. Good thing we were on the phone. "Dr. Yang might have sent this guy without telling you. Just because I don't trust your client doesn't mean I don't trust you."

"Methinks you're protesting too much, but I'll take it. I'll also take the warning at face value, and I appreciate it."

"It really was why I called."

After an awkward moment, Jack asked, "What did Bill say?"

"About Samuel Wing? I left him a message. He's incommunicado, tied up with Shayna Dylan."

"You think she's into that?"

"Yuck!"

"Sorry. Listen, what I'm doing up here—and I'm telling you this because now that you think I'm offended you're afraid to ask because it'll sound like you're checking up on me—is I'm trying to track any recent interest in Chau, see who the buyers and sellers have been, the last few years."

"Oh. Thanks, and thanks."

"Nothing interesting's coming up, though. I'm ready to move on. If you're not planning to spend the rest of the day with gangsters or at the pistol range or something, do you want to go over to Red Sky and see if we can find where the rumors came from that Jen Beril heard? They're open until six, which believe me is plenty of time to see the current show."

"You know, that's a really good idea."

"You don't have to sound surprised. Red Sky, forty-five minutes?"

"In the same building as Baxter/Haig, right? Meet you outside."

I'd been heading back along Canal while we talked, to my office. I had some time, so I clicked the computer on to try a couple of things.

First I checked my archived Samuel Wings. Two were in their twenties, and one was eighty-three, so I scrapped them. The fourth, in a stroke of luck, had won a bowling tournament on Long Island last year. His smiling puss was in a newspaper photo, and I'd never seen it before. So much for that. I moved on to my next bright idea.

New York City has devised all sorts of online and phone-related ways of making itself more user-friendly over the last few years. Some work and some don't, but as a PI it's my duty to keep up with them. I'd never used this one before and I was eager to try it.

Three-one-one is the city's information number. You can ask all sorts of questions and get all sorts of answers. Or you can do it online. Tap a few keys, for example, and you're at the find-your-stuff page, which exists to hook you up with the bus, train, or taxi you left your stuff in. I went to "taxi," filled in a form that asked for the medallion number, which I'd memorized from the top of Samuel Wing's cab, and the time of day, plus a description of the stuff in question and a way to get in touch. It claimed it would automatically text the cabbie or his garage. I could only see this working under two conditions: the cabbie was conscientious and honest; or the searcher was offering a reward. I went the reward route, not describing my stuff but suggesting there'd be something in it for the cabbie if I found what I was looking for. Then I locked up the office and headed west again.

9

In the slanted sunlight I walked past cheap electronics stores, hawkers of bootleg purses and bogus perfumes, and immigrants at sidewalk tables waiting to paint your name in bright brushstrokes and surround it with carp or dragons. Or to fold long leaves of grass into curled pythons; or dollar bills—that you supplied—into butterflies. As I passed them, the painters and folders, I wondered about their lives back in China: whether they were landscape painters, calligraphers, weavers, what their work was like when it wasn't butterflies and tourists' names. Whether they kept up that work here, on their own, when their Canal Street day was done.

Another few blocks and the crowds thinned out. I'd considered walking up to Chelsea, but decided I'd hate it if Jack beat me to the gallery. The subway got me there in a flash. I took up a station in front of the gallery building to wait.

Actually, not directly in front, a few yards east. I'd glanced into Baxter/Haig and seen that Nick Greenbank was still guarding the gates. It wasn't like it would blow my cover if he saw me; there was no reason that, in my role as an art consultant, I shouldn't accompany yet another client to yet another gallery, even one that happened to be in his building. But I'd had a thought and I was working out its implications: Doug Haig, and little Nick himself, courtesy of Vladimir Oblomov, had my cell phone number.

A few minutes more waiting and thinking, and here came Jack, unfolding from a taxi at the curb. I was about to make a subway-vs-cab wisecrack but, luckily for him, my phone rang. I checked the readout: my client, Jeff Dunbar. I held up a finger to Jack and answered.

"Sorry to take so long returning your call," he said. "I was in a meeting." He spoke eagerly. And gave me a bit too much of an explanation for someone so eager. "Do you have something to report?"

"A number of things. Can we meet later?"

"You've found the paintings?"

"If I had I wouldn't keep you in suspense. No, but I want to discuss some other issues."

"What kind of 'issues'?" His voice became wary.

"I'd like to meet you later, if that's all right. It's important or I wouldn't be calling."

"Yes. Yes, of course." He paused. I could have suggested a meeting place but I was curious what would happen if I left that to him. He gave it a few seconds; then since I wasn't coming through, he said, "There's a bar on West Street and Eleventh called The Fraying Rope. Do you know it?"

"No, but I can find it. About an hour?"

"Yes, that's fine."

"See you then." I clicked off, aware of Jack hovering at my elbow. "Excuse me," I said as I put the phone away. "Do I know you?"

"Not well enough." He was grinning, so I guessed the twin traumas of the gunshot and Dr. Yang's dressing-down had faded. "Sorry to keep you waiting. Though I'm actually five minutes early."

"I was ten."

"Does anyone ever get over on you?"

I sighed. "People do it all the time. That's why I have to win when I can."

"I guess that's not unreasonable. Uh-oh. Eagle-eyed Nick's spotted us." Cheerily, Jack waved through the glass door.

I turned to see Nick Greenbank scowling. I waved, too, and said to Jack, "Good thing he doesn't have Vladimir Oblomov's cell number or he'd be calling him to rat me out for two-timing."

"He doesn't?"

"No," I said. "He has mine."

Jack's eyebrows went up. "Oh. Oh ho ho ho. Is that an apology?"

"No way. But it's an interesting fact."

"That's true. Should we discuss it with him?"

"I think so."

"Any special gag?"

"I haven't thought of one. He knows you, right? He knows what you do?"

"Yes. Does he know what you do?"

"Not unless he Googled me. I was here as Vladimir's art consultant."

"Nick doesn't have that kind of enterprise. If you were convincing, he believed you."

"So how do you want to go in?"

After a second he grinned. "Winging it, like you and Bill. Walk this way." He turned and pushed through Baxter/Haig's oversized doors.

Nick's scowl fizzled around the edges as we approached. He was clearly happier expressing his disdain through an inch and a half of glass.

"Hi, Nick." Jack stuck out his hand. "Jack Lee. We've met a couple of times."

"I remember." Nick gave Jack a perfunctory limp mitt.

"And you know Lydia Chin. She's a consultant, she was here this morning. With Vladimir Oblomov. The Russian guy."

Nick licked his lips. "Yeah."

"The thing is, Lydia's an old friend of mine. This Vladimir, he was making her nervous. So she asked me to check up on him."

"Is that why you're here? He hasn't been back or anything. Made me nervous, too." Nick gave a weak laugh, seeming relieved that he and I were on the same side.

"From what I found, he's a nervous-making guy," Jack said. "Though actually, no, we didn't come here to talk about him. We weren't headed here at all. We're going upstairs to see the show at Red Sky. 'Bright Sun, Still Sea, Green Homeland'?"

Nick nodded. "It's good. If any of those three guys gets a following over the next year, we might take him on."

"Really, you liked it? I hated it. But no accounting for taste. Anyway, on the way here, something weird happened. Lydia got a phone call. So we thought we'd stop and see you before we go up."

Nick looked unhappily bewildered, as though he wasn't sure what to respond to: the fact that Jack hated a show he liked, or the weirdness of me getting a phone call. In the interest of progress I helped him out. "A man named Samuel Wing. The odd part is, he called my cell phone. I keep that number kind of close. But Vladimir gave it to you before."

It took Nick a minute. "You think I gave it to him?"

"Yeah," said Jack, leaning on the counter. "Yeah, Nick, I do."

"Oh, Jack, back off!" I snapped. "You know that he-man stuff drives me nuts. I may have to put up with it from clients, but not from you." Jack, startled, turned to me. I spoke to Nick. "I don't know what makes some guys think I need a prince riding to the rescue all the time. Is that how I come across to you? I mean, because I'm small, or what? Anyway, Jack has it wrong. As usual. He thinks I'm upset. So he can, I don't know, beat you up and save me or something."

Jack started to protest. "I thought—"

"You always do. Do you ever ask? No." I gave him an exasperated glare, and gave Nick, pointedly, a smile. "If this Wing guy were just some jerk, maybe I'd be mad. But it turns out he's kind of a big deal. A new collector with lots of money. It might develop into something. So I was wondering who he's a friend of. I told Jack that, but of course he didn't listen."

As I chattered, Nick caught on. If a new collector had come into my art consultant life, I might want to show my appreciation. I could practically see the gears grinding as he tried to figure a way to get in on it. In the end, though, he shook his head. "It wasn't me. I don't know the guy."

"Oh. That's disappointing. I'd hoped—"

"But what about Doug? Did you give him your number?"

"Mr. Haig?" I said that as though it were a new and clever thought. "Well, yes, we did."

"Then it was probably him." If Nick couldn't pocket my gratitude directly, at least he could make sure I knew which gallery to bring my new client to.

"Well, then, I'd like to thank him. He's in the office?"

"Gone for the day. He'll be back in the morning."

"Oh, I have a meeting in the morning. Give me his cell, I'll call him now." I took out my phone and waited.

"Sorry, no can do."

"What?" I acted like this was a first, being refused someone's cell number.

Nick squirmed but shook his head. "He really doesn't like that."

"Oh." I blinked. I glanced at Jack, who still stood there looking confused. "Well, I guess it doesn't matter. I'll catch up with him sometime. Just to thank him." I waited, giving Nick another chance, but he didn't bite. I stuck the phone back in my bag, said, "Jack, are you coming or what?" and walked out.

Jack followed me out of Baxter/Haig and then in the door to the upstairs galleries. Once Nick couldn't see us, he laughed. "Hey, Porthos, nice work."

"Same to you, Aramis."

"Why, thanks. Can I hit the elevator button, or is that too macho for you?"

"No, go right ahead."

He did. "A real twerp, Nick, and an ass-kisser and backbiter besides. He'll rise to the top in no time."

"Is that how the gallery business works?"

"What business doesn't?"

"Oh, good, another cynic."

"That's just so you won't miss your real partner while you're working with me. I'm actually an upbeat, positive sort of guy."

"I don't miss him a bit," I said, though I was wondering a tad edgily how long Bill needed to extract some simple information from Shayna Dylan. "If you're all that positive, though, tell me something. What am I supposed to think about the work in that gallery?"

The elevator arrived to fetch us. As it started jerkily up, Jack said, "Where, Baxter/Haig? The Pang Ping-Pong show? You can think whatever you want. Wait. Are you asking what *I* think?"

"Of course I am."

"Ah. Well. His technique, especially in the control of line weights in the smallest details, is terrific. That's real old-school stuff. And his color choices are fresh and his composition can be really strong."

"So you like it."

"No."

"No?"

"Just judged visually, it's great to look at. But the content's a one-liner. He's been doing this for years and he's done. Nothing new to say. If you look at the most recent ones you can tell even he's getting bored."

"You can? How?"

"The composition's slipping. Those three along the back wall? Too overall even, too balanced. Busy, bright, and sarcastic, but no aesthetic risk." The elevator bumped to a halt. "Why are you looking at me like that?"

"I guess I expected a wiseass answer. Not something that serious."

"Hey, I'm not just a pretty face."

I was saved from having to comment on Jack's face by the elevator door, which slid open into a huge loft. I stepped out and stood, taking in the skylights, the unpainted concrete floors, and the art.

Behind the reception desk, giant silver springs curved upward, topped with mylar strips streaming in the breeze made by rotating silver ceiling fans. To the right, multicolored acrylic tanks held multicolored plastic fish standing on their tails; occasionally one did a pirouette, then they all stood motionless again. To the left, taking up fully a third of the room, little patterned red boxes on big white wheels scooted through a forest of blue posts plastered with Chinese product labels.

"I can't wait for you to explain this to me," I whispered to Jack as a smiling young Asian man left the desk and came over to greet us.

"Inexplicable," Jack said. "Hi, Eddie. Lydia, this is Eddie To. This is his gallery, his and his partner Frank's. Eddie, Lydia Chin."

"Hey, what's up, Lydia? Jack, I'm surpised to see you back here. Frank said you didn't like this show." Eddie To, lithe and small, wore round black-framed glasses and a diamond stud in his ear. He had no more of a Chinese accent than Jack did. Or me.

"Hate it," Jack said. "Especially the dancing fish. I thought you ought to know, though, that Baxter/Haig is planning to poach your artists once their prices rise."

"Why, Jack. I'm touched by your concern, but not to worry. Doug Haig puts the moves on all our artists just to keep in practice. Mostly it's caca. Even that big giant diva Jon-Jon Jie's been running around lately telling people how much Haig loves him."

"Jie? I don't know him."

"Yes, you saw his show. Last winter. Don't deny it. 'Extra/ordinary.' "

"Wait. Blades, arrows? Animal skins? That's him? He's from Texas."

"So? They have divas in Texas."

"Haig's taking on Chinese-Americans?"

"Not. That's the point. Haig will string him along and then break his heart. Frank and I are keeping out of it, we're hoping it might make a man of him."

"Haig?"

"As if. Anyway," Eddie To said slyly, "I'm not sure the time is ripe for dear Doug to try something new. Not that I'm one to take joy in another's misfortune—"

"You're not?"

"All right, I am." He lowered his voice, though we were alone in the room. "If you listen, you can hear the walls murmuring that Doug Haig is deep in doo-doo. His backers, who helped him buy Brad Baxter out? The walls say they're getting antsy. The art market's not gushing cash as fast as they thought it would and they're tired of waiting. Or maybe they're just tired of Doug Haig pawing all their women. Haig's already discreetly had a fire sale of some older work he's had around. I guarantee you the chance of him stepping outside his comfort zone to start showing Chinese-Americans right now is exactly less than shit." Eddie raised his voice to a normal level and spread his arms to the work in his gallery. "Now, these fine fellows are from China, so technically they're Doug Haig's natural prey. But utilizing our super-secret weapon, Frank discovered them, so we're counting on a little Chinese loyalty."

"What's your super-secret weapon?"

"Jack. If I tell you it won't be a secret. Oh, all right, since you insist. You remember when Frank was in Beijing two years ago for the China Contemporary conference? He struck up a warm friendship with the head of the Art History Department at the Central University in Hohhot. So warm, in fact, I had to wonder if my domestic bliss was threatened." He gave a little sigh.

Jack asked, "Where's Hohhot?"

"Inner Mongolia," I said. When they both looked at me, I added, "Hey, I'm not just a pretty face."

"Whatever positions Frank offered Dr. Lin," Eddie To went on, "the only one he agreed to, as told to me, was to be our exclusive consultant in the field of bleeding-edge Chinese art. Dr. Lin Qiao-xiang. And doesn't Doug Haig wish he knew. Q.X. is the only reason we find artists Doug the Slug hasn't gotten to yet. We have to keep him secret or he'd be stolen in a heartbeat."

"How secret can you keep him, if he's an expert in Haig's field?"

"Please. Haig doesn't have a field. He has a market. He doesn't speak Chinese and Lord knows he doesn't go to conferences. He's above all that. So maybe we can remain a step ahead long enough to get established and stay out of the poorhouse. Possibly even to be able to afford some of the artists Q.X. has found us who, by the time we get to them, are beyond our means. Though as I said, with the gentlemen in this show we're counting on gratitude and a Chinese sense of duty."

Jack said, "I think you can count on their prices not rising."

"Oh, Jack, you're such a stiff. Hey, Frank named the spotted robot after you."

"Really? If that's a bribe he'd be better off naming them after critics."

"Don't be absurd. You're a tastemaker." Eddie cocked his head. "Odd for a stiff, hmm? Anyway, he did name a few after critics. The one that keeps crashing into that post, like it can't see it? That's Gross, from *ARTnews*."

I watched a red box drive itself into a blue post, back up, and do it again. "Why is the spotted one Jack?"

"Its job is to tail the striped one."

Sure enough, wherever the striped red box went, the spotted box zoomed after a few moments later. "They all have jobs?"

Eddie To went to the desk and brought over three stapled sheets. "Artists' statements. English on one side, Chinese on the other."

"The Chinese makes more sense," Jack said. "Especially if you don't read Chinese. Listen, Eddie, love chatting with you but we're here on a case."

"Seriously? I don't think I've ever seen you working. I've had to watch the robot to get any sense of what you do."

"Here's your chance. I want to ask you something."

"Well, isn't this exciting? Frank will be jealous. How can I help?"

"You've heard the rumors that there are new Chau Chuns floating around?"

"Of course. Who hasn't?"

"Jen Beril heard them, too. She heard them here, at your opening last week. She just can't remember who from."

Eddie To clutched his chest. "That's just heartbreaking."

"Why?"

Eddie pointed an accusing finger toward the elevator. "Ms. Thing made her entrance—vogueing in the doorway like RuPaul—took one quick spin, guzzled some Vigonier, and left. Frank would've named a robot after her but none of them's enough of an ice queen. Of course I mean that in the nicest possible way."

"Do you remember her talking to anyone?"

"I remember it well. Though obviously she doesn't. Shows you where I am on the food chain. The only person she spoke to was—*me*."

"It was you who told her about the Chaus?"

"Was that bad of me? I was trying to impress her with my up-to-the-second inside-track type of knowledge."

"I'm sure she was impressed. Where'd you hear it?"

"Yes, so impressed I've slipped her mind entirely. Remind me not to save the Vigonier for her next time. She can suck up Chablis and like it. As for me, to go back an earlier conversational motif, I heard about the Chaus from the wellspring of all self-importance. Jabba the Hutt down there on the first floor: Doug Haig."

As soon as the elevator door closed behind us I exploded. "That revolting creepy fat sleazebag ugly creepy liar!"

"You said fat, so I know you don't mean Eddie. And you said 'creepy' twice, by the way."

"Doug Haig! He is creepy twice. He told Eddie To about the Chaus last week? He acted like the first he'd heard of them was from Bill."

"You guys believed him?"

"Not at all. Unless Nick's wrong, Haig found out about them from Shayna Dylan, even though she doesn't know she knows. But Haig's spreading the rumors himself? I mean, what is that?"

"Why? Rumors create buzz and buzz drives up prices."

"And brings you people like Vladimir Oblomov, and then you act like you don't know what he's talking about?"

"Maybe Haig already has a buyer."

"Then why not say, 'I already have a buyer'? instead of, 'Don't be ridiculous, you silly Russian, there are no such paintings'? And besides, you aren't telling me Doug Haig would put loyalty to an existing buyer above profit from a brainless mobster? Especially if it's true he's in trouble." The elevator opened at the lobby. "No," I said, "here's what I think. I think Haig absolutely does know about the paintings. I think he's seen them and I bet he knows where they are. But he hasn't got his hands on them yet, so he can't sell them, to Bill or anyone else. Something makes him pretty sure he will, though. So he's trying to create buzz now, for then. Then he'll try to reel Vladimir in, and whoever else. But I don't want him to find them."

"If you're right he's already found them."

"Don't split hairs! I mean, to get his hands on them! I want to steal them out from under him."

"For our clients, you mean."

"Yes. Absolutely. For our clients. And also, as part of my plan to reduce Doug Haig to a grease spot on his own gallery floor."

"Remind me," Jack said thoughtfully, "not to get in your way."

"Don't worry, I will. Besides," I said, starting to calm down, "my client's whole point in hiring me was to get to these paintings first. Not to have to bid in public against some crazy Russian."

"Bill's not really a Russian, you know. And are you sure that's what your client's after?"

I looked at him. "What?"

"Phony name, prepaid cell, thin cover story—it must have occurred to you he was hiding something."

"Yes, and we told you—"

"What you told me isn't worth hiding. That's a lot of trouble to go to just so his own PI doesn't find out his name."

"We—"

"Look, I know you're smart because Bill's smart and he says you are. No way you guys haven't been wondering about Dunbar's angle. He wants something else, not just the paintings. Most likely, it's the painter."

In the setting sun the spring breeze was chilly. I zipped my jacket. "Yes," I admitted. "That's how we figured it."

"I wish you'd just told me."

"Does it matter? To the investigation?"

"Maybe not. But to me. 'All for one, one for all'?"

"I'm sorry. Really." I looked off down the street, then back to Jack. "But I didn't know you. I wasn't sure . . ."

"How far you could trust me?"

"I guess so, yes."

Surprisingly, he grinned. "Well, that's good."

"It is? Why?"

"Bill must have told you you could trust me. In fact, you said he said I was stand-up."

"He did."

"But you still had reservations."

"Yes. I'm sorry. I—"

"Au contraire, it's excellent. Because what that means is, you and Bill aren't quite as tight as I thought. And *that* means maybe there's room for someone else to slip in there."

I felt my cheeks grow hot. "Jack—"

"Okay, never mind, I was out of line, sorry." He spoke briskly but he was still grinning. "I'm all about business. So what's our next move?"

"Our next—I—" *Oh, stop stammering, Lydia! You'd think a smart good-looking ABC PI had never come on to you before!* "We—" While I was collecting myself so I could be all about business, too, Jack's cell phone rang.

He checked it, told me, "Dr. Yang."

I said, "Don't tell him yet."

Jack made a face at me while he said, "Professor. How are you?" Then his tone changed. "I don't . . . No, we're . . ." Dr. Yang was obviously talking, Jack trying to get a word in sideways. "What are you . . . I think . . . That's . . . *No.*" He raised his voice. "I'm sorry, it's just not acceptable." The volume seemed to have an effect; Jack got to say a whole sentence. "I think you owe me a real explanation. A few hours ago we . . . No, I . . . Wait, I'm . . . Hello? Dr. Yang?"

Jack lowered the phone. He stared at it for a moment, then looked at me. "He fired me."

"*Fired* you?" I was momentarily wordless, too. "Did he say why?"

"He changed his mind."

"That's it? Changed his mind?"

"So he says."

"That's ridiculous."

"You think?" Jack rubbed the back of his neck and breathed, "Damn! You know, I was already thinking you guys weren't good for my health. Now I'm not sure you're good for business."

"Did he say it was because of us?"

"I didn't mean specifically, I meant in a jinxy sort of way. Dr. Yang didn't say anything. He changed his mind."

I shook my head. "Something's going on."

"I know. Two hours ago he was so mad he'd have ripped the stripes off my sleeves if I'd had any, but he didn't fire me. But just now he was perfectly calm. He didn't say it was my fault, or your fault, or anybody's fault. He just said he didn't want this looked into anymore and he didn't need my services." Jack frowned. "I have half a mind to go down there and make him tell me what the hell is up."

"And the other half?"

"Is smarter than that. It wants to think."

"Is that the half that has Doug Haig's cell phone number?"

He looked at me. "Both halves do. How'd you know?"

"You didn't help at all when I was trying to pry it out of Nick Greenbank."

"I may have to rethink." Jack took out his phone. "You might be good for business after all."

I tried not to notice the little glow I felt when he said that.

10

As it turned out, Doug Haig wasn't available, at least not to us, not right then. While Jack was leaving a message I had another thought.

"If I bought you a martini," I said, "would you mind drinking it by yourself?"

"That's got to be the most ridiculous offer anyone's ever made me. Or maybe, the most oblique brush-off."

"You don't get oblique from me. I'm not that clever. What I was thinking was, I have a date with Jeff Dunbar. At six, at this bar on West Street. I'd be very interested to find out if he's someone you know from the art world. You obviously can't come to the meeting, but there's no reason you couldn't be sitting at the bar."

"Keeping an eye on things! Observing without being observed! Like Bill did in Dr. Yang's office."

"You caught that?"

"Did Mao wear a jacket? You guys do that all the time?"

"Whenever we can."

"Hmm. I guess a partner can come in handy."

"Come on," I said, starting down the sidewalk.

"Where are we going?" He didn't move.

"This bar," I stated the obvious. "On West Street."

"The Fraying Rope?"

"You know it?" I stopped. "Is it famous?"

"Among certain people. It's a bogus waterfront dive in a new condo building down there. Cheap beer, plywood paneling, and a stuffed fish on the wall, but no danger of running into any actual longshoremen."

"I think I hear a faint a note of disdain. You're a fan of long-shoremen?"

"I don't know any. Neither does anyone at The Fraying Rope. A pretentious crowd that plays it safe, that's all I'm saying."

"Look at you, moralizing."

Jack grinned. "Wow, I am, aren't I? Sorry. They do make a good martini, I'll give them that."

Leaving aside the question of how many trips to The Fraying Rope his assessment of the crowd and the martini was based on, I asked something else. "How did you know that was where Jeff Dunbar said to meet?"

"The area's changing but it hasn't changed yet. Most of the West Street bars are the real thing, genuinely sleazy. Your man Dunbar doesn't sound like the sleazy bar type."

"No, you're right, he's more the new condo type. Not particularly pretentious, though. But plays it safe, definitely that."

"Okay, you're on," Jack said. "Just one thing."

"What?"

"The subway's four blocks east. When it gets us downtown The Fraying Rope will be four blocks west again. Your date is in fifteen minutes. Let's take a cab."

In order to maintain a harmonious working relationship I gave in. Anyway, it was a lovely afternoon for a cab ride down by the river, with the trees freshly green and the water sparkling. We left the cab a block north and Jack strode on ahead of me. By the time I pushed through the door of The Fraying Rope, he was already leaning over a martini, as relaxed as if he'd been hanging out here all his life and actually liked the place.

From what I could see, Jack had nailed it. Cheesy ersatz-nautical. Actually, ersatz-cheesy, too. Not just the stuffed fish, but the linoleum floor, the plaid lamps with ship's wheels, and a variety of thick, looped, fraying ropes. The jukebox played Jimmy Buffett over a noise level loud but bearable. Glossy-haired blondes sipped pink drinks, and frat boys in suits or polo shirts swigged from beer bottles with lime slices in them. Chrome stools lined the bar, and cane chairs surrounded coffee tables. One of the stools was under Jack, and one of the chairs held Jeff Dunbar.

I spotted him right away, but lingered in the doorway as though I hadn't to give Jack a chance to notice me. Jeff Dunbar waved, discreetly. I waved back and crossed the room to his table, though Jack had shown no sign he knew I was there.

"Mr. Dunbar," I said as I sat. "How are you? Interesting place. Is it your local?"

"Friends brought me here, and I liked it." Neatly sidestepping the question of whether he lived nearby. "I'm hoping you have good news for me."

A waiter drifted over and I ordered cranberry juice. Dunbar was drinking one of those lime beers.

"I have news," I said. "I don't know if it's good. For one thing, I thought you ought to know that someone else had the same idea you did."

"What idea?"

"There's another PI on the case."

A pause. "Searching for the Chaus?"

"Yes."

"For another collector?"

"No. For Kah Ching." To his blank look, I said, "The Columbia professor?"

"Oh. Oh, right, of course."

"He wants to debunk them. He thinks they're phonies. I also thought you should know that someone took a shot at him."

Dunbar's beer stopped halfway to his mouth. "Took a— What are you talking about? At who? The professor?"

"At the other PI. Through his office window. Made a mess, but didn't hit him."

"Who? Who shot at him?"

"I don't know. And a couple of other things I don't know. For example: Who are you?"

"I—wait, what's going on here?"

My cranberry juice arrived, perfectly timed. I steered the straw to my mouth, gave my client another moment to stew. "Jeff Dunbar's not your name and you're not a collector. There's no such person as Jeff Dunbar. For your information there's no Professor Kah Ching, either. There is another PI on the case, though, and if you knew anything about the art world you'd have hired him, not me. I don't know what your real interest is, whether it's the paintings, because they're worth a fortune, or something else." I sipped again, gave him just enough time to open his mouth, and went on before he could speak. "Now, that doesn't necessarily matter. You're not required to tell me the truth. But I'm also not required to tell you anything. I've picked up a few leads. Since people are shooting guns around, though, and since someone came to my office and tried to buy me off, and threatened me when I refused—"

"Threatened you?"

"Yes. So you can understand that I'm reluctant to take this any further until I know what's really going on."

Jeff Dunbar looked at me with a steady gaze. "You took my money. Anything you learned, you learned on my dime."

"And the man who came to my office and told me I'd be sorry if I didn't stop? He was on your dime, too."

A slight pause. "Who was he?"

"I don't know. A Chinese gent calling himself Samuel Wing, though I have a feeling that's as phony as 'Jeff Dunbar.'" I met his eyes and I shut up.

After a few long moments, Dunbar nodded. He drank some beer and said, "You're right." His tone was conciliatory. "Jeff Dunbar's an alias. For reasons I don't want to go into I'd rather keep my name out of this. My interest in the paintings is legitimate. I don't know anyone named Wing, I don't know why someone would threaten you, and I certainly have no idea who'd shoot at some other detective. I'm absolutely sure, in fact, that that has nothing to do with me."

"You could be right." I softened, too, to show that while we may not be on the same page, we might be able to arrive there. "But that doesn't mean it has nothing to do with the paintings."

"But it does mean I can't be held responsible for it."

"Maybe you can't, but it did happen. In view of that, and of Mr. Wing's visit and his threats, your blamelessness doesn't necessarily make me feel secure. And 'legitimate' is a nice-sounding word but I'm not sure what it means in this context."

Dunbar looked to the windows. Cars whizzed by on the highway; beyond them, the river gleamed in the late sun. "The other investigator. Do you know who hired him?"

"Yes, but I'm not sure why. And I'm not going to tell you." He started to object, so I added, "Any more than I told him who you are."

"He knows I exist?"

"He knows I have a client interested in the same thing he is. His PI told him. That's one of the reasons I wanted to get together with you. To even up the flow of information."

We sat in our own cone of silence in the noisy bar. Finally, Dunbar said, "You say you've picked up some leads. Information about where the paintings are?"

"Possibly. I haven't checked them out yet."

"Why don't you give them to me? That can be the end. I'll follow through. You'll be out of it, and no one will have any reason to threaten you. It's only been one day, but you can keep the whole retainer. To compensate for the trouble this has caused you."

From the corner of my eye I saw Jack take out his phone, slip off his barstool, and thread his unhurried way to the door. I wondered what was up. He'd gotten a call and it was too noisy to talk in here? With my back to the door I couldn't see him leave, but I did see a brightening in the bar when the door opened. Whatever. He was a grown-up. I turned my focus back to my client. "That's a generous offer."

"No more than deserved, I'd say."

"Samuel Wing, before he tried very elegantly to bully me, offered me ten times what you'd paid."

"I see." Jeff Dunbar took a long pull on his beer. "All right, point taken. You can't be bought."

"Yes, I can. Just not with money. I want to know what's going on. Why you want me to find these paintings, why Samuel Wing doesn't, what the other PI's client wants." Or wanted. And doesn't now. "Who you are. Whether Ghost Hero Chau is still alive."

He gave a small smile. "That last question, that's the big one, isn't it? The rest, I know some of those answers, and I don't know others. But I'm not going to tell you any of them until you tell me what you know about where the paintings are."

"I don't know anything. I have some leads. They might turn out to be total dead ends."

"Still, I want them."

"And I want to know who I'm giving them to."

"The client who's paid for them."

After a stand-off moment I slung my bag up from the floor. "I'll return your money." I ran the zipper. It was one heck of a bluff; of course I wasn't carrying his thousand dollars around.

"No," he said quickly. "No, don't do that."

Slowly, I zipped the bag again. "What, then?"

He looked across the room, across the highway. "Samuel Wing. I may know who that is."

"You just said you didn't."

"I said I don't know anyone by that name. But I might know who's using it. If I'm right, I promise you he's not dangerous."

From the ineptitude of Samuel Wing's menace I'd come to the same conclusion, but I didn't see why I should share that. "Maybe he's not. But maybe he is. And maybe he's not who you think. Tell me about him."

"No. But I'll find out. If I'm wrong I'll let you know."

"And if you're right?"

"I'd like you to continue your investigation."

"Just like that? I'm supposed to believe you that Samuel Who-ever's not a threat, and the guy who is, who's spraying bullets around, isn't going to come for me? And that you're the good guys and this whole investigation's 'legitimate'?"

Jeff Dunbar sighed. "Ms. Chin, it's important those paintings be found. Not just to me. There are other . . . interested parties. I can't tell you why, not right now. I can tell you, it's not about money."

"No?"

"No."

"What is it about?"

He shook his head. "I'm sorry."

I considered digging in, but the set of his mouth told me that would go nowhere. "All right," I said. "Maybe I believe that: It's not about money to *you*. Or your interested parties. But Samuel Wing claimed to be representing interested parties, too. And the guy with the bullets? Or the other PI's client? It could be about money to them, couldn't it?"

And speaking of the other PI, where had Jack gone?

"I don't know," Jeff Dunbar said. "But I'll try to find out."

"You can find out what those people want, but you can't find the Chaus?"

He shook his head. "No. What I can try to find out is whether any of my interested parties are any of those people. Wing, or the shooter, or the other client."

"Well," I said after a long pause, "you do that. And here's what I'll do. I'll keep looking. As long as no one shoots at me." Not that that's ever stopped me before, but that was another thing I felt no need to share. "But if I find the Chaus, I'll need more than 'it's im-portant' before I give the information to someone whose name I don't even know. Is that a deal?"

He nodded. "For now."

He took a last swig of his beer, dropped a twenty on the table—from a money clip, not a wallet, which was just as well, because I might have swiped it to get at the driver's license—and stood. "Why don't you stay and finish your drink? Instead of following me." He smiled. "I'll be in touch."

"Fine," I said. "But one more thing."

He paused, waited.

"What should I call you?"

He cocked his head. "Jeff Dunbar. I always liked the name Jeff."

He turned and left.

I had, of course, been planning to count to ten, dash out after him, and tiptoe up the sidewalk to see where he went. But he'd stuck a pin in that idea.

So I stayed, drank up my cranberry juice, and let Jimmy Buffett work his way through "Margaritaville." Jack wasn't anywhere. Maybe that meant he'd stayed outside, and had at least seen which direction my client had fled in. I hefted my bag and gave up my chair, to the smiling gratitude of the young couple who'd been vulturing this spot ever since Jeff Dunbar left.

Outside, no Jack. The guy abandoned me? That call had better have been important. A cruising taxi slowed, but nuts to him. I headed for the subway.

On the way I called Bill. Voice mail yet again. His date must be going swimmingly. I left a message. Then I tried Jack.

"Lee."

"Chin. You hate that bar that much?"

"You have to admit I was right about it."

"So what?"

"Good point. No, I'm tailing your boy."

"You're doing what?"

"As soon as I saw you sit down I'd answered the main question, which was that I don't know him. I wasn't sure you were getting anywhere, though. I might be wrong, but it didn't look like he was giving much away."

"No, almost nothing."

"So it occurred to me this might be a chance we didn't want to miss. You strike me as tough enough to fight your way alone out of a candy-ass bar if you need to."

"Thanks, I think."

"No problem. So I got in a cab and told the driver to wait until I pointed out a guy and then follow him. Meter plus fifty bucks. If it turned out Dunbar told you everything, no harm done except I'm out a few bucks. Should I knock it off?"

"No," I said. "No, I'm in awe. Are you still on him?"

"Yes. Going up the highway, near Lincoln Center."

"Stay with him. Let me know what happens. What about the phone call?"

"What phone call?"

"You took out your phone when you left."

"You saw me?"

"Hey, I'm not just a pretty face."

"Um. Well, no phone call, and not just your face, pretty as it is. Dunbar's. I snapped a few pix. You're in one, though. Sweet."

I clicked off, pocketed the phone, and walked through the Village in the last of the light. Bill was right, it seemed to me. Jack was good at his job.

And speaking of Bill, the phone gave out with "My Heroes Have Always Been Cowboys" just as I reached Sheridan Square. I grabbed it and flipped it open. "Oh ho ho, is this you?"

"Hey, I've been working really hard here."

"Don't tell me about what's been hard."

"Oh my God, is that a dirty joke from you?"

"I've changed. I've spent the afternoon drinking in a dive bar on the waterfront."

"The whole afternoon?"

"No. First I had to give a stranger some perfectly good oolong tea in my office so he could threaten me without mentioning my mother, then I had to go watch a robot crashing into a pole."

"Are you speaking English?"

"Where are you? Still tied up with Shayna?"

"You think she's into that?"

"Why does everyone want to know that?"

"Well, it's an interesting question. No, she had dinner plans."

"You weren't charming enough for her to cancel them?"

"I didn't want to waste the charm if I didn't need to."

"Yes, I can see you'd want to conserve scarce resources. Why didn't you need to?"

"You know, I don't think drink agrees with you."

"It was cranberry juice."

"That changes things? I didn't need to because I got what we wanted."

I drew a sharp breath. "The Chaus? You found out where they are?"

"Where they were, when Shayna saw them. That was a one-week show, though, so they may not be there now."

"Still, that's huge. Where are you?"

"Upper East Side. Where are you?"

"West Village. You want to meet in Chinatown? I'm starving."

"Good idea. What about Aramis?"

"He's in a cab near Lincoln Center. I'll call him."

He didn't even ask me how I knew that.

I called Jack, who reported that the cab caravan had left the highway at Seventy-second Street and was heading across town.

"This driver's a rock star," he said. "Changes lanes, hangs back, all the good stuff. Rajneesh Jha, from Hyderabad. Grew up on American movies. Thinks he died and went to heaven, tailing another cab for a PI."

"Lucky you, lucky him," I said. "When you're done, Bill and I are going for noodles to New Chao Chow on Mott, north of Canal. Bill knows where the Chaus were when Shayna saw them."

"You think you have enough Chaus there?"

"If you spoke Chinese like a New Yorker you'd be able to tell them apart." I spelled the restaurant for him.

"If I spoke Chinese like a New Yorker my mother wouldn't understand me."

"Does she understand you now?"

"Everything but my profession. She shudders. She wishes I were respectable, like my older sisters."

"Mine, too! How many sisters?"

"Two. An endocrinologist and a lawyer. You have sisters?"

"No, four older brothers. Also a doctor and a lawyer, and two more besides."

"All respectable?"

"Spotlessly."

"My sympathies. Hey! Hey, I think Dunbar's cab's pulling over. Rajneesh, go around the corner and stop."

"Where are you?"

"Second and Seventy-third. Save me a bowl of noodles. I'll call you."

He clicked off.

11

Bill was waiting when I got to New Chao Chow. Rich aromas of pork and fish circled around me. I greeted the chubby manager. "Hey, Tau."

"Hey, Lydia. You bring appetite? Got good rice stick today. You eat two bowls?" We spoke in English because Tau's dialect is Fujianese, as incomprehensible to a native Cantonese speaker as, say, Russian would be.

"I'm starved, Tau, so maybe." There was no possible way I could eat two bowls of Tau's soups, not rice stick fish soup, pork tendon stew, or anything else, but he was always hopeful.

I dropped into the chair opposite Bill and eyed him critically. "You look worn out. The charm thing takes it out of you, huh?"

"You kidding? I feel great. Like Maurice Chevalier in *Gigi*."

"Am I glad I don't get the reference?"

"Probably." He took out his phone, handed it to me. "Somewhere in here are the photos."

"You really should learn to do this," I said, poking buttons. "Against the day when I'm not around."

"Am I expecting that day?"

I looked up, thinking I'd heard an odd note in his voice. He seemed normal, though. Not even tired, actually; that had just been me giving him the regular hard time. "No." A brief mutual pause, then I went back to his phone. A grumpy waiter came over and tried to hand us menus. Bill waved his away, ordered the beef stew noodle soup and a beer. I asked for fish cake rice stick soup and jasmine tea, but then grabbed one of the menus as the waiter turned to leave. "For Jack," I told Bill.

"He's joining us?"

"When his workday's done."

"Where is he now?"

"Still uptown, tailing Jeff Dunbar."

"How did that come about?"

"Because he's as smart as you said. I'd tell you but I can't do two things at once and I want to see these famous photos. How did you get her to send them to you?"

"Shayna? I told her I was interested in moving into the Chinese-American area. That I was attracted by the hybridized, mongrel nature of it. I implied I was ready to spend money, but I wasn't sure of myself in the field so I'd need an advisor, a specialist. Threw a bunch of art words around, then said I'd gotten the idea from Doug Haig, my drinking buddy, that Shayna Dylan was the person to ask about contemporary Chinese-American."

"Her ego's big enough that she bought that? A big-time dealer directing you to a temporary gallery assistant?"

"Without blinking. Like your client said, Chinese contemporary's a small world. Haig has no interest in Chinese-American but he'd know who does. Why not throw some business her way? Doesn't cost anything and now she owes him."

"The idea of owing Doug Haig almost makes me feel bad for her."

The waiter plunked down our beer and tea. "Shayna sipped her way through a cosmo and a half, explaining the difference between what the mainland Chinese are doing and what's happening here. She's not an airhead, you know."

"Please don't feel required to enumerate her good points. I bet you're planning to put in for a reimbursement for the drinks."

"Damn right I am. She mentioned one of the artists Linus had me buying. Just in passing, probably to prove we were on the same wavelength."

"Did she say she'd Googled you?"

"Does anyone ever?"

"Say it or do it? Everyone does it, but mostly people don't talk about it. She probably assumes you Googled her, too."

"Really? Maybe I should have."

"If only someone taught you how."

He raised his beer in a toast. "She described the newest developments on the Chinese-American scene and offered to take me around looking. She even asked whether I thought you'd want to come."

"Would I?"

"Not a chance. You only like tomb trash. Fusty stuff."

"That explains why I hang out with you, no doubt."

"She said she'd gotten that idea about you, but of course everyone has a right to their own taste. She said that with a lovely, tolerant smile."

"Showing her pointy little teeth."

"I kept asking for descriptions of the art, this absolute newest cutting-edge stuff, and finally she remembered she had some photos on her phone. She'd shown them to Doug. He'd actually been interested in one, but she didn't think anything had come of it."

"'Doug'?"

"Hey, Shayna's on a first name basis with the best."

"She call you Vlad?"

"Of course. So she showed me what she had—"

"Meaning the photos—"

"And I oohed and aahed over about a dozen—"

"I'd like to have seen that. You oohing and ahhing."

"—and I asked her to send them to me. Including but not making a big deal out of the one she said Doug liked."

"Here." I finally found Shayna's e-mail in the mess on Bill's phone, and downloaded the photos. "You know you have two text messages from her, too?"

"No, I didn't. What do they say?"

I opened them. "The first says, 'Here u go. Thnx 4 the drink—had a gr8 time.' The next says, 'When u want 2 see work, call me.'" I clicked through the photos, stopped when Bill said, "That one. There, in the background on the right."

"Well." I squinted. "Well. The mummy's treasure. Okay, they definitely look like what I saw when I Googled Chau. He had a distinctive style. I suppose if you were Haig and you knew his work you'd know whether you'd ever seen them, and if you hadn't you'd think they might be new. But in the background and tiny like this—how could anyone be sure they were real?"

"I don't think anyone could. Given their value if they were, though, they'd be worth checking out."

"So where were they when she took this?"

"At an open studio in Flushing. About two dozen artists rent a warehouse communally out there. It's Chinese Artist Central—ABCs, Chinese-born immigrants, a couple of Taiwanese, a pair of twins from Singapore. The place calls itself East Village, after an artist's district in Beijing in the eighties that named itself after the East Village here in New York. Very meta, you know?"

"I don't know, but okay. Go on."

"Two weeks ago another two dozen artists moved in for the week, and everyone hung work all over the place and waited for the buyers and dealers and critics to come."

"Did they?"

"To a certain extent, apparently. Not the biggest names, but the hip and the cool. That's why Shayna went. Contemporary's her passion, remember, not antiquities."

"And yet she dated you. So whose studio were these in?"

"She doesn't know. What she was shooting was that sculpture there. The aluminum foil one? She gave me his name, that artist. But the papercuttings where the Chaus are, she wasn't interested so she doesn't remember who made them."

"And this was what Doug Haig was excited about? This photo?"

"Yes, though Shayna thinks it was the aluminum foil that lit his flame. She tried to get me worked up about it, too. I think I disappointed her when I asked about the papercuttings."

I studied the tiny photo. "It must be one of the artists who rent the building," I said. "That must be his studio."

"Or one of the visitors."

"Well, but why would anyone bring phony Chaus to a temporary show? If they were trying to get people to notice their own work? And even less, why would they bring real ones? I think that's someone's studio and, real or fake, the artist put them up for inspiration while he works. Artists do that, right?"

"They do. Or they may be his. Not in the sense that he owns them, but that he made them. It's a Chinese tradition to copy famous works. It helps train the artist's eye."

"Really?" I sat back. "So maybe that's all these are, then. Somebody's really good copies. And everybody got carried away." I frowned. "They'd have to be awfully good, though, to fool Doug Haig."

"If he's actually seen them."

"He has. He's the one spreading the rumors."

"He is?"

I recounted what Jack and I had been told by Eddie To. "And the whole thing about the political content, too. You can't tell that from these tiny photos. If he's saying that he'd have to have seen them."

Our soup arrived. The monster basins of steaming broth sloshed over with noodles, rice sticks, meat, fish, and greens. The briny tang of my soup and the gamey scent of Bill's nearly knocked me over.

"But," I said, arguing with myself as I doctored my bowl with fish flakes, "if the Chaus were hanging in someone's studio for who knows how long, how come no one noticed them before? Maybe I'm wrong. Maybe they really were brought out to Flushing for that show."

"Or maybe all these cutting-edge people don't know what a Chau looks like. Shayna went right past them."

"The artists, though? You'd think they would. He's part of their cultural heritage."

"Maybe not. They're young. Chau may have been a hero around Tiananmen, but that was more than twenty years ago. Especially if he worked in traditional media with traditional subjects—"

"—politicized, though—"

"—doesn't matter. I bet he's been pretty much forgotten. You know," he said, winding noodles onto his chopsticks, "that group studio and that show, they sound right up Jack's alley. Even if he didn't go, I'll bet he heard about it."

"We can ask him when he gets here."

"Ask him what? Because he's here," said Jack, his shadow falling over the fluorescent-lit table. "Wow. I'll have one of each."

"The soup? Or us?"

"Sorry, but I'm hungry. The soup." He slid onto a chair and studied the menu. "What's good here?"

"Anything in a bowl. Tell me who my client is."

"Hmm," he said. "What's wrong with that sentence? Eight treasure soup with bean curd," he said to the waiter. "And a Tsingtao." He peered at Bill. "You don't look any the worse for wear. Have fun?"

"Are you kidding? It was exhausting. Sitting in a hushed bar over a Booker's, watching a beautiful woman sip a pink drink?"

"Your dedication is noted," I said. "Jack?"

"Hey, come on. Didn't you say something on the phone about knowing where the Chaus are? Isn't that why I came all the way to Chinatown?"

"You came for noodles, don't lie to me. And we know where they *were*. Which we'll share, after you share."

"Seriously? You're going to hold out until I tell?"

"I wouldn't, but you're obviously bursting to tell."

"How well you know me. Must be the long acquaintance." Grinning, Jack sat back and stretched his long legs under the table. "Dennis Jerrold."

"That's his real name? He just reversed his initials? That shows a singular lack of imagination. Who is he?"

"I don't know who he is, and that's not necessarily his real name. It's the name he lives under."

"Talmudic," I said. "And you know that how?"

"Is this where we start exchanging trade secrets?" The waiter clanked Jack's beer onto the tabletop. After a long pull on the bottle, he said, "I left my cab around the corner and saw him go into one of those white brick apartment buildings on Second."

"And someone's going to tell me how you came to be tailing him in the first place, right?" Bill stuck in.

"Maybe," I said. "Go on."

"I gave him a minute and then went to the doorman. 'Guy just come in,' I said. 'Just at my lestalant. Reave his cledit cald.'"

"You didn't. The Chinese waiter scam? With that accent?"

"Works every time. 'You mean Mr. Jerrold?' 'No, Mistah Dunbal. Medium guy, glay suit, brue tie. Just come in.' 'The man in the gray suit who just came in, that was Mr. Jerrold.' 'Oh. You shoe?' Big glare. 'Oh, so solly. Must be mistaken. Good-bye, got to find Mistah Dunbal.'"

"That's really, really awful," I said.

"Reary," Bill agreed.

Jack drank more beer. "We do what we have to. Some suffer with blondes in dim bars, some use politically incorrect accents. I checked whitepages.com on my way here, found his first name. Haven't gotten any further than that yet."

"Don't worry about it," I said. "That's what cousins are for." I took out my phone and hit the speed-dial number.

"Wong Security."

"Linus, hi. Thanks for that stuff before. It seems to have worked."

"Awesome! Bill got the girl?"

"He got the info, which is what we were after. Listen, I know it's late—you up for another job?"

"He needs to be somebody else now?"

"No, this would be totally different, and easier."

"We're thinking of going to a club at, like, nine, can I do it before that?"

"I think you can do it in five minutes. A guy named Dennis Jerrold, lives on Second Avenue." I relayed the address Jack gave me. "Who he is, what he does—I want to know whatever you can find by whenever you have to leave."

"Easy peasy, call you later."

"Wait! I just thought of something. Have to put you on hold."

"'K."

I did, checked my outgoing call record, and thumbed him back in. "Can you trace a phone number?"

"Is that a trick question?"

I gave him Samuel Wing's cell.

"Who's that?"

"That's what I want to know."

As I clicked off, Jack's soup arrived. "Umm." He sniffed. "Smells as good as my mother's."

"Your mother's from Fujian?"

"My mother's from Chicago. She takes a lot of cooking classes. Makes a hell of a pile of potato latkes, too. Now, your turn."

Bill reached for his phone so I could show Jack the Chaus. Before he got it out of his pocket, though, my own phone rang. An unfamiliar number, so I answered in both languages.

"Hello, this is R. T. Singh calling." The voice spoke English with the lilt of India. "You have said you lost an object in my taxi this afternoon?"

Samuel Wing's cabbie! I'd just about forgotten. "Yes, Mr. Singh, thank you for calling. Yes, I think I might have lost something. Though it wasn't an object."

"I don't understand, I am sorry."

"It was my husband."

Cautiously, he said, "Please?" while the men at my table exchanged surprised looks.

"Mr. Singh, you picked up a Chinese man at four on Hudson Street. He's thin, with gray hair. He was wearing a gray suit? That's my husband. I'm afraid—" I let my voice catch, then went on. "I'm afraid he was going to see . . . He was on his way . . . Mr. Singh, I think he has a mistress!"

"Oh. Oh, my. I—" said R. T. Singh. Bill and Jack were grinning, so I turned to the wall. Unfortunately, it was a mirror. They were inescapable.

"All I want, Mr. Singh, is to know where he was going. I'll pay you for that. It's just, not knowing, do you understand? It's driving me crazy!" As were Jack's and Bill's merry stares.

"Now I see," R. T. Singh said slowly. "Because when I received the e-mail, I said to myself, you did not have a woman passenger this afternoon at the time the alert is telling you, I think so. But Mrs. Chin—"

"Please, call me Lydia."

"Mrs. Chin, I do not like to be indiscreet."

"Of course not. And I wouldn't ask you. But I have to know! Maybe I'm wrong. That's what I'm hoping, you see. That I have it all wrong and we can laugh about it later. But I look at the children— our youngest looks just like him—and I start to cry. Please? I'll send you a reward, I really will. I just have to know! Where did he go?"

After a short pause, he said, "Please. No reward. I prefer not to become involved in affairs such as these. I will tell you where I took the gentleman and after that I will delete your telephone number. If mine has appeared in your telephone record I ask that you delete it, also."

"I promise! Can you check now?"

"There is nothing I need check. I remember because I was saying a prayer, that he does not want to turn about and go downtown. To get stuck in the Holland Tunnel traffic, you see, that was my worry. Luck was by my side, however. The address the gentleman requested allowed us to take the West Side Highway not south, but north. The Lincoln Tunnel can of course be a problem at that hour, also, but the tie-up was not bad, and we reached his destination soon after passing through that jam."

To a woodpecker, the world's a tree. To a cabbie, it's all about the traffic. "Yes," I said, with impressive self-control. "His destination, which was where?"

"Right at the next exit beyond the tunnel. Twelfth Avenue, at the foot of Forty-second Street. I left him on the south side, as that was where I turned. But he crossed to the north side while I drove away."

I was temporarily speechless. "Did he go into the building there? On the northeast corner?"

"I believe he did. I am sorry, Mrs. Chin, if this is what you feared."

"I—no, Mr. Singh, I'm better off knowing. Are you sure I can't send you something to show my gratitude?"

"No, as I say, I don't want to become involved, I think so. I hope for you everything works out well."

"Thank you," I said automatically. "I hope the same for you."

I clicked off and stared at the guys. They exchanged glances. "What's up?" Bill said. "You look a little stunned. What was that about?"

"I'm not sure," I said slowly. "Remember I told you someone came to my office and threatened me?"

"Circuitously, yes. I wasn't sure you were serious. You didn't sound worried."

"I didn't think *he* was serious, so I wasn't."

"Are you now?"

"I honestly don't know. The guy—he said his name was Samuel Wing—told me he represented some people who wanted me to stop looking for the Chaus. He wouldn't say who or why they cared but he was ready to hand me ten thousand in cash and when I turned him down he sweetened the offer. When I threw him out he suggested I reconsider or else, but there was no or else."

"That was when he didn't mention your mother? Now I get it."

"Yes." I pointed at my phone. "That was his cab driver. I left him a message before. He dropped Wing, or whoever he is, on Twelfth and Forty-second and saw him go into the building on the northeast corner."

"Oh," said Bill. "Damn."

"What?" Jack demanded.

I asked, "You've never been to the mother ship, have you?"

"Hong Kong," Jack said. "Not the mainland. Why?"

"You don't need a visa for Hong Kong. I haven't been to the mainland, either. But I've had relatives go back and forth over the years. Sometimes they need someone to pick up visas, papers, something, at the Chinese Consulate here."

"At the— Is that it? Where Wing went?"

"Forty-second and Twelfth. Northeast corner. There's nothing else there."

Silence covered our table in the clinking and slurping around us. "You called it," Jack said. "You said, from the mainland, but here a long time."

"You knew about this guy?" Bill asked Jack.

"You'd have known, too, if the bar you were in hadn't been quite so hushed," I retorted. "Listen, you guys. The Chinese government?"

"Or, one diplomat, freelancing," Bill said.

"To what end?"

"The same end as our other interested parties? He sees a chance to hit it big?"

"Well, but hold it," Jack said. "Maybe we're jumping to the wrong conclusion. Why can't it be just one guy, a civilian, doing two errands in one afternoon? Trying to buy you off: bad. And picking up papers from the Consulate: innocent. Unrelated."

I shook my head. "Nice try, but too late in the day. They close to the public at three. I've been on lines there often enough. If he got in the building this late, he works there. But come on. The Chinese government?"

Bill shook his head. "If he's really a diplomat he's got to be free-lancing. If the Chinese government wanted you to knock some-thing off they'd go to our government. The State Department or the CIA."

"Maybe they tried, but the State Department doesn't want to do the PRC's dirty work."

"I have to think they'd rather do that than let the PRC do its own, going up in the face of an American citizen."

"Or maybe this is about something the PRC doesn't want to share with the State Department," Jack said.

"Like what?" I asked.

"Chau was a political pain when he was alive. Maybe he'd be a pain again if he were alive again."

"But then, wouldn't Wing be trying to buy my information, not scare me off? Wouldn't he want to find out where the paintings are and whether he has a problem?"

Bill said, "Not if he knows already."

"Oh." I stopped a spoonful of salty broth on its way to my mouth. "Oh." I was considering the ramifications of that when my phone rang again. In some restaurants this much cell phone usage might fetch dirty looks, or even get us ejected. But this was a Chinatown noodle dive. Half the customers, the waiter, and Tau at the front, were working their own hustles on their own cell phones. "Linus," I answered it. "You have something?"

"I'm still working. But I found some stuff you want right away."

"I do? Tell me."

"I don't know what you're into, but you might want to, like, tiptoe. First, that phone number. I hit a wall. But not a regular wall. My phone company dude said, 'Dude, you can't have that and you don't want it.'"

"What does that mean?"

"Well, see, most of what my phone company dudes do for me, it's technically, you know, illegal?"

"Technically?"

"Yeah, but, see, there's like a line. Stuff they'll do, and the other stuff. Like, this number, giving me anything about it, it's not just illegal. It's, like, deeply illegal. You dig?"

His earnestness as he tried to explain the nuances was almost funny. "Okay, I get it, and back off it. I don't want you doing anything *deeply* illegal because of me. But what does it mean?"

"It means it's, like, a government phone."

"It's *like* a government phone? Or it *is* a government phone?"

"No, not it is, necessarily. But it's, like, a phone the Feds care about. Guys like me can't trace it and neither, by the way, can the NYPD, unless the Feds say they can. Not the owner or the call history. By 'can't,'" he added quickly, "I mean my phone company dude won't help. But I know some other dudes. Serious guys." Reestablishing his bona fides. "You want me to find someone, or what?"

"Don't sound so eager. I don't think we need to. Just tell me, is this the kind of protection a foreign diplomat's phone would have?"

That made him pause. "'Zactly. What, you're like, Dancing with Spies?"

"It would be a spy?"

"Not necessarily. Actually, probably not a spy, they'd have their own tech. This, it's just to be polite. Something our guys do for VIPs when someone asks them to, so when they make a date to go to, like, Stringfellows, it doesn't end up on Page Six. But what I mean, they don't just do it for anybody. If this dude that has this phone is from somewhere else, he's probably pretty high up in whoever's government we're talking about. What's going on?"

"I'm not telling you so you don't have to deny anything."

"Hey! Uncool! I—"

"Did you say you had something else?"

"Oh, man, I should hold out on you until you talk. Uh-oh, Trella's giving me a look. Never mind, here's the rest: the government. They're, like, everywhere. Your Dennis Jerrold dude? That's where he works. But not some foreign government. Our government. He's with the State Department."

12

Linus filled me in, I told him to keep digging, hung up, and turned to the guys. "Hoo boy."

"What's up?" Bill echoed himself from my last phone call.

"I wish I knew." I told them what Linus had said about Samuel Wing's phone, and then about Dennis Jerrold. "Chances are this won't surprise you, but Linus says Jerrold's on the China desk. Cultural affairs. Mid-level. Not a newbie, but not senior."

Jack gave his drawn-out, "Re-eally?" Then he said, "But the PRC guy, Wing, he *is* senior. According to Linus."

"To have that phone protection. Seems that way."

Jack looked at Bill. "You said if the PRC government wanted to stop Lydia, they'd have gone to the State Department. Well, here's the State Department."

"But not trying to stop me," I objected. "Dunbar, or Jerrold or whoever he is, is the one who got all this started in the first place."

Bill said, "Unless he's freelancing, too."

"You think there's that much of that going around?"

"It makes sense. Otherwise why meet you in a tea shop and use a phony name? If the State Department wants to find the Chaus, they have all kinds of resources. Why go to a PI? But if Dunbar heard about the Chaus in the course of his work and is trying to get over without his bosses finding out, that makes the stakes pretty high if he gets caught. Even if he's not committing a crime, it would be the end of his diplomatic career." Bill turned to Jack. "I wonder if your client's working for someone's government, too."

Quick swallow of soup. "You must have missed it. I don't have a client."

"What?"

"I got canned."

"I thought you specifically *didn't* get canned."

"Until Dr. Yang thought about it. He called about five-thirty and told me I specifically was canned."

"Why?"

"He changed his mind."

"About?"

"Me. No, I don't believe it and no, I don't know what's going on." Jack scooped up the last of his eight-treasure tofu.

"So why are you here?"

"Instead of back in my office, washing my hands of all this? You think, just for the chance of finding something to do that might turn out to be both safe and profitable—not to mention actually doable—I'd miss noodles this good?"

"You didn't know how good they were when you came down here," I pointed out.

"Hey, do I have to remind you which of us got shot at?" Jack crumpled his napkin into his empty bowl. "I have a stake in this and getting pink-slipped just fanned my flame."

"I knew I liked you." I signaled Tau for the check.

Jack grinned. "Almost worth getting shot at, to hear that."

"Really?"

"No. Well, maybe once."

Our grumpy waiter dropped a greasy scrap of paper onto the table. Bill picked it up and stood. He took out his phone and handed it to Jack. "Shayna's photo of the Chaus is on there somewhere."

"Say *what*? You've been sitting here with photos this whole time and you didn't tell me?"

"Only one. And it's not very good. Anyway, there you go. Lydia found it."

"Is that a dare? How fast?"

"Took her close to two minutes."

"Piece of cake."

Bill grinned and headed for the counter to pay up. I grabbed the phone from Jack. "For Pete's sake, save the chest-thumping for something important."

"It's all important," Jack said. "That's how guys roll."

"Don't I know it. Okay, here. In fact, this show was what we were going to ask you about." I found Shayna's photo and turned the phone to face Jack. "It was Chinese-American artists, in Queens. The Chaus are on the right there—what's the matter?"

Jack's smile had faded. Silent, he stared at the image on the screen. "These are the Chaus?"

"Don't they look like Chaus?"

"They sure do." He rubbed the back of his neck. "And I think they answer another question, too."

"What question?" said Bill, coming back from the counter.

"Why I was fired. These papercuttings in the studio with the Chaus?" He looked up. "They're Anna Yang's."

Night had fallen while we ate, and so had the roll-down gates on Chinatown's shops. The tourists had either gone happily back uptown with their fake Pradas and Rolexes, or were working their way through dinner at Red Egg or the Peking Duck House. The locals were home supervising homework. On the way to Bill's car we were able to walk side by side by side.

I said to Jack, "So I guess you became superfluous because your client found the Chaus himself. In his daughter's studio."

"Looks that way."

"*If* those are the ones the fuss is about. They might just be copies of early ones she keeps around for inspiration."

"No. I know Chau's work. Maybe not every piece, but enough that if these were a set of repros there'd be something I'd recognize. And remember, they got Doug Haig's Calvins all in a knot, too, and he knows Chau better than I do. At the very least, and even if they are copies, they're copies of unknown works."

"But possibly old ones? That would make sense, for her to have unknown old ones. If her dad brought them from China with him."

"And she what, stole them out of the attic without telling him?" Bill asked. "To stick on her studio wall in a shared warehouse?"

"Well, when you put it that way . . . Though maybe she doesn't know? Maybe she just took some old paintings that she'd always liked one day when she was visiting her mom? Dad wasn't there, she didn't think to tell him? Weren't you just saying this generation might not know about Chau?"

"Anna would," Jack said. "Bernard Yang's daughter? Trust me, she'd know."

"All right, then maybe she knows, but she took them anyway. For inspiration."

"I have to agree with Bill," Jack said. "Without telling Dr. Yang?

They're worth a fortune, old or new, if they're real. You don't just walk off with that and pin it to your studio wall."

"Maybe she told him and he said it was cool."

"Why?"

"Because he feels bad about her husband being in jail in China?"

"Are you serious? And then why the hell hire me?"

"Because these have nothing to do with the ones we're looking for?"

"Then why the hell fire me?"

"Because your boundless joy in asking unanswerable questions drove him crazy?" Bill suggested. "You two, there's no point in this. We'll go see the paintings, Anna will tell us why she has them, and at least we'll know whether they're real and whether they're old."

"How will we know that?" Jack asked.

"You're the expert," Bill said, as we reached the lot where his car was waiting. "You're going to tell us."

Papercutting's an ancient Chinese art. Flowers, phoenixes, entire lacelike villages emerge under the cutter's blade. The artist's skill and patience determine how complex the piece will be. It's painstaking and slow and one mistake ruins everything. I knew that because kids learn papercutting at Saturday Chinese school, ending up with stars and snowflakes to bring home for the fridge. Unless in their rushed impatience they've made that one mistake. I was too young to remember what my two oldest brothers brought home, but stodgy Tim, now a corporate lawyer, excelled in papercutting, smugly crafting trees filled with chirping birds. Andrew, who's a photographer and was always a little off the wall, made fizzy, wild science-fiction visions. My torn-and-Scotch-taped snowflakes rarely made it to the fridge.

Jack knew papercutting, too, though he'd never gone to Chinese school. "I did a graduate lab in paper conservation," he said. "They're a bitch to work with."

"Did you ever tear one?"

"Of course not."

"Silly me for asking." We were in Bill's car on our way to Flushing, me riding shotgun, Jack in back. I asked him, "Do many people still do it?"

"There are still classically trained masters in China. That's who Anna went to study with. And there are papercutters on the streets in China, just like on Canal Street. Tourists love it everywhere. But mostly it's seen as a craft and artists don't bother with it, or if they do, it's just to show off. Anna's different. She took it up in the first place as a political statement because it's a non-Western form. And what she does has political content, too."

"You mean, Mao's silhouette, things like that?"

"More subtle, and not particularly Chinese. She mostly cuts from advertising posters or magazines. She'll work against the content of the original image. Last year she did a series of those tiny slippers women used to wear when they had bound feet. They were beautiful. She cut them from glossy ads for spike-heeled shoes."

"Oh. Now I see why her work didn't appeal to Shayna."

Bill said, "Meow."

"Come on, did you see her shoes?"

"I wasn't looking at her shoes."

"Why does that not comfort me?"

"You want to be even less comfortable?" he asked. "We have a tail."

Jack whipped his head around to peer out the back window. I looked into the rearview mirror, staring at the headlights behind us. "Watch," Bill said. He steered the car into the passing lane, overtook a cab, and slipped back in.

"Dark SUV?" I said. "Jersey plates? Two cars back now?"

"That's the one."

"How long?"

"Since at least the bridge, maybe since Manhattan. What do you want to do?"

My case, my call. I know Bill's driving; he could lose the guy without breaking a sweat. I asked, "How close are we to where we're going?"

"Two more exits, then local streets."

"Is the next exit a residential neighborhood?"

"Yes."

"Take it, and drive around like we're looking for something. Jack, don't look back again. I don't want him to know we're onto him."

"Them."

"You sure?"

"The driver and a guy beside him."

"They got off with us," Bill reported a few minutes later, on the exit ramp. "He's hanging back."

"Okay," I said. "Make a turn and drop Jack and me off. You drive away. Let's see who he's following."

Bill drove a few blocks, let us out on a corner, and pulled away. Jack and I ambled down a quiet street of small, neat brick houses. We walked uncertainly, checking address numbers. Bill's taillights dwindled and no one passed us. "Well, it's not Bill," I said to Jack. "At the end of the block, you go right."

We paused at the corner to look like we were conferring. The tail car was down the block behind us and it stopped, too. "What if it's the guy who shot at me, come to finish the job?" Jack asked.

"I thought we decided he wasn't really trying to kill you, just scare you. Look at your watch like you're saying you have to go."

"That's the job I meant." He turned his wrist over.

"A tough guy like you? Okay, now walk away."

"No, the tough guy's you. See you around." Jack headed right. I turned left. A few seconds' pause. Then headlights swept around the corner.

So. It was me.

The headlights didn't keep coming, though. Were they just trying to find out where I was headed? Well, then I'd lead them on awhile. I continued down the block. Blue glows in the windows told me a lot of TV-watching was going on. I stopped in front of a house with no lights on, looked up at it, took out my phone and stood there as though I were making a call. Actually, I was.

"You or Jack?" Bill asked when he answered.

"Me. He's idling at the corner two blocks up from where you dropped us. I went left."

"I'm three blocks down. Be right there."

"A door's opening. One of them just got out."

"Anyone we know?"

"I can't tell but I don't think so. Big. I'm still walking and I'm going to stay on the phone. Maybe he'll want to wait until I'm not connected to anyone before he clobbers me. See if you can come around and get a look at him first."

"See you soon."

But not soon enough. Whoever this guy was, the fact that I was on the phone with someone who could presumably call a cop if I screamed—or suddenly went silent—must not have worried him. He was quiet and quick, and as I turned my head to look at a house number I found him at my elbow.

I took a sharp leap backward, said breathlessly, "You really should learn to knock." I dropped the phone in my pocket, still on. I thought he might overlook that while he focused on the .25 now in my hand. I checked him out: a big, broadshouldered Asian man, not handsome, not hideous. Sportcoat, white shirt, no tie. In his hand, a gun also, and bigger than mine.

"I can shoot faster," I said. "Also, I have more incentive."

He smiled quizzically. "Incentive? For shoot me? You don't even know me." His intonations rang of Mandarin.

"That's the point. You've been following me. You could've shot me already but you didn't. So you don't want me dead, you want something from me. I, on the other hand, don't like to be followed, don't know you, and don't want anything from you. Why shouldn't I shoot you?"

"But you don't shoot. Just stand there."

"Who are you?"

"Oh, now you want something?"

Yes, I wanted to know where the hell Bill was.

"Why are you following me?"

"You want two thing! I only want one. Want to talk to you."

"Who sent you?"

"Boss. Have couple questions, say, Go ask."

"You work for the government like everybody else?"

He looked surprised at the question, then laughed. "Government? Can't make no money, work for government."

"What do you want to talk about?"

"Got some questions about guy you work for. Also, advice. Come now, dark street dangerous place for lady. I drive you home."

"I don't think so."

But his driver did. He stomped the gas and in three seconds had swerved up the block and onto the sidewalk behind me. His door blew open and I was thinking, *Damn, I* am *going to have to shoot one of these guys* when the big guy yelped and spun around, staring wildly into the dark. I didn't know what was up, but whatever it was, it gave me a chance to spin, too. I slammed my gun up under the chin of the driver, off-balance as he left the car. His head snapped back. I kicked him in the belly and when he folded I smashed him on top of the head. That should hold him. I ducked in case the big guy had solved his problem and decided it was time to shoot me. In fact, I wondered why he hadn't already. But he wasn't even looking at me. He was shouting and cursing in the other direction, half-turned, one arm up to ward off a stone flying at his head. It bounced off his shoulder and so did the one after it. He waved his gun around, looking for his target. Another stone came soaring out of the dark and smacked his knee, and when his hand dropped there, he got clonked on the temple.

With a howl he took off after the thrower. He ran into a hailstorm of pebbles. Another big stone hit him square in the face. He fired into the dark, the gunshot thundering. In answer, a stone clipped his ear. He cursed again; when another skipped off his skull he turned back, racing for his car. I stepped to block his way but he plowed into me, then grabbed my jacket to drag me with him. Stumbling, I tried to break his hold. Whether I could have, I don't know, but it didn't matter: A rock walloped his back, making him stagger and slacken his grip. I pulled loose and stuck my leg out to trip him. He did a little jig but kept his footing, screaming to his driver as he reached the car door. The driver, still dazed, lurched in behind the wheel. He started the car as the big guy dove into the back under a rain of rocks. The car screeched into reverse, bounced off the curb, and roared away.

I peered after it. It swerved around the corner and vanished. I turned to look in the other direction. A lanky figure was saunter-ing out of the dark, hands in his pockets.

"That," I said, "was pretty impressive."

"Little League all-star," said Jack. "Middle school travel team. High school all-state. College varsity."

"Starter?"

"And relief both. Kid Iron, they called me. My high school se-nior season's still the Wisconsin state record."

"So all this whining about flying bullets—"

"I said I couldn't shoot a gun. I didn't say I was helpless. As long as there's a gravel driveway and a little landscaping, I'm good. You think maybe we should keep walking?" He nodded at the houses around us, where lights had come on. One front door was open, a figure silhouetted in it, but no one was saying anything. "One of these citizens might have called the cops."

"Over some cursing, a few squealing tires, and a single gunshot? They probably all think the neighbors have their TVs on too loud." But I fell in nonchalantly beside him, a couple enjoying a peaceful stroll, not a care in the world.

Headlights swept around the corner and we both tensed up. "Oh." I relaxed. "It's Bill." He slammed his brakes and threw his door open while I demanded, "Where have you been?"

"Got here as fast as I could. Wasn't more than two minutes." He climbed out. "I heard a shot. What the hell happened?"

"A couple of Chinese guys wanted to take me away from all this, but it turns out Jack's a stone sniper."

Bill turned to Jack. "Aren't you the guy who's been saying all day you don't know anything about guns?"

"Not 'stone' metaphorically," I said. "Stone, literally. He brained 'em with somebody's rock garden."

Jack pulled back his arm, his fingers curled around an imaginary baseball.

"Enterprising," Bill said.

"The shot came from the bad guy," I told Bill. "At Jack."

"Just like the batters I used to fan," Jack said. "Spun him until he was dizzy. He had no idea where to look."

"You're taking this much better than the previous gunshot," I said.

"Ice water in his veins," Bill agreed.

"Actually, I think I'm in shock. Wait until the numbness wears off. *What?*" Jack's eyes suddenly widened. "Someone shot at me? *Again?*"

"No," I said. "It was all a dream. Listen, you guys, I hear sirens. Maybe we should get out of here before the homeowner comes to get his rocks back?"

"There's a dirty joke in there somewhere," Bill said.

"I'd rather you didn't find it."

We got in the car and drove away.

13

"So," Bill said as we wound our way through Queens, "who was he, your Mighty Casey?"

"I have an idea, but I don't like it."

"In that case, by all means share it."

"I never saw him before. He said his boss had some questions about, and some advice for, the guy I work for. I asked him if he worked for the government, and he said there's no money in it."

"He's never heard of corruption?" Jack asked.

"I'm sure he has. I'm thinking he's some kind of Chinese gangster. He's unhappy about something Jeff Dunbar's doing—or Dennis Jerrold, or whoever he is—and he wants me to do something about it."

"Why doesn't he go to Dunbar?"

"If Dunbar's really with the State Department, that's got to be overstepping, no matter how big a deal Mighty Casey's boss is in China. I got a partial plate, four of, I think, six numbers. Can you find someone to run it?"

I have my own cop contacts, like my best friend Mary, but doing this kind of thing gives her hives. Bill's contacts are more straightforward: He slips them Knicks tickets and guy stuff like that. He made a call, left a message, made another, left another. "One of those guys will do it," he said. "But it looks like neither one's on tonight, so it'll be tomorrow."

"I guess we can wait." I had a thought. "Or not." I took out my phone, speed-dialed Linus.

"You've reached Wong Security," Trella's voice told me. "We're sorry we can't take your call right now, but it *is* important to us. Please leave your name and number and we'll get back to you as soon as we can."

"It's Lydia," I told the microchip. "Sorry to interrupt your night, but I have something I'd like Linus to do. Give me a call?" I clicked off, said to the guys, "Maybe that will get us something," and found my phone beeping as I started to put it away. It was Linus, but not a call, a text:

Hi cuz, @ club, cant hear a thing. Txt me.

So I did, typing in the partial plate I'd made out while the SUV careened away. Jack looked over my shoulder. I was typing

blck navgtor, late modl

when Jack said, "Last year."

I raised an eyebrow and he shrugged.

Last yr. C what u cn do. I know this illegal. Dont do deeply illegal. If cant do, ok. If u find sumthing, call whenever.

I put the phone away without interruption this time and said, "That may get us somewhere. Jack, you're a car guy?"

"It's a Midwest suburban thing."

"I see." I settled back, leaned my head on the seat. "You guys? I'm getting tired of this."

"Of what?" Jack asked. "Me getting shot at?"

"That, too. Of being confused. Of not knowing who any of these people really are and what they really want."

"I have an idea," Jack said, snapping his fingers. "Let's go to Anna's studio, find the Chaus, have her tell us what's going on, and all go out for a drink after the big dance number."

"Good plan." I closed my eyes, and opened them briefly to add, "I'll have a cosmo."

Bill meandered randomly through Queens until he was satisfied we weren't being followed. As that was going on, Jack and I filled him in on what he'd missed while he was exchanging pleasantries with Shayna Dylan. By the time we pulled over in front of the artists' converted warehouse it was half-past nine, but light still glowed through the industrial windows.

"Behold the midnight oil of inspiration," I said.

"Most of these people have day jobs," Jack said. "They make work when they can."

"It's more romantic my way."

Bill said to Jack, "What did I tell you?"

I couldn't remember what he'd told him but I was sure it was something unflattering about me, so I instructed them both to go jump in a lake.

We'd parked at the building's long side. Jack led us around the corner to a loading dock with a huge roll-down door and a smaller door beside it. He punched a couple of buttons on the keypad.

Only silence, so he did it again. "No answer from Anna. I assume we want to get in even if she's not here?"

"As opposed to coming all this way," I said, "exchanging rocks and bullets with who knows who, and then going home empty-handed? You better believe it."

He read down the list beside the keypad, pressed another combination, and when that didn't work he tried a third.

"Who's there?" squawked the speaker.

"Francie, it's Jack Lee. Can you let me in?"

"Jack Lee? What are you doing in an outer borough at this hour? Don't tell me there are no hip parties in Manhattan tonight." The buzzer buzzed and Jack pushed the door open.

We walked into a cavernous space, windowed along the long walls from waist height to the overhead steel beams hung with metal-shaded lights. The broad entryway held a few sagging chairs and battered couches, a bookcase, and a bulletin board covered with announcements and flyers. Off it, in both directions, corridors turned the corner and ran past a series of large, ceilingless cubicles in the center of the paint-splattered concrete floor. Skylights punctuated the roof. The place smelled of turpentine, sawdust, and frying garlic. I could hear the high-pitched whirr of some industrial tool, drifts of music, various bits of unidentifiable clatter, and the opening of a door. Then footsteps, and a compact, cheerful-looking Asian woman appeared around the corner, bowl in one hand, chopsticks in the other.

"Hi, Jack. Want a dumpling? Oh, you didn't say you brought people. Hi, I'm Francie See." She shifted the chopsticks to her left hand where the bowl was and stuck out her right.

"Lydia Chin," I said as we shook. "And this is Bill Smith."

"Good to meet you. You folks want some dumplings? I have lots."

"No, thanks," Jack said. "We just had some great noodle soup." I was a little sorry to hear him turn her down; the dumplings, seared and glistening with sesame oil, looked great.

"At Lucky Gardens?" Francie See asked.

"No, in Manhattan."

"Oh, right, I should have known."

"You outer-borough people, so touchy. Listen, Francie, we're looking for Anna Yang. Is she here? Bill and Lydia wanted to see her work."

"I don't think so. Unless she came back." Francie See stepped back to peer down the corridor. "Her door's closed. Want to see mine instead?"

"Sure," said Jack, as though seeing art were why we'd come. "Still doing landscapes?"

"In a way." She led us back in the direction she'd come from. "That's Anna's studio, down there past the kitchen," she said over her shoulder. "She came in this afternoon and I thought she was staying to work but she left pretty fast. I got the feeling she was upset about something. Did she know you were coming?"

"No. Bill and Lydia just met her, and we were in the neighborhood so I suggested we come over. Is she okay?"

"I don't know what's going on. You could ask Pete, they're pretty tight." Francie See turned through an open door. "Voilà." She waved the chopsticks, then used them to lift a dumpling. "Hope you don't mind if I eat. I'm starved."

"No, go ahead," I said, looking around. Pinned to the walls, covering a table, and on three easels, were watercolor paintings, in every shade of blue imaginable, and all of them paintings of water. Oceans, fog, mist, clouds, waves, pools, pounding rain, racing brooks, water in every possible form, including glaciers, steam, and ice cubes. Serene, threatening, chilly, boiling, soft, hard, fast, and slow, changing from painting to painting but all water and all blue.

"Wow," said Jack. "This is what one of my professors would've called 'bloody-minded.'"

"Just tightening my focus," Francie said. "It's all about water, Jack. The twenty-first century's all about water."

"You always were so cutting-edge, Francie."

"I am, aren't I? Besides, something's got to wash down these dumplings. You sure you don't want any?"

The guys shook their heads, but I couldn't stand it. "I'd love one."

"That's what I'm talking about." Francie grinned and pointed to a jar of chopsticks beside a can of brushes.

"I don't believe you," Jack said. "After that soup?"

"Adrenaline makes Lydia hungry," Bill said.

"Adrenaline?" Francie asked. "You get a rush looking at art?"

I fetched some chopsticks and dug a dumpling from the bowl she held out.

"Bill does," Jack said. "The jury's still out on Lydia. But we had some excitement on the way here. We were sort of mugged."

"Seriously? Are you okay?"

"We're fine," I said, biting down on the salty, gamey dumpling. "*I* was sort of mugged, and Jack saved me."

"Ooh, Jack, you caveman, you. But you're okay?" Francie asked me.

I nodded, swallowed, and said, "This is great."

"Day job. I'm the dumpling queen of Lucky Gardens. See, this is why you should move to the outer boroughs. No one gets mugged in Flushing."

"For your information," Jack said, "we were in Flushing, not all that far from here."

"Oh. Well, I'm lying anyway. Why do you think we have all that fancy electronic stuff on the doors? None of the windows below ten feet open, either. And we have alarms on the skylights, in case someone tries a *Mission: Impossible*."

"Glad to hear it."

"Yeah, I guess it's good. It cost a fortune, though. A lot of people resisted, but that was partly because the security commissar's that jerk, Jon-Jon Jie. Oops, he a friend of yours?" Her smile made it clear she didn't care if he was or not.

Jack shook his head. "Seen his work, but don't know him. You have commissars?"

"It's funnier than 'committee chair.' Of course it would help if Big Yellow Hunter had a sense of humor. There were people holding out *because* he wouldn't shut up. We had to take an actual vote. Appalling. And now look, after all that, he's moving out."

"I didn't know he had a studio here."

"Down the hall. He came in with us because he thought we were the hip place to be. As though anything could make him hip. But now he's kissing us off for some high-rent broom closet in Chelsea. I say good riddance and he can take the armory with him."

"Armory?" I said. "He has guns in there?"

"He says he does. And bows and arrows, and spears. In case a buffalo herd charges through here, I don't know. Let his new A-list gallery worry about it."

"A-list gallery?" said Jack. "You don't mean Baxter/Haig?"

"You heard?"

"Eddie To said Doug Haig was just leading Jie on."

"That's what we all thought, but the deal's gone through. As of a few hours ago. Ink's still wet. He'll be Baxter/Haig's first Chinese-American. Everyone's disgusted. Jon-Jon's the kind of gateway drug that'll make Haig allergic."

"Haig's already allergic. I can't believe he's opening the sacred precincts to a hyphenated artist. And it's Jie? I only saw one show of his, but it was garbage."

"Literally. He buys Gucci's scraps."

Jack shook his head. "Are you sure this is true? Say what you want about Haig, but he has an eye. I've never known him to show bad work."

"Ah, well, he's not showing him yet, is he?"

"What do you mean?"

"There are reasons to put a horse in your stable even if you're not planning to ride him." Bill looked over from a painting he'd been examining. Francie said, "Sorry, it's Jon-Jon's Texas thing. I couldn't resist."

"No problem," said Jack. "Can you translate, though?"

"Jon-Jon's from money."

"You're saying he bought his way into Baxter/Haig?"

Francie put the empty dumpling bowl into a paint-streaked sink and turned the faucet on. Reaching for a stained towel to wipe her hands, she paused and cocked her head as water splattered and overflowed the bowl. I followed her gaze, admiring the way light glinted off the rivulets. "Mmm," Francie said. Leaving the water running and the bowl where it was, she unpinned an ice floe from an easel and laid it on a table. Dragging the easel to the sink, she said, "Just before the rumors about Jon-Jon's knighthood started, we'd been hearing a better rumor: that Haig was in trouble. Whoever'd loaned him the money to buy Baxter out wanted it back, plus. Or so we heard."

"We heard that, too. Who was it, do you know?"

"No." Francie fingered through the jar of brushes. "But inquiring minds agree it was Chinese money."

"Really? Listen, Francie, it sounds like you hear a lot of rumors. Have you heard that there are unknown Chau Chuns floating around?"

"Chau Chun? Who's that? Wait—Tiananmen? The Ghost Painter or something?"

"Ghost Hero."

"I thought he was dead."

"He is."

"I haven't heard anything about him." She pushed a rolling table over to the easel she'd just set up. Crowding it were pots of cobalt, azure, teal, turquoise, indigo, aquamarine. "That must not have made it out here to the boonies."

"All right," said Jack. "I can see we're losing you. We'll let you get back to work."

"Nothing personal."

"Of course not. I think we'll find Pete, just to make sure Anna's okay. Which studio's his?"

"At the very end. Two down from Anna." Francie pinned a sheet of paper to the easel. "You can help him celebrate."

"Celebrate what?"

"That he'll be able to breathe again. So will Anna. As soon as Jon-Jon packs up his mangy hides and moves out from the studio between them."

We left Francie's studio and headed along the corridor. "That was cool," I said. "I always wondered where artists get their ideas."

"Just turn on the faucet, they flow right out," Bill said.

"I was surprised she barely knew who Chau was, though. I guess you're right—this generation doesn't necessarily know him. That would explain how Anna could have a couple of Chaus, real or fake, pinned to her studio wall and no one here would notice."

"It explains how she could, but it doesn't explain why she does."

Jack stopped at a black door that said ANNA YANG in small neat red letters and, below them, in equally precise Chinese characters. He knocked, then tried the door, but it was locked. "Well, she's not here to ask."

"Too bad," I said. "Do you have her phone number?"

"Yes. But I want to talk to Pete before we call her."

Bill, examining the door, said, "Maybe not too bad."

Jack looked at Bill. "What?"

"No one's here on this end of the building," Bill pointed out. "Except that guy Pete, who you're going to see. Francie's all the way down there with the water running and someone on the other side has music on. Why don't you two go talk to Pete?"

Jack frowned. "I don't know."

"No. And what you don't know can't hurt you. Go."

So we went, past the studio that was still, briefly, Jon-Jon Jie's—with a curling fragment of brown and white cowhide tacked to the door—and knocked at the open door of the studio beyond it.

Inside, a thin young Asian man in a blue work shirt sat drawing loose, fast pencil lines on a sheet of paper. He glanced up sharply. His intense, silent stare made me think maybe we should get lost. We might be interrupting an artist in the middle of an inspiration. But he relaxed, though he didn't smile. "Jack. Hey, what's up?"

"Hey, Pete. This is Lydia Chin. Lydia, Pete Tsang."

"Hi," I said. Pete Tsang, sharp dark eyes on me, nodded.

"We were looking for Anna," Jack told him, "but Francie See said she came and went. She also said she seemed upset. I just wanted to make sure she's okay."

Pete put his pencil down. "I didn't see her, just heard her. Sometimes when she gets in I take a break, we have coffee or something before she sets up. I was half-waiting, but she just locked up again and left."

"So you don't know what was wrong?"

"Could be nothing's wrong. Maybe she just came in to get something."

"When we saw her before she was headed here, said she had a lot to do. But maybe you're right. I'll call her." Jack turned to me. "Pete's a painter." I might have guessed that from the two large canvases, one in burning yellows, one in jagged reds, on opposite sides of the studio. Jack asked Pete, "What are you working on? Anything new?"

"Nothing right now. Planning something out, but I'm not ready to start." Pete didn't elaborate, and his glance flicked back to the sketch on his desk. He seemed taut, Pete Tsang did, like an arrow waiting for the bowstring to snap.

It occurred to me, if this case didn't end soon I'd be talking in nature metaphors, myself.

That wasn't my immediate problem, though. That was that it was clear Pete Tsang would rather we left. Which would leave Pete Tsang alone with his studio door open, two down from Anna Yang's, and who knew what was going on there? Jack, obviously thinking along the same lines, had strolled over to examine the yellow canvas. I looked around. There was nothing remotely intelligent I could say about Pete Tsang's paintings. That was my lack of art vocabulary, not the paintings. I liked the huge range of colors I could now see within what had seemed at first like two or three shades of a single color; and I liked the suggestion of small, shadowy human forms I thought I saw. The canvases struck me as radiating the same tightly coiled vigilance the painter did. Maybe; but that wasn't a promising conversational path. Then I spied a flyer tacked to the wall: a photo of a handsome young Asian man with wire-frame glasses, smiling on a sunny day. Below the picture, heavy black type read FREE LIU MAI-KE! At the bottom was a Web site address.

"Mike Liu," I said. "Are you involved in that?"

Pete looked me over as though maybe he'd missed something the first time. "You know about him?"

"He's that poet. He's married to Jack's friend Anna, who we came to see. 'The world calls this China's century, but if China's people are denied the right to think and to express their thoughts, if they cannot count on basic human rights and human dignity, China's century will be worthless dust.' He got seven years."

Jack's eyes were on me. Pete Tsang asked, "Are you an artist?"

"No. But I'm Chinese."

"You followed Mike's case?"

"The sentence was outrageous. It would have been a joke if it hadn't been a tragedy."

Pete looked at me another few moments, then reached to a long counter holding neat cans of brushes and pencils. He picked up a couple of sheets of paper, which turned out to be the same flyer as on the wall. "Have you been to our Web site?"

"No."

"Check it out. There's a rally next week. It'll be big. Important. You'll want to be there. Jack, you will, too."

Jack didn't say anything, but he walked over and took a flyer.

"You think it'll help?" I asked. "The Chinese government doesn't respond to much. Rallies and letter-writing, with other dissidents it sometimes looks like they don't even notice."

Pete's hard gaze held me. "I don't know. But I know doing nothing won't work." After another moment: "And this time, I'm pretty sure they'll notice."

He stood up and walked to the door, where he just waited. So we actually had to leave. By then I wasn't too worried. Bill's fast, especially when he's breaking the law.

Jack and I walked back down the hall the way we'd come. We both threw quick looks at Anna Yang's door, saw nothing but her name. We waved to Francie See as we passed her studio. She didn't respond, just kept feathering pale blue onto the emerging painting on her easel.

Jack said, "I didn't know you could do that. Quote Mike Liu."

"I read the open letter."

"I read it, too. But I can't quote it."

"I can do it in Chinese, too. You want to hear?"

Jack sighed. "No, I believe you."

"But actually," I admitted, "I read it twice."

We turned the corner and found Bill lounging on an entryway sofa, leafing through a book on the history of Chinese fireworks. A FREE LIU MAI-KE flyer, I now noticed, was pinned to the bulletin board.

"Hey," Bill said, getting up. "How's Pete Tsang?"

"Curt," said Jack.

"Handsome," said I.

"Really?" said Jack.

"I'm just reporting." I handed Bill the flyer as we headed for the door. "He wants us to come to a rally next week. He says it'll be big."

"For Anna Yang's husband?" Bill looked at Jack.

"Lydia can quote his whole manifesto by heart. In two languages."

"I'm translating it into Italian, too, right now in my head. No, seriously, that passage is the only part I can quote. It just grabbed me." I repeated the passage for Bill. "And now that we're outside"—which we were, on the sidewalk under the Flushing stars—"tell!" I wheeled on Bill. "Are they there? In Anna's studio?"

"The Chaus?"

"No, Jimmy Hoffa and Judge Crater! Of course the Chaus!"

"No."

I stopped. "No? Wait. No?"

"Not on the walls, and as far as I can see, not in the file drawers. That wall you'd have seen from about where Shayna took the photo? It's empty."

"Maybe they're what Anna came to get."

Jack said to Bill, "What about you? Will there be any way for Anna to know you were there?"

"If I didn't know you were asking that question out of concern for your friend Anna's nerves," Bill said, lighting a cigarette, "I'd take offense."

"Bill does a very clean B and E," I reassured Jack. "It's a point of pride with him. And you're sure that's where they were, the Chaus? Those papercuttings were for sure Anna's?"

The question had been for Jack, but Bill nodded. "I saw the ones in the photo. They're still there. It's just the Chaus that're gone."

"Well, damn," I said. I'd have said more, but my phone rang. An unfamiliar number, so I answered in both languages. The voice that replied, speaking in English, was not unfamiliar, but I was glad it was on the phone and not up close and personal.

"Chin Ling Wan-ju, my apology. I think we start on bad foot. I don't try to scare you, just want to talk."

I covered the phone and whispered to the guys, "Mighty Casey." To Casey himself, I said, "How did you get this number?"

"Just want to talk," he repeated. "About your client."

"Okay, we're talking."

"No, we meet. Have tea, be civilized."

"Your driver almost ran me down, you pointed a gun at me, you tried to kidnap me, and you shot at my friend. You might have tried this 'civilized' approach first."

"I say, I apologize. Sometime, get too . . . involved, my work."

"Who are you?"

"We have tea, I explain."

I thought. "Okay. Tea. In a public place."

A pause. "Yes. Okay. You come alone."

"So do you. And," I added, "not tonight. Tomorrow. In daylight." After, maybe, we'd heard from Linus, or one of Bill's cop friends, and I had some idea of with whom I was having the pleasure.

That didn't seem to bother him. In fact, he sounded amused. "Tomorrow, nine o'clock. Sun up high enough?"

"Maria's, on Walker Street."

"Happy to see you then."

I didn't share the sentiment, but I agreed to the time and place and clicked off.

"You set up a meet with that guy?" Jack asked.

"Don't you want to know why he was shooting at you?"

"He was shooting at me because I was throwing rocks at him. Who is he and what does he want?"

"He'll tell me tomorrow. Nine o'clock, Maria's on Walker."

"Well, you're not going alone."

I raised an eyebrow. "For Pete's sake, you don't have to get all John Wayne about it. Of course I'm not. You're going to come and do the same thing you did at the bar. Get there first, blend into the scenery. It could be you," I said to Bill, "but Jack will blend better at Maria's."

Maria's is a Taiwanese tea shop and Bill's been there with me any number of times. He's almost always the only non-Chinese person in the place, and he's big besides. He sticks out like a buzzard in a flock of swallows. That's if you ask me. If you ask him, the whole thing has more to do with lions and Hello Kitties.

That settled, Jack checked his watch. "It's past eleven. Hope Anna doesn't mind the late call." He made the late call, and Anna didn't get the chance to tell us how much she minded because she didn't pick up. Jack left a message, calm but using the words "really important" twice.

"When she calls back," I said, "whether it's tonight or tomorrow morning, let me know."

"What do you mean? You won't be with me when it happens? We're not going to end the night in some enormously chichi boîte over a couple of single malts, discussing exactly where we are in this case?"

"You've actually ever been to a boîte? Never mind. Besides, do you have any idea exactly where we are in this case? Me neither. Listen, you guys, this has been fun, chasing around with you, getting shot at and stuff—"

"I don't recall *you* getting shot at," Jack said.

"No, I think that's right," said Bill.

"Oh, so sorry. I'll try to position myself better next time. But right now, I'm going to leave you guys to have all the fun and I'm going home to sleep."

So Bill, dedicated chauffeur that he was, took me back to Chinatown. Nothing untoward happened on our drive, and the universe was clearly telling me I'd made the right choice because my mother was asleep when I unlocked the door, slipped off my shoes, and tiptoed in. Or at least, she was in bed pretending not to be waiting up. Either way was fine with me.

14

In the morning my mother's cover was blown. I woke full of energy, pulled on my bathrobe, and headed into the kitchen. My mother wandered in fully dressed suspiciously soon thereafter and with wide-eyed artlessness said, "Oh, are you home? I didn't hear you come in last night. I thought you were still out, working overnight on your new case." She says stuff like that to remind me that she's not interfering in my life, professional or personal. But when I peeked into the teapot I found about five times as much tea as my mother, alone in the apartment, would ever drink before lunch.

Being the big tea drinker in the family, I poured myself a cup, gave her a kiss, and said, "It's an interesting case. It involves art." I dumped granola in a bowl and sat down at the table.

"Oh, really?" She spoke offhandedly, puttering around the kitchen doing things that clearly absorbed her attention way more than anything I was saying. "Do you know many things about art, Ling Wan-ju?"

"No, Ma. But I'm learning. I went to a gallery yesterday and saw little red boxes chasing each other around."

My mother turned to look at me, waiting for the part about the art.

"It was sort of a sculpture. By a Chinese artist, in fact."

That the home team was responsible for this incomprehensible item didn't impress her. "Your cousin Yong Xiao is an artist. He painted a beautiful scarf for me."

My third cousin twice removed, Yong Xiao, is a twenty-year-old fashionista wannabe working for pennies at the atelier of a hot designer barely older than he is. In his off hours he paints chrysanthemums on cheap silk scarves to sell to tourists so he can pay his rent.

Casually, because of course she takes so little interest in that which is not her business, my mother asked, "Are you working alone on your new case?"

"Or, you mean, is Bill working with me?"

She gave me the wide-eyed innocent look again. Her brow has permanent grooves from that look. "Oh, yes," she said, as though she hadn't given that possibility a thought. "I suppose you might be getting help from the white baboon." She hasn't said Bill's name in years. She refers to him in other ways that would be endearing if she actually liked him.

"Bill's on the case, yes." I poked around for raisins in my granola bowl.

"I see." She sounded relieved, which surprised me. One of the things she dislikes about my profession is that she thinks it's dangerous. Almost as high on her dislike list, though, is the people I'm forced by the job to associate with, and on the top of *that* list is Bill. That he's big and strong and bodyguardish and could help with the "dangerous" problem has never cut any ice with her. So what was the relief about?

"But this case is not urgent? It allows you time for yourself? Perhaps to see your friends?" She spoke coyly and I had no idea what she was talking about. Keeping a quizzical eye on her, I scooped up another mouthful.

Then I got it. "The Chinatown telegraph." I put my spoon down. "Someone saw us at New Chao Chow, didn't they? Me, and Bill, and Jack?" The relief must have been at the idea that I was hanging with Bill out of professional necessity, not personal choice. And the reason for the coyness was now blindingly clear.

Absorbed in measuring rice into the cooker, my mother answered vaguely. "I think your auntie Ying-le might have mentioned it. Yes, I remember now. She saw you when she was shopping on Mott Street yesterday."

Mao Ying-le, a friend of my mother's from her sewing days and in no way my aunt, was one of Chinatown's biggest gossips. But it didn't matter. If not Ying-le, my mother would have gotten the word from someone else. It should have occurred to me that I couldn't dine in the neighborhood with a handsome Asian guy and expect my mother not to know about it before the check came.

"Jack Lee," I said.

"Your auntie said he looked very nice."

"She did?"

"Not exactly. She said *you* looked as though *you* thought he was very nice."

My face grew hot, which annoyed me. "She stood there and watched us?"

My mother smiled. "Is he very nice?"

Some things you can't fight. I'd have to talk to myself about the color in my cheeks later. "Yes."

"And he is Chinese?" Just checking. Because he might be Japanese, or Korean. From a different planet, in her universe, but still light-years ahead of Bill.

"Jack Lee Yat-sen," I confirmed. "From Wisconsin. He's second generation, parents born here, too. But, Ma, it was work. Jack's also on the case. He's another PI."

Her face fell. My mother's been to California twice, to visit relatives, and to New England to view the fall leaves, but she has only a vague idea where Wisconsin is. "Second generation" clearly worried her, too. But Jack's job was the final blow.

"Chinese, is he?" She sniffed. "Hollow bamboo." Hollow bamboo: Chinese-looking outside, empty inside.

"Ma, you don't even know him! He speaks and reads Chinese. And his field is Chinese art." I didn't tell her that in most other ways Jack was the guy who put the "A" in "ABC."

"I thought his field was detecting."

"In the art world. He finds stolen paintings, things like that."

"So he's involved with criminals, then."

"No more than I am."

"There, you see?" She plugged in the rice cooker emphatically, with bitter triumph.

I gave up. Whatever we were arguing about, I wasn't going to win. And why, I suddenly asked myself, did I care whether my mother thought well of Jack Lee, anyway?

I was finishing my tea when the cell phone in my robe pocket chirped out Arcade Fire's "The Suburbs." That would be Linus.

"Cuz!" he said. "Too early?"

"Not at all. Have a good time last night?"

"Dudess, it was sick! Dum Dum Girls at the Mercury Lounge! They tore it up! We didn't get back until, like, five a.m."

"And you're up working? I'm impressed."

"No way. We just didn't crash yet. A little wired, you know? So I thought I'd check out your dude first, to kinda bring me down."

"So does he? Bring you down?"

"Well, yeah. I mean, the dude himself, I don't know anything about him. You didn't get, like, cell phone pix or something?" His voice was hopeful.

"Linus, we were—" I almost said, *pointing guns at each other,* but I remembered where I was. "It was dark."

"Oh. Well." He sounded like he wasn't sure why that mattered, and to a tech geek I guess it wouldn't. But he moved on. "Okay, so, I found the car. This dude I know, he has a dude he rolls with— sorry, TMI. A Navigator—last year's, like you said. Plate number you gave me plus six-eight at the end? It's registered to Tiger Holdings, LLC. Addresses in Beijing, Hong Kong, Manhattan, and Basking Ridge, New Jersey."

"Who are they, Tiger Holdings? What do they do?"

"Well, I don't know who they are, but a couple of their honchos, you can see photos on their Web site." He gave me the URL. "Maybe your guy's there."

"Okay, I'll check it out. Anything else?"

"Well, sort of. I mean, I could be wrong."

"But?"

"Well, you remember that Web site I built for Vassily Imports? So Bill could be a shady Russian?"

"Sure."

"It kind of . . . smells the same."

"What do you mean? You think the Tiger Holdings Web site's a fake?"

"Not really. There's got to be a real Tiger Holdings, because they own at least one car, right? But you said, make Bill's look dubious, so I did. This one, it's like they're hiding the same things. Who the boss really is, all that. I mean, I was fake hiding, but I think they're real hiding. Cuz, I think they're gangsters."

I didn't finish the tea in my mother's pot because I was headed out soon to Maria's to meet Mighty Casey the Gangster. This disappointed my mother, but there's not much I do that doesn't. I had about twenty minutes before I needed to leave, so I sat down at my computer and brought up the Tiger Holdings Web site.

Linus's conclusion didn't surprise me. We'd figured Casey for a gangster last night. That whole kidnap thing, it was kind of a clue. Interesting to have it confirmed through the smell of a Web site, though. And Linus's worried tone made me glad I hadn't gotten to tell him the part about the guns.

I clicked through the bios of Tiger Holdings's officers, each page topped by a photo of a confident Asian man in a costly suit. A prosperous crowd, though I could see what Linus meant: They made it easy to get in touch with them to discuss investment and partnership opportunities, but exactly what they did was hard to tell.

I did find Casey, though. His broad face and thick shoulders were labeled as belonging to one Woo Long. Title: Corporate Liaison. If last night was illustrative of his liaising technique, I'd be surprised to find Tiger Holdings actually doing all that well.

Figuring Linus had already followed Tiger Holdings as far as he could, I Googled Woo Long, but found nothing. Linus had been heading for bed, an unorthodox sleep schedule being his MO and one of the perks of running your own e-business. This wasn't worth waking him for, but I sent him a note so when he resurfaced he'd know which of these guys I was interested in. Just because Google came up empty didn't mean Linus would.

I got dressed, clipping on my small-of-the-back holster with the .25 that had come in so handy last night. I surveyed my closet for a drapey jacket loose enough to hide them. I have a bunch of those, mostly made by my mother. She sews them out of fabric I buy and to specs I describe while I wave my hands around. When I was young she taught me embroidery, knitting, and other handwork, but she never let me touch the sewing machine. Her theory was if I couldn't sew I wouldn't end up in the factory. Now that she's retired, dressing my brothers' wives and me is her chief joy. Though making things for my sisters-in-law seems to be the more gratifying: When she's sewing my clothes she never stops grumbling about girls not finding husbands if they walk around wearing trousers and tents.

If she has any idea why I really like my jackets baggy, she's never said.

I chose one of my favorites, a black cotton twill that swings at the hem. It looks particularly good with black pants and a white shirt, and I added a red scarf because black-white-and-red is a power-color combination and I was, after all, meeting a gangster. The fact that Jack Lee would be sitting at a back table watching me barely crossed my mind.

"So long, Ma," I called, hopping around one-legged in the foyer, putting on my shoes.

"You are going to work?" She appeared from the kitchen, cleaver in hand.

"Yes."

"With the white baboon? Or the hollow bamboo?"

"Both. Aren't I lucky?"

She frowned. "Ling Wan-ju. You think you have been lucky, on your road in life. But take care. What looks like the path to good fortune can often be the opposite. And to bad luck, the same." With that she turned and walked back to the kitchen. Wow, I thought. All that was missing were crickets and ants.

In the bright spring sunlight I cut a path—to what kind of fortune, I didn't know. Pushing through the crowds of morning shoppers and early-bird tourists, I called Jack to ask if he'd heard from Anna Yang.

"Nope. I called her this morning again, just got voice mail. After I get through bodyguarding you here I'll try again."

"Here? You're at Maria's already?"

"The egg custard tarts come out of the oven at eight-thirty. Didn't you know that?"

I was early, too, and as I planned, I hit Maria's before Mighty Woo Long Casey. Inside the bakery things were only slightly less chaotic than on the street. I found Jack spread out over a cup of coffee, an egg custard tart, and *The Times*. His leather jacket hung over the back of his chair and he seemed completely absorbed in the news and caffeine, oblivious to the din around him, which included me ordering milk tea and a red bean bun.

I paid and stood with my tray, waiting for a table to clear. Jack, of course, could have gotten up and given me his, but then he wouldn't have been able to watch over the meeting. If I couldn't find one, though, Casey and I would have to take this meeting out to the street, in which case, what good was Jack having one? Quite a conundrum. I wondered if Jeff Dunbar, in the delicate diplomacy of the State Department, had ever faced one like it. Maybe after I'd filled him in on Tiger Holdings's concerns about him, and passed on their advice, I could ask him.

Luckily, as I stood there, a young couple got up from a table by the window. I sped over, plunking my tray down ahead of the countergirl who was coming to pile their dishes up and push their crumbs onto the floor with a cloth. I thanked her. She nodded and turned to leave, nearly bumping into Casey as she did.

"Ms. Chin," he grinned. "So nice, see you again."

"Not all that nice." I tried to play it tough, but it was hard to keep from smiling at the white bandage on his forehead. Nice work, Jack. "I trust you feel all right."

"Feel great, thank you." He pulled out a chair and deposited himself in it. Not far from Jack, a squarish young guy looked up from a Chinese-language newspaper and looked down again quickly. So we were both cheating: Casey had a second here, too. Not suprising. I hoped Jack had noticed. I thought he might have, because, still reading his paper, he shifted in his seat to where both our table and the square guy's were within his sight.

Casey stuck a straw in his plastic cup of bubble tea. I don't like that stuff anyway, and certainly not for breakfast. And the one he had was purple.

"What do you want?" I said.

"No," he contradicted me after a slurp. "Question is, what do your client want?"

"That's private business."

"Some private business, he telling everybody."

"Who?" I said, confused. "He's telling who?"

"Everybody. Go around saying, I looking new Chaus, you know where to find?"

"Not as far as I know, he's not. That's supposed to be my job. Do you, by the way? Know where to find them?"

Casey laughed cheerily, as though I'd made a good joke. "Of

course. Boss know. But not telling you." He wagged a finger in front of my face. "Not telling your client, too. You tell him, go away."

"No."

The smile dropped from his face. His voice hardened to ice. "Yes."

What, we're not friends anymore? Then enough of this. "Mr. Woo—oh, you're surprised? Don't be. I know all about you, you and Tiger Holdings." "All" was exaggerating, but I let it stand. "Mr. Woo, if you want something, you have to give something. That's how it works. Who is Tiger Holdings, how do you know who my client is, and why do you and your boss care if I find the Chaus for him?" Because they could be worth a ton, I suggested to myself; but I wanted to hear what he had to say.

He stared at me. "Think you pretty damn smart, Lydia Chin?"

"Why, is Tiger Holdings a big secret? Then you shouldn't have a Web site. Who are you people?"

Eyes still on mine, he took another slurp of his purple bubble tea. Some tough guy, I thought. Except I was glad there were three dozen other people crowded into the shop here. And that one of them was Jack.

"We same people as your client," Woo finally said.

"Interesting. Last night you said you weren't."

His brows knit. "Said I weren't, what?"

"With the government. When I asked who you worked for. So, what, did Samuel Wing send you because I didn't fold fast enough?"

"Samuel Wing? Who is he?"

"Yeah, I don't know his real name either. The skinny guy in the gray suit. Came to see me yesterday afternoon, to tell me to back off. He sent you because I threw him out? You're the stick?"

"Pah. Stick, what is stick? You don't make sense. Don't know

Samuel Wing. Boss sends me." He blotted his thick lips on a napkin. "Last night, you don't ask *who* I work for. You ask me, do I work for government. Government, big joke. I work for Tiger Holdings. Tiger Holdings just like . . ." He paused, searching for the right words. "Just like business interest your client work for." He gave a humorless smile. "Tiger Holdings want that business interest to go away. Save everybody trouble."

A light was beginning to dawn for me, but one dawned for him, too, and faster.

"Samuel Wing." He frowned and held up a thick finger to stop me from saying anything. "You telling this guy come, say you stop looking for Chaus, you telling he work for government? American government?"

"Chinese government. I don't know his real name or what his job is, but he's at the Consulate. And you're telling me you're not?"

"Of course not." He dismissed that with a wave of his purple tea. "Chinese government come bother you? Chinese government care about Chaus? Why?"

"I have no idea. You're a gangster, right?"

His eyes widened. "Lydia Chin—"

"No, don't bother. Tiger Holdings is a criminal organization, one way or another, and that's what you mean by, you're in the same business as my client. And Tiger Holdings is working for itself on this, not for the Chinese government."

He rested his gaze on me, slurped, and smiled. "Yes. Tiger Holdings don't want no trouble with Vassily Imports."

No, who would?

"So you want me to tell Vladimir to back off."

Because Vladimir Oblomov was a Russian mobster and Lydia Chin, as far as Tiger Holdings was concerned, was the art consultant helping him look for the Chaus. And State Department middle-manager Jeff Dunbar, aka Dennis Jerrold, and Lydia Chin, his PI, were nowhere to be seen.

"And you called me instead of Vladimir," I said, "because mine was the number you had. He hasn't been giving his out." Except to Shayna. But Nick Greenbank and Doug Haig only had mine. Either of those fellows, it seemed to me, would hand it over without a squeak if a guy like Casey rose up on their horizon; but how would he know to rise? "Who told you Vassily Imports is interested in the Chaus?"

"Little birdie." Woo seemed to relax a bit, now that I was catching on. He leaned back in his chair. "We understand, Vassily Imports want paintings. Chaus very valuable. We regret, Tiger Holdings got to protect investment. Sorry for inconvenience. Maybe Tiger Holdings can make up to Vassily Imports, some other time."

"Oh? I'm sure Vladimir will be pleased to hear that. It might make your . . . suggestion . . . more palatable. Mr. Woo, what investment?"

"Not making suggestion. Giving advice."

"And I'm asking a question. What investment?"

He shook his head. "Like you say, private business."

I ignored that. "Your investment in the paintings? I don't think so. You said you knew where they were but I don't believe you. If you had them you wouldn't care what Vladimir's doing. You might even try to sell them to him. Or is your investment in the artist? Mr. Woo, is Chau alive? Do you know where he is?"

"Too many question." Woo pushed away from the table and stood, throwing a shadow over my red bean bun. "Ms. Chin, you tell Oblomov, forget about Chaus. He do that, next time he need friends, Tiger Holdings don't forget about him. He don't do that . . ."

Woo stared down at me. "He don't do that, no one be happy." He nodded, then turned, working his way between tables to the door, not looking back. I sat watching him, sipping my tea. The young square guy with the Chinese newspaper stood when Woo did and followed him out, leaving the paper and mooncake crumbs all over the tabletop. Outside the door he turned right, as Woo had. Jack got up, too. He shrugged into his jacket and left Maria's as well; though, being a responsible citizen, he bused his tray and took his newspaper with him.

15

Jack didn't get far. I caught up with him on the corner of Mulberry. He was peering after a black SUV as it disappeared east along Canal.

"I got the plate this time," he said.

"Don't worry about it. Linus ran it already."

"Seriously? From what he had?" Jack stuffed his pen and paper back in his pocket. "I guess he really is all that."

"And a bag of chips. He's my cousin, what did you expect?"

"So who is this guy?"

"Who he is is interesting. Who he thinks his competition is is even better." I gave him the rundown: Tiger Holdings, Vassily Imports, the warning left with me to pass on to Vladimir Oblomov. "Obviously Tiger Holdings isn't a Chinatown outfit, or they'd know who I am."

"She says modestly. No, I know what you mean. But you're telling me that atrocious accent of Bill's has the Chinese mob on the run from the Russian mob?"

"Well, technically, the Chinese mob is telling the Russian mob to be on the run from them."

Jack rubbed the back of his neck. "There really ought to be some way we can make something off of this."

"If you think of it, let me know. I'm calling Bill. Did you hear from Anna Yang?"

"Maybe. Someone called while we were in Maria's, but I let it go to voice mail so I wouldn't get distracted. In case I needed to leap to the rescue or something." He pulled out his cell phone.

"And don't think I didn't appreciate it. Did you notice Woo had someone there, too?"

"Messy guy in front of the pastry case?"

"That's the one. I was concerned he might be between you and your only ammunition if it came to a battle again."

"I never threw a cream puff in my life."

"That's a baseball joke."

We focused on our phones. I called Bill while Jack listened to his message. "Hey," Bill said. "Done already? How'd it go?"

"Let me speak to Vladimir. He's the big star."

"Vat?"

"Casey's a Chinese gangster and he never heard of Jeff Dunbar. It's Vladimir and Vassily Imports he wants off his back. Wait. Hold on."

I stopped because I was looking at Jack. In the background I'd heard, "Hey, Anna, thanks for getting back to me," and then watched Jack's face darken as he listened in silence. Now he was offering an impressively reassuring, "Of course I will. Anna, calm down. Whatever it is, we'll take care of it. Give us half an hour, we'll be there."

"Unless you have other plans, meet us at the car," I told Bill. "I think we have business."

It took Bill, following Jack's directions, just over twenty minutes to get us from his parking lot to Anna's apartment in Flushing. It had taken Jack the entire walk from the bakery to the lot to persuade Anna to let me and Bill come along. In the end he had to both throw around the word "partners"—which he was beginning to use with not just abandon but also a certain élan—and to promise he'd toss us out if, after she told us what it was all about, he thought we should go.

"Doesn't want to know us, huh? Did you ask her about the Chaus?" I'd said when he finally hung up. We stood on the sidewalk waiting for Bill.

"She was too upset for me to ask her anything. And she knows you already. She says it's bad enough now, and having you involved will only make it worse."

"Us, anyone? Or us, us?"

"I got the feeling you, you. But remember, she doesn't know what you already know."

"When you put it that way, I don't either. Did she say what was wrong?"

"No. She just said it was bad trouble and there's no one else she could call."

"I hate it when people say that. Does it mean their first thought was to send up the Bat Signal and hope you'd come? Or does it mean, if there *were* anyone else they could have called, they would have called them?"

"Hmmm. Breakfast with a hard case makes you paranoid, does it?"

"I have breakfast at home every day. You only say that because you've never met my mother."

"No," he grinned, "but I'd like to."

Luckily, at that moment Bill came loping down the block, saving me from having to answer Jack and, I hoped, from Jack noticing the sudden heat in my face.

Anna Yang's apartment was the downstairs of a two-family house in a blue-collar Flushing neighborhood, not far from the East Village communal studio. By the time we got there I'd filled Bill in on Woo, Tiger Holdings, and Vassily Imports.

"And you scoffed at my accent," he said.

"I still do."

"Me, too," said Jack.

"Jack thinks we should find some way to make something off this," I told Bill.

"Scamming the Chinese mob?" Bill asked. "Well, if you think of a way, I'm in."

"Seriously?"

"Of course not. You think I'm crazy?"

"I don't know, you guys," said Jack. "I think we're missing a bet here."

"Give me a break," I said. "You're the one who was complaining all day yesterday about how serene your life was until you met us."

"Met you. I already knew him."

"Well, if you think this stream's that much rougher than your peaceful pond was, you are totally not ready for the Chinese mob white water."

For a moment, silence in the car. Then both Jack and Bill cracked up.

"Hey," I said huffily. "I'm trying. This nature metaphor stuff, it's not so easy."

Bill found a parking spot on Anna's block, a well-kept street of narrow houses and tiny yards. We rang the bell and, as she had at her father's office, Anna Yang opened the door to us. This time she didn't light up at the sight of Jack, though. She didn't react at all. She just stayed standing in the doorway. Her eyes were dry, but puffy lids and a red-tipped nose made it clear she'd been crying. Guys sometimes miss that, or pretend they have, but, after a soft, "Hi, Anna," Jack reached out and hugged her. I think I'd have found that comforting, myself, but Anna started to cry again.

"Come on," Jack said, moving into the apartment with his arm around her. "Let's go sit down." Bill and I followed them through a small entryway into a spare, bright living room: pale wood floor, ivory sofa and chairs, a scroll painting of wild geese in flight on one wall and a hazy, peaceful watercolor of a wooded lakeshore on another. That one had a familiar feel and I wondered if it was Francie See's, from before she tightened her focus. The coffee table was crowded with photos of Mike Liu: with Anna, with friends, alone. In most, he was smiling.

Anna wiped her eyes, smoothed her skirt under her, and sat on the sofa. Jack sat protectively close beside her. That left me with a choice of armchairs, so I organized myself in one. Bill, as usual, didn't sit, but wandered a distance away, as though he wanted to examine the paintings.

"Okay," Jack said to Anna. "Tell us. Whatever it is, we'll fix it."

I was a little alarmed to hear him say that so categorically. This was a woman whose husband was in prison in China. It was possible her problems were beyond the three of us.

Or, the four of us. From the hall an older Chinese woman appeared, thin and, while not quite as tall as Anna, not a tiny Cantonese like me. Jack stood immediately, so I did the same. "Mrs. Yang," he said.

"Hello, Jack." Her voice was deep, steady, and heavily Mandarin-accented. She wore her salt-and-pepper hair pulled back into a bun. Standing stick-straight, she carried a tray with a white pot and five no-handle teacups, so she couldn't bow, but she inclined her head to Jack. He, apparently without thinking, bowed to her. This was a well-trained Midwesterner.

"This is Lydia Chin, and Bill Smith," Jack said. "Yang Yu-feng. Anna's mother."

Yang Yu-feng deposited her tray on the coffee table. She shook our hands and now she bowed. She gestured us to sit again, which she also did, back straight, and she poured the tea. Jack picked up a cup, holding it one hand bottom, one hand side as good manners demanded. Whatever he said, I'd bet he'd have passed the lidded-cup test on his first go. "You're looking well, Mrs. Yang. Anna didn't say you'd be here. It's an unexpected pleasure."

Well, well. Straight-up suburban Jack, suddenly going all Chinese on us. He was smiling at Yang Yu-feng but the message was for Anna: If her mother's presence wasn't part of the plan and she didn't want to discuss her troubles with her there, she should send up a flare. We'd make small talk and get back with her later.

"Jack." Anna's mother spoke with a calm that could equally have been born of confidence or despair. "Anna has a problem. She thinks you will be able to help her."

Okay, so that was our answer. Jack glanced at Anna, and nodded. "I hope so."

Yang Yu-feng didn't respond. She waited until we all had our
teacups—Bill came across the room, picked one up, and held it correctly, also, just like I'd taught him—and then she lifted her own.
After we'd taken our ceremonial first sips—tea before trouble, oh,
would my mother have approved—she put her cup on the table and
turned to her daughter, waiting.

Anna looked at Jack, and then at Bill and me. She didn't say
anything, but her lip began to tremble.

Jack followed her gaze. "Lydia and Bill and I are working together on a case," he said evenly. "It has to do with Chau Chun, new
paintings that are supposed to be his. If the reason you called me
has nothing to do with Chau, they'll leave. If it does, you need them
as much as you need me." He added, "I promise you can trust them."

I gave Anna what I hoped was a reassuring smile, Chinese
woman to Chinese woman. Jack she already knew and trusted; her
mother, she also knew, and had had twenty-two years to decide
whether she could trust. That pretty much left Bill on his own, but
sometimes he can be just a big, heartening presence. After hearing
what Jack said, though, Anna suddenly seemed to stop caring
about me and Bill, and even her mom. Pale, she was staring at Jack.

"You already know? Is that—that's why you came to see Daddy
yesterday? To ask him if he knew anything about the Chaus?"

"Sort of. Not really. Lydia and Bill are working for a collector
who's looking for them."

"Someone's looking for them already? Who?"

I wasn't sure what that meant. They shouldn't be looking for
them yet? Later would be better? Later than what? Jack said, "It
seems like a number of collectors are. This one hired Lydia to find

them. I'm sorry, we can't tell you his name, but it doesn't matter. And I'm—I was—working for your dad."

"What?" Momentarily, she was wordless. "Working for Daddy? He didn't tell me. Working for him how?"

She hadn't known that. She had the Chaus, her father wanted the Chaus, and no one in this family talks to each other? Well, almost no one. Either Jack's client wasn't news to Anna's mother, or she had a good poker face.

"He'd heard rumors the paintings existed," Jack said. "Like the other collectors. He hired me to find out whether it was true."

"Where did he hear it? Why did he want to know?"

"I don't know where he heard it. But Chau Chun was his friend." Jack gave Anna and her mother the party line: "He thinks the paintings are phonies and this is all about someone trying to cash in on Chau's reputation. He's trying to protect his friend."

Mrs. Yang's gaze remained steady on her teacup. Anna opened her mouth, but covered it with her hand instead of speaking. Jack went on, "Your father's very protective about Chau. I think they must have been pretty close. He was with Chau when he died." Watching Anna, ashen and silent, Jack asked, "He's never told you that story?"

She shook her head. "No. They were close? He was there? Daddy was at Tiananmen? Oh, my God. Mom, did you know that?"

"Yes." Yang Yu-feng's dark calm was unshaken. "I knew them both, when we were young."

"Why didn't I know? Why didn't anyone ever tell me that?"

Mrs. Yang raised her eyes to her daughter. "The story of that night? A terrible night in terrible times. Your father and I left it behind us when we left China. You are an American child. A new land, a new life. Why should we burden you with such times?"

After a moment, Anna asked, "Did you know Daddy had hired Jack?"

"Yes."

"Why didn't you tell me?"

"Anna, tell you what?" Her mother's voice sharpened. "You were working again, you were eating, sleeping. For months you had been lost, so unhappy. Now you have been going to the studio eagerly, now you have . . ." She shook her head, said it in Mandarin, then switched back to English. "Come back to life, you have come back to life. Why would I tell you about your father's troubles, your father's anger? It had nothing to do with you. Or so I thought."

Anna didn't answer.

"Anna," Jack said gently, after a few moments, "it might help if I tell you we already know you have them. The paintings, the Chaus."

Anna shook her head without looking at him. "No, I don't."

Jack glanced at Bill, who walked over and handed Jack his phone. It took Jack about ten seconds to find Shayna's photo and show it to Anna. She didn't reach for the phone, just stared. In a voice almost too low to hear, she said, "What was I thinking? This whole thing, what was I thinking?"

"What were you thinking about what? Anna, are the paintings real? Where are they?"

For a moment, nothing. Then Anna stood unsteadily and began to wander around the room as though she were lost in a strange place. Her mother's gaze followed her. "They're not real," Anna said softly. "I made them."

Jack glanced at me and at Bill. "Okay." He nodded. "So someone spotted them and the rumors started and the whole thing got out of hand. But that's not your fault. I can't imagine you claimed they were real, right? So what's going on? What's wrong?"

When Anna didn't answer Jack looked to Mrs. Yang. She didn't turn his way, just kept watching her daughter.

Anna stood at the window, fingering the curtain, gazing at a couple walking down the street. When she finally spoke I had to strain to hear her words. "I always loved Chau. He's not really taught in art school but I grew up with him."

Jack threw me a glance. "Does Dr. Yang have paintings? Is that what you mean?"

Anna nodded. "Three. Literally, I grew up with them—they were in my room."

Paintings that valuable, in the nursery? Mrs. Yang must have spotted me trying to keep my jaw from dropping. She said, "We hung them there to remind us. What was really precious, what was valuable, what could be lost."

"I see," I said.

Anna flushed. "But no one ever said anything about him," she went on. "Chau, I mean. Until I was old enough to go through Daddy's books and start asking questions. That's Daddy's way anyhow, waiting for people to ask things. Then he told me Chau's story, the outlines of it. And that he knew him, back in China. But that's all. I never knew . . . Mom, why didn't you tell me?"

Mrs. Yang stayed silent. Asked and answered already; Anna wouldn't get a second response. I recognized that Chinese-mother policy.

Anna gave up, started again. "But always, as long as I can remember, I loved those paintings, and Chau's other work in the books I found. It just . . . it spoke to me, in some special way. In art school I started copying it, over and over. Chau's paintings are so beautiful. Do you know them? Graceful, controlled linework, and such precarious composition . . . and they're so entirely political.

Completely committed, but never at the expense of the art. I wanted to learn from that. I wanted my work to be like that." She paused. "When I got back from China . . ." A catch in her voice; she went on, "When I had to leave without Mike, I was so angry, and so helpless. Daddy tried, and other people, and there's the whole movement here, but it's all about begging and waiting, isn't it? It's horrible." Another pause, this time longer. "I didn't know anything to do except make art out of it all. So I tried, but nothing worked out. It was all garbage and I threw it away.

"Then I started to think about Chau. What would he do, what would he make? I started a painting, not a copy but something new, using everything I knew about him. I used the same paper he did, the same inks. You can still get them, they haven't changed in centuries. It was the discipline, you know? The painting was pine branches, and a wren. Nothing political, just a technique exercise, but it absorbed me. I can't tell you how grateful I was for that, just to be able to be out of my thoughts for a while, putting ink on paper." She stopped, fingering the curtain.

"As I was finishing up, wishing it weren't over, I heard Mike's voice. Oh, not really." She shook her head impatiently, though none of us had said anything. "I wasn't crazy. But he used to read his poems to me, and I heard him reciting one about a tree in autumn, tall against a gray sky, alone as the cold wind blew the leaves away and the birds flew south. So in Mike's calligraphy, as closely as I could, I put the poem on the painting. Partly just because it kept the painting time going, you understand? That was what I wanted most. Then when it was almost done, I came in to work on it one day and it caught me by surprise. It really looked like a Chau. Not that I'm that good. Obviously I'm not, no matter how hard I work at his techniques or his style. An expert could tell, of course he could."

Her voice caught again; then she went on. "But I realized. The poem was what made it a Chau. The balance of politics and art. The funny thing is, it's not one of Mike's political poems, not when he wrote it. You can read it that way now, but then it was only about a tree. Before his trial, if someone had put it on a painting, that's all it would have meant. But now, a painting in Chau's style with a poem of Mike's—in China I'd have been arrested."

Maybe it was the comfort in telling the story, in saying Mike's name; maybe it was the relief in getting through it without dissolving in tears; or maybe it was just exhaustion; but Anna now turned back, stood for a moment, and then walked over to once again sit beside Jack. I stole a glance at her mother, found her still face unreadable.

Jack angled toward Anna, elbows on his knees. "I can't wait to see these paintings. You are that good and I bet they're spectacular. But I still don't get the problem."

Anna reached toward the coffee table, straightening photographs that didn't need it. "I pinned the painting up and started a second one. That one, I had a poem of Mike's in mind, about how lions and tigers can rampage through the forest but they can't stop the cicadas from singing. Tiny bugs, dozens of them, and a wild tiger face, a paw. . . . I was working on it when Pete came in. Pete Tsang, you know him?"

"Yes. We saw him last night, at East Village."

She stopped. "You went to the studio?"

"Because of the photo. I knew the papercuttings were yours." He added, "Can't miss 'em."

I was glad he'd said that because it brought a small smile from Anna. Not from her mother, though, and Anna's smile faded as she went on. "Pete's been working with an artists' freedom network for years. The kind of international human rights group the Chinese government hates. They took up Mike's case as soon as he got arrested. They won't give up. I don't know if they can do any good but at least they keep trying." She ran out of photos to straighten, so she drew her hands back to her lap. "Pete saw the paintings, the pine one and the one I was working on. No one else in the studio had any idea but Pete knew right away what they were and he understood why I was making them. He was the one who suggested, a couple of weeks later, that if people thought they were really Chaus, that might work for Mike."

"Pete said to claim they were authentic?" Jack asked skeptically. "That doesn't sound like him. And what did he mean? Help how?"

"We weren't going to claim they were authentic. But we weren't going to announce to the world they weren't, either. We were just going to show them. Next week."

"Asian Art Week," I said. I looked at the guys. "That's the splash."

Anna said, "Splash?"

"My client thought someone might be planning to unveil them next week, to make a big splash. I think he was thinking more art world than political, though. Or," I paused, reflecting on who my client was turning out to be, "maybe not."

Anna nodded. "It would explode. It's more than just Asian Art Week, it's Beijing/NYC. You know about that?"

"There was a poster outside your father's office."

"The Chinese government's bringing over a group of officially approved artists. They're showing off, how vibrant the art scene is in China, all that. It's a big deal, big opening party, all the critics, everyone.

"Chau may not be taught much, people here might not know

him, but everyone in that world, the collectors, the academics, everyone the government's trying to impress, they all know who he was and what he stood for. How he died. New Chaus with Mike's poems on them, even if we admitted they weren't real—'homages,' Pete said we'd call them, not 'fakes,' 'homages'—new ones with the poems of a jailed dissident, shown just when the government's turning the spotlight on their own artists, it would be a huge embarrassment. It would be a big loss of face in the international community."

"Weren't you worried?" I couldn't help asking. "That they'd take it out on Mike somehow?"

"No." She shook her head emphatically. "To bring attention to Mike, that was the whole point. Since there's a spotlight, to turn it on *him*. Keep his name in the news, remind people he's still in prison, that nothing's changed. China wouldn't dare do anything to him while the world was watching. During his trial, the world was. But people forget. Nothing happens and they move on to something else. The government counts on that with dissidents, that people will forget about them. We were going to remind people in a way the government would hate."

"But they found out," I said. "And that's the problem, why you called Jack? Samuel Wing came to you?"

Mrs. Yang looked up. Anna blinked. "Samuel Wing? Who's that?"

"Maybe he was calling himself something else, because Samuel Wing's a phony name anyhow. The guy from the Chinese Consulate. The skinny guy. He came to me, too."

Anna looked completely blank. "What? From the Chinese Consulate? No. What guy?"

It seemed I was having a hard time selling Samuel Wing this

morning. "A guy calling himself Samuel Wing said he'd heard I was looking for the Chaus and the people he represented wanted me to stop. He offered me money if I did and trouble if I didn't. That's not what this is about? The Chinese government threatening you?"

Anna shook her head. "The government? No. They don't know yet."

"I'm afraid they do. Mrs. Yang? Does Samuel Wing mean anything to you?"

"I do not know this man," Mrs. Yang replied, though I'd asked because she seemed a micron paler than before. "He said he was from the Consulate?"

"No. But he was. Though as of yesterday," I said to Anna, "he didn't know where the paintings were. He didn't know you had them."

"I don't have them," she said wearily. "That's what's wrong. That's not who came to me."

"Who did?" Jack asked.

"Doug Haig."

Jack and I looked at each other. "That revolting sleazebag creep?" I said. "What did he want?"

Bill gave up the standing at a distance thing and came over and sat down in the other armchair.

"When he first came he just wanted to see the paintings. I guess someone told him they were there."

"He's seen the photo." Bill spoke for the first time and Anna turned to him. "The woman who took it was showing him the sculpture."

"Tony Ling's? The foil?"

"She thought he'd like it. She still thinks that's what he was excited about."

"Poor Tony. Haig almost knocked that piece over, bulldozing past it." She pushed some loose strands of hair back from her forehead. "Haig had probably never been to Queens before in his life. He came in a limo. Someone saw it pull up and word raced through the building before he got to the front door. Everyone ignored him, to not be uncool, but everyone was praying he'd come to their studio. They stuck their heads out after he passed, to see where he was going. We could tell from the way he was galloping along like a hippo in a hurry that he wasn't there out of curiosity, to check out the show. He was on a mission. It never crossed anyone's mind, especially mine, that he was coming to see me. I just kept cutting. I looked up when he got to my door, just to watch him pass. I almost sliced my finger when he actually came in."

"You were papercutting?" I asked. "Not painting Chaus?"

"I'd done four Chaus by then. I had them up in the studio. They were . . . comforting. But at an open studio show, when people are wandering in and out all day, they like to see you making your work. The work they'll write up if they're critics, or the collectors will buy. People like to see it being born. And anyway, the Chaus were just for me."

"Not for Pete Tsang's bombshell show?"

"He hadn't suggested it yet. That came later. Partly because of Haig."

"I'm not following. Haig knows what Pete's planning?"

"No, that's not what I mean. When Haig got to my studio he barely glanced at my papercuttings but he spent a long time with the Chaus. It made me uncomfortable. They were for me, they were about Mike. He was wearing a loupe around his neck on a gold chain, how ridiculous is that? He leaned close and examined them, every inch. Then he turned to me, all oil and smiles, and said those were nice paintings, where did I get them? I almost laughed. It seemed like he actually wasn't sure if they were real. I got the sense he was hoping they were and I didn't know what they were worth, so he could steal them cheap."

"Did you tell him you'd made them?"

"No. He was so taken with them that it felt like bragging to say they were mine. They were none of his business, anyway. I wished I'd thought to take them down. I told him a friend had done them."

"Did he ask who?"

"And he got really mad when I wouldn't tell. Bottled-up mad, like he'd have screamed at me except losing it was beneath him. He told me I wasn't doing my friend a favor, and who did I think I was to stand between an artist and interest from Baxter/Haig? I promised I'd tell my friend. He left steaming, but what could he do? After he'd crashed out through the halls, Pete came to my studio to find out what was going on. 'You could hear us?' I asked him. 'We could feel it,' he said. 'Like an electrical storm. Your studio was shooting off sparks.' So I told him. He thought it was pretty hilarious that the paintings had convinced Haig. Then he got thoughtful, and he came back the next day with the idea of the show. I wasn't sure I wanted to do it, but I did take the paintings down."

"Why?"

"Well, first, the open studio was still on and I didn't want anyone else to drool over them the way Haig had. And if I did decide to go ahead with Pete's idea, we'd want to spring them on people. We needed them to be a surprise."

"But Haig had already seen them."

"Pete said that wasn't a problem. In case they were real, Haig would keep them to himself for now, until he'd browbeaten me into giving them up. And when we unveiled them, we could count on Haig to add to the hype because he'd go around telling everyone he'd seen them first and known right away what they were."

"Self-aggrandizement R us," Jack agreed. "Except didn't Haig think they were fakes? Didn't he believe in your 'friend'?"

"I think for a while he thought my friend might be Chau himself."

"Those paintings must be damn good. Haig's a parasite but he has an eye."

"No," said Anna. "Or if they're good, they're good imitations. But eye or not, we all see what we want to see."

"Meaning?" asked Bill.

Anna said, "Haig's in trouble. He needs money. That's the rumor, anyway."

"We've heard it," I said.

"I think the idea that the Chaus might be real, it was like a lifeline. If they were and he could get them cheap and sell them all his troubles would be over."

"Well, too bad for him, then."

Anna shook her head again. "That's the problem. It's dawned on him that it doesn't matter if they're real, as long as people think they are."

"But people wouldn't," I said. "As soon as you said you'd made them."

She didn't answer that right away. "I don't have them," she said after a pause. "I came in yesterday to work, and opened the drawer I'd had them in, and they were gone."

Bill and I exchanged glances. Jack said, "Someone stole them?"

"Doug Haig called an hour later. He has them."

"Someone sold them to him already? That was quick work."

"No," said Jack slowly. "Not sold them to him. Stole them for him. Am I right, Anna?"

She nodded. "I think so."

"Jon-Jon Jie. He has the studio beside you. He climbed over the wall."

I thought of the quiet building, the ceilingless studios.

"The security commissar," Anna said bitterly. "We've never protected ourselves from each other. Artists? What was someone going to do, steal your brushes? We lend each other everything all the time anyway, who'd steal? The only reason we lock our studio doors is so you don't have to go round up your stuff every time you come in. But all the real security worries were about the bad guys outside."

"Jie's signed with Baxter/Haig," Jack said. "Francie See told us. Just yesterday. She said she thought he bought his way in."

"Looks like he did," I said. "Just not with money."

"Haig has them," Anna went on, her voice suddenly urgent, "and he wants to put them on the market. As authentic."

"But how can he?" I demanded. "You'll just say you painted them. You'll show everyone the paper, and the ink, that it's easily available. And your sketches, don't you do sketches? How can he pretend they're real if you do that?"

"He says if I do that, he'll tell everyone I already sold them to him as authentic, for a lot of money. Because I'm Bernard Yang's daughter, so I knew he'd believe me. I cheated him and the only reason I'm admitting it now is I'm mad and I want to make him look stupid because Baxter/Haig wouldn't take me on. He's got a whole story cooked up, bills of sale and everything."

"Would people believe that?" I looked to Jack.

"If he's got paperwork," Jack said. "And the paintings are good enough. Maybe they would."

"It would make him look like an idiot," Bill said. "Buying fakes."

"A trusting, honest idiot," said Jack, "bamboozled by a cold-blooded cheap thief trading on her father's reputation. He'd look stupid but it would pass. But it would end Anna's career. No gallery would take her on, no one would show her."

Anna and her mother sat silent, Anna pale, her mother seeming tight-packed, like TNT.

"Still," I said. "Suppose Anna doesn't say anything, then. No one will pay Chau's prices without getting the paintings appraised. Wouldn't it take more than the supposed word of an expert's daughter and some old paper to get some other expert to put his reputation on the line, authenticating new work by someone who's supposed to be dead?"

Jack nodded, as though what I'd said had confirmed something. "Yes." He looked at Anna, waiting.

"Yes," Anna also said, and she didn't look at anyone. "That's why I called you, Jack. I don't know what good you can do, though. I don't know how you can help me. He says Daddy has to authenticate them."

16

It took Jack as long to persuade Anna to sit still and do nothing until she heard from us as it had to convince her to let me and Bill come along in the first place. As soon as she finished her story she decided we couldn't, in fact, help her. So she wanted to help herself. She wanted to call her father. She wanted her mother to call her father. She wanted to call Pete Tsang. She wanted to call the police. She wanted to race up to Doug Haig's gallery with a meat cleaver.

"That's why Dr. Yang fired me," Jack said. "We thought it was just because he found out you had the paintings."

"Haig called Daddy. He was afraid I wouldn't, that I'd be a martyr no matter what he threatened me with. 'Like your idiotic husband,' he said. 'Two self-righteous peas in a two-bit pod.'" She flushed crimson. "So he called Daddy, and Daddy called me. We had a big fight but I couldn't lie to him. I guess that's when he fired you."

"He's not really going to do it, is he?" I asked.

She didn't answer that directly. "Haig says he has until tomorrow morning to decide."

"If he doesn't," Bill asked, "is there someone else Haig could go to?" Jack and I looked at him. "Well, I'm assuming that, much as he'd love to destroy Anna's career because he's just a mean SOB, he'd rather get the paintings authenticated and make a fortune."

"Maybe there's someone," Anna said. "I don't know."

Jack said, "There aren't a lot of experts in that area, people who really know Chau's work. There's Clarence Snyder, in Chicago—I studied under him, he was on my committee. But he'd spot them for fakes, or at best, if they're really good, he'd give them a question mark. No, Dr. Yang's perfect. He's the biggest name, plus he's in a corner."

"He can't even be considering it," I said. "He just can't. This is exactly what he was afraid of. It's why he hired you. Someone making a big profit off of Chau's reputation. And for that someone to be Haig, and for him, Dr. Yang, for him to make it possible by *lying*—he just can't."

"I said that," Anna said. "Not the part about Chau's reputation, and him hiring Jack—I didn't know that. But I told him to call Haig's bluff. I'm such a nobody. What could it matter?" Mrs. Yang stirred, but Anna frowned and her mother said nothing. "But Daddy was so mad. He didn't hear a word I said. He just told me to stay here and do nothing until he called me. That was last night. But I couldn't do nothing. I just couldn't. I didn't sleep, not at all. When I called you this morning, Jack, I was thinking . . . I don't know why. I don't know what I thought you could do. I just . . ." She trailed off. "I just needed someone to help me."

There was silence. In it, I heard my own voice say, "We will."

So there we were, Jack and Bill and I, back in Bill's car, rolling through Queens, trying to find a place where we could think. "There's a diner over there." Jack pointed from the backseat.

"Pro," Bill said. "Coffee."

"Mrs. Yang's osmanthus tea didn't do anything for you?" I asked.

"For me, either," Jack admitted.

"And just when I was beginning to think you really were Chinese," I said. "Anyway, veto. Walls have ears."

"Your paranoia knows no bounds?" Jack asked. "We're in the middle of Queens. Maybe you're famous in Flushing, but me, I'm pretty well unknown around here."

"First: I don't believe you're unknown anywhere. Second: *around here* is where yesterday afternoon the security commissar scaled a wall and stole the paintings, right before the Chinese mob slapped a tail on us, tried to kidnap me, and shot at you."

"You have such a vivid way of making your points." Jack sat back with a sigh.

"Compromise," Bill said. "We stop at the diner, pick up coffee, and sit in the park. Unless you think the trees have ears."

"Tree ears," Jack said helpfully. "Those black mushrooms. My mother makes soup from them."

So with two coffees, a tea, and a giant cherry cheese Danish—Bill had apparently not had breakfast—we repaired to Flushing Meadow Park, where in the middle of a fresh spring morning you can sit on a lawn with toddlers chasing dogs, dogs chasing Frisbees, and, if you're lucky, no one chasing you.

"Okay, bigmouth," Jack said to me as he peeled back the tab on his coffee lid. "You told her we'd help her. What's the plan?"

"Me? You're the one who said, 'Whatever it is, we'll fix it.'"

"I was hoping you'd forgotten that." He turned to Bill. "How come you didn't make any promises?"

"I never do."

I said, "That way when he saves the day it's more of a wow because no one expects it."

"But you do have a plan?" Jack asked.

"Nope." Bill took a bite of the Danish, which was the size of his head. "Don't you?"

"What, a plan? To quote you, nope."

"Come on, use your imagination," I said.

Jack pondered. "Well, how about this? You could distract Doug Haig with your mind-blowing legs while Bill breaks into the gallery and resteals the Chaus."

"You've never seen my legs."

"You said to use my imagination."

"Besides, where are you in that plan?"

"Monitoring the proceedings from my office. Wearing a bullet-proof vest."

I sighed. "You mean, it's up to me as usual? Why is everything my job? Okay, but you'll have to give me a piece of that."

Bill held out the Danish. I tore off a fistful. Bill offered the hardly diminished hubcap to Jack, but he declined.

"Okay," I said. "The problem is, Haig has the paintings. I'm just thinking out loud here. But at least I'm thinking."

Jack said, "Ouch." Bill shrugged.

"If he didn't have them he could yell and threaten to expose people and throw as many hissy fits as he wanted and no one would care."

"Vladimir Oblomov could go to him, to buy zem," Bill said.

"If Haig thinks he can get them authenticated, he'll wait," said Jack. "He'll stall any buyers until he knows how high he can go."

"Besides, we don't have a couple of million dollars to buy zem vit," I said. "No, I'm thinking we really might have to steal them.

Jack's idea about my legs was ridiculous, but we could try something like it."

"How about my legs?" Bill offered.

"You mean, instead of seduction we try terror? No, we need a *real* idea."

A Frisbee flew long and landed on the pond with a plop. A shaggy black dog chased it to the shoreline, stood and barked, whined, and then, with a loud yip, charged in after it. He beelined across the water, clamped his jaws around the thing, and swam like hell for dry land.

"Or," I said.

"Or?"

"Or?"

"Or, we let Haig keep the paintings and get exactly what he wants."

"Which is what?"

"To have them authenticated."

I laid on them the scheme that had come to me. A lot of brow-furrowing and dog- and Frisbee-watching followed, and a great deal of discussion. Bill worked his way through two cigarettes while we did what he and I always do when we're making a plan: try to poke holes in it, look for solutions to all the problems we were likely to stumble over.

Jack joined in all that but he loved the idea from the start, as I knew he would.

"Because you get to show off," Bill said.

"Oh, like you didn't show off already, Lord of the Blings? But I do have an issue to raise."

I said, "And that would be?"

Jack leaned back on his elbows. "I want to remind you guys that

Doug the Slug, Anna, and Dr. Yang aren't the only people who're interested in these paintings. For reasons we haven't even learned yet, the US State Department, the PRC government, and the Chinese mob also care. And Pete Tsang's human rights group," he added. "Though them we can probably discount as a threat."

"And dere's da Russkie mob, too," said Bill.

"Please don't go native on us," I warned him. "Jack, once all those people know the paintings are fakes, don't you think they'll stop being interested?"

"I don't know. Since we don't know exactly what they were after in the first place."

I turned to Bill. He stubbed out his smoke. "He's right. It's not clear what we'd be getting in the middle of."

"But then what are you guys saying? It's too dangerous, this whole thing, and we should back off? How can we? Leave Anna and Dr. Yang twisting in the wind? That's just wrong."

"Back off?" said Jack. "Are you kidding? That's just wrong. But since it *is* dangerous—I speak as the guy who's been shot at twice—"

"Yeah, yeah, okay."

"—as that guy, what I'm saying is, if we're going to take Haig on, and whoever else, using this undeniably brilliant strategy you've just outlined, then all I'm suggesting is, maybe we should consider playing for higher stakes."

I cocked my head, regarding him. "You said before, there ought to be some way we could make something off of this."

"It was one of the things my mentor drilled into me when I was working out my business plan. Risk should be commensurate with reward."

"You had a business plan? For a PI office?" I turned to Bill. "So much for the whole wild-man thing."

"He's crazy," Bill said. "Not stupid."

"Thank you," Jack said gravely.

"Did you have a business plan?" I asked Bill.

"Not a chance. For a PI office? Listen, guys. We don't know how big the risk actually is. The government men on both sides could still be freelancing. They might easily both just fade away if there were real trouble involved."

"I question the 'easily,'" Jack said. "And Mighty Casey Woo didn't sound like he was going to fade away. And he has a gun."

"Well," I said, "if that's the direction you want to go in . . ."

So we explored that direction, looking from many angles at a reasonable risk/return ratio. By the time the coffee and tea were gone and even the goliath Danish had disappeared, we'd come up with what we thought was one heck of a plan.

17

Our first step was to get all the good guys on the same page. We ran into trouble right away: We wouldn't be able to talk to Dr. Yang until lunchtime. "He has a seminar," Jack said, clicking off from a short conversation with the department secretary. "I made us an appointment. Meanwhile, at least we know where he is."

"You mean, at least he's not out trying to do Doug Haig grievous bodily harm? Because that thought crossed my mind, too."

Next good guy, Anna. Jack put his phone on speaker. He didn't tell her what we were planning, just to sit tight, not to answer the phone if Haig called, and to wait until she heard from us. She couldn't believe we really had an idea, and if we did, that it was any good; except she wanted to so badly she was willing to do what we asked.

One of the things we asked was that she call Pete Tsang and tell him about the stolen paintings.

"Haig said not to tell anyone," she protested. "Daddy did, too."

"I know," Jack said. "But if Pete talks to the wrong people he could screw this up. We'll explain the whole thing later, when we have it all lined up. Just ask Pete to call me, okay? And don't worry."

It was a no-brainer that she was going to disobey that last

instruction, but she said she'd follow the others. Our next call was to the good guy who'd need the most lead time: Linus. I got his voice mail and told it what we needed. "Another Web site. Call Jack Lee"—I gave him Jack's number—"and he'll tell you exactly what to say on it and where to get material. You don't know him but you can trust him." Jack delivered a thumbs-up when he heard that. "It can look a little primitive, in fact it probably should. But here's the important part. I need it by four this afternoon. And Linus, it needs to be in Chinese."

Bill gave me raised eyebrows as I clicked off. "Is his Chinese up to that? As I recall, it's kind of primitive itself."

"That's okay," said Jack. "No one who matters who'll see this site can read Chinese, either."

The action switched back to Jack's phone. First, he called Chicago.

He'd objected when I'd first brought up Clarence Snyder. "That other expert," I'd said. "The one you studied with. Are you on good enough terms to call him?"

"Not to ask him to lie, no."

"Nothing like that. He's just insurance." I explained what I had in mind. Jack was skeptical, but my logic was irrefutably sound. He made the call, skirting the details but letting Dr. Snyder know he was working for the Yangs (which was sort of true) and that Doug Haig was trying to get over on them. In the end, since Jack promised to reveal all once the case was over and since Dr. Snyder wasn't being asked to do anything except tell the literal truth, he agreed. "More than just agreed," Jack said, hanging up. "He was impressively enthusiastic."

"Well, you said he was a friend of Dr. Yang's."

"And also, he knows Doug Haig."

The next event on Jack's phone happened almost immediately. Pete Tsang called. Jack didn't put him on speaker but the gist of the discussion wasn't hard to follow.

"I know," Jack said. "Well, you could do that. Or you could let Haig hang them out to dry. . . . Yes, we do. . . . Anna's on board. She told you? . . . No, because she doesn't know the details. . . . Pete. If you see Jon-Jon Jie, or Doug Haig . . . I said *if* . . . No, that would screw everything up. Just be your normal warm and fuzzy self. . . . Pete? Please? . . . Later on today. . . . Okay, great. Thanks."

"Reluctant?" I asked when Jack clicked off.

"Oh, he's fine. I just had to talk him out of blowing Jon-Jon Jie's brains out and stuffing what's left down Doug Haig's throat."

"Creative solution."

"He's an artist."

So our first three good guys were relatively easy pickings.

The fourth, we weren't even sure was a good guy.

"If he is, it'll be a lot simpler," I said. "He lied and we don't know what he's up to, but if he's on our side the whole thing will be easier."

The guys agreed, so I called my client.

He answered on the second ring. "Ms. Chin! News?"

"A whole lot of it. Mr. Jerrold."

Into the silence while he was thinking up how to respond, I said, "Don't bother. But we have to talk. I'd like you to meet me at my office."

A pause, then just, "When?"

"An hour from now."

What could he say?

We were about to pack up and leave our little paradise when an unexpected good guy called us. Jack's phone rang, and he answered it with, "Hi, Eddie. What's up? . . . Say again? . . . Seriously? . . .

Holy cow. Eddie, can I put you on speaker? I'm here with Lydia and her other partner."

That brought a snort from Bill. I swatted him. Jack pressed the button and lowered the phone, holding it so we could all hear. "Guys, this is Eddie To. Eddie, if you hear a voice you don't know, it's Bill Smith. Eddie, go ahead and tell Lydia and Bill what you just told me."

"Hi, Lydia, and good to meet you, Bill," Eddie To said politely. I pictured him in his gallery surrounded by giant springs and speeding red boxes. "I called Jack because I'm being a source. A gent from the Chinese Consulate was just up here. Wei-mai Jin. Jin Wei-mai it would be in the patois of Mother China, which I don't speak. He's the Cultural Attaché."

"Eddie, it's Lydia," I interrupted. "About five-nine, skinny, receding gray hair?"

"No. Smaller, chubby, bald."

I glanced at the guys. "Okay, go on."

"He's been here before, has Mr. Jin, in his position as culture vulture. I've also seen him at receptions and such, once or twice in the company of a fellow like you're describing, if that helps."

"That other fellow, do you know his name?"

"No. Frank's fluent in four dialects of the mother tongue, plus Japanese, so he gets the eastern hemisphere VIPs. I get the French and all those stodgy Germans, plus the occasional Argentine, olé. But Frank's not here today, so Mr. Jin was all mine. I thought it would interest Jack and Co. to know he was after Chau Chun."

"Chau himself? He said that?"

"No, I'm sorry, the paintings. The rumored ones you and Jack were up here asking about yesterday."

"Eddie, this is Bill. What did he say, exactly?"

"Hi, Bill. Exactly, he said he'd heard someone was trying to pass off forged Chaus as real and was that a circumstance we here at Red Sky were familiar with?"

"It sounds almost like an accusation," I said.

"From the PRC Cultural Attaché, it's always an accusation. Understand, the role of Cultural Attaché is rarely played by anyone cultured. Mr. Jin's the third in that job since Frank and I opened this gallery. It's a reward position they give to party-liners who can be trusted out of the country and might enjoy a little capitalist R & R. Just like *Ninotchka*. There are other people at the Consulate whose job is to actually know things, but knowledge can be dangerous, so they have the Cultural Attaché to keep an eye on those people and to look after the government's and the Party's interests. At least that's what Frank always says, while I'm filling him full of martinis after an afternoon at the Consulate trying to get visas for our artists."

"So this Mr. Jin, he thought you had the Chaus?"

"I doubt it. It's a reflex with him, to make threats."

"Did he make a specific threat?"

"Why waste the opportunity? He told me regretfully that 'a lot of Chinese artists might have to be protected from the corruption of the Western art markets'—which means they'd have trouble getting visas—'if forged paintings falsely attributed to a discredited bourgeois counterrevolutionary were exhibited in New York in a blatant attempt by calculating capitalists to embarrass the People's Republic.' Which, by the way, is a direct quote. I liked it so much I wrote it down as soon as he left, so Frank could hear it."

"It sounds to me like he does think you know something about the paintings."

"No, he's probably going to all the galleries where they might

turn up, to see if he can learn anything and to make sure everyone's disinclined to get involved with them if they do. Except to
call him. That, it seems, would put him in our debt. So? How'd
I do? Now you know the Chinese Consulate cares, too. Is that important news? Can I be Deep Throat?"

"Eddie, you're the very epiglottis," Jack said. He didn't mention
we already knew the Chinese Consulate, or at least someone up
there, was interested in this case. "Thanks. Stand by and keep your
ear to the ground. Report in if you hear anything else."

"Yes, sir, Mr. Bond. Over and out."

The phone went silent and we all three looked at each other.
"Well," said Jack.

"No kidding," I answered.

"What now?" Bill asked.

I thought. "We have to go see Dr. Yang, but before that, I have
to get back to Chinatown to meet with my client. Maybe after *that,*
we should consider dropping in at the Chinese Consulate."

"Right up in their faces?" Jack asked.

"Maybe. First things first."

We gathered up our garbage and our cell phones and headed for
the car. Bill unlocked it, said, "Saddle up!" and we were back on the
road.

We'd reached the Manhattan Bridge and were admiring the
view when Jack's phone rang once more. He checked it. "A 718
number I don't know. Maybe it's your cousin. Jack Lee," he told the
phone. "Yes, hi, Linus, good to meet you. . . . I know. You ready? . . .
Well, but it doesn't have to be good Chinese. . . . No, not even . . .
Great. Here's what we need. Go to my Web site . . ." The conversation got art-technical from there, Jack directing Linus to a few
places online, listening to Linus's questions and suggestions, re-

sponding with his own. By the time we'd reached Bill's parking lot they were done. "He thanks you for your faith in him," Jack said to me, slipping his phone into his pocket.

"Was he being sarcastic?"

"No, just nineteen."

18

We'd debated whether the guys should be in on my confab with my client.

"I've never even seen the guy," Bill said.

"I have, but I bet he couldn't tell me from Daniel Dae Kim," Jack said.

"A common mistake, no doubt."

"It's the broad shoulders and smoldering brow. Still, it could be useful. Him not knowing what we look like."

"You could hide in the closet," I suggested.

"Both of us?" Jack said. "I think it would have to be the bathroom."

"What if her client has to pee?" Bill asked.

So we decided to come clean with Dunbar/Jerrold, in the hopes that he'd come clean with us.

Bill stuck his head in at Golden Adventure as we passed and was rewarded with the usual waves and smiles.

"Guess you don't need panic button today, Lydia!" Andi Gee called.

"No, I'm good," I agreed, unlocking my door.

"I don't get it," Bill complained as he followed me in. "They all like me. Why doesn't your mother?"

"You flirt with them."

"I could flirt with your mother," he offered. The idea did not merit a reply.

"I'm going to hear about you, too," I told Jack. "You know our dinner last night was all over the Chinatown telegraph? The aunties think you're cute."

Jack gave Bill a smug grin.

Bill, in response, went to my desk drawer and retrieved his ashtray. He'd just lit up when the doorbell buzzed. I buzzed back, and we waited.

Dennis Jerrold, aka Jeff Dunbar, pushed my door open but stopped with his hand on the knob when he saw Jack and Bill.

"Come in, Mr. Jerrold."

"Who're they?" He showed no sign of recognizing either of them, which I guessed spoke well of Jack's lurking-and-tailing talents.

"Colleagues," I said. "Bill Smith, Jack Lee. Guys, this is Dennis Jerrold, who likes to be called Jeff Dunbar."

"What are they doing here?" Jerrold/Dunbar ignored the introduction.

"Working the same case."

"What does that mean?"

"I told you there was another investigator with another client. Bill's my partner; Jack's the other investigator." This time the smug smile went from Bill to Jack.

"Who's the other client?"

"I didn't tell you before and I'm not going to tell you now. But I do have other things to tell you. And some to ask you."

"I don't want them here."

"I don't care. The three of us are working on this together. I'm following through on what I've found no matter what you think about it and don't start with the stuff about your dime. I offered you your money back and you said no. Unless you've changed your mind, come in and sit down, Mr. Jerrold."

So much for the whole Jeff Dunbar thing. Another hesitating moment, and Dennis Jerrold shut the door and sat. Jack was in the other chair; Bill, of course, was standing, though there's not much to be seen through my pebbled alley window.

"We found the paintings," I said.

Jerrold halfway stood again. "You have them?"

"No. I said we found them. We know where they are but there are complications."

"What do you mean, 'complications'?" He settled back down, recognition in his eyes. "A shakedown, is that it? Now that you have them it's going to cost me?"

I sat back in my springy chair. "Why is it," I asked the air, "that everyone involved in this case is so hard to help? So *suspicious*? But come to think of it, maybe this is a shakedown. Yes, sure, call it that. It's going to cost you, Mr. Jerrold. Just not money. A lot of that going around, too. I'll tell you what we know if you tell us what you know. And you have to go first. Why did you come to me and why use a false name? Why does the State Department care about a dead Chinese artist?"

He stared. "The State Department?"

"You know, if you start denying everything this could take all morning. State Department, Assistant Deputy Director, East Asia Section, China specialist. And speaking of China: the PRC government, why do they care? The phony Mr. Wing is from the Chinese Consulate and I'm pretty sure you know that, and you were supposed to call and tell me and you never did. The real Mr. Jin, is, too, do you know him? Now either tell me what's going on or take your money back and get out of here."

Jerrold's expression was that of a man trying to choose a path through uninviting but unavoidable terrain. He extemporized. "Is it considered professional in your field to talk that way to people who hire you?"

"Is it in yours, to lie to people you hire?"

"He's a diplomat," said Bill. "I think it is."

"That was unnecessary," Jack said. "Sorry, Mr. Jerrold. But you can see how it's frustrating to try to do your job when your client doesn't even trust you to know his name."

What was this? They were doing Good Cop/Bad Cop without me?

"Whoever you are, I'm not your client," Jerrold said.

"And you're about to not be mine in a minute," I said. "Unless we get some answers." When Good Cop and Bad Cop are already taken, there's always Steamroller. "Besides the guy with the gun I told you about yesterday, there's the matter of the Chinese gangster."

"Who also had a gun," Jack said.

"He suggested I stop looking for the Chaus because he has an investment to protect. What investment, Mr. Jerrold? And the so-called Samuel Wing, who made the same suggestion, though he wouldn't say why, and the mysterious Mr. Jin, who'd also rather these paintings didn't see the light of day. Who are all these people and what the hell is going on here?"

The question, besides being phrased in stronger language than I generally use, was admittedly disingenuous. I had, in essence, the information Jerrold had paid me to get: where the paintings were.

And the bonus fact, that they were fakes. Nevertheless, we waited, all three of us staring my client down.

Dennis Jerrold drummed his fingers on the arm of his chair. "How did you find out my name? Where I work?"

"Oh, please, Mr. Jerrold. You're a diplomat, we're investigators. Would I be surprised if you negotiated a treaty, or whatever it is you people do? Okay, nuts to the whole thing." I spun in my chair to reach my safe, which doubled as the sideboard with the tea set I wasn't serving Dennis Jerrold tea from. Turning my back on a client isn't something I consider good practice, but it's great drama and with Bill and Jack there I wasn't worried. I ran the dial, extracted the envelope holding Jerrold's thousand dollars and tossed it on my desk. "If this is the level of trust we've got going you'll be happier with some other PI anyway."

He made no move to take it. "The paintings," he said. "Were you able to ascertain whether they're real?"

"Yes."

"And?"

I waited a moment, then gave it to him: "They're fakes."

He visibly relaxed.

"But they're about to come on the market as real. Authenticated by an expert. Next week. Asian Art Week, Beijing/NYC."

"But you say they're fakes. What expert would put his reputation on the line like that?"

"That's not really the question. The question is, how bad would it be for you if it happened?"

After a moment he gave a soft laugh. "The funny thing is, it wouldn't matter. In my situation, I can be a hero—though that's looking less and less likely—but I can't really be the goat. Nice work if you can get it, huh? No, keep the money, Ms. Chin. If it's true you've found the paintings. It would be nice if we could keep them from hitting the market, but if they're fakes the authentication won't—"

"We might be able to."

"What?"

"Keep them off the market. Or maybe not, but we can probably discredit them with a bang. And the person who's going to be selling them. If we had a reason to. Would that work for you?"

He leaned back in his chair. "Do tell."

"No, you tell. Give us that reason. What so-called heroics are you engaged in here and how was I supposed to be helping?"

"Well," he said. "Well." He looked around. "I suppose it's reasonable to hope for a certain amount of discretion from all of you, even though I'm only paying Ms. Chin?"

"Actually, you're paying Bill, too. And Jack's one of us, so don't worry about it." I didn't look to see who was smug-smiling whom.

"Fine. Not that it really matters. I wasn't doing anything wrong, just . . . unauthorized. Going to you could earn me a reprimand, or, on the other hand, a commendation for creativity. If I tell you what I know—which I can already see won't answer all your questions—then what? You'll tell me where the paintings are?"

If I'd had any doubt Jerrold was a diplomat I'd be over it by now. Everything was a negotiation. I decided to stonewall.

We sat in silence; then Jerrold smiled. "Okay. Point made." He crossed one leg over the other, settling in more comfortably. "As you surmised, I'm with the State Department."

Surmised? We knew his job title.

"I've been there eight years. I'm not an art collector, in fact I'm not in the visual arts at all. Literature's my field. But we all talk, and you hear things."

"We all talk, who?"

"State Department staff, and our Consulate counterparts. In my case, the PRC Consulate. That's where I heard about the Chaus, at a reception. Buzz in the air, worried looks, things like that. The Cultural Attaché, Jin, had heard rumors and he wasn't happy. They have that Beijing/NYC show coming up, the whole Asian art world's watching. If the PRC gets embarrassed here in New York it's on Jin's head. Xi Xao, the guy at my level in the visual arts over there, dismissed the whole thing. He tried to persuade Jin not to worry about it. He said no one could possibly take these paintings seriously, everyone knew Chau was dead. I guess he changed his mind, though, or at least, he couldn't convince Jin, because I think Xi's who came to you as Samuel Wing."

"Older, skinny, receding gray hair?"

"Yes."

"I'm still not clear. If they decided to look for the paintings after all and asked you for help, why did Xi come to me to get me to lay off?"

"They didn't ask for help. First off, it wouldn't have been me, it would've been one of our visual arts people. But they didn't. Jin just scowled and Xi tried to jolly him up and they both drank scotch. No, what happened was, I was watching Xi fawning on his boss—a guy at least ten years younger than Xi, and nowhere near as educated or as smart—and my boss came over to join us and I had a lightbulb moment. It hit me that if I didn't watch out I'd be Xi before I knew it. You know the difference between staff jobs and line jobs?" I shook my head. Bill and Jack, I noticed, both nodded. "Well, it's what it sounds like." Seemingly instinctively, Jerrold offered his explanation to all three of us, so I wouldn't feel like the only dummy in the room. Very diplomatic. "Line does. Staff supports. At State you almost always start as staff but, like anywhere, line's where the action is. Eight years, I suddenly realized, was borderline too long to still be staff. There's a point beyond which you don't get promoted because you haven't been promoted, and I'm getting near it. I needed to make a move."

"And Chau was your move?"

"Xi kept telling Jin he should ignore the rumors, that the paintings were obviously fakes and any notice they paid would do nothing but stir up interest in them. Jin was unhappy but he agreed that he didn't want to draw attention. Someone poured another round and the talk moved on to other things.

"And I thought, well, okay. The PRC government looking for these paintings did have the potential to raise the paintings' profile. Xi was right about that. But if collectors were already looking, one more collector wouldn't matter."

"So it wasn't about their value? And it wasn't about making a name for yourself?"

He smiled. "It absolutely was, both things. But their value's not in money, it's in the PRC's diplomatic face, and the name I'm looking to make isn't in the art world."

"If you had the paintings, what would you do with them? Take them to Xi, at the Consulate?"

"No, to Jin. If I went to Xi he'd go to Jin, and that would get him some of the credit, diluting things for me."

I nodded, considering that. "Speaking of Xi, Mr. Jerrold, how did Xi find out about me and why did he want me to stop?"

"I don't know about the first. The second, I suppose it's because, as he said, he thinks making waves is the wrong approach."

"It was a lot of money to stop some waves that might turn out not to matter. His, I wonder, or the PRC's?"

"Well, probably his. Like what I gave you was mine. The PRC isn't that free with its purse strings."

I sat back. "All right, Mr. Jerrold. Here's what I think we can do. The paintings are fakes but they're about to be authenticated. Then they'll be shown."

"I thought you said you might be able to stop that."

"We'll be able to keep them off the market. Maybe not to stop their being shown. But they'll be discredited and the whole thing will look like a high school prank. But you can still be a hero."

"Oh? How's that?"

"The paintings have poems on them. Chinese classical paintings often do," I added loftily. "Since the Yuan Dynasty."

"I do know that much, Ms. Chin."

"These particular poems are by Liu Mai-ke. Mike Liu."

"Ah." Jerrold rubbed at his chin. "Ah, damn."

"It's true, then? That might be a problem?"

"Chau and Liu, together? A dissident double-team. Jin'll hate it."

"If it turns out the paintings will be shown, I'll warn you and you can warn Mr. Jin. Or tell your boss to warn him. At least it won't be a surprise. The PRC can prepare a response. That should win you points."

"Interesting thought. Not as many points as I'd hoped for from this, but it can't hurt. Although if you told me where the paintings are—"

"Not going to happen." I pointed to the money-stuffed envelope on my desk. "You can take that back if you want to, but right now that's all you're getting. If things change, I'll call you."

He eyed me. "They might?"

"You never know."

Chinatown's so near NYU that we walked up. As we neared Dr.
Yang's building I called his office. First hurdle jumped: he answered.
I asked in a breathy voice for an appointment because I was an unde-
cided student looking for guidance about my major. He blew me off,
suggesting—really, ordering—that I talk to Dr. Somebody Else.
Didn't matter, though. By then we were in the building and we knew
he was, too.

We caught him eating lunch behind his desk: pork dumplings
from the Rickshaw truck accompanied by green tea in a rough pottery cup. The room smelled terrific, salt and onions, very homelike,
but the comforting nature of his lunch mellowed Dr. Yang out not
one bit.

"What are you doing here, Jack?" Dr. Yang lowered his chopsticks to glare at us.

"We know what's going on," Jack said without preamble. "We
want to help. We have a plan."

After a moment: "Get out."

"No." Not only didn't Jack leave, he sat. I admired his courage
and then realized I needed to do something, too, so I parked on the
other chair. Bill wandered over to the window to look down at the
world. "We've just come from Anna's," Jack told Dr. Yang. "We knew
about the paintings before we went, the phony Chaus. We found out
about them more or less the same way Doug Haig did. Anna tried
not to tell us anything but she was too upset to fake it. We know
what Haig wants and we can stop him."

That was a tricky amalgam of three-quarter truths, but we
wouldn't get anywhere if, as it was threatening to, the top of Dr.
Yang's head blew off.

Dr. Yang, stiff-arming his desk, said in a voice he was obviously trying to control, "You don't know what you're dealing with. Or who's involved. I fired you for a reason. Keep out of this, Jack."

"You fired me to protect Anna. That's what I'm trying to do. And we do know. Government people from all directions. Chinese gangsters. And Doug Haig. We can deal. We're just asking you not to do anything right now. Haig wants you to appraise and authenticate the fake Chaus. Just stall him. That's all."

After a six-ton silence, Dr. Yang, oddly, picked up on just one of Jack's points. "Government people?" He stared as though Jack had turned into a Klingon. "What do you mean, government people? They went to you? You didn't tell me?"

"Not to Jack. To me," I said. Dr. Yang snapped his head toward me. His expression made me think I might be a Klingon, too. "From two governments. My client, who isn't a collector. He's with the State Department. And a fellow from the Chinese Consulate, too."

Fury, bafflement, fear, and a need to know battled it out on Dr. Yang's face. Maybe because he was an academic, the need to know won out. "From the Chinese Consulate? Who?"

"He said his name is Samuel Wing, but we think it's really Xi Xao."

It seemed to me a light dawned in Dr. Yang's eyes and was quickly not extinguished, but hidden. "What did he want?"

"You know him," I said.

"Don't be ridiculous. How would I know him? What did he want?"

"He wanted me to stop looking for the Chaus. Who is he?"

"To stop, on behalf of the Chinese government?"

"I don't know. He didn't tell me he was a diplomat. He gave me a phony name so I wouldn't find out. But on the other hand he said he was representing 'interested parties,' and he threatened me. Who are his interested parties?"

"He threatened you?"

"If I kept looking. And offered me a lot of money if I'd stop. Why does he care?"

"If he didn't tell you he was a diplomat, how did you find out?"

"Why do people keep asking how I find things out? I'm a private eye. Like Jack. Like Bill. People hire us to find things out. I looked into Mr. Wing because I don't respond well to being threatened. Or to being bribed."

"Like me," said Jack.

"Or me," said Bill.

"I can go to the Consulate and ask him what's going on. Or you can tell us. We want to help. Please let us. Tell us who he is. Tell us why he cares."

"No." Dr. Yang looked us over. "You can't help. You can only create a disaster out of what's already a bad situation. Clearly worse than I thought, and I can tell you it was already grim. The State Department man. Does he want you to stop looking, too?"

I didn't anwer, just met his angry eyes. If there'd been a heat differential between our glares there'd have been a thunderstorm in the middle of the room. Surprisingly, Bill stepped in.

"The State Department man doesn't want us to stop, no. He's Lydia's original client. The one who claimed to be a collector. He wanted us to find the paintings. We just came from a meeting with him. We told him we'd found them."

Dr. Yang went white. "You told him about Anna?"

"No," I said. "We said we'd found the paintings and ascertained that they were fakes. We told him that's all he gets right now."

"Right now? When does he get more?"

"I don't know. Maybe soon, maybe never. It depends on you."

After a long stare, Dr. Yang asked, "What was his interest in the paintings?"

"I'm not going to tell you that. But you don't have to worry about him. You have to worry about Doug Haig and what he wants from you. Just give us an inch or two, Dr. Yang. We really are here to help you. And Anna."

Dr. Yang, dumplings forgotten, laid his palms carefully on his desk. "All right, I appreciate that you're trying to help. And that you think you can. But you can't. As I told you, you can only make things worse. I have to ask you again not to interfere."

He stared at us, ranged around the far side of his desk, and we all stared back. It's a good thing stubbornness has no smell or you'd have needed a gas mask to breathe in there.

"With all respect, sir," Jack said evenly, "I'm not sure how we could make things worse. Isn't it already a disaster? What are your options? To junk your principles to save your daughter's future? Or stick to your guns and watch Anna go down in flames? Ghost Hero Chau—your *friend*—died for his beliefs, why? So Doug Haig can pay off his house in the Hamptons? And you'd better have negotiated a job as his houseboy, because if you do what Haig wants and it ever comes out, your career's in the toilet, too."

From Dr. Yang's bugging eyes I guessed people didn't generally talk to him this way. "If it comes out? Are you threatening me, Jack?"

"No," Jack said. "None of us would stitch you up like that. But it wouldn't have to be us. Lots of people saw Anna working on those paintings. All the artists out at East Village saw them. Mostly they didn't know what they were, but as soon as they're splashed all over *ARTnews,* sold for half a million each and authenticated by you, you're toast."

Dr. Yang replied through clenched teeth. "*With all respect*. Jack. There is nothing you can do. There is *nothing* you can do but make things worse. You're taking a risk you don't understand. You'll—"

"You're wrong! We can take Haig down. At least we can try. Just give us a chance. If we screw up, we come out looking like idiots and your so-called options are still open. What could we make worse?"

It was a persuasive argument, I thought, but it didn't move Dr. Yang. He looked like he was struggling not to explode out of his chair, leap the desk, and stomp Jack into a puddle.

Chinese standoff, I thought, in the loaded silence that followed. Locked eyes across the generations. Kind of like me and my mother.

"Dr. Yang," I said, reaching for an answer I thought I was starting to see, "Doug Haig isn't the only threat here, is he? These paintings have put Anna in some other kind of danger, too. Something to do with Samuel Wing, or Xi Xao, or whoever he is. So something to do with the Chinese government. Is it about her husband? Mike Liu? Is he at risk, or is she, because of these paintings?"

Dr. Yang's face got darker. I braced for an explosion but it didn't come. Without warning he slumped back against his chair. "Not Anna." He spoke low, sounding defeated. I was surprised to see him that way and I wasn't sure I liked it. "The only threat to Anna is the one you know. Nor Mike. The man in danger is Xi Xao."

19

"Xi Xao?" I asked. "Samuel Wing?"

After a silence, the professor nodded. "The man who came to you calling himself Samuel Wing is a career PRC government official and a ranking Party member. For the last nine years he's been in New York, assigned to the Cultural Section of the Chinese Consulate, but at the time of the Tiananmen Square protests he was a middle-level commissioner working out of the central government offices in Beijing." His words rasped; he reached for his tea, by now long cold. "His father and mine were sworn brothers. Not related by blood, but as close as if they had been. Xi Xao is older than I, but we were each our parents' only child and we lived on the same lane. We grew up as elder and younger brother, as close as our fathers were.

"I was in Tiananmen Square when the tanks came, trying to persuade my friend and my students to leave. However, my motives didn't matter. Like the true protestors, I was fired on, I ran, and the next day orders had been issued for my arrest.

"I went into hiding, moving furtively from place to place, thinking I'd be discovered every minute. Almost hoping for it, because at least that would end the fear. But I wasn't. When weeks had passed and government vigilance had slackened, I went to Xi Xao for help. It wasn't the right thing to do. It put him in an impossible position. But there were . . . reasons." He looked away. "My wife was pregnant. If I had been arrested she might have been, also. A baby born in a Chinese prison . . ." He trailed off, but it wasn't a sentence he really had to finish. "Xi Xao helped me hide, and, finally, with false documents, helped Yu-feng and myself leave the country. As an obligation of friendship, his and mine, and our fathers', too."

Dr. Yang stopped and picked up his cold tea. "Three days ago he came to see me. He'd heard these rumors, about the new Chaus, and he was bothered. He'd rather that whole era did not get stirred up again. I told him I hadn't heard anything, but that I'd look into it, something that in his position he couldn't risk doing."

"So you came to me," said Jack.

"Yes, Jack. I went to you." Dr. Yang drank his cold tea in small, deliberate sips. Just before he spoke again I realized what he was really doing: refilling his reservoir of steely resolve. Now he once more looked around the room, impaling each of us with his you-fail eyes. As though this were a group thesis exam and he were asking the question on which our doctorates would rise or fall, he said, "Do you understand what will happen to this man, my friend, who saved my life, and my wife's, and my daughter's, if this becomes known?"

Jack, the only one of us to actually have a doctorate, and thus to have been through this before, was first to break the silence. "Yes, sir, I think we do."

"Do you, Jack? Well, let me make it clear." The tea and the break had worked; we were back to full frontal Bernard Yang in all his ferocious glory. "He'll be called back to China. He'll be tried, and he'll be executed. Executed. Are any of you prepared to take responsibility for that? I didn't think so. Then do as I say. Get up now and leave." He waved us away with the back of his hand. "Don't repeat what you've just heard, go about your business, forget Chau Chun. It will be better for everyone."

I looked at Jack, and at Bill. A brief flurry of eyeball discussion, and then I turned to Dr. Yang. "Professor, if Xi Xao were the only person with a stake in this, we might agree to back off. But he's not. There's my client, who brings the American State Department in. There are Chinese gangsters who claim to have an investment, in what we're not sure, but they're part of this one way or another and they care enough to shoot guns around."

"Is that who shot at Jack yesterday?"

"Maybe. They for sure shot at him last night."

"Last night? You didn't tell me that." Dr. Yang sent a look at Jack, who shrugged.

"Yes," I said. "In Queens. They said they wanted to 'talk.' We scared them off—Jack did—and we're not sure what they're really up to, but it can't be good. And there's Doug Haig, and of course, you and your daughter. Our turning our backs won't make any of those people go away, or make the situation any less complicated."

"And your continuing to stir up these waters?" Dr. Yang said scornfully. "You can see a way that that will help?"

"If you stir the water vigorously enough," I said with care, "you can drag mud up from the bottom. In all that swirling, muddy water, a lot of things might be able to escape."

I didn't dare look at Jack or Bill, though I could hear Bill softly stifling a snort, and from the corner of my eye I saw Jack's eyebrows shoot up. So what? The look Dr. Yang was giving me had gone from angry disdain to guarded interest. The interest was tinged with desperation, true, but then, his position was desperate. I pressed on before he had a chance to regroup. "When we came in here, we had a plan," I said. "Now we have new information, so we need to amend it. But I think we can still make it work."

"You *think*? 'Make it work'? No. That's unacceptable."

"Sir," said Jack, cutting me and my frustration off, "Doug Haig gave you until tomorrow morning to answer him. He's expecting you to stew, look at your options, realize you don't have any, and agree. All we're asking you to do is not answer him until then. For our part, once we have things worked out, we won't make a move until we run the whole plan by you. If you're afraid it'll make things worse or you just plain think it won't work, we'll drop it and you can handle things however you want." Jack gazed evenly at Dr. Yang across the desk. "Fair enough?"

After a very, very long silence, Dr. Yang spoke. "Will my daughter be in danger at any time?"

"Danger? You mean, physical danger?"

"There are gangsters and guns involved. From what you say."

The "from what you say" wasn't lost on Jack, but he didn't rise to it. "I don't think they have any interest in Anna. The biggest danger she's in is to her career, and it's from Haig."

"And Xi Xao?"

"We understand." Jack leaned forward again. "Please, Dr. Yang. Give us a few hours. That's all we need."

Another long silence. Then, almost imperceptibly, Dr. Yang nodded.

Back outside, us Three Musketeers stood near the fountain, where a trio of jugglers tossed bowling pins and baseball bats back and forth.

"So, what do you think, guys?" I said. "Can we run this scam and not jeopardize Xi? I didn't like his threats and bribes and all, but if his life's at stake I guess I can cut him some slack."

Jack said, "I think we can, just the way we set it up. Whatever excitement it creates about the old days, it'll die down when we're through and everyone will look silly. That's the whole point, isn't it?"

He and I looked at each other, and then both of us turned to Bill. "What do you think?"

"I'm with Jack. If this works no one will be looking past it."

"If?" said Jack. "Hold it, I didn't sign on for 'if.' We're not doing 'if.'"

"Fine. *When* this works. How's that?"

"Much better. Because after all, isn't this a plan of Lydia's? So the chances of it working, aren't they like one hundred percent?"

So we split up. Each of us had work to do. And I had to change.

"Hi, Ma," I said, leaving my shoes by the door and entering the living room in my slippers.

"Oh, have you come home in the middle of the day? Why, are you ill?" She must not have been too terribly worried because after a glance she went back to ironing in front of the TV, watching two handsome Chinese actors in Tang Dynasty outfits having a low-voiced discussion. The camera lingered on them so portentously that it could only mean a conspiracy was in the making and an emperor was going to fall. Or else these two guys would end up with their heads chopped off.

"I'm fine, Ma. I just need some things."

She didn't say a word, so why did I hear disapproval?

In my room I put the phone on speaker, turned the computer on, and called Linus.

"Cuz!" he greeted me. "Just about done. You want to see it?"

"I sure do."

"'K, here comes the link."

I opened my e-mail, found the Web site URL he'd sent, and clicked on it. "Wow, Linus, I'm impressed. You did all this in two hours?"

"Hey, it's what we do here. I used a template I had from some other site I made for a guy. This one wasn't a big deal, 'cause it doesn't really say anything."

"I can see that." I was scanning the Chinese text.

"You sure that's okay? I mean, I just stole chunks from Chinese Web sites, I don't even know about what."

"Positive, it's fine."

"But in case your guys want to check a little deeper I put in a couple of links, like to the University, and to some artists. Even if they don't read Chinese they can tell they're links, so they can click. I also put in a bunch that don't work, they give you an error message. So it looks like they're supposed to be live but it's a crappy Web site."

"Excellent."

"And I paid a few bucks to a couple of search engine companies, so this site'll come up first if you Google him. The real guy, he doesn't have a site, so you lucked out there. He does have a Wikipedia page, so I put a link on it." Linus burst into song: "If you liked it then you shoulda put a link on it!"

"Okay, thanks, Linus."

"Sorry. Anyway, the University, I couldn't hack their site to put a link back to here."

"I thought you could do anything. No, I'm just kidding, we don't need that."

"My Chinese isn't good enough, is all," he said defensively. "I could totally hack it if it was English. But I know some guys. Do you—"

"No, really, the people this is for, their Chinese is way worse than yours. I don't see them bothering with the University site, and if they do they won't be able to navigate it so they won't know what they're not finding. Listen, really, Linus, thanks. The whole thing looks great. Especially the picture."

"Just a little Photoshop," he said modestly. "So, Cuz, who is that guy? Is he really another Chinese PI?"

"I'll tell you all about it. Later."

"That's what Trella said you'd say. Does Bill know about him?"

"Know what about him?"

"That's what Trella said you'd say! Dudess!" I heard him call across the room. "I owe you five bucks! So, Cuz, you need me anymore?"

"I don't think so, but I don't know," I answered truthfully.

"If you do, you know where to find me. I'm going back to bed."

I changed my clothes, called Jack, got his voice mail, and left him a message to check the new Web site. There was no point in telling Bill that, but I called him anyway, just to say it was done and that I was heading out.

"You okay?" he wanted to know.

"Raging adrenaline. And my feet hurt in these heels."

"I'll be right over."

"To carry me?"

"No, to watch you walk."

I hung up and headed uptown, passing through the living room where my mother did a double take based on my outfit. "Why do you look so nice?" she asked suspiciously.

"I need a reason?"

"Many daughters would not. Do you have a date with the white baboon?"

"Have you ever known me to dress up for him?"

If she'd been anyone else I'd have had her. That I didn't put on heels and a skirt for Bill should have signaled a lack of interest in what he thought of me, and should also have reassured her because he wasn't getting any free peeks at my legs.

But this was my mother. "Pah. When you see him you look like a gang boy but he doesn't stop calling you. He is a hyena with no understanding of beauty."

I splurged on a cab, because of the shoes.

Outside Baxter/Haig I smoothed my skirt, elegantly mussed my hair, and pulled back the heavy glass door. I gave Nick Greenbank a sweet, sweet smile. He returned a scowl and muttered, "He's here."

"Yes, I know he is," I said.

Little Nicky called the back office. When he hung up he jabbed his head in that direction, with a spreading smile so nastily predatory I began to wonder if Doug Haig had said to send me in, the bear trap was set. Nevertheless, I sashayed to the back where I was met by jittery Caitlin. She knocked on Haig's private door, got a barked, "Come!" and opened it.

And there was the bear trap: Mighty Casey Woo.

20

Woo sat in a chair in the corner of Doug Haig's inner office, where the take-out coffee he was sipping didn't threaten the art. He smiled at me, a smile uncomfortably similar to Nick's.

Doug Haig, meanwhile, sat examining a gold-and-pink pastel drawing just long enough for me to get it that the work on his table was far more important than I was and then slipped it with great care back into a portfolio, at which moment he finally looked up at me.

"Mr. Haig," I said, blasé and serene. Or I hoped I conveyed that impression. My heart was racing and my brain was outpacing it in an attempt to deal with this turn of events. "Thank you for seeing me." I nodded to the corner. "And Mr. Woo. What a nice surprise." I pulled out a chair at Haig's worktable, sat primly and waited.

Wielding his chunky fingers with impressive delicacy, Haig tied the portfolio's boards shut and laid it flat. He rejiggled his bulk to face me, showing Woo his wide back.

"Yes," he said. "Well, Caitlin told me you said I'd be happy if I met with you. So far, I'm not."

"You're an impatient man. And," I added, my brain reorganizing data like crazy, "you have such interesting friends."

"A busy man. And my friends aren't your business." Haig didn't look in Woo's direction, as though the man weren't there.

"No," I said. "It's not my business. It's yours, and they're not your friends. When Mr. Woo and I met, he told me he had an investment to protect. This is it. Your gallery. In my mind I had things more complicated than they needed to be. Now I get it. Tiger Holdings is your investor."

"I don't know why my financial arrangements were on your mind at all. You can't really be expecting me to discuss them with you? Now, if you're here about buying the Chaus for Mr. Oblomov, I'm not in a position yet—"

"I think you are."

He stopped. "I am what?"

"In a position to sell them. Well, let me qualify that. You have them. But it's true you can't sell them yet. And without my help I don't believe you'll be able to."

Woo sat forward. "You have Chaus? This true, what she say?"

"Why is he here?" I asked Haig.

Still without a glance at Woo, Haig said, "Certainly not at my invitation."

"And yet, here he is. You, who threatened to have *Vladimir Oblomov* thrown out yesterday, you who bullied a terrified young woman into leaving just because you could, you're putting up with this coffee-swilling klutz in your pristine inner sanctum. It's killing you, I can see that. But there's nothing you can do. He's here because his boss is getting impatient. You owe Tiger Holdings a lot of money and they've heard about the Chaus."

Woo, who'd let "coffee-swilling klutz" whizz right by him, jumped again on "Chaus." "You have Chaus? You have, don't tell Mr. Lau? That don't make him happy."

Haig's tongue darted out and licked his lips. He didn't seem to like the thought of Mr. Lau being unhappy.

"Why, Mr. Haig," I marveled. "They're afraid you'll cheat them. Mr. Woo's here because Mr. Lau—that's the boss, right?—isn't going to let you make a move anymore without him knowing about it. They suspect you of being the lying, cheating worm you are. I bet Woo's even supposed to follow you home. At least he buys his own coffee. Mr. Woo, please sit down." Haig whipped his head around. Woo, out of his chair, stopped uncertainly. "Mr. Woo, you won't get what you want by physical intimidation. Not because Mr. Haig is a brave man by any means, but because you can't squeeze blood from a turnip. Do you know that expression in English? Well, it doesn't matter. Please sit down. I'm here to help you both."

After a moment, Woo sat, scowling. Haig, who'd paled at the word "blood," slowly turned back to me, showing great self-control by not rearranging his chair to bring Woo into his line of sight. Maybe he was braver than I gave him credit for.

"As I say," I told Haig, "you'll need my help to sell the Chaus. Without me," I spoke to Woo, "he can't sell them and Mr. Lau can't get his money back." I gave him a significant look. I wasn't sure what it signified but he seemed to be. When I turned back to Haig, Woo stayed silent.

"Your help?" Haig said, starting to recover. "I cannot think of a situation in which I'd need your help. Oblomov's not the only interested party, you know."

"I do know that. But finding a buyer's not the problem, is it?"

"Ms. Chin. If I did have the Chaus," he flicked an involuntary glance in Woo's direction, "why couldn't I sell them? And if you think I can't sell them, why are you here?"

"You do have them," I repeated. "You knew all about them,

even where they were, when Vladimir and I were first here, but you didn't have them yet. Now you do. But you can't sell them because you can't get them authenticated. And I'm here because I can help." I crossed my legs, letting my skirt ride up a tiny bit. *Oh, Lydia, sometimes you're just so cheesy.*

Haig zeroed in on my leg-crossing operation. When it was over he switched his attention back to my face. "I can't imagine how."

I fingered the jade on its gold chain around my neck and smiled again. "Then I'll explain. You can't get the Chaus authenticated because they're not authentic." Movement in the corner caused me to turn my head. "Mr. Woo, sit down!" He scowled, but after a moment, he sat. "Thank you. You didn't know they were fakes? Don't worry, we can still make Mr. Lau happy." I turned back. "But you, Mr. Haig, you knew all along. Anna Yang painted them, Bernard Yang's daughter. Please, Mr. Haig, don't insult me by looking affronted. Or surprised. Thank you. Or by asking me how I know this or anything else I'm about to say, because of course I'm not going to tell you. You've asked Dr. Yang to authenticate them, but he won't. But maybe I should be more precise. You didn't ask him to determine whether they're authentic. You asked him to say that they are. To put his stamp of approval on them, so you can sell them for the fortune they'd be worth if they weren't fakes. Your threat, if he didn't, was that you'd claim Anna Yang already rooked you, sold them to you as real, using his name to pull the wool over your eyes. You'd look like a fool and be stuck with worthless junk paintings—which by the way you stole, she didn't sell to you, but that's another issue entirely and in fact I commend you on your resourcefulness."

Haig made a strangled sound.

"Please, Mr. Haig, this really will go better if you just let me finish." I bounced my high-heeled foot impatiently.

"Again, thank you. You'd be stuck, but Anna Yang's reputation would be ruined and her career would be over. You thought that would be a persuasive argument, forcing Dr. Yang into this bit of chicanery. But it wasn't. His own reputation means more to him, it seems, than you were banking on. More than his daughter's, and more than her career. In any case, there's a rift between them since her wedding in Beijing. Apparently, when she married that dissident poet, Liu Mai-ke, it was without her father's permission."

Haig's eyes widened.

"You didn't know that?" I asked. "You were at the wedding banquet. I've seen the footage on YouTube. It didn't strike you as odd that Dr. Yang wasn't there?"

"I understood he couldn't get a visa. May I speak now? Well, thank *you*. That wedding was a ridiculous public spectacle. I went because I had to go. A lot of my artists were there. It would have been unseemly for me to refuse. I assume she did it for the notoriety and he did it for the green card, and I really don't care. Unless you're accusing me of some crime in connection with that, too? I should have you thrown out of here on your compact little ass for the slander you're slinging around."

"Who would do that? Nicky Greenbank? Call him, why don't you? Or maybe you'll ask Mr. Woo for a favor? He'd probably enjoy it. But no, why would you? I'm right. Whatever hole you were in with Tiger Holdings that got you so hot and bothered you had those paintings stolen, you're still in it if you can't get them authenticated. You're desperate and you're wondering what I'm here to offer you. Not, I assure you, my compact little ass."

We stared at each other: he calculating, though pale; me smug, though I was getting tired of my heart racing.

"What, then?"

I smiled, taking my time before I spoke. "Vladimir Oblomov, as I'm sure you noticed, is an oaf."

"Oh, my. Really?"

"I promise you. An oaf with money. I do a lot of work with Russians. They're all the same. Vladimir's different only in his interest in Chinese art. He's a complete ignoramus, but he's decided it's his 'field.' Probably because Americans and Europeans collect it, but none of the other Russians do, so he can be a big cutting-edge deal. If the Chaus were real, or he thought they were, he'd buy them in a flash. At whatever price I told him was a good one. Which, of course, you and I would agree upon in advance."

"Lovely. And you're planning on getting around the eight-hundred-pound forged-painting gorilla exactly how?"

I leaned forward, hoping my eyes were glittering. "I can get them authenticated."

For a moment Haig didn't move. Then he shifted his vastness again, crossing his legs at the ankles. Woo sat up straight. I held up a finger to shush him. Haig said, "You have something to hold over Bernard Yang better than what I have?"

I tick-tocked my finger back and forth. "Not Dr. Yang."

Haig frowned. "The only other name in this area big enough to be believed is Clarence Snyder, in Chicago. These paintings are goddamn good, but I don't think they're good enough to fool him. Are you telling me you have him in your pocket? Or"—Haig's small eyes caressed my legs—"you can put him there?"

"Mr. Haig, if you weren't a potential source of a lot of money I'd slap your face and walk out of here." I said that, but I didn't pull my skirt down. "But you're also a narrow-minded moron. Yang and Snyder aren't the only two big experts. There's Lin, in Hohhot. And him, yes, I can get to him."

"Lin? Who the hell is Lin?"

"You see? That's what I mean. You've never heard of him, and though that speaks much worse of you than of him, it makes you assume that he's nobody. Dr. Lin Qiao-xiang. At the Central University in Hohhot. Of course Hohhot is a minor Chinese city, and the University isn't Shanghai U., so you don't know a thing about it. Beneath you, right? Lin's a rising star. Young, but he's built himself quite a reputation in late-twentieth-century Chinese art, which is a big study area at Hohhot. You can Google him. His work's largely theoretical and historical, not involved with the gallery and commercial world. You'd know him if you went to conferences, if you studied in the area, if you were actually interested in the art in any way except as a money trough you can wallow in."

"Oh, spare me." The acid in Haig's voice practically dissolved the words. "The opinion of a slutty art consultant whose clients are third-rate Russian pigs doesn't interest me in the least. I'll look at this Dr. Lin. If he's as impressive as you say maybe there's something there to talk about. But if he's a true expert he'll know the paintings are fake. Why would he do it?"

"Because, frankly, he cares as little for Hohhot as you do. Although his is an educated opinion. As things stand, though, he's forced to stay there. There aren't very many positions he could rise to in China. There are tenured professorships in his area in Shanghai and Beijing, but they're full. Or he could open his own gallery, but in China that involves dealing with the government, which makes even Hohhot seem appealing. Go ahead, check him out. Have little Nicky or poor scared Caitlin take a look and give you a full report. But be quick. For one thing, you want these paintings ready for sale next week, don't you? To take full advantage of all the sharks in the water. For another, he's here now."

"He's here? Who's here? This Dr. Lin?"

"In New York. He got in two days ago. For Asian Art Week. And he wants to stay."

An unappetizing, upper-hand look of understanding settled on Doug Haig's face. "He wants to stay?"

"There you go," I said approvingly. "Now you've got it. He came here hoping for an offer from a university or college. He did get one from Oberlin—they have a major art collection, and ties to China—but it's in Ohio. Really, he'd rather be in New York. If someone here were to offer him a job, in an area of expertise so esoteric he'd be able to get past the INS—for example, writing a catalogue raisonné on a few decades' worth of contemporary Chinese art—if, even, they agreed to sponsor him for his green card—it's entirely possible he might overcome his scruples and authenticate some paintings that are, anyway, as you so eloquently put it earlier, goddamn good."

I gave it a few beats while I watched Doug Haig's gears creak. "Of course, if he accepts Oberlin's offer first—"

"Yes, all right, I get it. When can you have him here?"

"As it happens we're meeting for coffee in the morning."

"Does he know you're here on his behalf right now?"

"His behalf? I'm not here on his behalf. Or yours. Or, god help me, Vladimir's. I'm here for me. No, Dr. Lin has no clue. He has a serious poker up his compact little ass. He's a lot like you—he thinks he's all that. The difference is, he is. Still, if he gets any whiff that he's being played, it's all over. When he comes here you'll have to handle him very carefully. I'll be here to help, of course."

"How kind of you. All right, I'll check on him, as I said. You call early tomorrow and I'll let you know whether I want you to bring him over."

"I'm a busy woman." I got up to leave. "Being a slutty art consultant is a fast-paced life. I may have another appointment, any number of other appointments, by the time you get around to calling. We'll do it this way: Unless I hear from you I'm going to bring Dr. Lin here at ten a.m. If you decide you don't want to see him, don't. Do whatever you think best, but in my opinion, not seeing him would be a big, big mistake. Mr. Woo, I think you can see how this arrangement will benefit Mr. Lau, also?"

Woo shook his head. "Not so sure."

"Don't worry." I smiled. "I'm sure Mr. Lau will be happy. Gentlemen." I nodded to them both and left them staring after me as I walked away.

21

I dropped the hip-swinging as soon as I got around the corner, and I called Bill.

"How'd it go?"

"Give me Oblomov."

"Vat's wrong?"

"Unexpected glitch. We need a meeting. Can you be ready soon?"

"Girlchik, I vass born ready. Meetink vit whom?"

"I'll set it up and call you back. Wear the bling," I added. "All of it."

Next, I called Jack.

"How'd it go?"

"You guys use the same dialogue coach? Listen, there's a problem. Haig's gallery is the investment Mighty Casey Woo's protecting from Vladimir Oblomov."

"Woo's the investor?"

"His boss. A Mr. Lau."

"Damn. How do you know?"

"He's there. Woo. He's sticking to Doug Haig like a bad smell. It seems his boss is worried Haig will dispose of the Chaus without cutting him in, as soon as he finds them."

"Haig? Double-dealing?"

"I know, it rocks your world. It didn't make either of them happy when I announced I knew he'd already found them."

"Either of them, Woo or his boss?"

"Either of them, Woo or Haig. His boss wasn't there. Woo's probably on the phone to him right now. Bill and I are going to go up and see him. Vladimir and I, I mean. Actually, this might turn out not to be a bad thing."

"You don't think so? Gangsters wanting a piece of Haig?"

"As far as I'm concerned everyone can cut him into lots of little pieces."

"Be practical."

"I'm trying. Right now, I think we should go ahead. Momentum's on our side."

"Sometimes they call that the slippery slope."

"You want out?"

"Why do you guys keep asking me that? Anyway, you can't do this without me."

"We'd do something else."

"See," he sighed, "in every species on earth, it's that carefully calculated who-needs-you attitude on the part of the female that keeps the male strutting, sticking his neck out trying to prove himself."

"It's not calculated. It's instinctive. Are you still in?"

"Was there ever any real question?"

"And so the real reason I'm calling: Did you speak to Dr. Yang?"

"Which is the real reason I'm still in. After the trouble he gave me? Now that I've talked him into getting with the program, the rest of this is going to be like taking candy from a baby."

"That usually results in a lot of deafening squalling."

On that encouraging note, we hung up.

I smartphoned my way to the Tiger Holdings Web site and checked out Lau's photo so I'd know him when I saw him. Then I called. By dropping "Baxter/Haig" a couple of times, I leapfrogged through levels of secretary to the secretary to the man himself. When I hung up Vladimir Oblomov and I had an as-soon-as-we-can-get-there appointment with Lionel Lau.

We got there soon, meeting at Lau's midtown building so we could saunter in together.

"Does your mother know you dress like that?" Bill asked when he saw me.

"You mean, parading my well-rounded calves for all the world to see?"

"And your dimpled knees, and not inconsiderable amounts of thigh."

"She thought I looked very nice. She just hoped I wasn't meeting you. You should consider piercing your ear, by the way. A nice diamond stud would complement the rings and chains."

"Uh-huh. In your dreams."

On the twenty-ninth floor the elevator opened into a hushed lobby. Glass doors guarded by a pair of marble lions announced "Tiger Holdings" at the far side of a carpet no bigger than a town square or softer than a summer evening. Bill peered around in smiling, fellow-gangster approval at the gaudy gold dragons on crimson columns, the blue-painted vases big enough for assassins to hide in, and the young woman at the desk, whose scarlet

lipstick accentuated her Ming-princess cheekbones and porcelain skin.

"Lydia Chin and Vladimir Oblomov for Lionel Lau," I told her.
She arched an eyebrow and spoke into an elegant 1930's desk phone,
listened, then pointed a fingernail at the door behind her. A moment later it opened and a familiar squarish Asian man beckoned
us in. I smiled at him. "My, my. So nice to see you again. I'm sorry,
at the bakery I didn't catch your name."

He didn't offer it now, either, just scowled and stood waiting.
He and Bill sized each other up with identical nice-to-meet-you-
I-wouldn't-try-it looks. I ignored the rising scent of testosterone
and walked past them into a large room where a wall of windows
spread Manhattan below me. Bill followed me in. The young man
shut the door and stood beside it.

I smiled at the man who stood between us and the view: an
older, sharp-nosed Asian gent who looked exactly like his Web site
photo. He wore short graying hair and a fine navy suit my mother
would have admired.

"Mr. Lau? Thank you for seeing us. I'm Lydia Chin. This is
Vladimir Oblomov."

Bill came forward and enthusiastically shook Lionel Lau's hand.
"Meester Lau! A real pleasure, dis is."

Lionel Lau, face impassive, returned the handshake in a more
restrained manner and gestured us to large leather chairs. As we
sat, he asked in accent-free English, "May I offer you tea?" He
might be shady, Mr. Lau, but he was Chinese.

Before I could answer, Bill said, "Yah, tenks, but you got *real* tea? I
mean bleck, vit a sugar cube? Dis tea you people drink, she like it," he
thumbed at me, "but it don't got no punch, you know vat I mean?"

The younger man darkened, and internally I questioned the

wisdom of throwing around the word "punch," but Lionel Lau just said, "Mr. Zu, will you see to it, please?" Young Mr. Zu stuck his head out the door and spoke briefly to the Ming princess.

Bill cheerfully shifted his chair so he could see both Lau and Zu. "Dis iss big honor, Mr. Lau. Vassily Imports got great respect for Tiger Holdinks. My boss tell me, 'Oblomov, you verk hard, you lucky, someday you be like Lionel Lau.'"

"I appreciate the compliment," Lionel Lau said, sitting behind his ornate desk. "In that case, however, I wonder why you—or your boss . . ." He waited, but Bill did nothing but grin, so Lau continued, ". . . would want to interfere with one of my business ventures."

"You mean, det gellery. Vere Fetso has de Chaus."

"I do."

A knock sounded, and Zu opened the door to a young woman who brought a tea tray to the sideboard, bowed, and backed out. Zu lifted from it a smaller tray with a glass of tea in a silver-handled holder and a bowl of sugar cubes, and brought it to the coffee table near Bill. From the larger tray he poured green tea into tiny cups, brought one to Lau and one to me. There was no cup for Zu; he must not drink on duty.

I gave the tea my full attention, out of courtesy to our host. It was sharp, sweet, and uncomplicated. "Lovely," I said. Bill was busy positioning a sugar cube between his teeth and noisily sucking his tea across it, so after a second sip, I spoke. "Mr. Lau, we appreciate your situation and we don't mean to cause trouble for you."

"No, sir!" Bill stored the sugar cube temporarily in his cheek. "Vassily Imports vant to be friends vit Tiger Holdinks. But problem vass, my boss, he vanted Chaus, too." He shrugged. What can a working stiff do? He went back to his tea.

"The problem runs deeper than you might think," I told Lau.

"We came here to warn you that there's about to be unavoidable trouble at Baxter/Haig."

"Warn me? Are you making threats?"

"No, I'm sorry, that was a bad choice of words. Perhaps 'alert you' would have been better. This trouble, you see, is unavoidable because the forces involved are some with whom Vassily Imports will go some distance to remain in good standing."

"Da," Bill agreed. "Big shots, you know?" He winked at Lau.

"If keeping these relationships untroubled involves Vassily Imports stepping aside in certain situations, I'm sure you can see that that's an investment well worth making," I went on. "And worth urging others to make."

"Ms. Chin—"

"Vat she sayink, Meester Lau—she beat across da bush all da time, I know—she sayink, vat's about to go down at Baxter/Haig, pleeze, you and Meester Voo chust stay out uff it, okay?"

"Vlad, please," I said. "Mr. Lau, we're in a position to help some friends with an operation that matters a great deal to them, and we'd like to do it. To this end Mr. Oblomov's employer has already abandoned his pursuit of the paintings. We do understand, however, that Tiger Holdings has a significant and legitimate investment in Baxter/Haig."

"All my investments are legitimate," Lau said. When Bill and I glanced at each other, Lau added, "If Mr. Woo's eagerness to complete his assignment had led you to think otherwise, I apologize. As, I'm sure, would he, if he'd understood that he'd upset you."

"His willingness to shoot me was a trifle upsetting, yes," I said. "In view of his self-restraint an hour ago in Mr. Haig's office, though, it's possible he and I just got off on the wrong foot. I'm willing to let bygones be bygones."

"I'm glad to hear it. Rest assured I'll be speaking to him about his approach. However, that's really neither here nor there concerning my investment in Baxter/Haig. I'm sure you understand, I must protect my business interests."

Bill said, "By heving Voo, or some udder jeckess, henging around dere all da time?"

"If that's required."

Shooting Bill a dark look, I said, "In that case I think you'll understand the value of the arrangement we came here to discuss."

"And what would that be?" Lau placed his teacup on his desk and tapped his fingertips together, the very picture of a reasonable executive willing to consider a deal.

"As I understand it, if Mr. Haig can't repay your loan, you'll own the gallery."

"That's correct."

"Vell, dere you go," said Bill. "All de paintinks, dey gotta be worth lots uff money. You don't need Fetso to sell de Chaus."

"Technically correct. But if I wanted to own a gallery I'd have bought one. Art isn't my business. I'd much prefer it if Doug Haig could sell the Chaus, pay off his debt, and go about his business while I go about mine."

"He can't, though," I said. "They're worth nothing. They're fakes."

Lau regarded me steadily. "Mr. Woo said you told Haig you could get them authenticated."

"Mr. Lau, my . . . arrangement . . . with Mr. Haig is predicated on Vassily Imports' relationship with the other forces I mentioned, and is not as straightforward as it appears. Tiger Holdings would be best served to stay far from the proceedings. In view of the fact that you do have a legitimate investment to protect, however, Vassily Imports is prepared to guarantee that, should Mr. Haig's debt to you become uncollectible, his assets will simultaneously become a great deal more valuable than they are at the moment."

"I'm not sure, Ms. Chin, just what you mean by that."

"She mean, iff you stay beck und vatch from da sidevays—iss dat right Eenglish?"

"Sidelines," I said.

"Da, de sidelines. Iff you don't mess us up, Meester Lau, you end up vit golden goose."

"And if I choose not to permit whatever is about to happen to go forward?"

"Den, my friend," Bill smiled, clinking his empty glass gently onto the silver tray, "I tink you find yourself vit goose egg."

22

I called Jack as soon as Bill and I hit the street.

"Life and limb still intact?" Jack asked.

"Yes," I said. "All we need to do now is find a golden egg for Lionel Lau before he makes fritters out of all of us."

When I heard the buzzer at nine-thirty the next morning I didn't ask who it was, just buzzed to let Jack in. I looked up when my office door opened and, fast, slid my chair closer to my desk, making sure I could reach the panic button. The stranger in the doorway was tall and Asian, but that was about all he shared with Jack Lee.

"Ms. Chin?" The man spoke in nasal, accented tones. "I think you expect me, we have appointment?" Disdain written all over his tanned face, he stood just inside my door in a cheap suit a few years out of date. It fit poorly over his wide shoulders, and his shirt strained over the early stages of beer belly. Polished loafers and showy tie said clueless foreign fop. His hair, combed straight onto his forehead, was Extreme Nerd. Black-framed yellow-tinted glasses rested on his nose, below which drooped a thin Fu Manchu mustache. He held himself tightly, as though stepping into my back-alley office was an action he didn't think he should be asked to undertake. "Dr. Lin Qiao-xiang," he announced with impatience. "You want see me, so I understand. Or maybe," suddenly relaxing the rigid pose, walking in and sprawling onto a chair, "I should send Aramis in?"

"Well," I managed. "Don't you look splendid."

"Do I?" Jack grinned. "If I didn't know better I'd have thought you didn't recognize me there for a minute."

"I must admit you're quite the apparition. How did you get to be that color, stage makeup?"

"Insta-Tan."

"That stuff's bad for you."

"Line of duty. Like Bill drinking with Shayna."

"And padding in the jacket? Or you gained twenty pounds overnight?"

"In the jacket and under the shirt. You don't buy the Daniel Dae Kim shoulders?"

"I'd have to wonder where you were hiding them for the last two days. The real question is, where did you get that terrible suit?"

"At a thrift shop, for occasions like this. Hey, as great as Linus's Photoshop work is, I thought I ought to look at least something like the real Dr. Lin."

"You think his mustache is that ridiculous? And he has that bad taste in clothes?"

"I also needed to look not like me."

"Ah, and chic would have given you away."

"Don't you think? I told you, Haig and I have met."

"Only once, you said."

"But we've been in the same room any number of times, grabbing off the same hors d'oeuvre trays. Haig's generally too self-absorbed to notice anyone he's not on the make for, but in case I did something unforgettable I don't remember I wanted to play it safe. Also, there's Nick. Be a bummer if that little punk derailed us." He took off the glasses and handed them to me. "Near the hinge," he said. I examined the decorative screw holding the earpiece on and found the tiny camera lens in its center.

"How do you—"

"Remotely. From my pocket." He held up a pen and clicked the top as though he wanted to write something. "You just took a picture of the junk on your desk."

"Hey, very cool. If the glasses weren't so ugly I'd get myself a pair." I handed them back.

"Come on. You can't tell me any of this is nearly as bad as Bill's bling and his accent."

"Can't I? But as long as it works on Haig. Which, let me remind you, Bill's bling did."

Jack grinned at me for another few moments. Then, as though I'd said something unbearably foolish, his smile vanished into a look of arrogant irritation. Jack Lee disappeared. Lin Qiao-xiang stood stiffly and replied, "In that case, we go now, see if can make this work, too."

Dr. Lin apparently shared Jack's penchant for cabs, and I didn't want to argue with so eminent a foreign expert. Also, I had those heels on again. We pulled up in front of Baxter/Haig, where Jack, without a care, got out, leaving me to pay the driver. On the sidewalk I once again smoothed my skirt, mussed my hair, and let my lips bloom into a superior smile. I waited for Jack to open the gallery door for me, but in his role as self-important overseas hick he was gawking through the glass at the art inside. So I yanked the handle and stalked into Baxter/Haig. Jack blinked and hurried after. I was surprised to see Nick at the front desk so early, but maybe Haig liked his first-string players here for VIPs. "Mr. Haig's expecting us," I told him nicely.

Jack didn't even look at Nick, so busy was he rotating his head and craning his neck to take in Pang Ping-Pong's giant canvases. The yellow-tinted glasses threatened to fall off, so he had to hold them on. If that meant his hand was in front of his face, well, he wasn't just a pretty face anyhow. Not that he gave Nick much opportunity to inspect him. Jack found himself immediately drawn to the canvas on the far wall. I myself loomed at Nick's counter much the way Bill had, though at five-three it's not as easy for me. Still, I managed to fill a good deal of Nick's field of vision, and by the time he was off the phone with the inner sanctum Jack was safely tucked behind a protruding wall, leaning forward to study a painting of Spider-man dancing one of the *Eight Revolutionary Ballets*.

"He says you can go on back," Nick resentfully admitted.

"I'm delighted," I chirped. "Is that charming Mr. Woo still with him?"

Nick curled his lip, which was answer enough.

I marched toward the rear, calling across the room, "Q. X., come on now, we have a meeting. We can look at the art later." Jack joined me with an air of fusty impatience, as though I'd been the one holding up the proceedings. Jumpy Caitlin came out to meet us and escort us into the presence of the potentate.

Doug Haig, as usual, was examining art on his worktable, from which, as usual, he didn't look up immediately. Mighty Casey Woo, in what might by now have become usual, clogged up the corner chair, drinking a Coke. When sufficient eons had passed for all to understand who was boss, Doug Haig raised his head to take in the vision of Jack and myself. The waiting time, I was not pleased to note, was about half of what it had been for me alone, now that I was accompanied by Dr. Lin Qiao-xiang.

"Mr. Haig," I said when he'd finally laid a sheet of tissue paper over his drawing and languidly fixed his attention on us. "This is Dr. Lin, from the Central University at Hohhot, in Inner Mongolia, China. Dr. Lin, I'd like you to meet Mr. Haig." Did I put emphasis on the "Dr." and the "Mr."? Perhaps a tiny bit.

Haig extended a pudgy paw, but Jack, as though he hadn't seen it, snapped Haig a bow. Speaking that nasal, accented English, he said formally, "It is great honor for small scholar as myself to meet such eminent American art dealer." He managed to make "small scholar" sound like "King Tut" and "art dealer" like "ditch digger." He held the bow a few moments; by the time he stood straight again Haig's right hand had folded itself over his left as though it had been on its way there all along.

"The pleasure is mine, Dr. Lin, to meet such an eminent authority. I've been looking forward to this for some time." Haig gave a bland smile. "Just yesterday, in fact, I was talking with Clarence Snyder. He speaks very highly of you."

"Dr. Snyder, generous man. Must call him later, thank him for helpfulness. Never lets friend down."

Jack sat, his jacket gaping over his chest-padding. He surveyed Haig's office with a fusion of burning envy and icy disdain. "Very interesting work, this gallery," he said, speaking like a man who'd been in and out of every important art venue in New York before coming down to this one. "Pang Ping-Pong, of course, does no new work now, five years, just recycles. Still, I suppose he still sells well in West? Here, though," he gestured at the drawings on the table, "this work new, maybe good. Find in China? You travel good deal to China, Mr. Haig, so I understand. More than most dealer."

"I have to," Haig answered. "To find the artists before other dealers do. I can't say I enjoy your country all that much"—a thin smile—"but those trips are my edge. How about you, Dr. Lin? Is it possible for you to travel outside China often?" He added innocently, "Does your schedule allow it?"

Schedule, my eye: that crack was about power, reminding Dr. Q. X. Lin who wanted what from whom. As Jack's about Pang Ping-Pong and the work on the table had been, reminding Haig who had what to give.

"Inside China, travel often," Jack said stiffly. "Outside, as you say, no time. Two years ago, go to conference in Berlin. This second trip to U.S."

"And how do you like it?"

"Like very well. Trip too short, only two week. Would be better, much longer. So much to see in U.S. In New York." Through the yellow lenses he stared straight at Haig.

"Yes," Haig said, "and for a scholar of your eminence, I imagine the U.S. holds a great deal of opportunity. It would be a shame if you couldn't take advantage of it."

"Speaking of taking advantage," I said, "I mentioned to Dr. Lin the paintings you were telling me about, the ones you thought would interest him. The unattributed works that might be by Chau Gwai Ying Shung, the Ghost Hero? I suggested we might take advantage of the fact that we were in your neighborhood to come look at them."

"She tell me," said Jack, "you not sure, authenticity. She say, if someone, large knowledge, all parts of field, appraises, authenticates, paintings extremely valuable. If true Chaus, of course, I don't need her tell me that."

"No question about it," Haig said, wetting his rubbery lips and giving me a look that said no one really needed me to tell them much of anything. "This is my area, of course, but I'm not an authority, not in the academic sense." He managed, in keeping with the ongoing war of intonation, to make "academic" an insult. "From the moment I saw these pieces I was convinced of their authenticity, but I wouldn't feel comfortable putting them on the market on the basis of only my own instinct. If, on the other hand, they were to be examined by an academic authority who came to the same conclusion I did, I'd feel on firm ground going forward. And," he added, with a cold smile, "I'd be quite grateful."

"I see." Jack nodded.

"In fact," Haig said, as though the idea had only just occurred to him, "an expert like that could be a great asset to this gallery. Over the years I've acquired a great deal of work—artists I handle and also work I've bought for my own collection—but my passion seems to have outpaced my paperwork. I'm afraid there's a tremendous amount of scholarship to be done within these walls. I'd do it myself but I just don't have the time."

"I see," Jack said again, more slowly. "How much time, Mr. Haig? How long you estimate this scholarship takes?"

"At least a year," Haig said without hesitation. "Perhaps two."

"Long time. If paintings she tell me about turn out be real, I suppose you very busy to sell them, have even less time for scholarship?"

"Absolutely true. If they're real, I'll definitely need expert help in the gallery into the forseeable future."

"So fascinating," Jack reflected, as though all of this were of purely abstract interest. "All this conversation, make me very curious, see paintings. Is possible you have time, can show me?"

"Dr. Lin, when I heard you were in New York I demanded that

Ms. Chin bring you here. I refused to take no for an answer." History Rewrites R Us. "I've canceled all my other appointments for this morning. A gentleman of your erudition, your cultivation—it would be my pleasure to show you the Chaus." Not the alleged Chaus, the putative Chaus, the I-know-damn-well-they're-not Chaus. For a moment I longed to forget the whole plan and have Jack take one look at the paintings and say they were garbage, just to see Haig's face.

Haig didn't get up right away; first he looked from me to Woo. I could see in his eyes the hope that somehow, magically, we might leave, that he might not have to share his treasure with us, to have our peasant eyes raking over his resplendent paper and ink. *You posturing prig,* I wanted to yell, *they're fake, remember? And you stole them, remember that, too?* I didn't say anything, though, just stared back at him, tired of smiling. Woo slurped his Coke and acted as though he hadn't heard a word of the entire conversation. Haig sighed, threw a long-suffering glance to Dr. Q. X. Lin, and rose. He moved with a surprisingly bouncy gait, as though his bulk were partially helium. At a set of flat files along the wall he unlocked a drawer, extracted a large leather portfolio, and brought it back to the table. He laid it carefully down, unzipped it, and took out a cardboard folder. The folder was tied with a cloth ribbon and I almost busted a gasket waiting for his ceremonial undoing of the bow. Finally he lifted the top board and slowly slid out an ink painting.

The left third of the paper was covered with grasses and rocks, some in shadow, some seeming to glow backlit in sun. Cicadas dotted them. You could almost hear their rhythmic singing on the hot, peaceful afternoon. They didn't react in any way to the fierce tiger clawing the center of the page while his ferocious face half-entered the painting from the right. Three rows of Chinese characters, written vertically in the old style, occupied the space above the tiger's head. I saw Jack's eyes widen and wasn't sure whether that response was from Q. X. Lin or Jack Lee.

"Well," Doug Haig spoke with satisfaction, "Ms. Chin, I see you're impressed, anyway. Dr. Lin, do you like it?"

"Quite amazing," Jack said, sounding as though he meant it. "Control of line, sharpness where brush lifts from page—see here?—black of ink, fierceness of eyes of tiger. Extraordinary." He leaned close, then stood up again. "Is possible I may see others?"

Of course it was possible. Doug Haig slid them out one by one. A stream rushing down a mountainside in great clouds of mist; plum blossoms on a tree limb echoed by a few fallen to the ground; and the willow branch and wren that had started it all. The paintings each had lines of Chinese verse on them, sometimes tucked in the corner, other times blazoned across the top. I cocked my head to read them—nature poems, all, with themes of courage, loneliness, resolve—while Jack moved back and forth along the table, scrutinizing one painting, then another, leaning down, then stepping back for a longer view. Done with the poems, I examined the images also, knowing little about what I was looking at, except for two things: the tightly controlled brushstrokes in the wild, idiosyncratic compositions gave the paintings a tension and an exhilarating energy; and though I'd only seen real Chaus briefly online during my research, these paintings looked just like those.

"Mr. Haig," Jack said, after a long silence. "These paintings, astonishing. May I ask, where do you get them?"

"They came to me from a client," Haig blithely lied. "He's not a collector. The paintings were left to him at the death of a relative. He'd like to sell them if they're worth anything."

"Worth anything?" Jack peered at the willow-and-wren painting once more. "If real Chaus, among most accomplished, impressive work of Chau. Mature period, probably painted close to time Chau died. But Mr. Haig. Verses here, by Liu Mai-ke. Who puts?"

"Liu Mai-ke?" Haig mangled the Chinese so badly he was temporarily unable to understand himself. "Who—that poet? Anna Yang's husband? The one who's in prison?"

"Yes, dissident, in prison. Married to American artist, daughter of Professor Bernard Yang Ji-tong. Anna Yang her name?" He looked at me and I nodded. Back to Haig: "You don't know, these his poems? Oh, my apology. I thought you can read Chinese." A smarmily superior smile. "Mr. Haig, who puts Liu poems on Chaus?"

"I—I don't know. But does it matter?" Haig had gone from ashen to an angry flush, but Jack's "Chaus"—not alleged Chaus, not putative Chaus—hadn't escaped him and he recovered fast. "But it's an old Chinese tradition, adding poems to paintings."

"Yes, goes back to Yuan Dynasty. Starts as protest against barbarian invaders." Again, Jack stared straight at Haig.

Haig chose to ignore the "barbarian" reference. "Perhaps the original owner was an admirer of Liu's." *Damn right she was.* "I can't see that the poems will affect the value of the paintings, though. If they're real, I mean."

"On contrary. In China, you, me, her, even him"—jabbing a thumb at Woo—"all detained, security officers find this. But here in West," Jack went on before Woo could protest his inclusion in the mass arrest, "Liu poems *add* to value. Dissident poet, dissident painter—if Chaus real, Western collector eats up. Right expression?" He looked over his glasses at me. "'Eats up'?"

"Yes, Q. X., that's right. He's practicing his slang," I explained to Haig, "for when he gets a chance at a long stay in the U.S. He has a job offer from Oberlin College, you know."

"Yes, long stay. Maybe professor, Oberlin College. In Ohio," Jack muttered, gazing at the arching willow branches and the singing wren. He looked up. "Mr. Haig, you understand, this exact period, my field? Of course, don't want put myself forward, just small scholar of Inner Mongolia." Which he managed to make sound less remote than "Ohio." "But possible, I can be of service, help you and client. If you allow me?"

"Allow you? Dr. Lin, let me understand—are you offering to appraise these paintings?" Haig's innocent surprise would have done credit to Shirley Temple.

"If would be useful to you," Jack said gravely.

"It would be exceedingly useful. My client and I would be very, very grateful."

Jack said nothing.

"Of course," Haig hurried on, "you'd have to permit me to compensate you for your trouble. And also, the minute I find out these paintings are real—if they are—the burden on me will increase tenfold, as we said earlier. I'll need that expert we were talking about, need him right away."

"Ah," Jack said. "Of course. Well, just let me look little while longer. Just need few more minutes, be sure."

"Sure?" Haig's voice had risen a whole register. I almost laughed.

"Impossible, of course, be totally sure, anything in this world," Jack retreated. "Looking now, things to say, definitely *not* Chau. Don't find, well . . ."

"Yes, of course. Please, take your time," Haig said, so obviously meaning the opposite that even Woo snickered.

Jack leaned down once more, this time over the waterfall painting. Haig's eyes stayed riveted on him as though he were afraid Jack was a mirage and might evaporate. Woo and I sat silent, on the edge of our respective chairs.

We all jumped when the phone rang.

Jack raised an offended eyebrow at this infringement on his concentration. Haig, scowling, spun to the desk and grabbed the receiver. "*What,* Nick? I said not—what? *Who* is?" He listened briefly, then smiled. "No, Nick, you don't know what deal he's talking about, because I didn't tell you. Well, how delicious. By all means, send him back." He hung up, gave me a special, slimy wink, and announced, "We have a visitor. I'm sure you won't mind, Dr. Lin. This will be very interesting." A moment later we heard Caitlin's timid knock, and after Haig's barked "Come!" the door opened to admit Dr. Bernard Yang.

23

His clenched jaw broadcasting equal parts determination and fury, Dr. Yang took one step in and stopped short, apparently unprepared for the population explosion in Doug Haig's office. Haig waved Caitlin away and, all relaxed geniality, held out welcoming arms to the professor. "Dr. Yang! It's an honor, sir. Please, please, come in."

"Mr. Haig. I've come about our . . . business. But perhaps this is not a good time." Dr. Yang seemed to take a tighter grip on the portfolio he held.

"No, it's an excellent time. To receive a scholar as prominent as yourself? A perfect time. Dr. Yang, you probably already know Dr. Lin, from China?" Haig didn't even attempt "Qiao-xiang."

Without missing a beat, Jack bowed low, and Dr. Yang, in reflex, bowed also. Bent over, Jack said, "Have not yet had pleasure, meet reknowned Dr. Bernard Yang." Slowly, he straightened. Dr. Yang straightened also, looked at Jack, and frowned. I realized I was holding my breath. "Lin Qiao-xiang," said Jack, his voice about as nasal and accented as he could make it without sounding like Mr. Moto. "From Central University in Hohhot, Inner Mongolia."

"Dr. Lin," Dr. Yang answered after a pause. "I've heard of you, of course."

"This old friend, Lydia Chin," Jack said, indicating me.

"Dr. Yang and I have met, Q. X.," I told Jack. "An unexpected pleasure to see you here, Professor."

"Unexpected, yes." Dr. Yang glanced from me to Jack again. "What exactly is—"

"Dr. Lin and I were just looking over some paintings," Haig said. "Perhaps you'd like to see them, also?"

Jack cooperatively stepped away, which put him out of Dr. Yang's line of sight. I wanted to catch Jack's eyes behind Dr. Yang's back but I was afraid to. Then I realized that at that moment we could have had a shouting match about anything we wanted right out in the open. When Jack moved, Dr. Yang had caught sight of what was on the table, and he'd lost all interest in us.

The professor leaned over the paintings, moving from one to another, his face draining of color as he examined them. Of course, I thought; this is the first time he's seen them, seen the quality of his daughter's work. Doug Haig's face, on the other hand, was suffused with a gloating joy so powerful I wanted to break a chair over his head. "These are the paintings I was telling you about," he said casually to Dr. Yang. "The Chaus."

Dr. Yang slowly straightened up and took a step closer to the triumphant mound of flesh that was Doug Haig. In a dark and quiet voice he said, "These are not Chaus."

"Really? I'm surprised to hear you say that. Considering what Nick told me about your willingness to . . . reopen yesterday's discussion. Also, considering what Dr. Lin said about these paintings."

Not that Dr. Lin had actually said it yet, but Haig turned confidently to Jack.

"Don't like to contradict eminent scholar," Jack said, looking away from Dr. Yang as though embarrassed by his own effrontery. "But my belief, paintings are Chaus."

"They are not."

"Your belief, Dr. Lin?" prompted Haig.

"My opinion." Jack spoke more strongly. "Professional, academic opinion."

"Which Dr. Lin, as my consultant, will be putting in writing," Haig assured Dr. Yang. "So while you're welcome in the gallery anytime, of course, Professor, it turns out you needn't have troubled yourself to come here today. In fact, unless you're interested in the art once we have it on exhibit"—he pointed at Anna's paintings—"you don't need to bother to come back. Ever." Haig gave the professor a smile he must have stolen from the Cheshire cat's evil twin.

The vein I'd seen pulsing in Dr. Yang's forehead yesterday was pounding away now. "I'd like to speak to you privately, Mr. Haig."

"Yes," Jack said, "can see you have many private thing to discuss. I must be getting to next meeting now, also. Mr. Haig, tomorrow maybe will call you—"

"No," said Haig. "Dr. Lin, you've only just met your distinguished colleague. You two must have so much to talk about, I won't hear of your leaving. Dr. Yang, whatever you have to say, I'm sure Dr. Lin will be utterly fascinated. Please, speak freely."

It was like being at a train wreck; I couldn't turn away. I had the sense that Dr. Yang, if he'd known a martial art, would be practicing it on Doug Haig as the rest of us watched.

"All right," he said icily, eyes still on Haig. "Dr. Lin, I believe what I've brought will interest you, too." He gestured to the table and waited. Jack, quicker to catch on than the rest of us, started to replace Anna's paintings in their portfolio to clear a space. Haig gave a strangled gurgle and almost slapped Jack's hand. With great ceremony, handling them delicately by their edges, he placed the paintings on the far side of the table where they were out of the way but still visible. Dr. Yang didn't spare Haig a glance, just waited until he was done. Then he laid down the portfolio he'd brought, unzipped it, and from its inner cardboard folder pulled another ink painting.

The paper, with a fine toothed surface, was the same as Anna's. The pure black ink, powerfully thick or delicately thin, or soft gray wash where the artist wanted it to be, looked identical. The meticulously controlled brushstrokes created exactly the same tension with the wild composition. The painting's subject, three large carp peering up through the water under a bridge, and the accompanying poem about flashes of silver and gold as fish jump and return to the same spot in the everchanging stream, put it in the same nature-metaphor category. But it wasn't the same.

Anna's paintings were undeniably beautiful. Next to this, though, they seemed childish, naïve. Her lines and forms had an arbitrary quality I wouldn't have understood if I hadn't seen this painting, where every stroke of ink was the right one, nothing was missing, and nothing was extra.

"This," said Dr. Yang, in his hard, quiet voice, "is a Chau."

Haig stared. Jack and I stared. Even Woo was out of his chair, tilting his head to see this wonder. No one moved or spoke until finally, with a grunt, Woo sat back down again. He resumed slurping, proving that in the face of the miraculous the world does go on.

Haig, as though unable to believe what was happening, said, "Dr. Lin?"

Jack looked up at him, nodded, looked back down. "Would have to examine, of course. But can be almost no question. Amazing. So skillful, so accomplished. Chau, but even better than any known. As though . . . Dr. Yang, where this comes from?"

"That doesn't matter." Dr. Yang dismissed the question, and Jack. His eyes riveted to Haig's, he said, "It's a Chau and I'll authenticate it."

"I also!" Jack said, the man from Hohhot suddenly seeing his year in America slipping away. "After examine, of course."

"Well." Haig folded his arms over his balloon belly. "Well. Dr. Yang, how do I know this is truly a Chau?"

"Dr. Lin just said it was. Isn't that enough for you? Although I suppose it's reasonable to mistrust his judgment, since a moment ago he was prepared to authenticate my daughter's paintings as Chaus." He spoke with disgust, including in it both Jack and Haig, and probably me, too. Not Woo; he was beneath the professor's contempt.

Dr. Yang's scorn rolled right off Haig, whose supercilious air didn't change. Jack, the offended academic, widened his eyes and began to protest. "My daughter's," Dr. Yang repeated firmly. "They're very good. But they're not Chaus." I almost smiled. Even under the circumstances, the father can't resist praising the daughter. "There are differences. A real expert could tell you." Quick, angry glance at Jack. "The control of the quantity of ink on the brush, to keep a line solid or break it up, as the artist chooses. The change of brushstroke angle around the sweep of a curve. If all that's too subtle for you, Mr. Haig, you can look to the poem. This, here, is Chau's calligraphy. That's Liu Mai-ke's, my daughter's husband's, as is the poem, though it was put there by my daughter in imitation of Liu's hand. Chau uses poems by classical masters, as he always did. This poem is by Wang Wei. But I'm sure you can see that."

I was sure Haig couldn't, and I was sure the professor knew that, too. I was tempted to give Haig a pass, though. I could read the Chinese, but my classical education was so poor I couldn't have told Wang Wei from Liu Mai-ke. Or, for that matter, from A. A. Milne.

"Yes, all right," Haig said, not even pretending to study the painting. "And you'll say all that? When you authenticate it?"

"I've brought a letter."

Haig seemed to try to put the brakes on, to think about this miracle the way he would any transaction. "What's the painting's provenance?"

"It's from my personal collection. It was painted the year Chau died. I brought it with me from China. That, too, is in the letter."

"I see. All very interesting. And Dr. Yang, you're offering to do what? Consign the painting to me? On what terms?"

"Don't be ridiculous. I wouldn't expect you to agree to anything as fair as a consignment. No, I'll give it to you. In exchange for these."

"Well." Haig rubbed his chins. "Well. A true, unknown Chau. Authenticated by two major experts." He looked at Jack, who nodded quickly. "If handled correctly, I imagine it could bring upwards of eight hundred thousand dollars." He looked from the carp painting to the others. "Oh," he said, as though a thought had occurred to him, "but these can be authenticated, too. Can't they?" Again, he looked at Jack. Jack swallowed, threw a quick look at Dr. Yang, and nodded again.

"They are not Chaus!" Dr. Yang barked.

"So *you* say," Haig answered equably. "Another expert says otherwise. And there are four of them. Not quite as good, but still, with proper attribution, they'll be worth close to two million together. I'm not sure the bargain is a good one, Dr. Yang."

Dr. Yang ground his jaw, making the vein in his forehead pop again. "Mr. Haig," he said quietly, "your greed doesn't surprise me.

I was prepared for it, though I suppose I'd hoped to find it less boundless than it appears. Consider this: One painting authenticated by Dr. Lin and myself will be worth a good deal more than four authenticated by Dr. Lin alone and challenged by me. Challenged also by the painter, my daughter, who, I must tell you, is prepared to sacrifice her career rather than allow you to commit this despicable crime. Since this situation is to some extent her fault, not for making the paintings but for failing to grasp the dangers of people's greed and malevolence, I'm prepared to permit her that sacrifice. However, if we can find another answer, that would be preferable." The professor slipped his hand into the portfolio again and brought out another painting.

On a page laid vertically, a path wound through pine trees and floating mists to a craggy peak. At the mountain's foot a river rushed, and on its banks stood a tiny figure, staring upstream. The three or four brushstrokes of which he was made created a palpable sense of longing. I read the poem, about yearning to see the spring in the poet's hometown, far away, and was surprised to find my eyes as misty as the mountain.

Haig had no such reaction. What filled his eyes were dollar signs. He practically broke into a happy dance when Dr. Yang brought out a third painting, this one so traditional in subject even I recognized it: The Three Friends of Winter. Curving branches of pine, plum, and bamboo swept across the page, the leaves of each delicately mounded with snow. Three Friends paintings are always about persistence and endurance, but the poem was about standing in the snow alone after bidding an exiled friend a last farewell.

Haig, after a long look at these paintings, didn't ask either expert about them. His only question, with almost comical inevitability, was, "How many more are there?"

Dr. Yang shook his head. "There are no more." He lifted the top board of the portfolio. We could all see it was empty. "I brought three from China. There are no more."

"And you've been hiding them all these years. You bad boy." Haig smiled. "Now the world will get a chance to see them. How wonderful. Professor, I believe we do, after all, have a deal."

Jack and I left Baxter/Haig soon after Dr. Yang brought out the last painting. Jack hailed the first cab he saw. It happened to be going in the wrong direction, but I was right there with him. As the cab sped around the block I threw myself back on the seat and kicked off my shoes. "What was he *thinking*? Three Chaus, in Doug Haig's hands?"

"Well, he read Haig right on that: One wouldn't have done it."

"I almost had a coronary! I thought you said he was with the program."

"I thought he was."

"And now he's freelancing, too." I rooted through my bag, then stopped to ask Jack, "Hey. You think we got away with it?"

"With Haig and Woo, yes. Who knows what was going on in Dr. Yang's head—who ever does, witness the three paintings—but what would he gain by ratting us out?"

"He wouldn't have Lin to worry about?"

"He's better off if Haig does believe in Lin. He said it himself, two experts are better than one."

I found my cell phone. "I'm calling Bill. And then I'm calling my client. If they all start doing improv this isn't going to be easy."

I did call Bill, brought him up to speed.

"Holy cow," he said. "Three?"

"I don't know what was more beautiful," I said. "The paintings, or Dr. Lin Qiao-xiang trying to ad lib around them."

By the time I got off the phone with Bill the cab was nearing Jack's office, so I put off the other call. "You've been quiet," I said to Jack. He'd taken off the glasses and run his hand through his hair, spiking up Dr. Lin's prissy man bangs. "Are you about to say something serious? Because the mustache is a problem."

"I can't take it off without solvent, so deal with it. No, just thinking."

"About what?"

"The paintings."

"It's a shame," I said. "Three new Chaus, falling into those hands."

"Three new Chaus," he nodded. "It sure is."

24

I paid the cabbie and we climbed the stairs to Jack's office. "The new window's not bad," I said, seeing it for the first time. "Trim all painted and everything."

"The new window stinks. My entire fee for this case is going for a real one."

"You think you're getting paid? By Dr. Yang?"

"He gave me a retainer. Damn lucky, because you're probably right, I shouldn't expect anything else."

"He might even sue you," I said cheerfully. "To get the retainer back."

I called my client while Jack went off to the bathroom to use his solvent.

"Ms. Chin!" Dennis Jerrold was cautiously eager as ever. "News?"

"Yes, Mr. Jerrold. Things have changed. We need a meeting."

"What's wrong? Are the Chaus about to be unveiled?"

"No. The good news for you is, it looks like the fake Chaus with Mike Liu's poems on them won't be shown at all."

"That *is* good news. In fact, it's terrific and it's better than I expected. So why do I get the feeling I'm not supposed to celebrate?"

"Don't pop the champagne yet. As I said, things have changed. There are three real Chaus that just turned up, and they will be shown."

"Oh. You're right, that's not great. Turned up from where?"

"I can't tell you that. But they're real, they're authenticated, and they're going on the market. However, I think I can still do right by you."

"Oh? How's that?"

I repeated, "We need a meeting."

Bill showed up at Jack's office twenty minutes later. I buzzed him in and met him at the door.

"Am I in time?"

"Plenty," I said. "Jerrold will be here in half an hour."

"Not for that. To see Jack's outfit."

"The outfit, yes," said Jack, coming out of the bathroom in black jeans and a white Oxford shirt. His wet hair was combed back and his face showed every sign of being freshly scrubbed. He pointed to the padded jacket and discount pants hanging over a chair.

"That's all I get?"

"Can get accent also." Jack bowed, speaking in Lin's nasal tones. "Small scholar of Hohhot does not wish to disappoint."

"He was great," I told Bill.

"Vass he chust as great as Vladimir Oblomov, do you tink?"

"Oblomov, forgive me say so, but is coarse man," Jack said. "Dr. Lin Qiao-xiang, much more refined."

"Dah, you mean, sissy. Real man tuff like Oblomov."

"Could you two pretend your native language is English?" I broke in. "We have work to do."

The English thing was put off a little, though, because for our next trick, Jack and I listened in while Vladimir Oblomov called Lionel Lau.

"Meester Lau, Oblomov here. Pleasure to talk to you. . . . Chust fillink you in, need to esk a favor. . . . Good, Meester Voo already told you about Chaus? He did great job, by de vay, keepink his mouth shut. . . . Oh, yes, two million dollars, cute leetle Lydia says." I gave Bill the stink-eye, but he was in character, so he just shrugged. "Vun tink, now, Meester Lau. Dose friends I vass tellink you about? Dey vould be very grateful, you do dis vun tink for dem. . . ."

Although Dennis Jerrold tried to keep his face pleasantly neutral as he stepped into Jack's office forty-five minutes later, it wasn't hard to tell he found the surroundings more congenial than my Canal Street back room. Well, nuts to him. "Hi, Mr. Jerrold," I said. "Thanks for coming."

"Thanks for making the meeting place so convenient. Is this your office?" That question, addressed to Bill, must have been diplomacy, because he couldn't have been serious. Even bling-free, Bill does not look like an uptown-office kind of guy.

"Mr. Jerrold," I said, "if we'd known from the start where you worked we could have made all our meetings more convenient. No, this is Jack Lee's office—you met him, remember?—and he was supposed to be back here by now. I don't see why we shouldn't start without him, though. Would you like some coffee? Tea?"

He wanted coffee, of course, and so did Bill, and I made myself some green tea from the supplies Jack had replenished specifically to make this afternoon run smoothly.

"The paintings," I said. "The Chaus you hired me to find. There are four, we found them, they're fakes, and as I said on the phone, they won't be authenticated and they won't be sold. Though they're really beautiful, as it happens." I sipped my tea: high-quality, but I'd made it too strong.

"Beauty's not the point," Jerrold said.

"That's the problem with politics," said Bill.

"Yes, fine, we'll debate that some other time. Where did they come from?"

"I can't tell you who made them," I said. "What I can say is, they do have Mike Liu's poems on them, and not only would showing them next week have embarrassed the PRC, it seems that was the whole point."

"That's why they were made?"

"No, but it's why they were going to be shown. If you want to tell your boss, and he wants to tell Mr. Jin at the Consulate, and you want to modestly take credit for saving the PRC some serious face, we'll back you up."

"Well, I'll certainly do that if it's the best I can get. Though I'd really like to know—"

"You're not going to know, so forget it."

He pursed his lips. A sticky point in the negotiations; pass it by, accomplish something else so you and the other party can feel good about each other, return later. "But don't we still have a problem?" We. Give the other party the sense you're on the same team. "You said there were three real Chaus about to come on the market."

"Yes. From a private collection."

"The interest in Chau brought them into the open?"

"In a way, it did. I don't think we can stop their sale. But forewarned is forearmed. We can tell you where they'll be shown and who's doing the authentication. You can tell the people at the Consulate. They can get their own experts, pooh-pooh the whole thing, whatever they want to do. Cast some doubt, be wet blankets."

"All right," Jerrold said, setting his cup down. "I think—"

I was interested to know what he thought, but I wasn't destined to find out. The door popped open and Jack popped through it.

"Hi!" he said. "Mr. Jerrold, sorry I wasn't here to greet you. Welcome to my world." He pulled off his leather jacket. "Hey, coffee! What a great idea."

He poured himself a cup and joined us, looking particularly bright-eyed and bushy-tailed.

"We were just telling Mr. Jerrold about the new Chaus," I said.

"The new Chaus!" Jack took a quick sip of coffee. "Hey, this is pretty good. You must have made it."

"No, Bill did."

"Oh. Well, it's good anyway. The new Chaus. I have a couple of things to say about them, myself. They're new." He sat back, beaming.

"Yes," I said. "We know that part."

"No, you don't. You mean unknown. I mean new." He jumped up and went to his desk, where he switched the computer on and rotated the monitor so we could all see. "These photos from the spy camera aren't great but they're good enough." On the screen, with a couple of mouse clicks, he called up the three paintings Dr. Yang had brought to the gallery. He added close-up details from each, and tiled everything on a single screen. "These paintings"—he tapped the screen with the back of his hand—"are new." He sat back down. "You said in the cab I was quiet. I was thinking. What I was thinking was, if Dr. Yang brought those paintings with him when he left China, I really am Lin from Hohhot."

"Who's Dr. Yang? Does he have these? Who's Lin?" My client was confused.

I ignored him. "What do you mean, Jack? We know he had three. Anna said so."

"Who's Anna?"

"He might." Jack ignored Jerrold, too. "But not those three. You saw them."

"They're beautiful."

"They sure are. Chau never painted like that."

"I thought all his paintings are supposed to be beautiful."

"They are. But they don't look like that. They don't have that pared-away quality, like the painter knows exactly what matters and what doesn't. Or that sense that he knows what he wanted to do and he did it and he doesn't give a damn if you like it." Jack grinned. "But they would have. In Chau's mature period. If he'd lived."

"What are you saying? You think these are fakes, too? Just better fakes?"

"No." He clearly wanted to keep the suspense going, make us keep asking, but he also clearly couldn't wait to tell. "This very is-sue was part of the full and frank exchange of views I had not an hour ago with Dr. Yang. They're not fakes and they're not old. They're Chaus. From his mature period. Painted within the last year. Chau's alive."

You could've heard a pin drop, if anything as messy as a loose pin were to be found in Jack's office. Then we all recovered at once.

"Jack—"

"Jack—"

"Mr. Lee!" My client was the guy with the loudest voice. "The Ghost Hero? He's alive?"

"Dr. Yang admitted it. He's an old friend of Chau's. Smuggled out of China around the same time, as it turns out, and by the same smuggler."

"*What?*" I said. "No. That story—you were there—"

"He said the story was true. But the man who died was someone else."

I sat openmouthed. Meanwhile Jerrold, with impressive diplomatic cool, said, "Where is he?"

"Chau? I can't tell you."

"Mr. Lee, you—"

"No, I mean I really can't. Dr. Yang absolutely drew the line at that. I'm assured, though, that he's been an American citizen for many years, under a shiny new name, living a shiny new life. Painting only in private, never showing. He was more than happy to give his old bud Dr. Yang those three paintings, though, to help him out of a hole. Like everyone else, he'd heard all the rumors about new Chaus, and he felt responsible for Dr. Yang's troubles."

"What troubles?"

"Trouble's all fixed, don't worry about it," Jack said, though worried wasn't how Jerrold looked.

"Whatever that means," Jerrold said, "this guy's a fugitive from a friendly foreign power and I want to know where to find him."

"You won't find him. You could ask Dr. Yang, but," Jack surveyed Jerrold, "I guarantee you wouldn't last a minute."

"I'd like to try."

"Oh, Mr. Jerrold!" I broke in. "Really, what good would it do?

Are you thinking that turning Chau over to the Chinese government would help your chances for promotion? If it's true he's a U.S. citizen, the Chinese government can't touch him."

"It is true," Jack affirmed. "Dr. Yang's one, too. Very efficient smuggler."

"We could agree to extradite them." Jerrold wasn't giving up.

"For Tiananmen crimes?" Jack was enjoying himself. "Just wait until *that* hits the news. You're with the government, Jerrold, so maybe you don't know this, but we're supposed to be the *good* guys. The Chinese government, during Tiananmen, they were the *bad* guys. Friendly foreign power, feh."

Jerrold fixed Jack with a hard stare. "You said they were smuggled in. If they entered the country illegally I could—"

"No, you couldn't." Bill got in the act. "Twenty years ago someone in the INS obviously decided whatever they were using for paperwork was good enough. Maybe even someone in your own Department told them it was. Gave Chau and Yang political asylum. While you were playing Little League."

"Pop Warner," Jack corrected. "Pee-wee football, not baseball, right? All thuggery, no finesse. Give it up, Jerrold. We have two smuggled Chinese Tiananmen intellectuals, right under our noses, and you can't touch 'em."

Dennis Jerrold, his face grim, watched Jack smile and sip coffee. A few moments of silence, then, "I want the smuggler."

I took a quick look at Jack, then said, "What?"

"The smuggler, Ms. Chin." Jerrold sat back in his chair. "Chau and Yang, whoever Yang is, may be U.S. citizens, they may be political heroes, they may be untouchable. Fine, you win. The smuggler's something else. Undocumented aliens coming into this country, that's a hot-button topic. For all we know the smuggler has been running a snakehead operation, flooding our shores with undesirables for two decades now."

"I doubt it."

"I don't care. No matter what heroes he smuggled in, no one will think the smuggler's a hero. The press on netting a human trafficker—it's all good. The PRC government won't be happy about Chau being out of their reach, but the smuggler's a good consolation prize."

"Forget it."

"No, you forget it. Entering the country illegally is a felony. If you know the smuggler's identity and refuse to reveal it you're committing one, too."

"You're not law enforcement," Bill said.

"So I'll call the Justice Department."

"We'll call our lawyers. This could go on a long time."

"Are you all prepared for that? Long legal cases are expensive. This office is nice, but it's a little minimal. And Ms. Chin's? You don't strike me as people with a lot of discretionary funds. I doubt if it will be good for the investigation business, either, to be involved in a drawn-out legal proceeding in which I paint you as less than patriotic. Give me his name."

"How would we know?" I said. "Jack just found out about Chau an hour ago."

"You've all apparently known about Yang, whoever that is, for much longer than that. Tell me who smuggled him in."

"I don't know," I said.

"Me either."

"Me either."

"For people who lie for a living you all do it pretty damn poorly."

I sipped my tea. It had grown bitter. "Mr. Jerrold," I said, "giving the PRC the smuggler's name might win you a promotion. It could also get the smuggler killed."

"That's the risk he took. Listen well. Even before I bring the Justice Department in—which I will do, believe me—I can make your lives miserable. Like to travel? I'll put you on the terrorist watch list, you'll never get on a plane again. In fact, no one in your family will. Any of your families. I'll put them all on the list. Or get a bank loan, a college loan, a mortgage . . . Not to mention your licenses, gone in a flash. You guys are screwed. Accept it. I want that name. Then we'll all be friends again."

"We were never friends," I said.

"So we'll never be friends. I don't give a damn." He waited another few moments, then took out his phone. "Okay, I'm calling Justice."

"Wait," said Jack.

"Yes?" Jerrold lowered the phone. "I'm waiting."

"I want to make a deal."

"What deal?"

"Jack!" I yelped.

Jack shook his head. "I'm sorry, Lydia. It would be hard enough on my family if I got arrested, but the rest of this stuff? You're from a Chinese family, you know. My sisters, their kids. My dad's an academic, flies everywhere all the time. I can't let this happen to them."

"He can't do it," Bill said.

"I sure as hell can," said Jerrold. *"What deal?"*

"Listen, Jack—"

"Oh, shut up, you guys. I'm sorry. I'm not big and tough like you. I'm a wimp and I can't do it." To Jerrold: "I'll give you the smuggler's name. But I need to get something in return."

"How about, you and your family don't end up on the terrorist watch list?"

Jack shook his head. "Not enough. Once it gets out who gave this guy up—"

"It won't get out."

"Bullshit. Of course it will." Jack rubbed the back of his neck. "I need to live in this community. The Chinese community, I mean. So does Lydia. Bill, well, what's the opposite of collateral damage? What I'm saying, we need something sweet to counteract the stench of ratting a guy out."

"I'm not ratting anyone out," I said.

"That's not the way it'll look." Jack didn't meet my glare.

"What do you want?" Jerrold asked.

"Who would you take this to? Jin, at the Consulate?" At Jerrold's nod, Jack said, "Call him. Get him over here."

"First of all, I don't just call the Cultural Attaché and tell him 'get over here.' Second, I'd need to hear what you have to say before I approach Jin."

"You won't. I have a deal to offer, and if I need to get a lawyer to help me offer it I'll do it in public. You'll get what you want, in the end, but I'll make the whole thing as embarrassing for the State Department as I possibly can. That won't do anything for your promotion, will it?"

"Promotion" was the magic word. Dennis Jerrold dialed the Consulate of the People's Republic of China.

25

It was a tense twenty minutes up there in Jack's office, waiting for Jin. I tried to talk to Jack but he cold-shouldered me. He made fresh coffee. Bill had some of the coffee. Jerrold, as though he were at the dentist, leafed through an art book. I didn't have more tea; the last thing I needed was caffeine to blend with the adrenaline already sizzling through me. I kind of felt like I was at the dentist, too.

Finally, the downstairs buzzer buzzed, and Jack answered it. He waited at the door as he had for us—was that only the day before yesterday?—and stepped aside to admit a sour-faced, bald Asian man. Jerrold rose to his feet. I did, also, before I could stop myself. Bill didn't.

"Mr. Jin. Thank you for coming." Dennis Jerrold executed a creditable bow, which Jin returned.

"Mr. Jerrold. You say, important." Jin looked around the room, then strode forward and took a chair.

Now Bill did stand, because there were only four chairs, and five of us. He went over to lean on the sill of the new window.

"It is important." Jerrold brought Jin a cup of my bitter green tea. He introduced each of us, and Jin gave us each an unsmiling nod, remaining seated. Jerrold said, "These people have a . . . proposal for us."

"Bill and I don't," I said.

"Lydia, you might as well get in on it, because it's happening anyway," Jack said. "And it's not a proposal. It's a deal. In response to a threat."

Jack brought Jin into the loop in a couple of sentences. Jin listened intently, interrupting only once—"Alive? Chau Chun is *alive*?"—and after Jack was done he sat grimly sipping tea. No one else spoke, either, until Jin finally said to Jerrold, "You cannot arrest Yang? Make him tell you location of Chau?"

"I'm sorry." Jerrold, shamefaced, apologized to Jin for the rule of law. "He'd get a lawyer immediately. I have certain . . . pressures . . . I can put on people"—he gave Jack a look—"but in this situation I doubt if they'd work. And if we did find him, Chau I mean, there's not much we could do anyway."

Jin pursed his lips, gestured at Jack. "What he say. Your government will not extradite. Is true?"

"I'm afraid it probably is. The events surrounding the Tiananmen riots are seen differently here from the way the Chinese people understand them—"

Jin waved him off with his teacup. To Jack, he said, "What do you want?"

Jack took a deep breath, and said, "Mike Liu."

This was beyond pins dropping. You could've dropped a piano through the ceiling and no one would have noticed.

Just to make sure Jin knew who he was talking about, Jack gave him the Chinese version. "Liu Mai-ke. I'll give you the smuggler's name if your government frees Liu Mai-ke."

"What the hell—" Jerrold started.

"Listen! There's going to be a big Free Liu Mai-ke rally next week. Designed to embarrass the PRC government." Jack turned to Jin. "Those paintings, the phony Chaus, have Mike Liu's poems on them. I don't suppose you knew that."

"No, I did not."

"Well, they do, and they'll probably have the paintings at the rally."

Jerrold pointed accusingly at me. "I thought she said they wouldn't—"

"As Chaus. They won't be exhibited or brought onto the market as Chaus. But they may well be shown as, I guess you'd say, homages. Just because they're not authentic doesn't mean they won't be used to make a political point."

He looked to me. I gave an irritated shrug. From Jerrold came a sharp, exasperated breath.

"And the real Chaus," Jack said. "They *are* going on the market. At exactly the same time as the rally. Which is smack in the middle of Beijing/NYC. Mr. Jin, your government is going to come off looking pretty bad, with Chaus and fake Chaus and Mike Liu's poetry all over the place, at exactly the moment when you're spending a lot of money to look good. Here," he added, "in New York."

New York, the Cultural Attaché's turf. From which, presumably, he'd rather not be called home in disgrace. You could tell from his stony face that these words were not lost on Jin.

"Or," Jack said, settling in his chair, "you can disarm the whole thing. Mike Liu's been off people's minds for a while now, so it won't look like you're yielding to pressure. Say he's sick, how's that? The PRC and the Communist Party can demonstrate your great humanitarian compassion by releasing him. Once he's out, he's useless as a symbol. Nothing to rally about, no reason to show the fake paintings."

"And the real ones?" Jerrold demanded.

Jack shrugged. "Not a lot we can do about that."

"You can tell me where they are. I might be able to delay the sale until after Beijing/NYC. There's pressure, and there's pressure. As you know."

Yeah, I thought, and I'd like to see you try it on the guy who ultimately owns them now: Lionel Lau.

"You guys are both diplomats." Jack was beginning to look pleased with himself again. "I'm sure you can spin this to your bosses. Explain how you saved the PRC all kinds of face. What a media crisis you averted. Get your own experts to refute the new Chaus. Beijing/NYC can go on, all the approved artists can sip white wine with the critics, and the PRC can sit back and rake in millions from the sale of tame art. Win-win. How about it?"

Jerrold exchanged a glance with Jin. Damn these people. I sent Bill a look, and then I said, "Not yet."

Everyone turned to me.

"Jack, if you're selling our souls here, the price isn't high enough. Mr. Jerrold, we'll give you the name of the smuggler, God help us. We'll also tell you who has the new paintings. But Mike Liu doesn't only get released from prison. He gets kicked out of the country. Well, come on, people. What's to keep the PRC from grabbing him up again as soon as this is over? You get what you want once Mike Liu lands here."

Way to raise the stakes, Lydia. The first to speak, coming from left field, was Bill. "If you agree to this," he said, "I can get the sale of the real Chaus delayed."

"What?"

"There's pressure," Bill said. "And there's pressure."

"You said you couldn't—what are you—" Jerrold was practically sputtering.

"Mr. Jerrold, you're a reputable diplomat." Under the circumstances Bill's tone wasn't nearly as sarcastic as it might have been. "I'm sure you understand what I'm saying when I tell you, you don't want to know."

"But he can do it, I guarantee," I said. "And the last thing is, as part of this deal, the State Department has to agree to accept Mike Liu. To give him asylum."

"No asylum!" Jin barked. "Stupid poet. That make him sound like political prisoner."

As opposed to what, I wondered, but I kept silent. I could see on Jerrold's face that he'd heard the same thing I had: If Jin was negotiating the terms of Mike Liu's release, he'd already agreed to it.

In Chinese, Jerrold asked Jin to step into the hall with him. That was almost funny, Bill being the only person here who didn't understand what he said; but I got the feeling the language choice was more out of courtesy than secrecy anyway. They left together, Jerrold holding the door for Jin. We three sat in silence, and after a while Jerrold came back in, picked up one of Jack's chairs, and carried it into the hall. Holding the door and carrying chairs? Maybe there was more than one reason why he was still staff, not line. Jerrold set the chair in the hallway alcove. Jin sat and took out his cell phone.

"This is a conversation Mr. Jin would understandably rather keep private," Jerrold said, coming back into the room and closing the door behind him. "We'll wait."

Once again, I wondered, *As opposed to what?*

If the twenty minutes before Jin had arrived were tense, the forty

Jin spent in the hall gave new meaning to I-need-to-jump-up-and-run-around-the-room-screaming. I didn't, though. I passed the time thinking about my mother's reaction to my face in *The New York Times* anywhere near the words "federal indictment." I don't know what Bill was thinking, but after about half an hour he pulled out a cigarette and nailed Jack with a look that squelched any protest Jack might've made. Jack glanced at the new window, but being only temporary, it didn't open. He sat back, rubbing his neck.

Finally the door opened and Jin strode back in. We all shot to attention, but Jin waited while Jerrold retrieved his chair from the hallway. He settled himself, not looking any more jovial than before.

"Have spoken, my superiors," Jin said. "Liu Mai-ke, pah, stupid man, bad poet. Nothing but irritation, stirs up other stupid people. Unlikely will be rehabilitated. People's Republic better without him. Will send him here. You"—he pointed a thick finger at Jack—"will tell us name of human trafficker. You"—moving to Bill—"will stop sale of Chaus."

"Delay," I said.

"*You*"—the finger swung to me—"will be silent!"

"And none of you," Jerrold added, visibly relieved and palpably taking charge, "will go anywhere until this deal is complete. Just in case you were thinking of running out on us. Or warning anybody."

"No problem," said Jack.

"You bet, no problem. This whole process shouldn't take more than twenty-four hours. Let's go."

"Wait," I said. "Go where?"

"Don't worry, the quarters are comfortable. And the food's not bad, and it's on us. Now, either you all accompany me voluntarily, or I'll ask the Nineteenth Precinct to detain you in *their* quarters.

I'll have to call Justice to get that to happen, and the whole process is kind of a pain, so I'll be even more aggravated than I am now. How aggravated do you want me? If this all works out, you'll be home in your own beds tomorrow night. If it doesn't, you'll want to practice being guests of Uncle Sam, anyway."

Which is how I came to be spending the night—without my cell phone—in a government-contracted four-star hotel on the Upper East Side. I ate grilled salmon in a small but, as promised, comfortable room with a giant TV, a lovely view over the East River, a disconnected phone, and a State Department security officer outside my door. Jack and Bill, I understood, were billeted together down the hall. Because they were both large guys, I hoped their room was bigger.

26

Morning's usually a busy time for me. I wake up early, go running, or rollerblading, or to the dojo. Get my blood moving before the action starts. Not today, though. The sunrise over the East River was gorgeous, the hotel bathrobe was comfy, the shower was fabulous, and breakfast was quite tasty, featuring a selection of premium teas. Lunch wasn't bad either. I was climbing the walls by the time the security officer knocked on the door at midafternoon to tell me the car was here.

Yesterday's final negotiation—besides one phone call to my mother, to tell her I was working overnight—was that we'd all, including the Yang family, be at the airport to see Mike Liu arrive.

"They're putting him on a plane that gets in at five," Jerrold said. "Direct flight. You don't trust me to call and tell you he's here?"

"You're kidding, right?"

So we all piled into a black government limo, Jerrold up front with the driver, Bill and me in the normal backseat, Jack in the one facing us. Which meant we all had to stare at each other on the hour-long drive.

When we finally got to Newark after sixty particularly long

minutes, the car dropped us and went off to park in some special diplomat place. Jerrold flashed credentials and we were led through blank hallways and up an elevator, then shown to a room with a one-way window overlooking the vast space where people wait to meet international travelers.

Jerrold checked his watch. "Plane should be just landing." The door opened, admitting Mr. Jin and Dr. Yang. The professor glared around the room, with just slightly more discernible anger and contempt for Jack than for the rest of us. Jin and Jerrold bowed to each other. No one spoke. We all stood at the window, watching the crowd below. A normal crowd, no press, no Mike Liu welcoming committee. That was part of the deal, too. And Jin had won on the no-asylum demand, but Mike Liu, being married to an American citizen, could start his naturalization process this same afternoon.

An unbroken stream of people pulled suitcases or pushed piled carts through the doors, looked around, got their bearings in America, and went on. Some spotted people waiting for them in the crowd; some had to look deeper, because their people were farther back. If your people happened to be Anna and Mrs. Yang, you'd have seen them in a second, Anna leaning over the waist-high barrier, her mother standing beside her. Anna was in constant motion, rising on her toes, tilting left and right, as though at a ball game tied in the final minutes when everyone's on their feet and you can't see. Finally, she saw.

The glass in our window was ballistic, an inch thick, but I'd swear I heard Anna shout Mike's name. A man just through the doors stopped. He was thinner and paler but otherwise looked exactly like the photos I'd seen of Mike Liu. Appearing dazed, he searched the crowd. Anna jumped, waved, shouted all at once. He spotted her, pushed his way over, and enveloped her in a huge, crushing hug. The little group disappeared out the terminal doors.

"Okay," Jerrold said. "That was touching. Now you owe us. And this information had better be good. Or—"

"We know," I snapped. "The terrorist watch list, the Justice Department, our families, we know."

Jack turned from the window. "Don't worry. It's good."

He waited for Dr. Yang, but the professor's mouth was drawn into a hard, flat line. He shook his head slowly: He wasn't going to speak.

So Jack nodded, rubbed the back of his neck, and gave Jerrold and Jin the name they'd been waiting for.

He said, "Doug Haig."

27

The debriefing was, well, not so brief. The four of us—the Three Musketeers and Dr. Yang—sat alone in separate rooms waiting for Jerrold, or Jin, or Jerrold and Jin, to stride in and hurl questions at us. We each told the story as we had it. I gave my version, messing up the details that were mine to mess up, forgetting the answers that were mine to forget. Our versions were unavoidably different, just as we'd planned. Nothing's more suspicious than four people whose stories match exactly, especially if three of them are supposed to have gotten the facts secondhand. Bill and Jack were pros, so I wasn't too worried about them screwing up. It was Dr. Yang, the academic with a certain professional stake in the truth, and little experience at interrogations, who concerned me. On the other hand, he had the most to lose; he was capable of improvising—witness the three paintings, when the plan had been for him to bring one—and as Jack pointed out, he had the scariest scowl.

To Jerrold, on his first visit to my windowless room, I gave the details of the investigation we were claiming we'd done. We'd looked into the situation, so the story went, after Dr. Yang told us about Doug Haig arranging for him to slip out of China. We didn't know about Chau then, I said, but his story must be substantially the same. I told Jerrold what was there to be found, most of it on the Web, which is where PI's do our background investigations these days, didn't he know that? All the evidence, of course, was circumstantial: records of Haig's China trips, meetings he'd had with young artists who'd been caught up in the Tiananmen violence or denounced afterward. Some of the information I directed Jerrold to was real. Haig had made a lot of trips, talked to a lot of people. The patterns that pointed to political activity, though— phone records, surveillance reports from not-quite-identified, now defunct Chinese agencies, newspaper photos documenting Haig's presence in this town or that—had been planted by Linus, to shore up reality.

It wasn't the nature of the evidence against Haig that brought the steam out of Jerrold's ears, however. It was Haig. "He's an American citizen!"

"You were thinking a Chinese person pulled this off?"

"I can't turn him over to the Chinese government! And you're not giving me anywhere near enough to arrest him here."

"Mr. Jerrold, we didn't promise we'd make your case for you. We just said we'd give you the smuggler's name. You'll have to do your own police work. Maybe you can get Haig to confess."

"Oh, sure! On what basis?"

Actually, I had no idea, so I held my tongue, and he stomped out. The really lucky break in all of this was that neither Jerrold nor Jin knew Haig particularly well. If they had, they'd never have bought for a minute the fantasy that Doug Haig would lift a finger, especially in the face of danger, to rescue anyone.

Finally, disgusted with my inability to deliver damning details, Jerrold told me I was free to go. I called Bill and Jack from the airport monorail, left messages on both their phones, and settled in for the ride home.

28

Threading through the boisterous crowd to reach our center-of-the-action banquette, a waiter lifted down a single-barrel bourbon, neat; a martini with three olives; and a pink cosmo in a wide-mouthed glass.

"Oh, come on, you guys," I said to Bill and Jack. "I'm supposed to drink that?"

"Do it," Jack said. "Don't be a wimp."

"Speaking of wimps"—I picked the glass up and sniffed at it—"Jack, I said it before but I'll say it again: You were *fabulous*."

"Completely convincing," Bill agreed. "Except you said 'smuggler' about three dozen times."

"I was trying to plant the seed and I wasn't sure Jerrold was catching on. I'm sorry, Lydia, but your client does seem a bit thick."

"He works for the government," I reminded him. "*Your* client, on the other hand, has an instinctive genius for the con. As do you. Jack, you *so* sold it!"

We all clinked glasses. Jack said, "I'm not sure that's a good thing."

"What, that your acting talents are Oscar-level?"

"That I can be that convincing as a sell-out lily-livered spineless rat."

"Bill was convincing as a Russian thug."

"I'm talking about *acting*."

"Guys?" That was a fourth voice. We looked up to see Eddie To standing at our table. "What just happened?" I slid over and Eddie slipped in next to me. He was introduced to Bill, whose hand he shook; then he looked around the table, blinked, and said, "Frank and I just had a long conversation with a gentleman, and I use the word dubiously, named Lionel Lau."

"So he did call," Jack said.

"Just the way you said he would. It's a good thing we were prepared or we'd have both been on the floor in a swoon. He represented himself as the new owner of Baxter/Haig, which he'll be liquidating as soon as he can. No, as soon as *we* can. He wants Red Sky to handle the sale of the current inventory, for a fee."

"A fair one?"

"Jack. Those works, I'd have paid *him* to have our name associated with. But very fair, thank you. And he tells us we're welcome after that to whatever artists are willing to sign with us, their existing contracts becoming null and void upon the dissolution of the gallery. Apparently Frank and I were highly recommended as experts in the field."

"Is that wrong?"

"No, of course it's not wrong. It's merely miraculous." A waiter appeared at his elbow. "Would it be out of line to order champagne?"

Jack said, "I don't think so, no."

The waiter was dispatched for some Tattinger's and a selection of munchies.

"Furthermore," Eddie To continued, "two also dubious gentlemen are reported to have appeared at Baxter/Haig within the hour, waving badges and wanting to discuss various things with the proprietor."

"Who reported that?"

"Caitlin Craig, when she called to inquire whether we'd be needing administrative help."

"Haig's nervous assistant?" I asked. "She's leaving the sinking ship already?"

"It seems so. Do you think we should take her on?"

"She probably knows a lot about the inventory. You'd have to nurse her through a case of PTSD, but it might be worth it. I wouldn't touch Nick Greenbank, though."

"Uck. Not with surgical gloves. But that's on principle. You have something specific in mind?"

"We think he was Lau's inside man. Probably ever since Haig first borrowed money from Lau. He's how Woo knew about me."

"Who's Woo?"

"Never mind," said Jack. "Just do this: Get things in writing with Lionel Lau and stick to the letter of the contract. In case of a tie, do it his way."

"Jack, what are you telling me? The man's a crook?"

"Yes."

"In the art world? How can that be?"

"And I'd suggest that when you're done with the liquidation, you be done with Lau, too," I said.

"I see. Well, you people have certainly proved to be fonts of wisdom so far. I'll tell Frank to do as you say."

The waiter returned with a champagne flute, and plates of prosciutto-wrapped figs, tiny *merguez* lamb meatballs, and boiled peanuts with salt and seaweed. This hip multi-culti bar was one of Jack's favorite haunts. Bill and I had let him pick the celebration spot because he'd had the hardest role in the con.

Eddie To lifted his glass, watched the bubbles rise, and took a swallow. "Yum. So tell me, besides being unable to pay his debt to a crook, is Haig in trouble? The men with the badges—has being a douchebag become a crime?"

"It hasn't, but he is," said Jack. "It won't last, though. For what he's accused of, there's no proof."

"Did he do it?"

"No. The trail's long, but it's mostly fresh brushstrokes to fit the picture we wanted to paint."

"Careful," I said. "That's awfully close to a nature metaphor."

"Well," Eddie said, "lucky for Haig, then."

"Sure," Jack said. "He only has two problems. One's Lau, but he expected that. His plan, if he couldn't pay him off, was to let Lau have Baxter/Haig and walk away. Find another sucker to finance him and start again."

"You speak of that plan in the past tense. As though it were over."

"It is. The other problem interferes. The PRC government's seriously irritated with him. I don't think he'll be getting any more visas."

Eddie To's eyes lit up behind the round glasses. "Doug Haig, PNG in the PRC?"

Jack nodded and stuck the silver martini sword into his mouth so he could pull the olives off.

"Can it be?" Eddie said. "Doug Haig's edge, gone? The era of Haig Hegemony over the field of contemporary Chinese art, coming to a close?"

"The sun sets on every empire," I said.

"Drink your cosmo," said Jack.

I held my pink drink up to the light as Eddie had his champagne and squinted at it.

"I'm not sure I want to hear any more," Eddie said. "It almost sounds like you people framed Doug Haig for something he didn't do."

"Would that bother you?"

"Are you serious? I just don't want to know too much because I don't want to be arrested when you are."

"We already were arrested," I said. "And look at us now."

"You were?"

"Well, close."

Eddie waited, but no more explanation was forthcoming. "All right," he shrugged and said. "The fact that Frank and I have suddenly become Rulers of the Universe is only one of the thunderbolts Lau threw. Among the items he wants us to unload are three new Chaus."

"He told you you can't do that until after next week, right?" said Bill.

"'Unload' is the least important word in that sentence." Eddie frowned at Bill. "Three! New! Chaus! *New*. Previously unknown. In fact, previously unpainted. Lau says they're new, like really, really new. He says Chau's alive."

"Well," I cautiously brought the cosmo closer, "there've always been those rumors. And Bernard Yang is ready to authenticate these as real, and possibly new. Of course, authentications are often disputed."

"These won't be," said Jack.

"Not that they're Chaus, no. But that they were painted in the last year or so. I just want Eddie to be prepared. He may get a different opinion from Dr. Snyder, or from the real Dr. Lin."

"There's a fake Dr. Lin?" Eddie asked.

Jack didn't answer that. Instead, he said, "He won't."

I'd been about to taste the pink thing, but I stopped. "Jack? What are you saying? Those are the Chaus from Anna's room. From the Tiananmen days. They're not new."

Jack paused before he spoke. "When I told Dr. Yang about the plan, after the first burst of Jack-that's-insane, he started arguing details. He said those three Chaus were Anna's, given to her before she was born so she'd never forget what's important. He couldn't give them away, they weren't his. Anyone else, I'd have thought he didn't want to part with them because they're worth so much. But Dr. Yang would do anything for Anna. So I thought maybe he wasn't interested in any scheme that would get Mike Liu out of prison."

"Mike Liu's getting out of prison?" Eddie broke in.

"He's out, Eddie."

"Let Jack finish," I said.

"But—" said Eddie, looking like the Red Queen had just suppressed him.

"It's not public yet," said Jack. "So keep it in your hat. It will be, in a few days."

"I—" Eddie stopped. "Am I supposed to have any idea what we're talking about?"

"No."

"Oh. Fine." He reached for a fig.

"So I asked him," Jack said. "About Mike. He told me to back off. He'd opposed the marriage because he didn't want Anna involved with a Chinese dissident, something he knew something about. But now Mike's his son-in-law, now he's family. I said, then for his son-in-law's freedom, Anna's happiness, and incidentally her career, this was his best shot. Now, Eddie, here's what matters to you. Where Dr. Yang got stuck every time was at claiming Chau was alive. I told him we had to, that we had to make them want badly something that they couldn't get, so they'd demand second best, which was the smuggler. He dug in and fought me. I thought his problem was the old idea of exploiting his friend."

"But?" I said.

"Finally he told me he had to think and he'd call me. When he did and agreed, I thought I'd just worn him down. Then at the gallery he pulled those paintings out, and I got it. You were blindsided because he brought three. For me it was the paintings themselves."

"Jack, really, you're not saying—"

"Yes, I am. The line quality, the composition—everything about those paintings screams the same painter, twenty years later. When I was supposed to be up the street having coffee while you guys messed with Jerrold's head in my office? I really *was* with Dr. Yang. I had to know. Then I came back and read from my script the way we'd made it up. Except it was all true."

"My God. Jack, really?" I stared at him. "The Ghost Hero is alive?"

Jack looked into the clear liquor of his drink, possibly because it was more attractive than the three pairs of bugging eyes around the table. Well, two—mine and Eddie's. And one narrowed: Bill's. He doesn't bug. Jack went on: "That's why Dr. Yang didn't want us to say it. Because it's true."

"Oh." I sank back against the banquette.

Eddie To sat openmouthed and speechless.

After a moment, Bill said, "The same smuggler? Around the same time?"

"That's right. Exactly what we said. Chau's been underground for twenty years. Painting, never showing, just the way we had it. He's a citizen, so he's not actually in danger, but Yang didn't want to out him."

"What made him change his mind?"

"He talked to Chau."

"Oh," I said again.

"Chau told him to get over himself. He said this was for Anna, what was the big deal? If a lot of problems could be solved by people thinking he was still alive, so fine. And by the way, don't use Anna's paintings from China, here are three actual new ones."

"Why?"

"He said Dr. Yang had never made a false attribution in his life and he wouldn't let him start now. If he was going to have to sign off on paintings as new to make gangsters happy—by which, apparently, he meant Jerrold and Jin as well as Lionel Lau—they were going to be new."

"You know," I said, "I think he really may be a hero."

"But not a ghost. The only thing he asked was that Dr. Yang not say where he was if at all possible. He likes his new life."

"Jack," said Eddie. "Jack. The Ghost Hero lives, he's still painting, and Red Sky will be showing the first new Chaus in twenty years? Do I have that essentially correct?"

"You do."

"Oh. My. *God!* Jack, if I weren't already married to Frank I'd marry you. You could marry us both! I'm sure Frank won't mind. Jack, will you marry us?"

"No. But maybe you should go home and break the good news to Frank."

"I will. I will." Eddie gulped the rest of his champagne and stood. "Though I get the feeling you're throwing me out. You want to be alone with your co-conspirators? Are you starting another conspiracy? I don't want to know. I'm leaving. Will you come to the opening? All of you. The wine will be excellent. It'll be invitation-only. Yes, I'm going. Frank! Oh, Frank!" He practically ran out of the bar.

29

The next morning I slept in. That's unlike me, but the celebration had gone on and on. After the drinks, Jack took us to a Lebanese restaurant for *tajines* and loud music from a joyous three-man band. Then I suggested coffee and tea at Silk Road. Then Bill had an after-hours club he recommended. The sun wasn't yet crawling up over the horizon by the time I got home, but it was nearing it. And I'd had a pink drink.

"Ling Wan-ju," my mother said, as I stumbled into the kitchen in search of the tea I knew she'd made. "You've slept quite soundly. Perhaps you came in late last night. I didn't hear you."

Uh-huh. "Pretty late." I kissed her, grabbed the teapot, and poured a cup.

"How is your case going?"

I took a sip, felt the heat cut its way down my innards. "It's over, Ma. It worked out well."

"You were successful?"

"Yes, we were." Caffeine began kick-starting my brain.

"I see. That is good. Professional success is important. No matter what one's profession."

Uh-huh, again.

"Now that the case is over," my mother said, her back to me as she sorted dishes from the dish rack onto cabinet shelves, "I suppose you will not be seeing the other detective? The Chinese one?"

"Jack? I guess I hadn't thought about it." I hadn't, and I had to say, my first reaction to the idea wasn't positive. "But Ma, I thought you didn't like him."

"Ling Wan-ju." She turned, wearing the wide-eyed look. "I do not know him."

This was true, and was the point at which, normally, I'd have given up. Now, though, maybe prompted by the still-circulating remains of my cosmo, or maybe by the not-yet-faded flush of victory, I found myself soldiering on. "Ma, you just seriously flip-flopped on the subject of Jack. A few days ago you were completely disenchanted when you found out he was an investigator, and second generation, too."

"I do not understand what you mean by 'disenchanted.' I have not been under a spell."

Bilingual communication failure: The Chinese word I'd dredged up to express that thought was obviously not quite right. "If you spoke English I wouldn't always be using the wrong Chinese word," I said. "I meant 'disappointed.'"

"If you spoke better Chinese, you would not, also. I *was* disappointed. I was hoping you had met a young man in a respectable profession. First generation, or possibly Chinese-born. More Chinese than American." She shut the cabinet. "However, you have not. You have met this Lee Yat-sen. You seem to enjoy his company. He appears to be a respectable young man."

"How do you—oh, no. You had someone Google him, didn't you?"

"Someone" could only be one of my brothers, and her affronted look told me I was right. "Ling Wan-ju, I don't know that word, goo-goo. I asked your brother on the telephone if he knew this Lee Yat-sen. He called me back to tell me that he had heard good things about him, as far as that is possible in your profession."

My mother never tells me which brother she's talking about; I'm supposed to just know. In this case, it could have been any of them, until she hit that last snide remark. That made it Tim, and I snorted.

My mother pursed her lips. "Your brother is concerned about you, Ling Wan-ju. He is interested in your happiness."

"He just doesn't want me to embarrass him."

"Bringing shame to your brother would cause you sorrow, would it not? So in this concern, he is interested in your happiness."

I could only stare. The woman was a natural wonder.

"Your brother cares for you," she insisted again. "All your brothers do."

"I suppose you're right. Sometimes they have odd ways of showing it, though." I sighed and finished my tea.

"That is a privilege of family. To express concern and be understood, even if the expression is odd."

"Yes, Ma." I got up, kissed her again, and went off to get dressed and face the day.

30

Three nights later, there was another celebration. As Asian Art Week opened with grand fanfare, and Beijing/NYC debuted to critical praise, the East Village communal studio in Flushing threw a party to welcome Mike Liu to New York. The PRC government had already issued a press release to the effect that, for humanitarian reasons involving his health, lawbreaker Liu Mai-ke had been released from his obligation to the Chinese people to serve his sentence and, by the benevolence of the government and the Party, been sent to the West for medical treatment. The press release had been Xeroxed a few hundred times at different sizes and pinned up all over the studio's corridors, where it had been painted and drawn on by the artists. In some places it was covered with glitter; in others it was folded into origami animals. A giant copy was suspended from the ceiling and hung with bells that tinkled in the breeze whenever the door opened. It kept opening, too, to admit the hippest of the hip; literary and art world stars; Chinese community movers and shakers; and all the downtown glitterati, every one of them dressed in black. The only other color you could see, spotted throughout the crowd, was red, the color of luck and joy.

The party was roaring by the time we arrived, me in black silk pants and sleeveless black blouse, with a chunky red glass necklace; Jack in black suit jacket, black jeans, white shirt and red tie. Bill was a bit out of place, in a charcoal suit with a gray shirt and no tie, but at least he wasn't wearing Vladimir's bling.

"I thought about it," he'd said when he picked me up. "But if Jack won't wear the fat suit, you're not getting the bling, either."

"How is it I'm so lucky?" I'd climbed in the car and we'd fetched Jack and made tracks to Queens.

Unlike our first visit to the studio, entrance tonight was through the loading dock doors. The party and its thumping soundtrack spilled out onto the sidewalk and into the street. "Hey, Jack!" Francie See waved from behind a long outdoor table crowded with wine bottles. "We're taking turns playing bartender. Hi, Lydia, Bill. What can I get you?"

Jack asked for Cabernet, Bill took a beer, and I got a Pellegrino with lime—I was forced to glare at Jack when he asked if I wouldn't rather have a cosmo—and we strolled on inside. Almost no one at this shindig understood the part we'd played in freeing Mike Liu, which was how we wanted it. As far as we knew, just he and Anna, Pete Tsang, and Dr. Yang had any idea at all. Of them, Dr. Yang knew the most, but even he was sketchy on the whole Lionel Lau thing. The less anyone knew, we'd decided, the safer everyone would be.

"Is that Mike Liu?" I pointed down the hall to a thin man with glasses. He was animated, laughing, talking. Radiant, you might say, as was Anna, at his side. "Gee, he doesn't look sick. Let's go get introduced." We headed over, but Mike and Anna were swept up by a writer I recognized from a profile in *The New Yorker*. "Oh," I said. "I guess we'll be later."

"That's the way it goes when you're on the B list," Bill shrugged.

Jack said, "Oh, really? I wouldn't know."

"Jack?" Someone had stepped out in front of us, an Asian woman in a red cheongsam. She raised her voice over the music to say, "Hello, Ms. Chin. Hello, Mr. Smith." It took me a moment, then I realized: Anna's mother.

"Mrs. Yang!" I said. "You look wonderful."

Her bearing was still subdued, dignified, but she no longer looked grim, as she had when we'd met her in Anna's living room. "Thank you. May I speak with you for just a minute?" She included all of us in her gaze, so we followed her through the door of the nearest open studio. It happened to be Francie See's, where the bowl-and-tap painting we'd seen the birth of was pinned to the wall, joining all the other paintings of water, infinitely yielding and yet, in the end, invincible. Mrs. Yang turned to face us.

"I wanted to thank you. For all you've done for Anna, and my family."

I said, "Dr. Yang told you?"

"Yes, he did. He keeps no secrets from me."

"Oh. Well, you're very welcome." The guys seemed to have elected me spokesperson, or maybe I did that myself; so to be properly Chinese about it, I went on, "We're honored to have had the opportunity to help. We were lucky to be able to come up with a fitting solution to the problem."

"Fitting." Mrs. Yang gave a small smile. "Yes, some solutions are more fitting than others. Anna's so happy now that Mike is here, it's hard to remember that my husband and I once opposed this marriage."

"You wanted to protect her," Bill said. "I'm sure she understood that, even if she didn't like the way you tried to do it."

"Of course she did," I said. To my surprise I found myself channeling my mother. "That's a privilege of family. To express concern and be understood, even if the expression's odd."

The look Mrs. Yang gave me was definitely odd. So was what she said: "And beyond family? Can one be understood, do you think, and maybe even forgiven, for expressions of concern that are . . . odd?"

I didn't know what to say because I didn't know what we were talking about. Bill just drank his beer, so I guessed he didn't either. Jack, though, leaned down, kissed Mrs. Yang's cheek, and said, "Forgiveness is always possible, even without understanding. When there's understanding, it's inevitable. Go back to your son-in-law's party, Yang Yu-feng."

After a moment she smiled; then she bowed. Jack bowed back, and she left the room.

I said, "Um?"

Jack smiled as he watched Mrs. Yang make her way down the hall. "She's the one who shot at me."

"What?"

"That's what she wants to be forgiven for. She said he has no secrets from her. But she kept a few from him. She knew Anna had made the paintings, and what Anna and Pete were planning to use them for. That's why the target was me, not Dr. Yang. For one thing, I'm not sure she could bring herself to shoot at him, even if no one was supposed to get hurt. For another, it didn't matter that there are other people who do what I do. By the time Dr. Yang found and hired one of them the Free Mike Liu rally would've happened and the paintings would've been shown. She just wanted to buy time for Anna by scaring me off."

"No, seriously? Where would Mrs. Yang even get a gun?"

"Oh, I don't think she personally did it. She hired it."

"Okay, then where would she get a person with a gun?"

"A gun, and a high slime factor. Right here, in the studio next to Anna's."

"Jon-Jon Jie?"

Jack nodded. "I'm sure Mrs. Yang paid him well. And he probably thought that this would, long-term, give him something to hold over Dr. Yang. For when he wants a show reviewed or something."

"Gunshots in the middle of the day on Madison Avenue? He'd take that kind of risk?"

"Come on, he's a Texas cowboy."

Bill said, "What are you going to do?"

"About her? Nothing. I forgave her. The end. About him?" Jack shrugged.

"Jack, he shot at you!" I said.

"Can't prove it. Besides," he grinned, "he's got enough problems. Every artist here knows he stole the paintings. He has an expensive lease on a Manhattan studio, and he's about to lose his gallery. He'll never drink white wine in this town again."

"You don't think Eddie To will take him on?"

"Not in this lifetime."

Probably conjured by my magical powers, Eddie To right then passed the doorway in the company of a familiar-looking Chinese woman. He took a step backward and leaned in. "Hey! Is this you guys' cabal office?" He led the young woman in. "Hu Mei-fan, this is Jack Lee, Lydia Chin, and Bill Smith. You need to meet them, they're very dangerous."

Hu Mei-fan smiled shyly, a smile that suddenly vanished when she got a look at me. Flushing, not meeting my eyes, she said, "We have met."

In Doug Haig's office, yes we had. "No," I said, "I don't think so."

"Mei-fan's a painter, fresh off the boat from Beijing." Eddie said as the young woman gave me a grateful smile and an almost imperceptible bow of the head. "Really good. We'll be giving her a show later this year, Frank and I. After, you know . . ." He winked and touched a finger to the side of his nose. "About which, by the way, Drs. Snyder and Lin said exactly what you said they'd say."

Jack asked, "They've seen the paintings? They're here?"

"Snyder's here for the week's festivities. Lin's in Hohhot. I sent him photos. Not so easy for him to travel, you know. Though now that he's advisor to the top dogs in Chinese contemporary, he thinks his government may cut him more slack. Listen, if you people don't have any crimes to plan right at the moment, let me buy you a drink."

"Drinks are free here, Eddie."

"All the more reason to get you the best. Come on, come say hi to Frank. Lydia and Bill, you haven't met him yet. He's right over there."

We started out of Francie's studio. "You guys go ahead," I said. "There's someone I want to talk to. I'll catch you up."

"Cool." The four of them walked away down the corridor. Only Bill gave me a lingering glance, and I gave him a tiny head shake. To which he responded with a minute nod. I was tempted to wink, just to confuse him, but the man I wanted to speak with was turning the corner and I went after him.

That man was Dr. Yang, and I found him outside. A few yards away, under a streetlight, a half-dozen people were taking a cigarette break.

"Getting some fresh air, Professor?"

He turned to me. "Ms. Chin. Good evening." He gestured at the others. "I used to smoke. After I stopped, I realized one of the things I missed most wasn't the cigarette itself, but the excuse to leave a room for a brief, unquestioned period."

"I understand the feeling completely. But if you were hoping for an unquestioned period right now, I'm afraid I'm going to mess you up. I have a question."

He didn't give me permission to ask it, but he didn't turn away. So I said, "Chau Chun is alive."

"Is that the question?"

"No, Jack's got me convinced that's true. But the other day in your office you gave us a very persuasive account of holding your friend's hand while he died. Either you're a terrific actor, or that story was also true."

"Performance has never been one of my talents."

"I disagree. I saw you in Haig's office. But that's not the point. That story was true."

"Yes."

"But it wasn't Chau Chun who died."

"No."

"But," I said, "Chau Chun was there."

A long pause. Dr. Yang looked down the quiet street. "Yes. He was there."

"And he's here now."

"Tonight? At this party? No, he—"

"No, Dr. Yang. Here. On this sidewalk. With me. You're Chau Chun."

The professor didn't speak, didn't move, didn't react at all.

"It was Yang who died," I said. "You took his identity. That's why there were rumors about Chau for months afterward. People saw you before you managed to leave the country."

"You're stating these hypotheses," the professor said quietly, "as facts. My students learn early on not to do that. You said you had a question."

"I have. What really happened that day?"

"I have a question, also: What gives you the right to ask that?"

"I could say, I just risked an awful lot to save your reputation, your daughter's career, and your son-in-law. But that's not really it. I took this case from the start to find out what was going on. I've found a lot, some of it complicated, little of it what I expected. But there's still something else. There's still something I don't know."

"And do you have to know?"

"Do you mean, will I shrivel up and die if I don't find out? Probably not. But I might keep looking, now that I know it's there to be found."

"Are you that tenacious?"

I told the simple truth. "Yes."

Another long pause, and I gave him time for it. "What happened," he finally said, "was what I told you. Chau had been in the square for days with our students; teaching, painting, chanting, encouraging. Yang went to persuade the demonstrators to leave. 'Violence will serve no purpose,' he said. 'We can build the movement with our art.' As they debated, the tanks came. There was gunfire, there was running, there was blood and screaming." The professor fell silent again, and again I waited. Staring into the night, he said, "Yang was shot. The gentle peacemaker. Bleeding to death on the paving stones. I held his hand."

The door behind us opened. Music thumped out of the party as a couple left laughing.

"But I didn't take his identity," the professor said. "He gave it to me."

"I'm sorry?"

"As he lay there. His name and his papers. 'They know you, Chau,' he said. 'They'll come for you. Everyone knows you've been here from the beginning. And Yang the Coward, back in the studio, everyone knows about me, too. Take my papers.' I refused. I told him he was being foolish, that I'd get him a doctor, that he'd be fine. 'I'm dying,' was his answer. 'It doesn't matter. But they'll come for you.' 'Then let them come.' 'And Yu-feng?' he said. 'They'll come for her, too. Your daughter, born in prison and taken away? Don't let me die with that fear in my mind.'"

"So you did what he asked."

"Yes. I exchanged our papers. He thanked me, and he died. Thanked me! Do you understand? I made my way out of the square and back to our offices, to do another thing, the last thing he asked of me. On his wall were three paintings I'd made for him to celebrate his faculty appointment. I took them. 'I have no gift for your child. Take the paintings. From you to me, and now from me to your daughter.' I stayed until he died, and then I did that."

"But his body," I said. "It was identified as Chau's."

"By me! Who better? I presented myself at the Public Security Bureau in the morning, claiming to seek information on my friend. It was chaos there, frightened people whose loved ones hadn't come home. They showed me bodies, a roomful of them, all laid along the floor. I recognized one of our students. And Yang. 'Chau Chun,' I said. 'From the Art Institute. A painter.' That was all they needed. All they wanted. I left Beijing within the hour, making my way circuitously to my hometown, to my wife. We went into hiding until it was safe to contact Xi Xao, the man who came to you as Samuel Wing. He brought us here. My wife needed false papers made. I didn't. I used Yang's."

Overhead the stars were bright; before us the street was empty.

Music pounded from the artists' studio, where a poet's freedom was being celebrated.

"That's why you wouldn't give Anna's Chaus to Haig."

"They weren't mine," he said simply. "I'd been painting all along, in any case, in a rented studio."

"And also, what Jack said was true. Your professional pride demanded those paintings be new, if you had to say they were."

He regarded me. "I think you know something about professional pride, Ms. Chin."

A compliment from the fierce professor? I tried to keep myself from falling over. "Does Anna know?"

"That I am Chau? No one knows but Xi Xao, my wife, and myself." Slowly, he asked, "Will you tell her?"

"No." I didn't have to think about it at all. "This story isn't mine to tell. Except to my partner. And my friend." Interesting, what I'd just heard myself say. I'd have to consider that later. "But they won't share it, I know. Chau Chun is Anna's hero, though. Now that she knows he's alive, she'll want to meet him."

"Many people will want to meet him. It will pass. Anna has other things to think about now. A career. A family. Thank you, Ms. Chin."

"On behalf of Bill, Jack, and myself, you're welcome." I bowed. "Maybe we should go back inside now." I added, "Dr. Yang."

He held the door for me. Probably it was the lights, and the music, and the giddiness of the party as we walked in, but I imagined I saw a sparkle in the professor's eyes as we went in search of his family.